SKYE'S WEST: BANNACK

RICHARD S. WHEELER

SKYE'S WEST: BANNACK

Copyright © 1989 by Richard S. Wheeler

A Tor Book
Published by Tom Doherty Associates, Inc.
175 Fifth Ave.
New York, N.Y. 10010

Cover art by Royo

ISBN: 0-812-51071-2   Can. ISBN: 0-812-51072-0

First Edition: October 1989

Printed in the United States of America

0 9 8 7 6 5 4 3

For Sue Hart

Chapter 1

Mister Skye lifted the new Henry, peered down the blued octagon barrel until the blade sight lined on the dusty glass eye of a royal elk, and squeezed the trigger. He was rewarded with a smooth hard click. Then he leveled the rifle at the low furry brow of the erect grizzly, with the late Mrs. Bullock's beflowered straw hat upon it, and squeezed again. Nothing happened. He had forgotten to lever the Henry. He levered it and aimed again and squeezed, and felt again the satisfying click. He loosed a fusillade at the grizzly, and deemed that he had stopped it in its tracks. Next he focused on the color lithograph of the Last Supper on the whitewashed plank wall behind Bullock's desk and he thought for a moment to dry-fire at Judas, who was holding the bag of silver, but he decided against it. Mister Skye was a reverent man.

Skye groaned, full of covet. "I'll take it, Bullock," he growled. His voice boomed too large for buildings, and anything he said rumbled through the gloomy cavern of the Fort Laramie sutler's store, cut down and measured.

Colonel Bullock sighed. He fidgeted beside his desk,

florid-faced, white-haired, in a gray swallowtail coat. "Ah'm sorry, suh, but Ah can't sell it to you. You're over two hundred in arrears on your accounts, Mistuh Skye."

"Hold it for me, then!"

"Ah can't do that, either. I've a dozen officers on the post salivating, Mister Skye. This is the first one I've laid hands on. Only fifteen hundred made last year, and all snapped up by the army back in the states. This was made in January sixty-three, and just came in with the freight. Ah'm truly sorry, Mister Skye."

The post sutler, a retired Southern colonel, had chosen the North in the current conflict, knowing exactly where his hominy grits were buttered.

Again Skye groaned. The lever-action repeater held enough shining brass cartridges in its magazine to hold off a whole war party of Bug's Boys. And now some shavetail from West Point with a pocketful of gold would snatch it.

"I need it worse," Mister Skye argued. "Out there by myself, much worse than your soldier boys, mate. Stash it away and I'll find the plunder somehow."

The courtly sutler shook his head. "Ah wish I could. Ah'll hold it for an hour or two, but Ah can't hang on—"

Commotion erupted out on the parade. Another wagon train arriving, Mister Skye thought. And in moments, a horde of westering pilgrims would flood in, men in homespun shirts, square-toed boots, and baggy britches; women in ginghams and bonnets, looking to trade, buy, sell. This was the place for it, he thought. Bullock's cavernous emporium sheltered whole rolls of canvas and barrels of pickles and wagon ironwork and axes and coiled hemp rope and burlap sacks of green coffee beans, cotton bags of flour and sugar, and whole shelves of airtights.

A man as burly as Skye burst through the open front door, peered around in the brown gloom, and finally spotted Colonel Bullock and Mister Skye.

"Where's the commander?" he shouted. "I'm Porter, Jarvis Porter, captain of this train, and I've a military matter to put to him."

"Suh? At headquarters, suh," Bullock replied.

"You some damned Southerner? What are you doing in a Union fort?"

Colonel Bullock drew himself up quietly. "My loyalty is beyond your consideration," he said. "The fort is barely garrisoned, suh. The rest are out patrolling the Oregon Trail for the safety of parties such as yours. There's only a lieutenant here at the moment. The colonel is up at the Platte River Bridge. Perhaps, suh, you could state the nature of your . . . business?"

Porter oozed choler. He glared darkly at Bullock, and then at Mister Skye, staring at Skye's shoulder-length gray hair, black silk stovepipe hat screwed rakishly on his head, and fringed buckskins, elaborately quilled and beaded. He looked pained.

"You're not the army, but maybe you'll steer me. I've captained a large train this far, some for Oregon, some for Idaho. Decent salt-of-the-earth people, upright farmers and their families, God-fearing. Some of them desperate and miserable war refugees. Well, gents, just before we left from Independence, three more wagons attached themselves to our party. One was a couple named Riddle chaperoning some women, mail-order brides, bound for the Grasshopper diggings. Mean-tempered and too slow, not able to keep up, and troublemakers. I don't mind them so much, but the others . . . the others! The whole lot should be hanged from the nearest cottonwood."

"That what you want the army for, Porter? Enforce your discipline on the wagon train? Won't work, suh. The army never interferes in civilian conflicts unless there's—mayhem."

Porter glared, outraged. "One wagon is owned by a woman named Goldtooth, and she has with her several, ah, ladies, ah, whores, sir. She has whores of the lowest sort. The other wagon is also owned by this—this—this Goldtooth slattern. In it are a gambler with the stinking audacity to call himself Cornelius Vanderbilt, a man who would steal his grandmother's wedding ring. Not only that, but a black banjo singer—who corrupts my sons with scandalous music—and worse, a giant Chinese, seven feet tall, they call Seven-Story Chang. It wouldn't be so bad if they minded themselves, but these lowlifes set up shop—do business, to put it bluntly—on the trail, causing havoc in decent families. The tinhorn gambler has fleeced everyone in sight. And the women, the slatterns, have—deflowered my boys and offended my Stella.

"We've tried to rid ourselves of them. We've threatened death if they continue to attach themselves. We've—we've attempted . . . but that heathen Chinese is like a demon. And so we want the army, we want the army to detain them. Stop them. Throw the whole unsavory lot into your stockade. Stop them from preying on decent people."

"Are they with the train now, suh?"

"A mile behind. I've ordered my people to shoot, shoot their stock, their mules, if they get any closer."

"Should be rolling in about now, then," said Mister Skye. "I think I'll have me a look. Give me two hours, Colonel. Don't sell that Henry just yet."

The faintest smile peeked through the sutler's white beard. "Mistuh Porter, suh, you can tell it to the lieutenant, Bates is his name, over yonder down the row there, where the colors are flying. Go tell him your woe, suh, and let me know what the army says."

"I'll do that," snapped Porter. "But we're not leaving here with those lowlifes. We'll shoot them if there's no other justice out here. I'm not just talking; I mean it."

He stormed out, pushing through a crowd of people examining the sutler's wares and hoping to strike bargains.

Colonel Bullock slid out from behind his rolltop desk. His office squatted in a corner separated from the store by a banister. A flood of customers demanded attention, far more than his two sallow clerks could handle. "Excuse me, Mister Skye," he said.

"Why, if it isn't dear old Colonel Bullock!" exclaimed a sweet female voice.

The lady accosting him was brown-haired and doe-eyed and full-figured, and wearing a skimpy summer dimity with a scoop neck that revealed the tops of her lush golden breasts. When she smiled, a gold tooth caught the light from Bullock's window.

"Imagine finding you here," she said brightly. "It's a long way from Memphis!"

Mister Skye was grinning.

"I don't believe I know you, ah, madam."

"Of course you don't, honey. I was Ella Lou Jones then. Now they call me Goldtooth."

The colonel reddened and appeared flustered. "Ah don't believe—ah, how shall I address you . . . Miss? Mrs.?"

"Call me Honey."

The colonel nodded slightly.

"I'm havin' a little trouble, sweetie, and I'm a-lookin' for some help. This little old wagon train just won't let some working girls go along. The wagon master wears cast-iron pants. We're a-goin' to Bannack City, Grasshopper Creek, to do a little business, and we're having the hardest time. The wagon master just won't have us along and we have no protection."

Colonel Bullock had turned crimson, much to Mister Skye's delight. He'd never seen the colonel hued in any color other than sallow indoors-white.

"If you'll excuse me, ah, madam, I've customers waiting. Good day."

He fled toward a knot of calicoed women standing at the footwear shelves.

"He doesn't remember me," she said to Mister Skye. "He used to be our neighbor in Memphis. We lived—my parents lived—up on the Chickasaw heights. That was before I went into business on Beale Street."

"The wagon master, Porter, was just here spilling woe," said Mister Skye.

"Woe and fire and brimstone. I don't know how we'll get to the Grasshopper diggings without the protection of a wagon train," she said. Then her eyes focused at last on the burly barrel of a frontiersman before her. "Hey, aren't you something. Do you live out here? Those quilled buckskins! All you'd need to be an Injun is a warbonnet instead of that stovepipe hat. How come you wear that?"

"To remind myself and others that I'm mister. Mister Skye," he rumbled.

"What do you do, Mister Skye?"

"Milk wayfarers of their money."

"I'm in business too," she said. "Honey, I got portable merchandise and the shelf is never bare." She laughed. "Or maybe it is."

"How many are in your party?"

"Why, myself and three ladies, Big Alice Roque, Mrs. Parkins, and Juliet Picard. And in my other wagon, Cornelius—Cornelius Vanderbilt—he's a sporting man—and Blueberry Hill, my pianist and friend, and Seven-Story Chang. And there's another wagon the wagon master won't have, also going to Bannack City. Full of mail-order brides. Now Mister Skye, why do you ask? Is there something I can sell you?" She flashed a knowing smile.

"Let's go look," said Mister Skye.

"The Riddles and their ladies are over there," she said, pointing at the dry-goods counters. "That's Alvah," she said, pointing at a ferret-faced balding skinny man. "And that's Gertrude," she added, pointing at a potbellied jowly scraggly haired female with mean gray eyes. "They are very virtuous," she added wearily. "And those are the brides. I forget their names. The Riddles are marriage brokers, taking those poor little old things to the mining camps. They're like me, only they peddle new merchandise and I sell the used." She grinned. "Everything I sell is properly broken in."

They emerged from the post sutler's into a blinding June sun and hiked toward the riverbank, where wagons were gathered in a long string. "I didn't let my people come in," she said. "For obvious reasons, honey."

"Mister Skye."

"Mister Skye, honey. Now tell me true, what do you do?"

"I'm a guide when there's guiding."

"We don't need a guide. They tell me the trail's perfectly clear. What we need is protection. I'd like about ten soldiers."

"We'll get you through," said Mister Skye.

"Who's we, honey?"

"I'll discuss that after I see whether I wish to do business with you."

Three fine wagons hunkered separately, about two hundred yards east of the rest of the wagon train. Even at a distance Mister Skye could see that these were all mule-drawn, three spans apiece with spare mules and horses tied on. Faster and better than oxen, when there was good grass on the trail. Two of the wagons were lacquered a dazzling red, and the wagon sheets spread over the bows had been dyed blushing pink. The other wagon was lacquered green with gilt filigree work.

Advertisements, Mister Skye thought. Advertisements.

Standing beside the wagons were the lowlifes. "There they are," said Goldtooth. "We're going to have the best parlor house in Bannack City. And mine all the gold in the gulch." She laughed amiably.

"What's in the wagons?"

"Why, in this one, nothing but the ladies and supplies. In my other one, some hogsheads of Kentucky bourbon, some vintage wine, and Cornelius's faro and roulette layouts."

Mister Skye experienced a stab of delight. Sometime along the trail, he'd tap a hogshead and disappear for a few days. Always assuming, of course, that he landed this business.

They were all staring at him, their gaze fastening on the silky stovepipe with the two bullet holes in it, his beefy face with the mashed and twisted prow that had been broken in a dozen brawls, at the golden-tanned skin garments, the shirt and leggins fringed, at his red-beaded loincloth, and heavy boots, as well as the Navy Colt holstered at his side and the battered heavy Sharps cradled in his arms. They saw, too, his sailor's roll, as if the earth were a pitching deck, and they sensed the menace about him. He could read it in their faces as he, in turn, surveyed this gaggle of outcasts.

"I want you-all to meet Mister Skye," said Goldtooth. "He's a guide just a-lookin' us over."

She introduced them all. Big Alice reached almost six feet, yellow-eyed and yellow-fleshed, and dressed entirely in lavender. Mrs. Parkins—Cleo Sylvanus Parkins—

seemed a patrician blonde, dressed in a svelte summer yellow dress with a deep vee at the neck. Perhaps thirty. She studied him with calculating gray eyes. Juliet Picard turned out to be a young sable-haired beauty with a voluptuous figure and shining eyes, dimples, and pouty open lips made to kiss.

He had been unprepared for this. He had not expected such dazzling beauty, such bright eyes and good humor. He turned then toward the sporting gents, and Goldtooth introduced. The gambler wore a gray swallowtail. He was a cadaverous pocked gent with oily black hair combed straight back, and darting brown eyes that never steadied on anything. Crooked as hell, Mister Skye thought.

"What's your real name, Vanderbilt?" he rumbled.

The man started. It was a question never asked. He glanced into Mister Skye's blue eyes, and surrendered. "Donk. Homer Donk. Brooklyn, New York. But I'd just as soon that weren't bandied about because of, ah, troubles back there."

Mister Skye nodded.

Beside him slouched a graying black as burly as himself, with hair like iron shavings. He wore a collarless white shirt, a black broadcloth suit, and white spats over patent-leather shoes.

"Blueberry Hill, our pianist," Goldtooth was saying. "Blueberry takes good care of us and is very strong. When there's trouble, why, we just call on Blueberry and he throws the troublemakers out, don't you, honeybunch?"

Blueberry smiled. Mister Skye saw the telltale bulge of a shoulder holster, and decided the man would be formidable in a brawl.

"I keep the ladies from going stale," said Blueberry, revealing a row of even white teeth.

Mister Skye nodded.

"And this is Lui Chang, but we call him Seven-Story Chang," Goldtooth continued.

Of all the people in this party, Seven-Story Chang commanded Mister Skye's attention. Powerfully built, lean, and all muscle. He wore a long queue that swung easily across the small of his back. But he wore Western clothing—denim britches and open-throated gray Bedford cord shirt. A pair of holstered shining revolvers, a sheathed dagger, and on his great white horse a Spencer carbine in a scabbard.

"It is an honor to meet Mister Skye, who is plainly a fighting man," said Seven-Story. "As am I."

"Seven-Story is a mandarin from Peking and the son of an officer of the Imperial Guard," Goldtooth explained. "He's not really with us permanently. He's adventuring, and we—exchange services."

Mister Skye found himself believing Chang could whip him, fists, clubs, knives, anything. He had that look about him, at once serene and assured, as if nothing on earth save a coward's bullet from ambush would ever fell him. A one-man army, Skye thought. No wonder Goldtooth was glad to include him.

Mister Skye hadn't met the Riddles yet, but he thought he knew the type, and they didn't concern him. He had seen what he wanted to see. He could get this party safely to Bannack City, especially with Seven-Story Chang beside him.

"Five hundred dollars," said Mister Skye. "In gold."

"For what?" said Goldtooth, astonished.

"For delivering you safely to Bannack City. My services include those of my wives, who will make meat and scout."

"Wives?"

"Mary, my beautiful young Shoshone, and Victoria, my beloved Crow lady."

"We were looking for protection, not a guide."

Mister Skye sighed. "Inquire about me at the fort. Ask Colonel Bullock."

"Hire him," said Cornelius Vanderbilt. "It doesn't matter what he charges. He'll enjoy our sport."

"That's more than we can afford." She smiled coyly. "How about a hundred dollars—and services? We'd all love to share the merchandise, wouldn't we, ladies?"

"Five hundred in gold."

She shook her head. "We'll find someone else, I think."

"Try it," said Mister Skye.

Something in the way he said it gave her pause. "I don't know anything about you," she said.

"Ask."

Seven-Story Chang said, "Don't ask, Madam Jones. This is a man I have heard of. I hear of all such men. He is exactly what we need. I am pleased to make his acquaintance."

Goldtooth sighed. "Four hundred fifty in greenbacks. We haven't gold. I'll charge the Riddles a hundred fifty for their wagon, and pay three hundred for mine. They'll complain, but they'll pay rather than be left behind."

"Gold," said Mister Skye. "In advance. Gold you skinned from the wagon train."

"Two hundred in gold and the rest in merchandise. Honey, I have the best merchandise west of the Mississippi."

Mister Skye yawned. "Find someone else," he said, and turned to leave.

Seven-Story hissed something at her. "Wait!" she cried. She lifted her dimity skirts, revealing a splendid golden thigh, and extracted some greenbacks from a purse strapped to the glowing flesh.

"Here!" she said. "We're leaving in the morning. We have some business to do with the soldiers at the fort tonight. Be ready!"

Mister Skye was taken aback. He always made the decisions once he agreed to captain a party into the wilderness.

"Goldtooth," he rumbled, "the safety of this party depends on strict obedience to my direction at all times. We will be in a wilderness infested by bandits, outlaws, hostiles, disease such as cholera, rattlesnakes, and more. Your lives will depend on my knowledge. Is that understood?"

"I trust you-all, honey."

He nodded and trotted off to Bullock to pay his bill, buy the Henry, and boxes of those shining brass cartridges. There'd be enough left over for supplies, and treats for his wives.

Chapter 2

It wasn't the fine brick parlor on Beale Street, but it'd do, she thought. She was open for business and getting it here at this makeshift parlor house on the Platte, perhaps half a mile from Fort Laramie. Cornelius had his faro game laid out on a light folding table brought along for the purpose, with a pair of coal-oil lamps on poles for light. Her ladies, in their skimpy wrappers, lounged around their wagon, now partitioned into two cribs with a canvas sheet. Display the merchandise, she had always told them, and they were doing it, a knee or thigh golden in the firelight now and then. Blueberry, when he wasn't tending the bar, sat up on the tailgate of the other wagon, plucked his banjo and sang. Out in the dark somewhere, Seven-Story Chang stalked the night like a yellow cat, making sure all was well. Goldtooth herself tended the bar, drew reluctant blue-clad corporals and sergeants to the girls, and drummed up trade for Cornelius. She envied her ladies—there were several of the Fort Laramie soldiers she'd have loved to bed.

It had gone on all evening. Cornelius, looking particularly sallow and pocked beneath the two lanterns, shuffled the greasy faro deck methodically and replaced it in the casebox and turned over the soda card and once again invited the troopers to lay coin on the oilcloth. But the pickings were slim. These soldiers drew eight dollars a month when they got paid at all. Cornelius knew that, of course, and traded chits for U.S.-issue boots and belts and holsters and anything else. He methodically milked them all, until a fine midden of army goods was heaped behind his layout.

Men and boys from the wagon train milled around too, mostly just looking because the ladies and Cornelius had long since skinned them all. And assorted Brulé Sioux from Squaw Town wandered through. They loved to gamble, but had little to wager with. Even so, Cornelius cleaned them out of their knives and blankets and belts and a few old revolvers, with his braced deck and his twitchy dealing. Every few minutes a spasm would wrack him, and he'd suck on a tin cup of raw bourbon, and go back to dealing and keeping cases with the little black abacus beads on their wires. After each cleaning, he gazed dolefully at the shorn victim, his brown eyes blinking, and sympathized. "Have a little drink on Goldtooth," he said. "We want sporting men to go away happy." And she would dish up a well-watered dose of popskull.

The trouble came close to midnight when the crowd tapered to an edge and Goldtooth was about to fold up the tents and count the loot. Before leaving, she intended to trade as much of the U.S.-issue stuff with the sutler, dear old Colonel Bullock, for whatever she could get. It had been a splendid evening, she thought, except that she didn't get a chance to bed. That made her cross. She needed two or three good customers a day.

A rush of hooves rattled from the darkness, on the flats along the river. Several muffled shots. At almost the same moment, armed men materialized around her outdoor parlor house, all of them carrying rifles at the ready, which glinted in the firelight. She recognized most of them at once. They were the bearded patriarchs of the wagon train, and foremost among them was Jarvis Porter, the wagon master. And among them a sprinkling of blue cavalry shirts, many with two or three yellow chevrons on their sleeves, noncoms who could be out at night, away from the fort, without getting into trouble. Every one of them, over thirty in all, brandished rifles or drawn revolvers.

Worse, they were leading Seven-Story Chang from out of the darkness, his hands bound behind him. The giant Celestial peered calmly at his silent captors and Goldtooth, and smiled faintly. An ominous silence pervaded these night visitors. Mrs. Parkins stared, and dived into the wagon, along with Juliet. But Big Alice stared back defiantly in a black kimono with a giant red dragon on its back, a gift from Seven-Story. Easily, they prodded Blueberry and Cornelius Vanderbilt into their circle.

Something glinted in Porter's eye. "You've been warned," he whispered softly. "You've been warned but didn't heed. Now the price."

At a nod from him, rough-hewn men wheeled off in all directions recovering booty. The wagon master himself searched her, his giant rough hands probing everywhere, ripping greenbacks and coin from her pockets and purses, yanking at everything, ruthless and cruel. When he finished, he shoved her into the grass. Cornelius endured the searching stoically, his hands in the air. Rough hands dug at his pockets, threw his hideout derringer into the grass, dropped his britches, ripped off his moneybelt, emptied the lining of his silk top hat. And then these silent avengers carried the U.S.-issue loot piled behind his faro layout off to a central collection depot near the wavering wind-whipped fire.

From inside the wagon came the screams of the ladies as others of these hard men probed and dug.

"I've had that all my life," cried Juliet Picard, from within.

"Shut up," came a voice.

Big Alice, still outside, simply opened her kimono and grinned. There was nothing underneath. God! thought Goldtooth, what great merchandise. Then one of them

slapped her down, and she sat with a thud. Next they dug
at Blueberry, yanking out his pockets, ripping off his black
broadcloth coat.

"Where's it hid, nigger?" snapped one.

Blueberry said nothing.

They threw him to the ground.

Several of these silent avengers climbed into the supply
wagon and rolled the hogsheads of bourbon out. They hit
the ground with a hard thump. One cracked as it landed
and began to leak. Porter himself caught up an axe and
began to swing.

"Hold it," yelled a burly old sergeant, menace in his
eye. "This here stuff is illegal in Injun country and I'm
confiscating it for the army."

No one laughed. Cornelius managed a faint smirk.
Seven blue-shirted noncoms with leveled revolvers held
the vengeful wagon train men at bay.

From inside the wagon came the shrill voice of Mrs.
Parkins. "You sonofabitch, that's a family heirloom," she
said.

Goldtooth wondered whether the Riddles were escaping
this. They and their mail-order brides had camped a couple hundred yards away, far enough to get sleep. None of
them showed up now, not that she expected them to. She
sighed. She had been through something like this before,
but not . . . this bad. Memphis had fallen to Union forces
led by Charles Henry Davis just a year earlier, June 6,
1862, and business on Beale Street had at once tailed off
under a reign of fear. But little by little the blue-clad army's curfew had relaxed, and in some small anemic way,
the sporting crowd revived, sliding in and out of her house.
Hard times. Food always ran short, and at times she
couldn't squeeze spirits out of a drunk. Then more and
more of the Union officers—the only ones who could afford her amazing prices—slipped in, magnetized by her
stunning ladies. She thought she'd weather the war that
way, taking in Union gold, but it was not to be. Davis
closed her down for various reasons—money, demorali-
zation, fear of disease, and above all, fear the Union Army

secrets were divulged in the cribs of Beale Street and were finding their way into the ears of the army of the Confederacy—which was true. One night they came, polished officers and a smart squad of infantry, and ransacked the place—some of them the very men she'd entertained—and told her to shut down. But not before carrying off everything of value. She had wasted no time leaving Memphis then, with the safety of the Western camps the end of their odyssey. Until now.

Jarvis Porter had found two shovels, and these he handed to Cornelius and Seven-Story.

"Dig," he said curtly.

The sallow gambler paled. "You aren't—you can't—" he blustered.

"You were warned," said the captain of the wagon train.

Seven-Story took his shovel, and somehow it looked like a weapon in his hand, she thought. He began calmly to lift sod and set it carefully aside, his eyes less on what he was doing than upon those whose rifles bored in at him.

"You wouldn't!" she gasped.

"You were warned."

"But why the Chinese? He's not even one of our party!"

"He was with you. And there's no room here for the heathen, the Celestials."

"You'd kill him for that?"

"This land is given to the God-fearing."

"I suppose you'll murder us all."

"Only the men."

"Blueberry too?"

"Is that his name?"

"All he does is make music and serve drinks. What has he done to any of you?"

"Corrupted our sons," said a black-bearded man.

Blueberry's eyes, yellow in the amber firelight, peered from face to face, and then he sagged. "Never was much hope for a man of color," he muttered.

"And what's my fate? and my ladies'?"

"We are confiscating your mules and horses and harness to repay—debts. And burning your slut-wagons. What you choose to do after that is your business.''

"That sounds about right!" she cried. "You're stealing about twenty times what was sold to you. And murdering three men.''

For an answer, be booted her. The heavy brogan caught her square in the ribs, a painful sickening jolt that shot nausea and fire through her. She thought, absurdly, that the bruise would turn yellow and purple and turn away trade.

Cornelius and Seven-Story dawdled with their spades, slowly lifting off turf but not producing holes.

"Get busy," snarled the wagon master, prodding Seven-Story with his rifle.

"If I am pleased to join my ancestors, then, gentleman, it makes no difference. You may have the honor of burying me." He bowed slightly and handed the shovel to the surprised Porter.

"Dig!" Porter handed back the spade.

"Ah, no, I will decline the great honor."

The wagon master pointed at Blueberry. "You—dig."

"I can't say that it makes much sense to dig my own grave," said Blueberry.

For a reply he got a wicked boot to the kidneys, and crumpled into the grass.

Vanderbilt thought otherwise, and dug feverishly, hoping Lady Luck might be kind.

"You and all your bible-thumpers are nothing but murderers," said Goldtooth. "And thieves."

Jarvis Porter grinned sallowly in the flickering light. "I'll wager that this sport here, Vanderbilt, has some hanging offenses behind him. As for the rest"—he shrugged—"they aren't whites."

Seven-Story's arcing spade landed on Porter's head with an awful thump, and the wagon captain toppled to earth. Several of the night visitors lifted rifles to shoot the Chinese, but shots crashing from the blackness burned their hands, shattered rifle stocks. They screamed. Others, especially the noncoms, wheeled toward the darkness, emptying revolvers at unseen targets.

Bodies slammed to earth, making themselves small. Blueberry flattened himself. Cornelius dove into the shallow hole that was to hold his bones. Goldtooth saw all this in a series of flashing impressions, and clutched the earth, bewildered.

From the blackness came the roar of a vaguely familiar voice. "Hands up, mates. Drop the guns." From out in the blackness came an insane shriek of a horse, eerie, unlike any horse Goldtooth had ever heard in her young life. Much to her astonishment the soldiers dropped their revolvers at once, all of them looking terrified. The wagon men were slower, some of them obeying but most of them firing blind into the night, a useless racket.

"Hands up, mates," came that rumble again, but from a different place. Now it became familiar, that voice. The guide she had hired, Mister Skye. Her heart hammered.

Still the wagon men clung to their rifles, peering into the darkness, many of them too stubborn and inept even to get out of the firelight that perfectly silhouetted them. Shots cracked again, shattering rifles, bloodying hands. More of the wagon men peered at their own bloodied hands and fingers, yelping in the night. And they surrendered.

A stretching silence. Goldtooth peered about and saw nothing. Closer at hand, disarmed men began to wrap shirting around hand wounds to stanch the blood.

"The two with the pistols in their holsters—pull them out and drop them," came the thunderous voice again. One of them did; the other tried to slip off into the night. A shot cracked. "Far enough, mate. Get back to the firelight."

Seven-Story stood, a commandeered revolver glinting in his hand.

Then at last a soft thump of hooves, and into the amber wind-whipped light rode an apparition, Mister Skye on a giant ugly blue roan so scarred and battered that all its furrows and pocks lay black-shadowed in the firelight. Its cruel yellow eyes caught the light and glowed like lanterns from hell, and its lips were drawn back around murderous teeth that clacked and clicked and snapped. What had she hired? What sort of hell-man and hell-horse had she engaged to guide them?

"Why are you here?" she whispered.

"We were paid to protect you."

She didn't know who the others were.

He addressed the several noncoms. "You. Pick up the government-issue and be glad you won't have to pay for it. And collect what this gambler took from you. To the penny."

"I won that fair and square," croaked Vanderbilt.

"With a braced deck, Homer Donk. Hand me the case-box."

Reluctantly the greasy cadaverous man handed the box up to Mister Skye, who pulled out an ace of diamonds and eight of clubs and held them up to the firelight. Pinpricks of light shone through. "Braced," he said. He pulled the rest of the filthy cards and tossed them into the fire, where they flared yellow.

The soldiers carefully claimed their goods and cash.

"You're square now," said Skye. "Go back. In the morning report it all.

"You—Porter—you've got three men with bloody hands as a result of your little murderous games. Be glad you are alive."

The choleric wagon master glared. "There's over twenty of us here. You think you can take us all?"

Two things happened. Mister Skye's giant blue roan, Jawbone, lurched, his hard chest slamming into Porter and toppling him again. And shots rang from the blackness, each plucking off a hat.

Mister Skye glared at them all. "Take what the gambler screwed out of you and not a penny more," he said. "You paid for the booze and you paid for the ladies, and they'll stay paid-for. Take what Donk here skinned out of you and get out. Go back to your families. Go nurse your fingers. If you sneak back here, you're dead."

Even as Skye addressed the night riders, Seven-Story

emptied their rifles and revolvers of their charges and pried caps off nipples. He handed the weapons back to them. The wagon men stared reluctantly, and finally began sorting out their own possessions, under Goldtooth's watchful eye. The ladies joined her.

Ten minutes later it was done. The wagon-train elders skulked off to their wagons, and the night held only the music of the crickets. The terror left Blueberry's eyes. Goldtooth felt more at ease, except for the dull ache where she had been booted. She would remember that little calling card forever, she thought savagely.

"I do believe I am alive," muttered Blueberry. "It is a surprise."

Seven-Story Chang glided in from the darkness. "The mules and horses are all at hand and picketed," he said. He turned to Mister Skye. "I have the honor to be in your debt. You and the others who are still out there. Mister Skye, I had heard of you from the day I arrived in San Francisco. And all the stories are true."

Mister Skye nodded.

The fire was reduced to embers, and the camp grew dark. The guide seemed to like it that way. "Goldtooth," he said softly, "I will get you all to Bannack City safely. And once you get there you can do as you please. But on the trail, I will have certain rules. There'll be a lot of people on the trail to Oregon and California. We'll be mixing with various wagon trains, camping close to all sorts. I will have no trouble. You and your ladies will avoid married men and boys, youths. Are we agreed?"

Goldtooth nodded, reluctantly. What he doesn't know won't hurt him, she thought.

"And you, Donk. That faro layout stays in the wagon as long as you're under my protection. And so do all your thimble-rigged games. If I catch you skinning the pilgrims, you'll be in trouble with me. Do we have a meeting of minds, Donk?"

The gambler stared back, sullen. "I will do what I want. You've no authority over me," he replied.

Mister Skye grinned, his teeth catching the vague orange of the embers. "I will not protect you from the consequences of your acts, as I did tonight. You were almost the late Cornelius Vanderbilt."

"I've always fended for myself," the gambler retorted.

"Until tonight, mate. Go lie down in that hole."

"What are you talking about?"

"Lie down in that hole or feel my fists, mate."

The gambler stared, and then slowly dragged himself to the long slash gouged from hard clay, and lay down.

"Throw some dirt on him, Seven-Story."

The Chinese grinned, and began shoveling enthusiastically.

"You're dirtying my suit! My swallowtail coat!"

"It's no dirtier than the man inside."

The Chinese stopped after unloading several shovels.

"I'm fitting you for your future, Cornelius Vanderbilt." Skye's voice mocked the name as he pronounced it.

The last embers faded, and Mister Skye became an unseen voice in the dark. "We'll be back 'round dawn. Be harnessed and ready. Have the others—the Riddles over yonder, and their women—ready too. If we get a fast start, we won't have to tangle with the wagon train you've managed to incite to murder."

"Amen, Mister Skye," muttered Blueberry. "I think I see stars up there."

Goldtooth smiled. Men like Mister Skye were hard to find. "Thank you, honey," she said. "You come visit."

Chapter 3

Alvah Riddle couldn't understand why he had been booted out of Porter's wagon train. Or, indeed, why he had been bounced from yet another train back on the coasts of Nebraska. To be sure, he was slow. He had to harness and hitch three span of mules each morning, and not a woman in his party helped him. And each evening he had to unhitch the six mules and pasture and picket them, also without help.

At first Porter had waited for him, but soon he hadn't, leaving the Riddles to fend for themselves and at the mercy of hostile Indians on the trail. Now, here he was, tied to some bawds and lowlifes for mutual protection, and he a respectable man, too. That Porter, now, he must have had some angle. People always had angles. Maybe someone in the wagon train had paid Porter off. Riddle figured he had just as much right to be in that train as anyone else, and a lot more right than those sluts, but they had all turned against him. Someone in that outfit had stirred up feelings against the Riddles, for sure. Probably some gain in it, someone who didn't want the Riddles to deliver their mail-order brides to Bannack City.

An angle lurked behind everything, anyone knew that. The train had been badly captained anyway—Porter hadn't the faintest idea how to run a wagon train. He bossed people around as if they were lackeys, and he continually made stupid decisions, such as driving the wagons far into the evenings, wearing down the footsore stock. Alvah figured if he'd been wagon boss, the whole party of forty-seven wagons would be better off.

He unrolled his bed each night under his enameled green wagon, mostly because all the women he chaperoned needed their privacy. And now, as usual, the early sun of June upended him long before the time they'd travel. Riddle had a protruding belly and bright glancing eyes that studied others and hunted the angles. The stubble on his face ran smoothly from his nose to his neck, without the interruption of a jaw. He hadn't slept well: he never slept well on the hard ground, and he'd explained to Porter that was why he was slow getting harnessed in the morning, but Porter kept playing some angle and wouldn't listen or sympathize.

Now he was stuck with the lowlifes, and that made him uneasy. Maybe when he rolled into Bannack City with his women, he'd try to be well ahead, or well behind, so the miners who had paid him good money to bring them respectable brides wouldn't get the wrong impression. Yes, he'd do that. Arrive separately. He had a wagonload of virgins and they had to be quarantined from those shopworn bawds. Not that he minded close contact with the bawds on the trail, though Gertrude and the brides complained. In fact that heathen Chinee might be a comfort. With him around, it would be like traveling with a squad of infantry. And he figured maybe that gambler and the black lowlife could be deadly if it came to that.

Yes, that would be his angle. Get what protection he could from them, but keep his distance. Three miners had contracted for the women, half down, half on delivery, and he intended to make sure they didn't have any angle that would work against him. It was hard enough making money in the bride business—finding the women and delivering them took all the string-pulling and sharp dealing he could muster—and the cost of delivery kept rising. Why, he'd have over a thousand of expenses and clear only two; less if any of the miners balked. Of course he'd written up an ironclad contract, empowering him to seize assets and keep the bride if they defaulted, but one never knew. The bride business bid fair to be troublesome because the husbands and brides sometimes recoiled when they met. But he had a default clause in his contracts, drawn up for him by the trickiest shyster in upstate New York, and if they defaulted he'd have them both over the barrel in any court.

It rankled him that this bawd, Goldtooth Jones, had gone and hired some lumbering guide to protect them en route, since they lacked the protection of a wagon train. A hundred fifty would reduce their profits all the more, and Gertrude would be peeved. Well, he hadn't paid Goldtooth, and didn't intend to. He would cook up his own angle to squirm out of it. Hadn't she struck the deal without his consent? She'd played the sucker. So he'd just profit. Who said madams were so smart? That guide had skinned her good, a whopping five hundred smackerinos for a little trip down the trail. He hadn't met this Mister Skye, but sort of admired him as a slick operator. If he could shoot, or haul in a little game, all the better. Alvah had heard there would be no game along the heavily traveled trail, except when they struck buffalo, so anything this slick frontier rube brought in would be a little bonus and fill the hollow bellies of those complaining women. They were eating up his profit, these women.

Life stammered within the wagon, and it rocked above him. That would be Drusilla Dinwiddie, always first up, and first to the bushes. She hadn't much in the beauty department, but in the dark they were all the same. That's what he told his clients. He told the women that, too. In the dark they were all the same. And of course his contract expressly stated that physical appearance would not be a ground to nullify the agreement. This one, Miss Dinwiddie, had taken a lot of persuading. New England bred, built like a pear, with a face like a mule. The bluestocking had eyeglasses, liked to read, and even kept a diary. She had left thirty-one behind and looked desperate. That's when he had them over the barrel, when they got desperate. He'd had to go clear from his home in Skaneateles, New York, to Bennington, Vermont, to persuade her, and then pay for a hoity-toity first-class rail ticket to Council Bluffs, Ioway, before she'd consent. Not much profit in her.

She clambered down from the wagon in her long wrapper, stared owlishly at him, and headed for the Platte River brush. He rolled out of his blankets, rubbed the mouse-stubble on his cheeks and stood in the moist dawn air. He wouldn't scrape his whiskers today. Most days he didn't scrape. That was just another angle people played, scrape your chin to do good business. She returned, glaring at him.

"You haven't even got the mules harnessed or breakfast started," she snapped. "No wonder they kicked us out. No wonder I'm forced to associate with—I won't say the name. Women who are beneath words. If you weren't so lazy, this would be a better trip. But no, I had to get stuck with a no-account."

That was her angle, he figured. The more she complained and nagged and demanded, the more people jumped to her word. He grinned, thinking of the unlucky future husband, one Amos Rasmussen of Bannack City in the new territory of Idaho.

He had to harness the blasted mules, but that could wait. Now that they were no longer with the wagon train, they could set their own pace and tell the guide, this Skye, that a few miles a day were plenty. Save the mules. He calculated that he could sell the mules for a better price fat and healthy than he could trail-gaunted. That was an angle hardly anyone else thought of.

He waited for breakfast, irked because as usual Gertrude and these lazy women were dawdling in there long after sunup. He wanted his hotcakes, doused with the ma-ple syrup they'd hauled clear from New York. She'd grumble at him because the fire wasn't built or the coffee on, but he couldn't see why he should be doing that kind of work, women's work. Here he was, supporting her, and filling the bellies of the merchandise, his shelf stock, and they would grumble because he didn't think it his duty or responsibility to build the fire. Women all had their angles too, and if you let them get away with it, they'd con a man out of his manhood. Let them build their own fire. He relented a moment and thought to fetch some wood, but hardened. He had enough burdens without adding that.

Next out, and predictably, he thought, was Flora Slade. He didn't like her. She lacked nineteen and thought the whole world should kiss her big toe. The war had wiped out her family and left her alone and destitute, and that was how he had cottoned onto her. Halfway pretty would describe her, but snobby as a dowager. Her father had been a slave broker, a slave auctioneer down somewhere in the South, but had been killed in the war, and her mother had died suddenly. What an evil thing, he thought, buying and selling flesh like that, brokering slaves. The father, Slade, deserved what he got. Alvah didn't hold with slavery. He suspected Flora was corrupted—she must have watched naked slaves bought and sold, and felt some sort of bizarre power and conceit, knowing her father could do that to people. Alvah could see it in her, a contempt for the world, a woman ready to buy and sell anything, up to and including God. Getting her north had been a problem, but Alvah had his angles. He'd picked her up in Council Bluffs. She had brought silks and satins, things utterly impractical for the trail, and he had been forced to buy other clothing. But he'd present a bill, padded generously thanks to a little token of esteem he gave the storekeeper, to Flora's fiancé, a placer miner named Yakima Cranston. Alvah didn't believe anyone would be baptized Yakima Cranston, and could hardly wait to find out what the man's angle was. If he balked at the clothing bill, Alvah would keep the bride and sell her elsewhere. That hunkered in the contract too, unusual expenses.

From within the wagon sheet arose a great caterwauling and snapping, and Alvah knew the last of his merchandise was awake. He'd gotten her cheap, right off the boat, though it took a small fee to another marriage broker to fetch her. Mary-Rita Flaherty was her moniker, red-headed, freckled, and plain as the snout of a pig. She'd arrived in Boston with scarcely a penny, and not much more than a pair of leather lungs and tonsils that howled at everything. He'd wormed the story out of her soon enough: her family in Tipperary had scraped together her passage. It had taken the combined savings of her father, uncles, aunts, plus her mother's gold wedding ring to do it. Alvah thought that sounded rather touching, a whole family sacrificing its last cent to let a lass fulfill her dream of going to a new and better life in the New World, until he found out that Mary-Rita hadn't wanted to go. They had bodily hauled her to the boat and locked her in, courtesy of the purser, who didn't open the door until the ship plowed the sea. Alvah loved that. Those micks always worked the angles. They'd simply got rid of her with that ticket. After a while he understood why. She had cater-wauled her way clear across the continent. It tickled Alvah to think he'd be foisting her off on some poor unsuspecting Irish miner out there, fellow named Tom O'Dougherty. Good thing he'd signed an ironclad, airtight, hellacious contract. Well, Alvah thought, those Papists deserved one another.

Alvah congratulated himself for setting up camp a couple hundred yards away from the lowlifes. There'd been wild times over there last night, even gunshots from some hell-raisers, and the noise of it hadn't been so bothersome here. A good angle, camping apart. He'd do that on the trail.

A voice from behind startled him. "Mister Riddle!"

Alvah turned, stared up at a man on a giant ugly blue roan with evil yellow eyes. Alvah had never seen such a man, built like a barrel, wearing dark buckskins and a black-silk stovepipe hat, set rakishly on gray hair that hung to his shoulders.

"I'm Mister Skye. I'll be guiding you and your ladies to Virginia City. We'd best be off, mate. Time's flying."

"You're Skye?"

"Mister Skye."

"Heard of you," Alvah said, craftily, playing the best angle. The man before him was astonishing. He wore fringed leggins and a breechclout, like the savages, instead of pants, and some thigh flesh shone umber in the sun. Indecent. And he cradled a new rifle in his arm, as if he expected Alvah to be dangerous or something.

"On the trail we'll be moving one hour after first light without fail," said Skye. "I see your people are barely up, and your mules aren't harnessed. I'll help you today, mate, but after this . . . " Skye's voice trailed off.

"Now just a minute!" said Alvah. "I didn't hire you. And we're going to be moving slower. I got delicate women to think of. And no help for the harnessing."

Mister Skye stared unblinkingly, and Alvah withered under the gaze. At once he despised this man, this barbaric guide.

"On the trail you'll follow instructions from me or my wives. Your lives will depend on it."

"Wives? Wives?"

"Mary of the Shoshone, and Victoria of the Crow."

"I didn't hire you. Wouldn't ever hire some bigamist, squawman, lowlife," said Alvah. Resist Skye, that would be a good angle. Resist this wilderness oaf.

"Suit yourself," said Mister Skye. "The other two wagons are leaving in a few minutes. Join us or go alone." He peered amiably at Alvah.

So that is his angle! thought Alvah. Threaten to leave him behind and helpless, without protection, so he could have his way on the trail. Alvah stared back shrewdly. Still, it was probably a bluff. Alvah liked to ferret out a bluff.

"We've employed you; we'll make the decisions, and you'll obey them," he said airily.

Mister Skye yawned. "Suit yourself." He turned the ugly horse and trotted off.

"Wait!" cried Alvah. That man and the Chinese looked like a whole army to Alvah, safety on the trail. But oh, the price. "We'll harness. We'll forget breakfast. We'll be right there."

"Who says we'll forget breakfast?" yelled Mary-Rita Flaherty. "You idjit, who do you think you are, starving me?"

Mister Skye smiled. "I will help you harness, Mister Riddle," he said.

Alvah couldn't understand Skye's angle, helping him harness. It made him suspicious.

But the guide slid off that terrible horse, which stood quietly, trailing a single rope rein on the grass. The burly man lumbered toward Alvah's mules, unhobbled one and led it to the pile of black harness and slipped on the collar and buckled the bellyband, and soon had the animal ready for the tugs, even while Alvah and his women gaped. Secretly Alvah exulted. He'd have this dumb guide, who didn't mind work, harness the six mules each day.

"Grab a collar, mate," said Mister Skye. "I'll fetch the next one."

Alvah did nothing. Let the rube do the work, he thought. The man's accent bothered him. What was it? Sailor-talk, that's what. And the way the man walked, too, rolling the way they do on the deck of a ship. Alvah squinted. This guide had been a sailor, but was now a Western man. Some angle there, maybe fraud. He'd worm it out of Skye and maybe use it.

"You a sailor once, Skye?" Alvah asked, carefully doing no work.

"It's Mister Skye, mate. British navy, until I jumped ship. I was pressed right off a dock on the Thames."

Jumped ship! The confession delighted Alvah. He'd turn the big dumb guide in, and collect a reward. Contact some Canadian Crown officials.

In minutes, Mister Skye had two mules harnessed. These would be the wheelers, so he added breeching and backed them up to the singletrees, fastened the tugs, secured the wagon tongue between them, and tied up the reins.

"You oaf," yowled Mary-Rita, "I'm going to eat me porridge. And cover up your flesh, you—you wildman."

Alvah permitted himself a smile. Mary-Rita Flaherty was having a normal day.

"Suit yourself," said Mister Skye.

Alvah Riddle plucked a long stem of timothy grass and pressed it between his yellowed teeth. "Some nag you got there," he said, as Skye lumbered off to fetch another mule. "Older'n creation. Guess you can't afford better, guiding business bad as it is. Never seen one so scarred up." He ambled over toward Jawbone, who laid his ears back and bared his teeth.

The next thing Alvah knew, he catapulted to the ground, thrown hard by some terrible force hitting from behind. It belched the wind out of him. When he finally caught his breath and stared up, Mister Skye loomed over him.

"Sorry, mate," said Skye. "Don't ever go near that horse. You and your party, never get closer than ten or fifteen feet. Is that clear?"

Alvah was peeved. "He probably kicks. Fine thing, we have to live with an unsafe horse that kicks."

"No, Mister Riddle, he kills."

Alvah chose silence. Then Gertrude Riddle, who had watched all this with alarm, helped Alvah up and faced Mister Skye. "We have decided to employ some other guide," she said primly.

"Now hold up, Gertie," said Alvah. "This fella must be hell on Injuns, and that's the kind we want."

"Take a whip to him," said Flora. "Some men just need whipping. Mister Riddle, if you don't whip this man, I will."

Alvah muttered unintelligibly.

Flora Slade lifted a long snaky plaited whip from the whipsocket on the fine enameled wagon, and cracked it a few times. "I'll teach hired men manners," she said, advancing on Skye.

Mister Skye unhobbled another brown mule and led it to the harness pile. He watched her coming. "I don't believe we've met," he said gently.

The tasseled whip snapped and hissed as she cracked it.
"Flora Slade, and you will address me as miss," she said.
The tassel hissed close to Mister Skye's face. The mule
reared, frightened.

"Very well, Miss Slade," he said, patiently leading the
mule.

The lash snapped angrily around Mister Skye's midriff,
whacking the buckskin with an awful pop.

"Stop that, Flora," muttered Alvah, but not too force-
fully. It seemed a good angle to be on record against it,
even though a good whipping might teach the oaf manners.

Mister Skye ignored the lash, and tied the skittery mule
to the wagon.

"I'm afraid you're frightening the mules, Miss Slade.
Perhaps you'd care to whip me after they're harnessed."

He dropped the collar over the mule, and began to harness the twitching animal. Flora Slade gaped.

"We are ladies and gentlemen, Skye," she yelled. "You
are a hired servant. You will do exactly what we tell you."
She cracked the whip hard over his head for emphasis,
knocking off his silk hat and denting it.

Mister Skye's gaze followed her. Then, like a giant cat
he clawed out at her, trapped a small hand in his giant
brown one and easily plucked the whip from her. "Save
the whipping, Miss Slade, until after the mules are harnessed." He smiled amiably, and screwed his hat back
down.

Flora Slade glared. The rest stared.

He addressed Alvah Riddle. "If you're coming with us,
have your wagon at the other camp in five minutes."

Alvah decided he would. Where else could he get a
savage lackey for free?

Chapter 4

Drusilla Dinwiddie hadn't yet made up her mind about Mister Skye. He behaved like any frontier oaf equipped with a pair of squaws to do his drudge work. That had been the lot of women, she knew—men had the fun and women drudged. Still, there seemed something competent about the man. He hefted that new repeater rifle as if he knew how to use it. In minutes he had done something Alvah Riddle couldn't do—organize this little party of three wagons into a small train and start westward on schedule.

She'd had more or less two months of experience with Alvah Riddle, and had come to conclusions about him. The paunchy proud man with the chinless ferret face and balding head seemed crafty and nasty. Drusilla rode in a fine wagon pulled by three span of prime mules because Riddle was clever and didn't want breakdowns. But no other virtues manifested themselves. He repelled her now that she knew him. He'd gotten them kicked out of Jarvis Porter's disciplined wagon train, and its safety. She loathed him for that. Now they were forced to travel with two wagons of unspeakable lowlifes, and with no safety at all.

They'd be easy prey to the restless Sioux or Cheyenne, prowling unhappily this year of 1863, especially since the frontier garrisons were gravely weakened by the great holocaust back East.

Still, this Skye, who insisted on being called mister but had a low-class British sailor twang to his voice, seemed commanding and competent, and her dread eased a bit. She knew nothing of weapons, but obviously a man with a repeater could do a lot of damage fast. He'd sent those squaws out on either flank as soon as they were clear of Fort Laramie and proceeding down the south bank of the Platte—or at least she thought they were, since the trail more and more distanced itself from the river and plunged through black hills covered with pine and cedar.

This Skye had done something else, too. He'd summoned that giant Chinese named Chang, who appeared to be of the warrior caste, and the two of them had ridden ahead of the procession, talking, taking the measure of each other. Behind Skye, who rode that awful blue roan horse, came several of Skye's mules, some with packs and others drawing travois with Skye's buffalo-skin lodge and lodgepoles on them. The squawman lived totally like an Indian. Drusilla peered ahead discreetly at Skye's breechclout and leggins and the bare flesh of the thigh. She'd never seen a white man like this, and had never seen breechclouts until far out on the plains, when beggar Indians had shown up in Jarvis Porter's camps.

Next rolled Alvah's wagon, and after that the red wagon of that infamous Cyprian, Goldtooth, and her bawds. And behind that, bringing up the rear, came the other red wagon driven by that crook, Cornelius Vanderbilt, and Blueberry Hill, who usually walked beside it, his white spats gleaming in the prairie sun. Tied to the rear of that wagon was a span of spare mules. How perfectly disgusting to have to travel with such people, and she scorned Alvah for it.

She blamed herself for signing that contract with the potbellied weasel. She had read his character instantly when he showed up at her cottage in Bennington, floppy hat in hand, leering around crooked yellow teeth. She debated now what to do about it. She feared for her life. This little party would be easy prey for even a small hunting party of fierce Plains tribesmen. It would depend on Skye, she thought. If he proved as inept as Riddle, she'd just jump this party and join any wagon train they overtook, or that overtook them, contract or not. Staying alive was more important than contracts. One thing about Skye she liked: he seemed to handle that rodent Alvah as if he scarcely existed.

Late today, Mister Skye had told them, they'd pass Register Cliff. For two decades now immigrants had stopped there to paint or carve their names on its face, and before that, the mountain men did it. But he said they wouldn't stop; if they wanted to carve their names, they could do that at Independence Rock a few days ahead. Tonight they would stay at a warm springs where people usually scrubbed laundry on the trail, and he wanted this party to arrive there ahead of any wagon trains. That made sense to her, although Alvah grumbled about Skye's relentless speed, faster by far than Porter's train with its ox-drawn wagons.

She'd do laundry then. And bathe, too, if she could manage it without all those oafs and lowlifes peering. Not that they'd want to peek at her anyway, she thought bitterly. When it came to beauty, Nature had dealt her the two of clubs. She'd grown so plain that her whole life had been affected by it, and she despaired of ever enjoying the normal pleasures and comforts of home and family given to other women. She had only two assets, one of them lustrous brown hair she wore long and divided at the center and hanging in ringlets. The other a smooth peachy complexion. Everything else was—dreadful. Her face too long, and with too much jaw. Her eyes too small and farsighted, so that she wore rimless spectacles. Her mouth naturally turned down, making her look sour no matter how amiable her mood. From neck to waist she stayed thin as a celery stalk, and almost without breasts, but below her waist her hips flared to ungainly size, and her legs swelled as thick as the variety that propped up pianos. The very thought of all this plainness plunged her into melancholy.

There were compensations, she thought. She read a great deal, and had become particularly familiar with the transcendentalists over in Massachusetts, especially Emerson and Thoreau. She had completed an education at Savoy Women's Academy, and could teach. She read voraciously and knew without a doubt that she possessed the best-informed and -educated mind of either sex in this party, or maybe even in this vast territory. She wrote melancholy poems, kept a diary with a lock on it so she could record her savage thoughts about Alvah—and Gertrude, who dabbled in spiritualism, tarot cards, séances, and the rest. And since Drusilla had the mental training to judge the worth of others, she did not hesitate to judge. She had no illusions at all about why she traveled here, on this wilderness trail, and why the other two brides were here as well, instead of back at their homes being courted and preparing for an amiable life. It embarrassed her faintly even to be in the same wagon with that howling immigrant girl and that incredible slave-seller's daughter. But that would pass, she told herself.

Alvah Riddle had shown up at a time of crisis, shortly after her father died, leaving her with a small Bennington cottage, a pittance of inheritance, and no means other than the possibility of a tiny living boarding somewhere else as a schoolmarm. The possibility of marriage had never occurred to her—she thought only of her plainness—until Alvah had discussed the miners in the Far West starving for a wife, any sort of respectable wife, of any description. Were any starved enough to marry the likes of her? It seemed so. Still, she thought the bulgy ferret was loathsome, and she appended all sorts of conditions, which Riddle reluctantly agreed to. Then she accepted. Men might make their destinies; why couldn't women? It scared her to think such bold thoughts. But the meeting, the confrontation at the end of this vast journey—that alarmed her even more. What if Amos Rasmussen stared, gasped—and embarrassed her?

Well, she thought, she'd deal with that when the time came. She didn't really want a consummated marriage anyway. That whole animal business seemed—messy. She'd be quite content to cook and sew and provide company, in exchange for his security. She felt indifferent about children. A good novel seemed better than a messy, sucking, demanding infant anyway. She wished she knew the means those soiled women used to prevent conception. Perhaps she'd nerve herself to find out before the trip was over. She'd read, write, live her own life of the intellect. If she got there alive, which she increasingly doubted.

They had toiled the last half hour up a long grade that took them away from the river and its valley. At the crest Mister Skye—why did she involuntarily call that oaf mister?—halted to let the mules blow. Drusilla clambered down from Alvah's enameled wagon and stood in the warm sun, enjoying the feel of the dry winds whipping her tan skirts. The wildness of the land struck her hard. From this vantage she could see the wide Platte coiling sleepily through a green valley, between arid blue hills dotted with silvery sage. Off on the western horizon rose purple saw-toothed mountains still capped with white, and another range stretched across the hazy north. And above her a sky so azure and intense that the color pierced into her spirit. Blue was the color of freedom, she thought. Those who loved liberty loved blue. Her colors were blue and white.

Mister Skye dismounted, and studied the members of this party. Drusilla had the feeling she would be observed, weighed, and—judged. It annoyed her. How dare he, a wilderness squawman, subject her to his judgment?

"What is it you don't like about me?" she said crossly.

The old guide gazed silently for a moment. "I don't rightly find any reason to dislike you, Miss Dinwiddie."

"Well, stop you staring, then. Am I too plain for you?"

Mister Skye grinned faintly. "I like to think I'm helping people make their dreams come true," he said quietly.

She would not buy his blarney. "I don't think so," she snapped. "I think you're studying each of us to see whether we're going to be helpful on the trail, or a problem you'll have to deal with.''

The guide looked faintly surprised. ''You may have something there,'' he admitted.

Drusilla felt the faint thrill she always did when her sharp mind had penetrated through to some truth, usually ill-concealed in the Aesopian language of someone else. She felt a strange power over this frontier oaf, Skye.

''Are we going to be safe in this wilderness?'' she asked.

''There is no safety here.''

That was not an answer she wanted to hear. ''We're outcasts. No wagon master would have us. I'm sure you understand why.''

''I do,'' he said. ''But traveling this way has some advantages. Disease, for instance. It can burn through a large wagon train like a prairie fire, killing as it goes. There's no cholera this year, so far. And speed. This party with its mules can go much faster than ox-drawn wagons. And convenience. At the warm springs tonight you won't have to wait for others to wash ahead of you or worry about muddied water.''

''But we're vulnerable—to even the smallest band of thieving Indians.''

Skye grinned. ''Depends how you look at it. Horse theft is a great honor among the Plains tribes. They will try us, for sure. And we'll try them.''

''You mean you'd steal?'' she asked indignantly.

''When in Rome, do as the Romans do,'' he replied.

''Where did you learn that?''

He grinned, saying nothing. Then, ''We have four superb warriors and three others who might or might not fight. I think Blueberry Hill might stand up and be counted, but the others will set too much store on preserving their precious hide.''

She peered around her at the others who stood near their wagons, enjoying the vast aching views. ''I don't follow your counting,'' she said crossly.

"My wives are better warriors and sureshots than I am. Ruthless. Between them, they've taken a dozen scalps."

She shuddered.

"The younger one is Mary, of the Shoshone, or Snake people. She's excited because she'll be seeing her people this trip. And the older is Victoria, of the Crow." He eyed her amiably. "Get to know them. You might learn a thing or two."

That miffed her, the subtle insult. But she knew how to deal with the barbs of this man.

"I will teach them more than I learn from them," she said archly.

He nodded, smiling. "You will excuse me, Miss Dinwiddie. There are people in this party I don't yet know and wish to meet."

She felt suddenly alone. How could a big halfwit do that to her? She had formed no friendships on this long trek. The immigrant girl appalled her. The daughter of the slave dealer thought only of social position. Gertrude Riddle was . . . peculiar. Drusilla peered in the direction of the dumpy woman and found her perched on the wagon seat. Tarot cards in hand, eyes pressed firmly shut, and mouth forming inchoate sounds. No, she thought. There'd be no bonds formed with that bizarre creature. As for the rest, the lowlifes, she hadn't yet nerved herself even to talk with them, though she found herself curious. Perhaps she would try it sometime. Now, on the trail, would be the time to study the other side of life and draw conclusions about it. She could examine these women and put them in the display cases of her orderly mind, much the way butterfly collectors netted specimens and pinned them down in glass-covered chests.

Mister Skye approached Alvah, who industriously greased his axles with a brush and tar bucket.

"That's always a good move, mate," Skye rumbled.

Alvah peered up, sharply. "I know what you're up to, Skye, but your compliments don't signify anything."

"Your mules are in fine shape, Mister Riddle."

The chinless man straightened. "I fed out oats the first

two hundred miles until two bags were used up. It pays,''
he said. ''But don't think soft words will get you the upper
hand of me, Skye.''

''Mister Skye.''

''Whatever,'' said Alvah.

''You haven't paid Goldtooth for my services yet,
mate.''

''I don't need your services. If she was sucker enough
to pay you your fee without my consent, that's her problem.''

''Pay her, Mister Riddle.''

''Who are you to be giving orders, Skye?''

''I'd hate to see you and these young ladies out alone
on the trail.''

''You've got some angle, Skye. Are you getting a rake-
off?''

''I guide and protect paying clients, mate.''

The thought of being alone in Riddle's wagon chilled
Drusilla.

Mister Skye stared off toward the dun horizon. ''No,
Mister Riddle. I've found that a party works together—
defends itself better—when the burdens are shared properly.''

''Don't ya fear for me, Skye. I got a loaded Spencer
repeater. That'd cut a whole party of Injuns in two.''

''An arrow travels far, Mister Riddle.''

''I know your angle and I ain't buyin'.''

''Then we will leave you behind in the morning,'' said
Mister Skye softly with the whisper of steel in his voice.

''I know your angle!'' the man croaked.

Drusilla grew alarmed. ''Mister Skye, if that happens I
wish to go with you and the—lowlifes.''

The guide grinned. ''It can be arranged,'' he said.

''You have a contract! I'll sue you from one end of the
territory to the other!''

Drusilla peered at the rodent and smiled.

That was when Gertrude Riddle cried out from the
wagon seat, and began to swoon. They all peered up at
her. Riddle did nothing, and acted as if he'd seen all this

before. The woman righted herself and stared out into blue space, as if she'd seen a specter. Others joined Drusilla now, Mary-Rita, and Flora, all of them staring at the woman clutching her chest and gasping up on the seat.

"You have another trance, Gertie?" asked Alvah.

"The cards. The cards!" she cried. "I asked the tarot cards about our safety. And the spirits replied. Yes, they answered!"

Drusilla yawned.

"Tell us," begged Flora.

The woman peered wildly around, her eyes on everything and nothing. "Trouble!" she cried. "Trouble aplenty. And . . . someone is going to die!"

They waited silently. Something wild and eerie possessed her, something commanding their attention and keening their senses.

"The spirits have told me that Mister Skye will not survive this trip."

A quick black silence. "Now, now, Gertie, half the time that blasted board tells nonsense," said Alvah. "Did Skye put you up to this? There's some angle to this."

Drusilla peered furtively at Skye, who frowned but otherwise revealed nothing. Then his face relaxed, and the faintest smile appeared on his crevassed mouth.

"I am a fatalist," he said. "The wilderness is like a catamount in the night. The best-prepared men go under."

"It's all nonsense," snapped Drusilla. "The universe operates on rational principles."

In minutes they were off again, wending down long grades and around sharp curves through the black hills. Word of Gertrude's revelation spread swiftly to the lowlifes, and all of them kept a sharp lookout through the breezy afternoon. But no matter how hard they peered, they did not find death lurking anywhere. They followed the rutted trail, hammered into a wide highway by thousands of wagons before them, and in the long June evening they rounded a claw of land and approached the warm springs which were nestled between dark dry bluffs that flamed orange in the low sun.

Drusilla chose to walk the last mile. She grew impatient. She itched to wash her clothing—why were women always surrounded by rags and constantly scrubbing? Men were lucky. Maybe she'd bathe, too, if suitable awnings could be erected. But not in the same water with those—those fallen women. She might catch something, something terrible! She'd insist on bathing first, before those lowlifes so much as dipped one of their petticoats—if they wore any—into the water.

But as they approached the spring they found horses hobbled nearby, a dozen of them. Not mustangs, either, but good solid bays and sorrels and blacks with some size. Distant figures lolled around a campfire, and even at a distance Drusilla could see they were all male. Ahead of her, Mister Skye loosened the thong that pinned his revolver in his holster. Up on the sunlit bluff she spied Skye's two squaws, sitting quietly on their ponies, and suddenly Drusilla grew afraid.

Chapter 5

It gladdened Mister Skye's heart to see his two women sitting their ponies on the far bluff. This was sudden country, even so close to Fort Laramie, and when he sent his women out on the flanks to scout and hunt, it was always with the gnawing fear that he'd never see one or the other again. So much could and did happen to lone riders in country like this—such as captivity or death at the hands of hunting or war parties. Ponies had a way of coming up lame. There were always sudden encounters with grizzlies or rattlers, not to mention flash floods or hailstorms or bad water.

But there they were, a mile or so above them on the high bluff. Old Victoria seemed to have meat slung over the rump of her pony, though he couldn't tell for sure just what. Antelope, probably. He thought of her as old now, with her face like lined brown parchment, and her black hair shot with gray. She'd lost weight and gotten smaller too, but still rode her ponies with feist and ease. And Mary! A woman in her prime, thirty now, still flashing the smiles exuding the bright happiness that had first galvanized him when he discovered her among her Shoshone people. He loved her, and even though he pushed toward sixty, she still built a fine fire in him. Nowhere on earth were there two women wiser on the trail, more experienced, cautious, and able to fight like male warriors. Time and again they'd rescued him, rescued parties he had guided. They found food where none existed, and water where it didn't flow.

Now their presence on the cliff above the warm springs signaled trouble, he thought. For the moment, they would not come in, but would lurk like ghosts out of sight of whoever squatted there, able in an emergency to send a bullet out of the night, or out of the brush. Somehow they knew, instinctively, what to do, and Mister Skye had only to fathom their ways to have a hand full of aces in any trouble.

He felt glad, as he always did in moments of potential danger, that his son, Dirk, wasn't here. Twelve winters now, and in Missouri being schooled. There wasn't money enough, but somehow things had been arranged. Mister Skye had friends, some of them from the fur-trade days, who were eager to help. How his Mary had wept, and hugged the boy, when they had put him on the steamer at Fort Union, but how proud she'd been that the blocky golden child would learn the mysteries of white men's medicine, and read the talking signs on paper. She wept that day but never again, and after that redoubled her efforts to bring happiness and comfort to the man she loved.

They judged right to be cautious, he thought. Who knew what sort of men hunkered ahead? Those at the warm springs could not see his women, who had retreated behind a low ridge. As always, he lifted his black stovepipe and screwed it down again, as a signal. The three of them had never discussed the gesture, but they all understood it to say, I see you, and be wary—there could be trouble. He watched the tiny figures turn their ponies and disappear beyond a saddle. For the time being, they would be watching all that transpired at the warm springs.

He glanced at Seven-Story Chang, riding beside him, and noted that the mandarin had not missed anything.

"Mister Skye likes to improve upon the Fates," he said, pulling his white stallion apart from Jawbone, who stayed strangely docile around the mandarin's horse. It was an instinctive move for a warrior, separating so as not to bunch up and become an easy target.

Mister Skye and his wagons pulled up near the springs, which were set in totally barren hills. Any trees that had once grown there had been long since stripped off by immigrants seeking firewood. Nonetheless the eight young men present there had a smoky fire wavering in the low light, feeding on buffalo chips and brush hauled some great distance.

They looked to be civilians but Mister Skye knew at once they were army in spite of their gray butternut shirts and britches and old laced high-top boots and floppy felt hats over long unkempt hair and beards. A single glance at the horses, with their US brand, and at the saddles, some of which were McClellans, told him that. A closer look revealed muzzle-loading Springfield carbines in cavalry-issue saddle-scabbards. One of them, a burly auburn-bearded man, had a Colt's Army revolver at his waist, and a faded blue shirt with darker blue chevrons on an arm where the marks of rank had been torn off.

Veterans, then. Wounded veterans, discharged, heading for the West and its bonanzas, Mister Skye thought. But he saw no wounds among them. They all had four intact limbs. They peered at him now, their gaze raking him and the wagons, wagons enameled a startling red, with dyed wagon sheets. Then he knew: *deserters*.

Men who, if caught, could be thrown into stockades— or shot. Men trained to battle and arms, and probably well disciplined by this deserting sergeant into a smooth fighting force. Mister Skye studied the surrounding country, looking for a ninth or tenth, but didn't see one. The land was so barren it would ill conceal a sentry. Deserters. No wonder he had not seen them at Fort Laramie. They had skirted the fort and ducked its patrols. Even now they were tempting fate, resting here at a popular stopping point on the Oregon Trail, between garrisoned outposts.

The burly one's cold gray eyes studied the Henry cradled in Mister Skye's arms, raked the giant Chinese, and glanced briefly at the rest, dismissing Riddle but assessing Blueberry, and then the women of all sorts. Cornelius Vanderbilt had vanished, and was in fact spread flat in his wagon, derringer in hand.

"Light and set," the man said suddenly, a smile forming in his curly beard. "I'm Twill. Conrad Twill. The boys and I could use some company. We just stopped here to wash up a bit, and boil up some parched corn. If you've got some chow to spare, we'd be plumb grateful."

Mister Skye nodded. "You're cavalry," he said.

"You see the McClellans and the cavalry mounts, I reckon. Yep, we are. Fort Kearney, Nebraska. On a little private foray for Gen'l Harney. Can't tell ye about it."

"Harney? The retired General Harney, mate?"

"One and the same, fella. You got a little chow to spare? We ain't seen hide nor hair of game along this trail. All shot out or skeered off."

General William Harney had sat out the war, bitter because the Union Army gave him no commands, not trusting him because of his Southern origins. That was common enough gossip around Fort Laramie, and Mister Skye well knew of the fate of the old frontier warrior.

"Where are you headed, mate?"

Twill didn't answer. Instead, he studied Skye and Jawbone and the rest. "I don't think I caught your name," he said.

"I am Mister Skye."

The name meant nothing to Twill. It usually meant a great deal to men familiar with the Northwest frontier.

"Well, Skye, it's confidential army business."

"Mister Skye."

The man laughed, and so did the others. "Well, if you want to be 'mister,' no skin off my back," he said. "You sure got yourself a passel of females here."

"Yes. They've engaged me to protect them."

"Looks like some of them lovelies don't want your protectin' very much."

Several of Twill's young colleagues laughed. Most of them were boys, Mister Skye thought. Eighteen, nineteen, fuzz-faced young toughs who decided to give the army the slip. And all the more dangerous because of their lack of scruple. Their carbines were not in hand, but close by.

The women had emerged from the wagons behind him, and Mister Skye knew these deserters would quickly understand Goldtooth's profession. It showed plain in their gaudy dress, in their manners or lack of them. All except Mrs. Parkins, who dressed severely and looked like a deacon's wife. Riddle's ladies had emerged too, and Mister Skye could see them being dismissed with a glance.

"I am engaged to do what I must do," said the guide amiably.

"Now, don't be hasty, Mister Skye," said Goldtooth. "These look like fine sporting men to me."

He said nothing. He couldn't stop incautious people, especially out on these wilderness trails where the constraints of the East seemed to fly away like dry cocoons and people's hidden natures emerged.

Alvah spoke up. "The name's Riddle," he said. "I already got yourn, but not the rest of these soldier-boys. Mrs. Riddle and me, we're chaperoning these young ladies to Bannack City, where their fiancés await them. We just happened to get caught in this—this"—he waved toward the lowlifes—"this other party, mutual protection of course, and we'll be pleased to have a visit with you. The ladies here—they do want to wash."

Mister Skye thought that for a man obsessed with angles, Alvah Riddle was being rash. Or blind.

Goldtooth said, "You boys come visit in a little while. The gals and I, we've got some scrubbin' to do, and don't you stare too hard at the laundry." She laughed amiably. "We'd like to get the undies scrubbed up and drying before some big train rolls in. Then you all come visitin' a little later, and we'll have us some dessert."

"I like dessert," said one of them, a youngster with

blond stubble over sunburnt cheeks, and an old six-gun hanging low.

"I'd sure take it kindly if you could spare some chow," said Twill again. "This parched corn ain't fit for hogs."

"It seems that General Harney didn't provision you properly, mate," said Mister Skye.

"This here's army business and you get your nose out, big fella. You hear me? Any more pushing and prodding and you'll get hurt."

Mister Skye grinned, feeling his pulse quicken as it always did in moments like this. Chang had already vanished somewhere to the rear of these men, managing to be invisible even in open space.

Another one of them, thin with wary brown eyes, broke in. "We don't want trouble, Twill. Remember? This is a quiet little mission."

"This big galoot Skye is proddy, and I thought to show him some army steel," Twill muttered. "But like you say, Callaghan, we got a mission to do." He turned to Skye. "All right, Skye. You and this bunch of wimmin and low-lifes mind your own business, and we'll mind ours, and you won't get hurt."

"It's Mister Skye, mate."

Twill laughed. "Sure enough, Mister Skye. And Mister Riddle. And my respects to these Virgin Marys."

The women carted bundles of clothing to the springs, along with balls of lye soap and washboards. For once no social distinction cleaved them, brides and bawds on their knees beside the purling waters.

Mister Skye shrugged. He enjoyed a brawl, just to be brawling, and the odds were about right. Maybe later. A few bloodied noses might straighten out the army. He'd brawled in the toughest brawl college in the world, the decks of British men-o'-war, and he'd brawl again, even near age sixty. But for the moment there were horses to care for, mules to unharness, travois to untie.

"You! Skye!"

Mister Skye turned.

"The army's requisitioning food. That's the way it is in war. You got any objections?"

Skye ignored him, and the sergeant laughed. Trotting down a game path now were Victoria and Mary on their ponies. A slain antelope drooped over Victoria's horse, the blood from an arrow wound in its chest dark and congealed. On Mary's horse teetered a tied bundle of deadwood, gathered in some distant place.

"Well, look here," said Twill. "We got us some meat. We'll have lots of meat tonight. Looks like you're a squawman. Two squaws, one for slaving and one for sport. Maybe you'll share all the meat with the army, eh, Skye?"

"It's Mister Skye, mate."

Twill laughed, and the other deserters, emboldened now, laughed too.

Mister Skye lifted the blood-soaked pronghorn carcass from Victoria's mount, and squeezed her hand.

"Sonofabitch," she muttered, and dismounted, glaring at the strangers with fierce proud eyes.

There were no trees, so Mister Skye hung the carcass from a propped-up wagon tongue and Victoria and Mary skinned it skillfully with deft cuts and tugs. Mary glanced fearfully at the rough men watching her, and at Mister Skye, who simply screwed his hat down on his gray head.

"You got 'em well trained, Skye. Well-trained squaws are like well-trained mules," said one.

"Mister Skye, mate." Patience, he thought. He had people under his care. He'd try to get free of this scum at dawn, get his assorted ladies miles away before the others stirred much.

It took an hour to butcher and cook the antelope on the economical fire Mary and Victoria built, and when it turned brown it yielded a small meal for all, but not enough to allay the hunger of men who had toiled outdoors all day. Cornelius Vanderbilt never showed, and lay hidden in his wagon. He'd gone coward, Skye thought, or else he recognized some soldiers he'd skinned some time or other. Well, let the thimblerigger starve. Blueberry took his meat but sat apart, finding some sort of safety simply in distance. The deserters eyed him from time to time, obviously adding up odds, calculating costs, if there should be a little fracas. In the end, they dismissed him as unimportant or an unknown quality. That was good, Mister Skye thought. And as twilight settled into darkness Seven-Story evaporated again into the night somewhere in the vicinity of the mules. Maybe even inside Skye's lodge, judging from the way Jawbone stood with laid-back ears and an alert glare in his evil yellow eyes. Good enough, then.

"I could sure use some meat," said one whose name Mister Skye knew to be McMaster. They laughed. The bawds grinned.

The three brides and the Riddles pretended not to hear or understand. They were peculiarly silent. Flora Slade said not a word, afraid that her Southern tongue would provoke these Union soldiers, or reveal her hatred of them. Alvah peered at them all, yellow-eyed and nervous and afraid. Even Mary-Rita Flaherty held her sharp tongue. Goldtooth itched to open her store for business, and Mister Skye wished she wouldn't, for the simple reason that these deserters would be penniless and likely to take what they couldn't pay for. But that wasn't Goldtooth's way, and now she sat beside the embers in her scoop-necked pink gown, provoking whatever lusts she could. Big Alice grinned and locked smoldering gazes with one man after another. Juliet Picard found ways to display her assets. Only the patrician Mrs. Parkins, dressed primly in a high-necked turquoise summer calico, didn't seem to invite trade, and that only provoked a great deal of attention from the young toughs, who recognized social caste when they saw it.

The June night air eddied languorous, and scented with fresh sage. It played with the clothing hung from lines stretched between the wagons, making the bawds' under-things of bright pink and purple and gold and silk shimmy in the lavender twilight. Such gauds delighted Mary and Victoria, who had studied the bawd clothing rapturously, fingering silky things, giggling at frills and peekaboos and transparent nothings and black net.

"Mister Skye," said Mary, "gimme one of them." She stabbed at something made entirely from black lace. "I never saw stuff like that at the sutler's store. How come they don't got it?"

The guide bellowed.

Over at the green wagon of Alvah Riddle hung another type of clothing altogether, primly white, dancing like ghosts in the night.

Alvah stood. "Well, ladies, it's time to retire. Guess I'll check my Greener shotgun before I turn in," he said in a slightly loud voice. "I got a fine new one, loaded with buckshot," he announced loudly. "Out on the trail, a man has to figure angles."

Several of the young deserters grinned through their beards, their teeth gleaming yellow from the embers of the fire.

"That's not the only protection we got," boasted Alvah loudly. "Got things that'd wipe out an army—ah, of Injun warriors and such."

He shepherded his uneasy women toward their wagon, after some detours into the darkness.

"I would have liked to write in my journal," said Drusilla, sounding annoyed.

But a few moments later the wagon stopped creaking, and there was silence.

"Well, ain't we gonna have fun," said Twill.

"I can hardly wait, honeyboy," said Goldtooth. "My good Kentucky bourbon is two bits, and other merchandise starts at a fancier price, U.S. dollars or gold."

It was coming, thought Mister Skye. He nodded slightly, and Mary and Victoria disappeared into the lodge. Jawbone snorted in the darkness. The rest were still seated around the dead fire, starlit shadows, the deserters rank with sweat and grime.

"I don't think I got me a thin dime," said Twill. "You got some coin to lend a poor suffering sarge, boys?"

"Ain't got a cent. Eight bucks a month in this man's

army, and it don't last through payday," came a voice in the dark.

Goldtooth replied, "Why, don't worry your poor heads about cash. I bargain, honeypots, for any old thing. Like those nice guns. We love to have guns, don't we, ladies. Big guns, little guns. Long as they shoot!"

"I think not," said Mister Skye softly, thinking how stolen army Springfields would look to any Union command inspecting wagons on the Oregon Trail. But he was trumped by Twill.

"Sorry, my little lady. We'll be keeping our Springfields. And our horses. And our saddles. We're the army, honey, and this is war, and we're just going to requisition everything we need."

"Yeah," came a voice from the dark. "Start dishing out that Kentuck, for starters. Get a jug of that, and we'll just have a fine old time."

"I think not," said Mister Skye.

The silence steepled. "Want to try us, Skye?" said Twill.

"I think you'll just turn in now," said the guide.

Chapter 5

A hard rough hand clamped over Mary-Rita Flaherty's mouth, even as a burly arm caught her in a vise, pinioning her arms to her side. She bolted awake in convulsed terror, and in seconds her heart slammed so fast and hard in her chest she thought she'd die. She twisted and wrenched in her white nightdress, the fear of death upon her. But the brutal force pressed her, and she lay trembling and helpless, feeling now the cold steel of a blade upon her throat.

Beside her she heard the others threshing helplessly, and knew that more than one attacker crawled inside the dark wagon, where the girls and Gertrude Riddle had pallets on top of a pile of supplies. She peered around wildly. Mrs. Riddle lay inert; she could see that much in the murky light.

"If you make a sound—you're dead," hissed a harsh male voice addressing them all. Then the brutal hands and arms hoisted her as if she were a feather, tossing her outside. The night air pierced through her thin white nightdress. Then all three brides emptied out of the wagon, trembling ghosts in the night. She saw Alvah pinioned to the ground beneath the wagon by three men. One of them hefted Alvah's glinting Greener shotgun. Others ransacked the wagon, no doubt hunting for money. One pinched coin in a purse and grunted. Then Mary-Rita was lifted bodily and hauled to a place where two others held saddled horses. She was thrown up over the withers of one, and a man who seemed a giant swung up behind her.

Just then Mister Skye's horse, Jawbone, shrieked crazily, squealing in the night as no other horse she had ever heard. The eerie howling frightened her worse than the cruel arms that bound her like a band of steel. They bolted off, the throb of the loping horse hard upon her soft thighs. She tried to see whether anyone followed, whether anyone would rescue or help, but when she twisted her head he cuffed her hard, a blow so jarring that she cried. She hadn't cried since she was a wee lass, but now she bubbled tears and wished she were back in green Ireland with her people.

Beside her raced other horses, and in the starlight—no moon lit the way—she saw the ghostly white forms of Drusilla and Flora, all of them being sped to their doom. They'd be used brutally and killed; she knew it. She knew she would be tormented and die. She tried muttering an Our Father but the words wouldn't form in her head, and she fought back panic. The brutal riding never stopped, the hard gait of the horse slamming into her, making her sore. She wanted desperately to relieve herself. She wanted desperately just to be put down, just to feel the earth beneath her bare feet. But it never stopped. She bit her lip until she tasted blood. She began to weep, and got cuffed for it, but wept anyway, even as the cuffings rocked her head.

She had fallen asleep thinking she had nothing to fear from these rough men. There had been one last drama, which she and the others had watched unfold in the darkness around the campfire, from the shadow of the wagon sheet as they peered through the loosened puckerstring hole. The soldier men had tried to work their will upon those sinful women, but Mister Skye had told them to forget it, go to bed. The burly guide had stood there, his gleaming repeater cradled in his arms, and resisted. They had laughed, but a voice in the darkness—Blueberry Hill's—told them that the first one to move would die. And another voice—it belonged to that slimy gambler, Cornelius—had announced that they were covered. That astonished them—a voice they'd never heard, because the gambler had never shown himself the whole evening. To cap it off, something out of the dark brained two of the soldiers, who fell with a thud, never uttering a word, and so they knew the heathen Chinee, plainly a man to be reckoned with, skulked behind them. Mary-Rita had sniffed. Heathen Chinee shouldn't be braining good Christian white men. She had blessed herself at the sacrilege. And finally, even that contemptible Alvah under their wagon had yelled, "My Greener's on you, gents, jist in case you try playing the angles."

And that wasn't the end of it either. That sinful woman had a pearl-handled little lady's revolver snug in her hand, aimed steadily at the sergeant, Twill. She had laughed gaily. "Sorry, honeys, we all shoot."

Mister Skye had told them to rest peaceable, or some of them would rest eternal. Mary-Rita liked that. He spoke poetry, and it flamed romantically in her Irish heart. She thought Skye a disgusting beast, him with a British way of talking, too, but at that moment she became an admirer.

She had fallen into uneasy sleep then, feeling protected enough by brave men. Until she had been so brutally awakened. And now she knew she'd die, after being abused. Saints in heaven, if they abused her she'd have a baby. That's what always came of it, her ma had said. She'd have a baby and not even be married, and that would be shame, worse even than, than . . . she couldn't think of anything worse. She wouldn't even have the courage to confess it to the father—if any father existed in this place she was being taken to. If only her ma and pa could see her now! Then they'd be sorry they stuffed her on the boat! If only they could see her now! All their fault!

"I have to go. Let me down," she said to the man behind her.

For an answer he cuffed her again, and her head rang with the noise of it.

"You . . . you swine!" she boiled. "You scum! You don't even know how to treat a lady. I'm a lady! I'll bite your ear off, I will! You think you'll have your way with me, but I'll fix you!" she bawled. For an answer she got socked so hard she tumbled, and was dragged back up onto the horse just before she slid off. She wept again. "You are a pig, is what!" She wheeled her head around and spat at him, seeing the glob of it land full in his bearded face.

"Bitch!" he muttered. "I'll take the starch out of you soon enough, you dumb mick."

She spat again and he slapped her.

"Don't you call me a mick, you swine."

She boiled clear through, and the mounting ache and chafing of her bare limbs only made her madder.

"Saint Joseph, Saint Jude, Saint Paul, Saint Peter," she howled.

"Saint Mary, Saint Rita, Saint Elizabeth, Saint Clare, Saint Teresa," she added.

"Jesus before me, Jesus behind me, Jesus beside me," she yelled for good measure.

"Shut up, you little bitch."

She got an arm loose, balled up a fist and smacked it into his gut, feeling the explosion of sour air as it landed. "I'll kill you," she yelled, howling like a demon on the moors.

This time an arm clamped around her neck and tightened, choking her until her breath bottled up, harder and harder.

"That's a lesson," came the voice behind her as the arm eased. She gasped fiery air into her lungs, sucked it in again, and slugged him.

"Goddamn you!" he cried.

"You got trouble with that mick, Leo?" Twill's voice, and a horse loomed beside.

"I can handle it. Little bitch needs a lesson," snarled the man clamping her.

"You need a little lesson, lady?" Twill's amused voice came to her in the darkness. "Why, in a little while we'll teach you lessons you won't forget, and you'll like them, too." He laughed. "But for now you be quiet. One more peep outa you, and we'll shoot you."

That seemed like a good idea to Mary-Rita, so she yelled, a fine lusty bawl into the night, a bawl just like all the ghosts and goblins and werewolves she'd heard prowling on All Souls' Eve back across the seas. She howled, a fine daffy howl, and when the crack came on her skull, she just kept on howling, dizzy or not. A hand clamped over her mouth and she bit it, tasting blood. It yanked away, and she heard cursing behind her, words she'd never heard before and which she knew would shock a priest if she used them.

She yelled them back at him, and could hear laughter in the night. So she yelled them louder, fine dirty words bayed into the night like wolf laughter, an endless stream of them, new dirty words that filled her mouth and rolled from her tongue. She wasn't sure of the meaning of them all, but she knew they were dirty and her ma'd wash her mouth out if she heard, but her ma lived across the seas and glad to be quit of her. So she howled and they laughed, and she could sense those other women staring. She peered around. It grew lighter now, with a crack of gray slitting the east. She saw the gray and knew they hauled her south, away from the Platte River, away from the man who would marry her, a man with a name as Irish as her own, and a Catholic too.

Now in the gloomy dawn she saw only the two others, Drusilla and Flora, white ghosts in their nightgowns, silent and terrified. So Gertrude Riddle wasn't here. And neither was that skunk Alvah who'd got her into this, bought her, he did. Just the three of them, and each one a pure virgin. At least for the moment. Her anger slipped away to despair. "Blessed Mother, Blessed Mother, protect me, protect me, spread your wings over me, Saint Mary . . . '' she muttered, and finally she wept.

Flora Slade had grown up with horses, and she found her perch on the slight pommel of the McClellan saddle not at all uncomfortable. Her thin white nightdress rode high on her thighs, though, and she deplored that. But nothing seemed possible with that lout of a Yankee pinning her in place with arms of iron.

War, she thought. She'd never escape the war. War had reduced her whole life to rubble in months, and now it came back to haunt her after she thought she was free of it. Using her! The same as they used a slave, she thought, and it shocked her. She was being taken somewhere—she, a white woman—taken somewhere against her will! How dare they? Had these Yankee soldiers no decency?

Unlike Mary-Rita, who howled and caterwauled, or Drusilla, who simply sobbed, Flora sat cold and calm and thinking of murder and mayhem. She took after her father. Her father had been a calculating man, who smiled when the occasion called for it, not particularly a cheerful sort. Her father had perfected a calculating command of human nature, and knew exactly how much he could demand for a slave; knew exactly how to deal with sullen, rebellious slaves without destroying the merchandise. Oh, that had always been a sight, the disciplining of slaves, and Flora thought back on it with a certain electric pleasure through her back and loins.

Her father, Conan, had been a tall wiry man with jet hair, and a long face so chalky white that some believed the sun never touched it. In fact the sun touched it a great deal, but he neither tanned nor burned. Slaving waxed more than profitable, it became a bonanza, though a tricky thing because a lot of merchandise had been damaged. He had built, in Biloxi, a fine red-brick auction market with a raised covered dais on the street front, where crowds of buyers could gather on auction day. Inside hulked his offices, pens, and a few barred calls for particularly bestial brutes. Also a kitchen and some crude sanitary facilities:

it wouldn't do for the place to stink too much, or for the merchandise to get ill. In the rear, cloistered from eye and ear, stood a small brick disciplinary room with things in it that always made Flora shiver. Occasionally slaves were shot there, either because they were weak or ill and not worth the care, or because they had turned into savage animals. But for the most part, they were whipped, after their arms and feet were pinioned to the walls with chained manacles. At first her father had shooed her away from these events, but she had sneaked back anyway, and eventually he gave up. So she knew exactly how to treat people beneath her, and knew all the special torments reserved for males, and other torments reserved for females.

The wealth generated by this lucrative trade had purchased a fine mansion with Doric columns in front, and a whole stable of blooded horses, some trained to saddle and some to driving, all with the ruthless discipline that had been applied to human beasts of burden in the auction yard. Flora knew, by the time she grew old enough to understand such things, that her family was richer than almost anyone save for a few plantation owners who rarely came to Biloxi anyway. She knew too that slavery was a great institution, not only the source of her family's comforts, but valuable to the whole South, and also a natural and beneficial way of life for the Africans themselves, who might otherwise be trapped in steaming jungles without the slightest enlightenment of religion and science.

By her teens, Flora had become a willful aristocrat who defied her soft and retiring mother, invited the courtship of numerous swain and beaux and gallants, promising and tantalizing and seducing them with endless adroitness, but actually giving them nothing at all save for an occasional chaste kiss. If a horse displeased her, she had it shot, until even her father protested the extravagance. But she always reminded him that he would do the same, and she took after him. She had her own retinue of slave women, none of whom pleased her for more than a few weeks, whereupon she caused them to be whipped or sold or sent back to the auction market to be sold, naked, to someone else.

She enjoyed the power of it. Let any one of them become too familiar with her, and she would swiftly show them the differences of caste, class . . . and power.

Then the war changed everything. Almost at its debut, her father had been killed by a Union minié ball that had passed through his left eye and emerged from the base of his skull. A month after the black-garlanded caisson had drawn his Stars-and-Bars-draped casket to the family graveyard, and he had been laid to rest with full military honors befitting a colonel of the Mississippi cavalry, her mother had taken ill and begun a lingering decline that had lasted six months. Meanwhile men stripped the great house of horses for Confederate cavalry; income from the slave dealership had ceased, the grim brick fortress became a hospital for the wounded; and finally she found herself alone in an abandoned mansion, selling off the last of her furniture, staring at untilled fields, damning surly slaves who no longer jumped to her whip. That's when she began to think of escape to a better life, somewhere, somehow. Preferably shooting a few blue-shirted Union soldiers en route. If she killed a thousand of them, she had thought, it would not atone for the murder of her father, death of her mother, and present poverty.

And now one of those despicable Yank soldiers pinned her familiarly in her nightdress, taking her against her will, and intended to do to her exactly what a slave woman might expect. She was a slave! The thought astonished her. They would force her onto her back just like the lowest slave women, and they would have their sport with her! She seethed at the thought of it, seethed that a person of her caste would be treated like a slave by these barbaric Northern louts. But as she seethed, she realized that she had not been bred humble or dumb, and that her salvation lay in her hands. They'd find her no slave, submitting dumbly to their lusts. She knew where to strike them to double them up. Knew exactly where to jab with a knife to ruin their manhood forever. She'd seen slaves and other animals gelded, and she'd geld these Yank pigs one by one.

So Flora didn't struggle or howl vile obscenities the way that stupid immigrant girl did, or weep the way that toad of a New England woman did. She calculated. Her maidenhead for sixteen balls. The only trouble was, she hadn't the faintest idea how to wreak her revenge.

"You're smart," said a rough voice behind her. "Not like that dumb girl fresh off the boat."

"Yes, I'm smart. And I'll find ways to kill you," she retorted.

He laughed.

The endless ride had become painful, even for her. They were hastening south; she knew that from the light cracking the east. It occurred to her that she might die. These barbarians might simply use the women and kill them.

"Are you going to kill us?" she asked.

"Only if they're dumb enough to follow. If those lowlifes and that Skye come after you, we might."

She peered behind to look at him, now that enough gray light allowed her to see. Twill, the one whose blue shirt showed where sergeant's chevrons had once been.

"You're cowards and deserters," she said. "That's what Yankees are."

"It'll be a pleasure to enjoy a Reb lady," he replied. "In fact, this is as good a place as any."

"You had better kill me when you're done. Because I'm going to remember your face. And I'm going to have you tracked down. I'm going to find you, wherever you hide, and have you killed, but not before you lose your balls."

"My, my," said Twill. "I thought you Southern belles were all blushes and kisses."

"Try me," she said.

He stopped the horse, and dumped her unceremoniously into a patch of prickly pear. She yelped, sprang to her feet, and landed a petite foot in the chest of the cavalry horse, which reared up and began pitching, while Twill cursed.

The others had stopped, tossing the other brides to earth. They halted in an open arid meadow, a shallow valley. Stiff-legged men stomped life back into their saddle-bound limbs, while the women huddled and drew their thin night-dresses tight about them. The air lay chill.

"Well, who's first?" asked Twill, after he had gotten his mount under control.

"Loser gets the ugly one," said one. They laughed. Drusilla looked tormented, Flora thought. No trees, no shrubs, no brush grew here, and whatever happened would happen in full sight of everyone. Now terror and rage crawled through her, and she felt a need to vomit.

She had no weapons, not even long fingernails to claw with; not a shoe or a belt. Leering, Twill approached her, and yanked her to her feet. She scarcely realized that the other women were being yanked up by other men and dragged, like her, to a sandy place. Then a single brutal rip yanked the nightdress off and spun her to earth.

"Halfway pretty—for a Reb lady," he said.

A moment later he was on her, and she fought with knee and claw and teeth and muscles inspired by rage. But it failed her, even as her screaming gained her nothing as it pierced out into a dawn-gray wilderness. He laughed and fenced and finally clubbed her, so that her head rang, and still she evaded him, evaded the piercing, until at last she ran out of breath, pinioned by hands other than Twill's, and she felt herself hammered and invaded.

She scarcely heard the weird shrieking of Skye's horse Jawbone from afar, and scarcely knew why the thing that hadn't yet succeeded was abandoned, why Twill leapt to his feet and yanked at his clothing. She sprang at him, and with the only weapon she possessed, bit him exactly where she wanted, and spit out flesh.

Chapter 7

He thought he was too late. The women sprawled whitely in the dirt, somehow luminous in the murk of dawn. On second glance he changed his mind. Each of them thrashed violently, far from inert. At the sound of Jawbone's insane screech, deserters scrambled to their feet and lumbered toward their stolen cavalry mounts with the sheathed Springfields hanging from the saddles.

Jawbone wheeled to cut them off, his demonic screeching stirring the cavalry horses until they danced at the end of their pickets. The evil blue roan terrified horses as well as men. Mister Skye dropped the big rope rein and let the animal have its head. Easily he lifted the new Henry and sent a bullet into the earth just ahead of the deserter closest to the horses. He levered another cartridge and fired at one who was wrestling one of the women to her feet, taking care where he aimed. The slug missed, plowing dirt close to the man. He dropped the woman. A revolver cracked, and Skye saw that Twill had his sidearm out and was shooting with one hand, even while clutching his naked groin where blood leaked between the fingers of his other hand.

The picketed mounts pulled loose and skittered away from the deserters, and Skye turned Jawbone toward Twill, who grappled with the Slade girl. The deserter yanked her to her feet and slid behind her, making her a living shield of soft white flesh, while his revolver pressed into her skull above the ear.

"She dies, Skye. Drop that Henry or she dies!" he barked.

The man had sand, Mister Skye granted him that. The sort of sand that had made him a sergeant. He leveled his Henry straight at the girl, straight at Sergeant Twill.

"If you kill her, mate, you'll die," he said softly.

One of the others had caught a horse and ripped the Army Springfield from its sheath. Skye swung slightly, shot, and the man's hands bloomed red even as the horse began pitching wildly from the splattering lead that had struck the sheath and carbine and sprayed in all directions, none fatal. Twill shot, and the slug tore Skye's hat off, along with some of his hair and the smallest furrow of scalp.

Now others were catching their horses, and that became the larger danger. He leapt free of Jawbone, who screeched his macabre howl and plummeted full tilt into the milling cavalry horses, bowling over deserters in the process. He wheeled through them, ears laid back, flailing hooves and teeth in every direction, spinning violently on any man who lifted himself from the ground.

Skye saw the other women, Drusilla and Mary-Rita, attempt to rise. "Stay low," he yelled, and they did. Twill was the problem. The sergeant shot again from behind the Slade girl, but it flew wild because she struggled. Mister Skye levered his Henry and lowered it again, straight at Flora Slade, straight at Sergeant Twill.

"She dies if you don't drop that rifle," snapped Twill.

"You die, Twill. If she dies, you die."

Skye crouched now, sliding in little panther steps toward the pair of them.

"Don't shoot me," screamed Flora. "You murderer, don't shoot me!" The terrible black bore of the Henry opened on her. The muzzle of the revolver shoved again into her skull above her ear.

"Miss Slade," said Skye quietly, "get out of the way." She gaped at him. Eternities passed.

"Stop where you are, Skye—" barked Twill, swinging the revolver from Flora's head to shoot at Skye again. Flora wrenched suddenly, spoiling the shot, then dropped herself violently, wrenching free from Twill's arm and falling in a heap on the ground before him. Mister Skye aimed down the octagonal barrel and slowly squeezed the trigger. The Henry cracked, and Twill crumpled, dead from the hole in his forehead before he hit earth.

Flora flapped her mouth wordlessly. She sprang up and leapt at Mister Skye like a lioness, her claws raking him. "Murderer!" she cried. "You would have killed me. You stupid oaf."

He pulled the powerful girl off him and pinioned her with his free arm.

"Stand down, now," he said quietly. "You're alive and safe."

Several of the others crawled toward the milling horses, even as Jawbone paraded murderously between the men and the animals.

He snapped a bullet into the earth before the most active one.

"The next bullet will not miss," he thundered at them.

Behind him he heard the soft progress of a horse, and a swift glance revealed Seven-Story Chang on his white stallion. That would be about right, he thought. At Jawbone's first screech in the night, Skye had catapulted from his lodge, thrown on the saddle that was always at his lodge door, and loped off only a minute or two after the deserters had pillaged the Riddle wagon and fled into utter blackness. He'd given Jawbone his head. The horse would track through the blackness, using its nostrils and senses to follow a trail that Mister Skye could not pick out of the inky night. He knew Chang, the warrior mandarin, would be along soon enough. Skye sometimes probed so close to the deserters he could hear them talking and jesting ahead, but he and Jawbone hung back until dawn, when he could see what to do, and do it.

"I see I am not needed," said Chang as he turned his stallion toward the cowering deserters and leveled a long-barreled blue revolver upon them.

"Needed you plenty, and sooner," replied Skye.

Mary-Rita and Drusilla lay huddled and naked in the dirt. The Irish girl simply stared, but Drusilla wept softly and clutched her whiteness with her hands as if to ward off the gaze of male eyes. Three thin nightgowns lay in white ruin in the bunchgrass. Flora stood, no longer caring, and railed at Skye.

"I'll horsewhip you," she snapped. "Aiming that gun at me! I'll see you in hell! I'll cut you to pieces, you and your stupid squaws. You big idiot. You risked my life!"

She was, in a way, a beautiful woman with a fine full lithe figure turning golden in the dawn, and Mister Skye found it difficult to address her. "Was I too late?" he said softly.

"I don't know," she snapped. "Yes, you were hours too late. You should have been protecting us, you swine. You're a murderer. You killed that man. And stop staring at me."

"That is hard to do."

She picked up her gown, now confetti in her fingers.

"Now what am I going to do?"

Mister Skye addressed Miss Dinwiddie. "Was I too late?" he asked softly.

She shook her head and wept again.

"Was I too late?" he asked Mary-Rita Flaherty.

"Of course you was," she snapped. "Here am I, without a stitch on me body and men staring at me like I'm some common slut. And God in heaven and all the saints peering at me naked body and the shame of it. Oh, was you too late? If you had an ounce of decency, you wouldn't even ask a poor lass. And stop your starin'. I haven't got fine full breasts like that one has, just these little things that won't suckle a mouse, and you ask, was you too late?''

Mister Skye sighed. He could face arrows and guns. He could plunge into war. He could shoot to kill. The sight of gouting blood, his own or others', didn't faze him. But these women did, and he retreated from their glares.

"You," he said to one of the deserters. "You are going to donate your shirt and britches to the lady standing there.''

"And what does that leave me in this wilderness?" the man muttered.

"That's your problem.''

Reluctantly the man shed his shirt and wrestled with the buttons of his cavalry britches.

"Saints preserve us, there's enough nakedness to go around,'' yelled Mary-Rita. "Are ya daft, Skye?''

"Mister Skye," he said.

He carried the britches and shirt to Flora, who swiftly put them on, rolling up trouser legs.

"You!" barked Mister Skye. The man he pointed to reluctantly stood and began sliding out of his shirt and britches, and moments later Drusilla stood before them in clothing.

"You left me to last so you could feast your sinful eyes on me," snapped Mary-Rita. "You pig.''

Moments later, another of the deserters doffed his shirt and britches, and Mary-Rita skinned them on, wallowing in the oversized garments. The third deserter had worn nothing underneath.

"I'll burn to death in this wilderness," he snapped.

"Three nightdresses over there, mates.'' He addressed Chang: "We may as well return the stolen mounts, saddles, and carbines to the army.''

Chang began to round up the horses and the cavalry gear. In Twill's saddlebags he found a black pigskin purse laden with greenbacks and some double eagles. No doubt Riddle's. Mister Skye picked up his black stovepipe hat, discovered new ventilation in it, and screwed it down on his head.

"You'd leave us here on foot?" yelled one.

"Should have thought of all that before you deserted. The army can use the horses and carbines. Can't use you, though. Shoddy goods."

"We'll starve!" cried another.

"You'll have Twill's revolver and cartridge belt," Skye said. "Which is more than you're worth. I will take it with me for a half a mile or so, and then drop it for you."

Once they were clad, the women recovered their dignity and courage swiftly. Somehow it had come out well enough, though he felt unsure about Flora. Maybe the slave trader's snotty daughter deserved what she got.

He helped them mount, and adjusted the stirrups on the McClellan saddles.

"You!" he barked at the surviving deserters. "Lie down. I'll shoot the first one that stands, for as long as you're in the range of this rifle."

They glowered at him, but obeyed. Skye watched them from Jawbone's back while Chang and the women distanced themselves, driving the unridden horses ahead. Then he caught up.

Noon passed before they reached the warm springs camp on the Oregon Trail. Old Victoria, always alert, sat her pony on the bluff above the springs, watching them come. Mister Skye doffed his hat, and she turned her little bay down the easy slope. They rode in silently, amid the gapes of the fallen doves, Cornelius Vanderbilt, Blueberry Hill, and his own lithe and dusky Mary. But the Riddles clucked and fussed and asked questions. Alvah hadn't scraped razor over flesh; Gertrude luffed like a loose sail.

"High time, Skye," he said. "High time. These women look badly used. I'll hold you responsible for it. I'm glad they're alive, at any rate . . . Are they in good marriageable condition?"

"They are unharmed," said Mister Skye wearily.

"Indecent in men's clothing," snapped Gertrude. "Wash up. We won't have you dressed like that."

The three brides dismounted. They didn't need encouragement to head for the warm springs. All of them were caught in a melancholy silence.

"You poor dears," said Goldtooth. "We can help you. If you wish. Come along, ladies—we'll help these girls."

Drusilla nodded. Flora and Mary-Rita acquiesced, silently.

"Stay away from those women of mine. I know your angle, and I ain't a-gonna permit it," snapped Alvah.

But Goldtooth had taken charge. She snapped instructions to her ladies, who brought awning for a screen, and bottles of mysterious salves and ointments.

"It ain't right. Women like that messing with my brides," muttered Alvah.

"What happened?" asked Blueberry Hill. Mister Skye told them the whole story, and how he and Chang rescued the women.

"Damaged goods! The women has got carnal knowledge now because you didn't get there fast enough. I know your angle, Skye. You was fixing to break me. Where's my shotgun that they took? Where's my purse that they robbed? You keeping it?"

Mister Skye stared at the chinless, unshaven man. "I don't recollect that you employed me, Riddle."

"What do you mean by that?"

"I don't recollect that you paid Goldtooth, there, your share of my fee."

Riddle glanced around craftily. "So that's your angle. I should have known. Not an ounce of decency in you; not a shred of charity for these poor abducted women. Not a care in you about my business, bringing virtuous folk together to unite in eternal wedlock." Riddle peered narrowly up at Skye. "I suppose you'll keep my purse. I didn't contract for your services—there was no contract, no agreement—and now you'll pay yourself from it."

Mister Skye laughed. He slid heavily off Jawbone, tired from a dozen miles of night riding, and lumbered over to Twill's cavalry mount. He dug around in the saddlebags, found Riddle's purse, and held it up.

"This what you're looking for?"

"It is. And there was three hundred and seventeen dollars and twenty-seven cents in it, in currency and specie. If it ain't all there, Skye, I'll see you in court."

"Mister Skye."

The guide opened the black pigskin, and extracted a hundred fifty in greenbacks, and handed the rest to Riddle.

"That goes to the madam, who paid your share."

Alvah could scarcely contain his rage. "I didn't make that contract; she did. I knew you had an angle, you and her teaming up to sucker an honest businessman. I know your kind, Skye."

Mister Skye grinned. "All right then," he said. He stuffed the bills back into the purse and handed it to Riddle. "Here it is. Count it if you wish."

"What's your angle, Skye?" Riddle said suspiciously, even as he furtively flicked through the contents with adroit fingers.

"Well, if you aren't employing me, Riddle, I thought I'd just take the girls back and leave them with the deserters. Take your purse back, too."

"You wouldn't!"

"You haven't employed me, Riddle."

"It's a bluff. I know your angle. You'd never abandon decent women to them kind of men."

Mister Skye scratched his head. "I do believe you're right, mate. Guess I'll deliver them back to Laramie. I imagine there'd be a heap of soldiers, officers maybe, who'd like to tie the knot."

"You can't do that, Skye. They're my property!"

"Mister Skye," he said, leading Jawbone toward his lodge, which Mary and Victoria were dismantling.

"We gonna go down the road now?" Victoria asked.

"You are a beautiful lady."

"Sonofabitch," she muttered. "You getting crazy in old age, Chief Skye. If you ain't going down the road, I am. Pretty quick that wagon train with that Jarvis Porter is gonna roll in here, and then they see these sporting women and all hell busts loose. Maybe you'll get drunk, and I'll get mad.''

Mister Skye laughed, and settled to earth in the glowing sun for a ten-minute snooze. That was the great thing about squaws, he thought. They did all the work and he had all the fun. He'd had a good life. The best of all lives, though it had begun brutally, when he'd been pressed into the British navy as a boy, and spent years as a virtual slave in a man-o'-war until he slid over the side one foggy night back in twenty-six, and swam to the south bank of the Columbia River, close to Hudson's Bay Company's Fort Vancouver. Thirty-seven years now, a man of the mountains and prairies, a squawman, living a life beyond the wildest imaginings of the London youth who'd been shanghied on the banks of the Thames. And he didn't regret a moment of it, not even when the likes of Alvah Riddle temporarily blotted out the sun.

The burly guide cocked one eye open and rolled to a sitting position, feeling the soft buckskin shirt that had been Mary's shy gift to him slide over his barrel staves. The paunchy matchmaker shifted uneasily from one foot to the other, clearing his throat, which bobbled beneath a day's whiskers.

''I've been working the angles. Don't think you're pulling one over on me, because I'm wise to you, Skye. I know what you're up to, better than most. You're not worth a hundred fifty. This here is a well-marked trail and we don't need no guide. Mebbe worth a little for protection. Not any hundred fifty. But I'll make an agreement. I'll pay that—that—woman the price, but deduct the price of my shotgun, which was just under fifty dollars, leaving a hundred. You didn't protect my property, get my scattergun back, so I'll deduct that.''

Mister Skye yawned, observing puffball June clouds in the aching blue beyond Riddle's head. ''I've been paid. Deal with the madam.''

Drusilla approached, encased now in a crisp gray cotton dress, her washed hair hanging lustrous and loose. ''Mister Skye,'' she said, ''I don't suppose anyone has thanked you. I wish to.''

The guide nodded, peering up at a plain woman with intelligent soft eyes, hidden behind small gold spectacles.

''That—woman—who runs the parlor house . . . '' She glanced helplessly at Mister Skye, and Riddle, and proceeded bravely on. ''She says that no one was—damaged. Miss Slade is . . . intact. We all owe that to you.''

Mister Skye felt embarrassed. He'd rather face a hunting party of Bug's Boys than this. He cleared his throat and flapped his lips. ''We'll travel in fifteen minutes,'' was all he could manage. ''Harness your mules, Riddle. I see that Blueberry and Vanderbilt have theirs all set to go.''

''But—but, you're to harness the mules. That is part of it, Skye. You did it yesterday morning. That's part of it. Otherwise—''

Mister Skye stood and slapped tan dust from his leggins.

''Miss Dinwiddie. I'll be escorting you and Miss Slade and Miss Flaherty back to Fort Laramie, where you will have your freedom. I will leave instructions with the post sutler, Colonel Bullock, to attend to your needs on my account. I think you'll find a good new life there.''

''I'll sue!'' croaked Riddle. ''These women are under bond, signed and sealed.''

''Harness your mules,'' said Mister Skye.

''I'll pay the bawd her extortion,'' Riddle muttered.

Chapter 8

Blueberry Hill had a great fondness for mules. Goldtooth's mules were long brown creatures with bowed noses, floppy ears, and powerful bodies. Like himself, he thought. Mules were smarter and feistier than horses, and that reminded him of himself. He understood mule minds much better than horse minds. Mules were opportunists, finding feed and comfort at times when horses stared stupidly from harness and ignored the grass at their feet. That also reminded him of himself. He prospered with no visible means of support.

Technically he had been a slave all his life, but actually he lived in a delicate limbo, neither a freeman nor in servitude. He had never been manumitted, and hadn't a single paper declaring his ownership of himself. But neither did his masters, from outside Biloxi, ever pursue. In fact he was owned by an elderly widow and she had been rather fond of him, and not inclined to set the hounds after him. Still, that could change in an instant. He had drifted off, found refuge in the demimonde of Beale Street in Memphis, and had settled down in the parlor house and saloon of Goldtooth Jones. There he lived one day at a time, doing everything. He plucked his banjo and sang; learned to tickle tunes on the black and white levers of the piano-forte; learned to mix spirits and pour slightly watered bourbon; found himself evicting unruly white men from the confines; hauled water and toted bales and cared for Miss Jones's fine trotters and coach. For all this he was fed and sheltered, had his choice of the merchandise, and picked up occasional tips. He never seemed to lack funds, though he never seemed to have any to spare, either.

But it proved to be a delicate existence, especially when war came and with it the possibility of being conscripted into slave-labor battalions in the service of Confederate army engineers, digging sanitary trenches and breast-works, cutting and hauling firewood, and toiling for those who wished to keep him in bonds. So when Memphis fell to the Union forces early in the war, he had quietly re-joiced, until he found that they had similar designs on him, and a moralistic fervor that threatened the livelihood of his patroness, Goldtooth Jones, and thereby threatened him. So he felt perfectly content to be where he rode now, far west of the conflict and organized society, sitting in the madam's flaming red wagon, reining the mules and spitting occasionally at the footboards, targeting a knot midway between his black patent-leather shoes and the white spats over them.

Each dewy dawn he and Seven-Story Chang harnessed the twelve mules, with no help from Cornelius Vanderbilt, who considered such labor beneath him and in any case liked to sleep until the very last moment before they struck camp. The evening unharnessing fell easier, and Blue-berry did that alone, picketing or hobbling each animal in good grass, near water if possible. Each hot day, Blue-berry drove Goldtooth and her ladies, while Vanderbilt drove the second red wagon. The giant Chinese, who rode along for adventure rather than for the madam, simply mounted his great white stallion and vanished one way or another, often stopping to consult with Mister Skye at the front of the small procession.

Behind him this day the ladies lolled on their makeshift pallets beneath the pink wagon sheet. Heat blanketed the land, making breath come short. Usually they walked, or sat beside him as the wagon rolled down the long westering ruts, but today the sun forged so fierce and the air lay so heavy with blistering heat that they left Blueberry to his own devices. He coaxed the goldbricking mules along, cussing them with his gravelly voice, singing them love songs. They responded by rotating giant cupped ears backward, listening for the vinegar voice that meant whip or lash, and not hearing it. Today all three wagons ambled at the pace of an ox train.

Customarily he wore his black broadcloth suit coat everywhere, on this long trail as well as in camps, just as he wore it as a sort of uniform in the parlor house on Beale Street. But by mid-morning, the coat had turned into a furnace, and he felt his cotton shirt drenching across his back and belly, and sweat collect under his armpits. And so he gingerly wrapped six reins around some scalded ironwork and doffed the coat, folding it neatly beside him. The wily mules decided the faint tremor of the reins could be interpreted as a lax hand, and Blueberry admired them for their craftiness, a craftiness well understood by any black man who had ever worked cottonfields in heat like this. He felt a faint coolness as the sweated white shirt began to dry in the furnace breezes.

"Move your lazy ass," he said softly to the mules, recalling when the exact phrase had been spoken to him in his boyhood. Not once but too many times to remember. The mules quickened slightly, for a few yards, and imperceptibly slowed down again, and Blueberry grinned. Mules were realists, but had a great sense of theater. Mules were four-footed magicians, expert at illusions and abracadabra. Mules were mountebanks, standing eagerly in their traces but plotting skulk and sloth. He knew the inside of a mule soul, and they knew the inside of his.

"Were you referring to me?" asked Big Alice, putting a bawdy coloration on it. "When it's a little cooler, honey, I'll move it fast enough."

Big Alice's mind went only in one direction. From any starting point on the compass, it vectored toward sex. In that respect she was a soul mate of Blueberry's, seeing life groin-to-groin. She liked herself, enjoyed what she did, and had no intention of leaving the life until old age forced her to. In that respect also she was Blueberry's soul mate. Alicia Roque rose almost to six feet of high yellow, a fine amber nectar of French and Spanish and African, raised half wild in the bayous, where she discovered her life's calling at age thirteen, and never looked back. Big Alice's approach to her trade seemed exhausting, and he did not wish to exhaust himself after a broiling day.

"I'm saving my virginity for Mrs. Parkins," he replied, rattling the reins.

Mrs. Parkins did not reply.

Blueberry could neither scribble his name nor extract sense from books and magazines and broadsides, except for numbers. He knew the exact difference between a one-dollar Confederate shinplaster and a ten. But he plumbed souls, and knew precisely what anyone around him was thinking. He constantly dumbfounded people by telling them their private thoughts, and he had long since discovered a certain power in it, this ability he alone shared with God. Thus he knew the minds of his mules. Not in general terms, but specifically. Right now, for example, the offside wheeler concentrated on murdering a horsefly that had landed on its nose and was crawling toward a nostril.

Blueberry closed his eyes for a moment, shutting out the arid sagebrushed hills and the long blue mountains as they approached the Platte River Bridge. He wanted to know whether Mrs. Parkins would welcome him tonight. He already knew everything else worth knowing about her. The others always welcomed him, but Cleo Sylvanus Parkins sometimes dithered. No more prominent families ruled Memphis than those named Parkins and Sylvanus, and no more beautiful belle resided in antebellum Memphis than young ice-blond Cleo Sylvanus. She crowned and sceptered Goldtooth's ménage. In 1859 she had been given in marriage to Hannibal Parkins, who had amassed a fortune by massacring hardwoods, notably black walnut, and by age thirty-four, having slaughtered forests, he built himself a fine porticoed red-brick manse on a slope of Chickasaw Heights overlooking the river town and the silvery river. Cleo had already discovered voluptuous pleasures, and supposed, as Hannibal carried her straight across the threshold to the fourposter upstairs, that she would now command an endless supply of this titillating commodity. But in fact nothing satiated her, and while Hannibal proved as virile as any man, she never felt satisfied. Given her position, she resigned herself to this state of affairs, except for minor flirting at balls. But with the onset of war, Hannibal became Colonel Parkins and marched off to slaughter Yankees. Cleo wasted no time, not even twenty-four hours, before finding satisfactions, and enjoying the game of it as well, as she flitted among young Confederate officers. In a trice she galvanized gossip. But people of her caste merely tut-tutted such things, and ignored her even while her conduct grew wanton.

Then Memphis fell, and with scarcely a breather Cleo seduced a Union Army captain, her thirty-eighth lover, to be precise. That set tongues wagging, so she invited him to move into the great red-brick house, just to make them wag harder. Hannibal was gone, and could not in fact return to Union-held Memphis. It all seemed amusing enough until the captain's wife appeared one day, trotting down the gangplank of a riverboat she had boarded at Dubuque, proceeded by carriage straight to the Parkins mansion, and shot the captain dead. Some said, dead in bed, with Cleo Parkins beside him. At that point, the tattered shreds of society in occupied Memphis froze Cleo out. She, in turn, chose a career that would fill her insatiable needs and let her thumb her nose at the silly snobs. She arrived in a liveried carriage one day before Goldtooth's door, and announced her intentions. Unlike most any other woman of her caste, she kept her full name out of spite. Business had been spectacular. Not every man had sampled high-society women. Goldtooth goosed the price to astronomical levels, fifty Union dollars a tickle, but the trade never slowed—and Cleo lusted more than ever.

Blueberry delighted as much as anyone else in the reckless fury of Mrs. Parkins's lovemaking. He closed his eyes, heard Cleo entertaining the prospect of a night with Blueberry, felt no objections emanating from the ice-blond bawd, and decided, with a small flick of his six reins, how he would spend the night.

Homer Donk had devoted his entire life to improving the odds. It was not just philosophy with him, it was religion. Look life over and find ways to bend Fate. It didn't really matter to him how Fate could be bent; only that the odds in his favor would multiply like rabbits.

He lacked the nature of a mule-driver or teamster, but Fate had decreed that he would drive Goldtooth's red wagon west, as the third and last wagon in the procession. Within the bowels of his wagon, fine stout oaken hogsheads of Tennessee bourbon clunked and whispered, along with his roulette wheel with the removable magnet under the seven, and faro layout. The wagon toted sundry other items that would elegantly furnish Goldtooth's next bordello, along with delicacies not available in Bannack City, such as tins of oysters. And beyond that, a supply of staples and trail foods for Goldtooth's entire ménage. The Celestial, Seven-Story Chang, had thrown his small affairs into the wagon as well. Blueberry possessed nothing and needed nothing, beyond a bedroll.

Homer Donk didn't like driving the last wagon. No guard marched behind to protect him from surprise. So he peered backward frequently, around one side and the other, staring past the wagon sheet sagging on its bows, beyond the saddle horses tied to the rear, and off to the dusty backtrail, where who knows what lurked. He had been doing that, looking over his shoulder, a long time, both as Homer Donk from Brooklyn, and Cornelius Vanderbilt. He had selected the name, Vanderbilt, as a classy way to hoist the odds. It didn't matter whether people took him for the famous financier; it festooned him with instant respect and recognition. It had a mellifluous ring, too, not at all like the dismal one he had inherited from his Dutch parents.

He meditated, with some satisfaction as the wagon seat battered his tailbone, that he had changed life's odds. He had been dealt deuces, and had managed to turn the business of living into jacks and queens. With luck, he might yet make kings and aces. There had been temporary setbacks, such as when Skye had snatched his braced faro deck from him at Fort Laramie, and burned it. He muttered. It would take a few days of painstaking labor to pinprick another deck, and thus restore the edge. Faro, when played square, offered the dealer only the slightest of odds, about half a percent or so. Plainly that needed improving if a man were to survive in the sporting world at all. The pinpricks allowed him a precise knowledge of what card lay just below the top one in the casebox, and then it was easy enough to palm one, or pluck seconds if the need arose, which it rarely did.

He thought from time to time to do something about his appearance, for life had dealt him deuces in that matter, also. The image in looking glasses had been a cadaverous, pale, pocked man possessed of a long horseface and aquiline nose with fur prospering around the nostrils. His jet hair grew straight as a shingle and looked greasy even after he had just scrubbed it with Castoria. He had squinty furtive brown eyes that focused on nothing for more than a split second, but saw everything. He lacked the face or physique that would swoon a woman, so he had abandoned all thought of domestic life and had tackled his pleasures in the demimonde. He did, however, sport the attire of his profession, a swallowtail black coat, boiled shirt, luxurious maroon cravat with a flashy two-carat headlight diamond stuck on it. And on his fingers glinted four rings, each with solitaires, except for the one with the flat gold surface, polished into a convenient mirror.

He normally fanged himself with three derringers, a single-shot in a special boot holster; an over-and-under in his swallowtail coat pocket; and another single-shot in a small underarm holster. But this artillery was insufficient, in his estimation. He lacked speed. The odds needed improving, at least in certain high-stakes games against dangerous sports. So he had gone to a smith and had some personal armor made to specification from sheet steel of sufficient gauge to stop a lead bullet fired at close range. The thing was slightly curved to the contours of his chest. It covered about a square foot of vital area, protecting heart and lungs. It draped from leather straps over his shoulders, and weighed so much—seven and a half pounds can become a strain on the shoulders over a period of time—that he anchored it under his boiled shirt only when the occasion called for it. Once it had saved his life. He had been ruthlessly skinning a teamster when, with no warning at all, the man pulled a Colt Navy and fired a .36-caliber ball into Cornelius Vanderbilt's heart. But it gonged on steel and the gambler had calmly extracted the over-and-under from his coat pocket and made a loser of him. The others in that Saratoga Springs game had sat perfectly astonished, and for a brief while people had called him Gongs. Now a fine pucker dimpled the device, and Cornelius took to improving odds the way Baptists took to total immersion.

Cornelius did not favor the wilderness. Danger could come at him from any quarter, and he had no way to adjust the odds. He inclined toward corner seats in sporting houses, with log or rock walls projecting to either side of him. All this open space made him antsy. Try as he might—and he devoted whole days to it while the wagon seat hammered his hemorrhoids—he could discover no way to embellish odds out here. At the warm springs he had simply vanished into the bowels of the wagon, lying flat for several miserable hours while those deserters—one of whom he had skinned once—reveled. Now he debated whether to doff his swallowtail coat. The heat lanced his vitals. But he had worn that coat like a second skin through all kinds of weather, and he hated to doff it now, even though his flesh craved cooler air. It would reveal his shoulder holster to the world. He did not want Mister Skye to know of the holster. He distrusted Mister Skye, and expected trouble from the burly guide. He might in any case shoot the man, as a small billet-doux for burning his braced deck, and treating him as some sort of scum.

But the heat triumphed. Ahead, Blueberry had shed his suit coat, and finally Cornelius did likewise, neatly folding the coat so that the pocket with the over-and-under derringer lay on top, the gun instantly available. For a while the swift evaporation of his soaked and soiled shirt cooled him, but then the forbidding heat crushed him again. He would not shoot Skye en route, he thought—the guide provided certain comforts in his brute way as a species of infantry. But later, on the very skirts of Bannack City, he'd have his revenge. He'd sidle up behind Skye and blow out the back of his head.

They had driven all that day along the south bank of the Platte, and the gumbo dust had bathed Cornelius in a fine powder, along with his mules, and the whole wagon. Another reason to despise Skye, who had put him at the tail end of the procession. Off to the left rose a high blue mountain, among the first of the Rockies, though ranges were now visible west and north as well. By late afternoon they had come to the Platte Bridge crossing, a toll operation run by toughs who were not inclined toward charity. They were raking in fifty cents per wagon, and lesser sums per animal.

There would be a wait. Ahead of them a wagon train spasmed forward, and many of the wagon owners harangued and argued fees with the ruddy-faced owners, who simply invited the objecting parties to swim or raft the river instead. Cornelius knew that Goldtooth would pay without even questioning the toll. Such things were of no consequence to her. Enterprise would recover whatever was lost. But that marriage broker would moan and connive, and that would be the day's entertainment. He studied the wagons ahead, concluding they were the usual westering riffraff, dullwits and their families planning to prong Mother Nature somewhere else. Easy marks, perhaps, if Skye would permit him a game or two, which he doubted. Another reason to get even with Skye when the right moment arrived. Maybe he could improve the odds a bit this evening, with a game or two on the sly. He could carry a whole shell game, not to mention a deck, in any pocket.

It looked like an hour wait. Sure enough, Riddle slithered ahead, tromping down to the riverbank looking for a ford, calculating angles. The weasel even waded into the Platte here and there, surprised by its sudden depth and the tug of its water. Sensible Blueberry unhitched a span of mules at a time and led them down to the river for a welcome drink on a scorching day. Riddle watched, apparently decided that was a good idea, and began to water his own mules. But that sort of stuff bored Cornelius, and he left his mules to stand, heads drooping, in the blistering sun while he ambled forward to case the wagon train ahead. In every train there was a mark or two.

Up ahead where the bridge operators extracted wealth, Skye stood listening. Riddle had caught up with him and was playing yet another angle as Cornelius arrived.

"Up to you to pay," said Alvah. "You're the guide, paid a mighty big fee to git us here, and you're the one should be paying these bloodsuckers. Else find us a ford somewheres."

"You can always build a raft, Riddle," boomed Mister Skye. Laughter rippled out. Any cottonwoods that had once prospered here had long since been stripped away. Some parties in this train had no cash, but that was commonplace on the Oregon Trail, and the tollmen accepted payment in kind. But it always took time to come to agreement about the worth of a highboy or barrel of flour or silver teapot, and more often than not, westering pioneers were driven to rage and their women to tears by the extractions.

An hour later they rattled over a crude wood bridge barely wide enough to accommodate a wagon, and were heading along the north bank through rough country. Two hours later, in June twilight, they halted at a likely camp spot already crowded with westering people. Mister Skye didn't like it. He hadn't missed the flinty stares at the red wagons and their inhabitants from the wagon master and various yeomen farmers. But the mules had played out in the heat. They'd have to compete for what remained of grass in this overgrazed spot. Skye pushed on a quarter of a mile or so beyond the wagon train, hoping for distance and grass, but bluffs hemmed the trail and he could go no farther. Cornelius could read Skye's mind easily enough, and from his wagon seat, laughed.

Chapter 9

Unlike some, this train of thirty-six wagons seemed to be a merry one. Drusilla wandered timidly among these people in the bright June evening, enjoying the sight of families eating or doing their chores, scampering boys, bearded men in trail-worn clothes out among the oxen and horses, weathered wagons with sun-bleached sheeting drooping between bows . . . and all of it an amiable cacophony with no shrill sounds of dissidence and rage in them, sounds she had picked up at once in other trains.

Some had gathered in a central place among the drooping wagons where a fiddler tuned up. People eyed her amiably, their gazes settling long on her rimless glasses, respectable tan dress, and the small book in her hand. No one bothered to talk; something about her discouraged approach. Drusilla knew only that she didn't really want to make small talk with these robust souls. She would simply satisfy her curiosity, retire to her own small camp with its disgusting denizens, and read her new Thoreau, *Excursions*, which she'd plucked from the stalls the day before she left Bennington. The sojourner at Walden Pond was dead, but this book had just appeared posthumously.

Thank heaven, she thought, Goldtooth and her bawds were discreet enough not to venture here and become a cynosure of shame. Blueberry had stayed away too, and the Chinese had simply vanished to prowl the country, as he often did. Not even his mandarin background would rescue him from savage treatment often accorded to Celestials in the Far West. But the Riddles were everywhere here, and Alvah rounded through the wagons like a rat terrier, sometimes leaving puzzled frowns behind him. She'd seen the gummy black gambler, Cornelius, sidle around the wagons, but now he was invisible.

What a disgusting thing to travel with such people, people so disreputable that they had to remain hidden away from the eyes of the virtuous, she thought. Perhaps all these people thought she was one of them! Mary-Rita had wandered through briefly and retreated to the wagon, but Flora wandered around somewhere, daring these people to make something of her Southern origins. Drusilla thought for a moment of retreating to her own camp, but she feared the bawds would be doing business over in their wagon, and maybe selling spirits to the men who sneaked over there. Unless she chose to crawl into her bedroll in the Riddle wagon, the options weren't good.

Earlier she'd witnessed a peculiar thing. After they'd made camp up against the bluff, Mister Skye had meandered toward the wagon train and had run into the wagon master, a perfectly disreputable man in grease-blackened buckskins with a salt-and-pepper beard and hair so long it draped over his shoulders. The pair of them had roared like young lions—she'd heard exactly such a roar when a circus with caged lions had rolled through Bennington—and embraced each other and hoorawed around until she thought they were quite mad. Mister Skye had called the wagon master Boudins, and seemed to know him from somewhere. She stood mesmerized, seeing conduct that would have been unthinkable in the East. Odder still, they began to roar at each other in a tongue she barely recognized as English, though it was plain they were insulting each other, calling each other ring-tailed coons and old niggurs and things that shriveled her abolitionist soul.

And they growled and jabbered and proffered perfectly odd sentiments, such as "that's the way the stick floats," and "hyar's damp powder and no way to dry it." The phrase "gone under" rang frequently, and it dawned on her they discussed the dead, dead comrades from some time and place. It annoyed her, this unintelligible babble of plews and skins and Hawkens and Bug's Boys and bull-boats and buffler and *aguardiente* and men named Broken Hand and Blanket Jim. Worse, Mister Skye had wrapped a giant paw around the shoulder of this wagon master and dragged him back to the sordid little skin camp and sat him down in front of Skye's conical skin lodge, and then, as bold as you please, filled a crockery jug from Goldtooth's hogshead, and sat at Victoria's fire, passing the raw whiskey back and forth with Boudins, all the while roaring and belching and—and relieving themselves in sight of everyone and burping and reducing themselves to pure savagery. Never had she seen such a disgusting thing! And even his squaw Victoria muttering "sonofabitch" and "now you gonna go away for a week," and "now I gotta run the wagons." Even the young squaw, Mary, swilling from that awful jug, and giggling and elbowing and—Drusilla's mind blanked—pawing Mister Skye.

It frightened her. She couldn't read there, with those two bull moose howling and baying. She felt her security melt away. What safety resided in a party led by a howling drunkard? She'd be murdered in her bed by any red- or white-skinned predator.

So she felt homeless, at least until that awful guide and his awful wagon master friend had imbibed so much spiritous liquor that they fell into a stupor. She hoped they'd have a monstrous headache in the morning. The fiddler tortured his squealing fiddle now, with merry notes punctuated by shrill squeaks, and some of the wagon-train people had started to jig and hop and behave in a most undignified manner. She couldn't read there, either, amidst such chaos. Had the whole world gone mad here? Even the women, the wives and daughters, were circling and bowing and linking arms, as if an exhausting hot day on the trail were not enough for them!

Daylight lingered, and she would read until dusk and hope things would settle down. It would be dangerous to wander far from camp—awful things happened to lone women—and men—who wandered beyond a kind of circle of safety. But she had a clear view of barren bluffs, and she slipped toward the Platte River, found a large smooth boulder, still sun-warm, and pulled out her slim new Thoreau.

Peace at last.

"Where did you get that!" exclaimed a male voice. Drusilla peered up through her small spectacles and beheld the most awkward and plainest young man she'd ever seen. Like her, he wore rimless spectacles. She gaped at a high white forehead and a skull that seemed to bulge over his ears, all of it set on a delicate jaw perched on a long stem of neck, which convulsed behind a prominent Adam's apple. He seemed young, probably younger than she. He peered at her from intelligent hazel eyes that blinked as regularly as a watch tick.

"I didn't know that was published," he said.

"I found it the day I left."

They talked about Henry David Thoreau and *Walden* and Thoreau's civil disobedience, and she found him intelligent and literate, and best of all, not one to notice her plainness. Perhaps he couldn't because in that respect he was just as plain as she, she thought. He seemed to possess a mysterious knowledge, as if he knew things about the universe that no one else did, especially these wagon-train families. She itched to find out what he knew and didn't know.

"I don't believe I know your name," she said.

"I am Parsimony McGahan."

"Oh," she said. He did not ask hers, and perhaps that meant he wasn't interested. A chance meeting on the Oregon Trail. Let them be ships passing in the night.

"Where are you from?" he asked. "I know it is New England because of the way you talk."

"Vermont, Bennington."

His eyes lit. "I know the place. That is where William Lloyd Garrison's pamphlets come from."

"You are an abolitionist?" She itched with curiosity.

"Of course. Of course I am. And the tracts are printed in Bennington. What did you say your name is?"

"I didn't. I am . . . Drusilla Dinwiddie." She loathed her name and slid past it quickly.

"You don't look like your name. You should have been named Venus or Diana."

She gaped at him.

"If you are done with that book, I will buy it from you on the spot."

"No . . . it's something I treasure, Mister McGahan."

"Call me Parsimony. The name makes the person, and I am too frugal for my own good. Don't call me Parse—I loathe it. My parents picked the wrong virtue, so I am heading west."

"I—I don't follow."

"I should like to be called Abundance, or Generosity, or one of the warmer virtues. When I am in the new land, I will change my name to one or another. I'm going to Comstock, Virginia City, Nevada, to open a lending library. A reading room, actually. I will charge members five dollars a month."

"Virginia City? Oh. Nevada. I'm going to Bannack, in Idaho Territory, or maybe the new camp they're calling Alder Gulch. A lending library?"

"In my wagon are eight hundred books, weighing over one thousand pounds, half a ton of books and more. I asked myself, what do they need in the Far West? What might I bring for a living they don't have, and the answer was, knowledge. Books of course. I've heard they all starve for books, for the latest novels, for science and the higher arts, and practical advice. All of it well salted with abolitionist literature. I will have none of slavery, I assure you, and if you were on the other side, why, I would have long since made my excuses."

"Where are you from, Parsimony?" She detected a quaver in her voice, and felt mortified by it.

"Boston of course. My father is an immigrant from Ireland, a perfectly common man with a great heart and a natural hilarity I happen to love and admire. My mother is a Boston patrician, a puritan, a rebel of sorts, a Congregationalist, and very rich. I love her also. Now what can the son of a proper Bostonian mother, born on Beacon Street, and an Irish pappy, do but head west?"

He laughed, and she realized she'd never even seen him smile. He seemed almost handsome, and his face burst into sunlight when he laughed his Irish laugh.

"But Parsimony—why aren't you in the war, if you feel so strongly?"

"Ah, you pierce to the heart of things and turn over a man's weaknesses like a plow turns soil. I am a coward. Physically, that is. And a snob. I don't wish to subject a fine mind to minié balls. I am no coward in the realm of ideas—in fact I am a radical and willing to stand on my beliefs. But uniforms and marching and orders and all the rest—why, we purchased my relief from the forthcoming draft. There are advantages to family wealth. I am perfectly corrupt, except that I have an uncorrupted mind with which to corrupt others."

He laughed again, and she heard music in it.

In short order they discussed the war, the abominable Mister Lincoln, Harriet Beecher Stowe, *Uncle Tom's Cabin*, and sundry other matters of large importance to both. She hung on to his every word, but only part of her listened. The other part, a part she wouldn't admit to owning, examined him, hearing the tone and lilt of his voice rather than what he said, studying his richly made clothing, listening for idiosyncrasy or foible that would make him weak and foolish, glancing into eyes to see whether there might be mockery or malice in those windows of the soul. She grew dimly aware that he scrutinized her with quick glances, quiet observations, leading questions. It occurred to her that she desperately wanted to pass muster, to meet his approval.

It grew dark and blue light traced the ridges of the western mountains, and now a fire flared where the fiddler sawed and people swung their partners right and left. And still they sat.

"You haven't told me why you are going to Bannack City, Idaho—or have they organized the new territory yet?"

"It's Idaho, but back at Fort Laramie we heard they're talking of a new territory that will be called Montana. And just a few months ago it was called Washington, and before that, why, Oregon! I'm not sure I have it all straight."

"You were saying—"

"To visit a relative!" she blurted out. Then she blushed in the dark.

She never lied. It stung her conscience to lie. She couldn't imagine what wild impulse impelled her to lie. But she was made of stern stuff, and corrected herself at once.

"I—didn't put that correctly," she said softly. "I am betrothed to a man I have not met, who is either at Bannack or the new Alder Gulch diggings."

The slightest pause. "I rejoice in your happiness," he said softly.

"I don't know that I will be happy," she responded tartly. "I don't know the man. I entered into a contract . . . because my circumstances required it."

"I think you will find a good life," he said amiably. "What happens if this liaison doesn't happen?"

"The contract treats me as merchandise! I am the marriage broker's shelf goods, to be offered again! And yet again if that fails."

He grinned, and she caught his humor in the dark. "And you an abolitionist!"

"I am!" she cried. "You do not know the special slavery of being female. In some places I could not even have signed that contract because women are wards, in law."

"What's to prevent your simply abandoning the contract?"

She recoiled. She knew he had a weakness, and here it was. "Mister McGahan," she retorted icily. "I abide by the contracts I make. I entered into it knowingly and willfully. I will not act dishonorably or unethically. I will not casually toss aside, as a result of my whim or will, a solemn agreement!"

He laughed. "You are like my mother," he said. "You puritans are impossible."

"Maybe it's the people who don't keep their word or their bond who sully civilization!" she cried. "Mister McGahan, good night."

"Don't leave! This night is young. You are the first woman I've ever met that I could talk to."

"Are we all so dumb?" she snapped.

"No, but the interests of so many lie in domestic things, and I am not domestic."

She laughed. She couldn't help but like him.

"I haven't a domestic bone in my body."

"I wasn't suggesting you break the contract. I think the contract might be unconstitutional and certainly unenforceable, that if you had a good lawyer, you might put it to a test. That's very different from simply breaking an agreement."

She knew where all this would lead. In the space of three hours they had gotten so far as to be considering each other for wedlock. That's how she put it to herself—considering each other for wedlock. A cool and sanitary way of putting it. She disdained sentiment. Well, it would never happen. Some aspects of marriage she didn't look forward to: its endless drudgery, cleaning, babies, jumping to a man's will . . . She intended to turn the marriage she had agreed to into kind of companionship that would permit her to have her own bookish life.

"Whatever I do will be in accordance with the highest standard of civilization," she said primly.

"Migawd, you puritans. I don't wish to marry. I wish to live in sin with a lady who loves books and liberty."

"Sir!"

"I told you—I'm a radical. I oppose bonds, including those of marriage."

"If your parents hadn't married you wouldn't be here," she retorted.

"Why, Drusilla, I'm not so sure about that."

"You are unthinkable and impossible—and I am going to retire."

"To the camp of the bawds and lowlifes. Oh, I listened to that Riddle when he skittered about."

In truth, she didn't want to return to her own camp and listen to the raucous laughter of the soiled doves and their men, or the wild fustian of the drunken guide and wagon master. She didn't want to stray an inch from Parsimony.

"When I went to my mother's church, I listened to long and brilliant sermons, the tenor of which was that I had to continually shape myself toward perfection to find favor with God. And when my pap slipped off to Mass with me, I learned that we were all going to sin, because of our nature, and if we went contritely to the communion rail, we would be cleansed. I don't know which I like better. I'm an abolitionist and a radical because I think the whole commonwealth, the people and our institutions, might be led toward wisdom and virtue. That's my puritan side. But I don't know whether it applies to persons. The thought of transforming myself into a moral paragon is simply— exhausting. I prefer to sin and find grace. That's my Catholic side. One thing my pap has is fun. He loves life."

Drusilla had never heard such talk.

"I think I am an agnostic anyway," he added.

That horrified her, but not terribly much after she'd thought about it.

"I don't think I wish to live . . . in scandalous circumstances with a man—no matter how pleasant a man. He would dishonor me by it."

"I thought so." He chuckled. "I also look like a frog. So we are ships passing in the twilight. Tomorrow you and your lowlifes will whip your mule teams and soon be far ahead of our ox-drawn train. And that will be the end of it. I'd like to write you, though. You're the only one. The only princess who would talk to an educated frog."

"We will probably lose track. My name is going to change, and you are going to change yours. I don't even know whether I'll be in Bannack, or the new Alder Gulch camp."

"I will always be Parsimony McGahan at the Virginia City, Nevada, post office. And you?"

"I am to become Mrs. Amos Rasmussen," she said slowly. "I understand him to be a pleasant and literate man."

"I will remember the name." He rose and stretched, and she realized he stood tall, like herself. "Drusilla, I am going to ask you a terrible question. . . . Would you like me to go to Alvah Riddle and propose to buy up the Rasmussen contract at a figure that would give Riddle more profit?"

"Parsimony!"

He laughed, infectiously, but hot tears welled up and she couldn't choke them back.

Chapter 10

Victoria knew she wouldn't be sleeping for a few days. Whenever Skye found the whiskey jug and disappeared to the other side for a while, everything fell to her. Now he was gone. He and Boudins had roared and guzzled at the campfire before Skye's buffalo-skin lodge, and now they sprawled. It was bad, she thought crossly. Mister Skye the guide, and Boudins the wagon master of the other people, passed-out drunk. And Skye only employed a few days, too. What would that madam say?

Mary slept heavily too, but that was all right. The young Shoshone had nothing to do now that the boy had been sent to St. Louis and put into a white men's school. She drank and laughed with Skye, and watched the stars spin. But Victoria was his Sits-Beside-Him-Wife. Now she was old and her flesh felt like dried and cracked rawhide, and she had nothing but old bones inside. Old Jawbone sagged like that too, but she doubted that Mister Skye noticed. He seemed to think Jawbone would last forever. But Jawbone's teeth grew long and his back sank and the ribs separated, and soon Jawbone would be gone. Like herself, like Skye.

She and Jawbone would watch camp, the way they always did when Mister Skye went over to the other side. She wouldn't sleep. She would go for days without real sleep, just tiny naps, her old brown eyes and leathery ears more alert than ever. They'd gotten this far through life, and she intended they'd get the rest of the way before being gathered into the spirit world. Mister Skye never apologized, or regretted these times. It was not in him. But he had given her a sawed-off double-barreled fowling piece, with many balls of lead in each barrel, for safety and comfort. It might be worth a hundred arrows. She had it in her lap now, as she peered into the windy night, and listened to the air move.

She knew Boudins from the old days, the times when he and Skye and she had trapped the beaver, and roamed the mountains and valleys, and every sun set on joy, except the times they ran into the Siksika, or Gros Ventre, or Arapaho. The names made a sour taste in her mouth, and she spat. It felt good to spit out hated names. Boudins had been a good trapper and got many plews, and had traded the plews for geegaws and that terrible stuff they drank at the rendezvous, with grain alcohol, peppers, and plugs of tobacco in it for flavor. Then, in debt for his next year's supplies, he roamed out into the hard mountains again, sometimes with Mister Skye and Victoria, sometimes with a girl of his own. Now he guided white men along trails, just like Mister Skye.

The rolling air cut sparks out of the embers and jammed them off like shooting stars. Nearby, Jawbone grew restless. She knew that without looking, but she peered back at him. His yellow eyes picked up light like glowing marbles, and his ears flattened back. That meant someone was coming, but not stealthily. When someone sneaked, he began his unearthly shrieking, and then she knew of trouble. She spotted a man, someone she'd seen with the wagon train. He peered behind him to see whether he walked alone, glanced briefly at her lodge and the sprawled

figures before it, and at the green wagon that was silent
and dark; then slipped onward to the red wagon with the
red lantern hanging from it. Victoria laughed. He was going to hire a woman. Her people, the Absaroka, knew all
about that. Many a warrior had hired out his squaw to the
trappers at the rendezvous, but it was all fun and not so
furtive as this. The white men acted sneaky about this,
and that had always puzzled her. Sonofabitch, what a good
thing those hired women stayed at their wagon and didn't
go parading around the wagon train, getting them white
women mad. Then there'd be trouble, and Skye and Boudins drunk as magpies, too.

She sniffed the air. There would be a hell of a damn big
storm, soon, and then Skye would get wet. She laughed.
Over at the red wagon, the women slipped out and stood
around in thin wrappers, so thin she could damn well see
right through, shadowy limbs in the lantern light.

They parleyed, he and Goldtooth, and he studied the
women and talked, and finally he dug into his britches
pocket and pulled out a sack and pressed something into
Goldtooth's hand, and then he and two of the women, that
Mrs. Parkins and that Juliet Picard, climbed into the red
wagon. It shook, and not from the wind, and the other
two, the madam and Big Alice, settled down in the grass
outside, and she heard yelps and laughter. Sonofabitch,
she wished she were young enough to have a good time
like that. But she had become dried out as old leather now.

The stars burnt out. Off to the south the sky lit white
and went black again. Pretty soon now, she thought,
smelling dampness in the freshets of air. She eyed the dark
terrain narrowly. This place might be no damn good in a
storm. They camped at the foot of a long draw that snaked
up the hills into the night. And too close to the Platte
River. Mister Skye as crazy as a magpie, too.

Jawbone snarled. His ears cocked forward. Victoria
didn't know what to make of that but she swung the fowling piece into the darkness where his ears pointed. Probably someone of this party, maybe that gambler Vanderbilt,
or the black man Blueberry or the big Chinese. Sonofa-

bitch, where did that yellow man go all the time? She liked him. He looked a little like the Absaroka, same eyes. A good man to cut throats or count coup.

Like a skunk one of the bride women padded to the green wagon. That startled her faintly. She'd kept track and thought they were all over there, Riddle and his medicine wife, and the women, all asleep. It was the strange one with the rimless spectacles. The one who carried a book all the time. Victoria pitied her because life pressed heavy upon her. She'd been having a damn bad time, she could see that from the way the woman walked, all slumped and weary. Dinwiddie, that was her name. Them whites had such funny names, no song, no music, no medicine in them. Just some damn sounds in the throat. Drusilla Dinwiddie stopped and stared at the red wagon and its lantern wavering in the wind, recoiled from some noise and the sight of half-covered women lounging in the night, and walked toward the green wagon. Something shone on her cheeks, wetness.

"Hey!" Victoria yelled. The woman turned, approached hesitantly. She stared uncertainly at the corpses of Boudins, Skye, and Mary.

"You're not feeling good. You sit down here and mebbe I can help."

She shook her head, but sat anyway, and Victoria waited. Lightning sheeted across the west now, and in the flashes she glimpsed towering thunderheads, the Thunder Spirits riding the bucking sky tonight.

"Them people over in the wagon train do something bad to you?" Victoria asked, squinting at the woman.

Drusilla shook her head, and Victoria waited.

"I met someone I care about. Someone who cares about me," Drusilla said. "It has never happened—and it will never happen again."

"How come that's bad?"

"Because I am under bond. I have made a contract."

"Go anyway. Go to this man and say you will be his woman."

"I can't. I am committed."

"Damn! You are a strange woman. I don't understand this stuff."

"My word is my bond."

"You go! Riddle, he ain't gonna come after you. You go to the other wagon train, and nothing will happen, and you'll be happy with this here man."

She shook her head slowly. "You don't understand. I don't suppose you—I mean, your background, I don't suppose—"

There she went, Victoria thought. Them whites always figured Indians were dumb, didn't know nothing about stuff.

"We got medicine vows," Victoria broke in. "Sometimes we lie like hell, and make big jokes against other Indians, against white men. But we got sacred vows too. When the men come back from battle, they tell what happened, how many scalps, how many times they count coup, they tell it all exactly true. We got people going on a vision-quest, making vows and doing them, mebbe die if they don't do what they vow. We got truth times, when our Spirit Helpers make us talk true and do what we say. You got a medicine vow, this contract, and you ain't gonna break it."

Drusilla stared. "You have said it very well, Mrs. Skye."

"Victoria, dammit."

"I'm a New England puritan, and it's the way I'm bred. I have given my word on paper, and I must keep it."

"You love this man over there?"

"I don't know what that word means. I know we could be lifelong friends and have a very good time."

"You keep your vow. I'm going to make medicine, love medicine. I'm gonna talk to my Helpers, and find out about you. I get a vision, I'll let you know, but I gotta have some time. The Helpers come when they come. You're doing good, young woman. Keep your sacred contract vow, and we'll see."

Drusilla smiled. "Nothing will come of it, I'm sure. But you are most kind." She rose.

"You whites never believe nothing. Thunder's coming, and the Thunder Spirits will tell me. Maybe they strike lightning on the Riddles."

Drusilla recoiled. "That is not what I wish," she replied sharply, and fled to her dark wagon.

That's a good woman, thought Victoria. Damn good woman who got ways to live and things figured good in her head. A woman like that made good medicine.

Lightning cannoned, scattering white glare off the land, and she knew she'd have to round up the mules swiftly before it was too late. She peered around sharply in the cavernous night. Yonder the red lantern swung. The man emerged from the red wagon and skittered off toward his own camp. The bawds snuffed the lamp, and darkness folded in, along with wind.

She set the fowling piece just inside the doorflap of her lodge, so it wouldn't get wet, and toiled up the slopes toward the mules. She'd have to both hobble and picket them, not only hers but all the rest. Lightning snapped, and she saw them all, restless and tugging on their pickets. A crackle like water snapping on a hot skillet came, and then the world turned white and an explosion rocked creation. It came too fast! Below, Jawbone shrieked. And Skye lost on the other side. Where were all them white men? Didn't that Riddle know nothing? She reached a picket line with two mules on it and began tugging it downslope, fighting the nervous mules every step. Another jolt hit and she felt the blast of it, hot air whiffing past and hissing, and a white ball rolling along grass and up on the mules' ears. They bucked and shrieked and yanked free and went clattering up the slope again.

Maybe she would go to the Spirit Lands herself. It might be the time. She started up the slope again, up to the ridges where the mules gathered. They'd all pulled their picket lines now, and headed up where lightning hissed. Crazy, going where the Lightning Spirits would strike them. Sheets of white rattled off the clouds now, rattled like gourds, light making noise or noise making light. She stumbled into one black mule, one of Skye's, down lower and grabbed the halter. One anyway. But it jabbed its head up and down, its teeth bared in the blue light, and refused to budge. A white crack knocked her flat and she left the world a moment. When she came to, she smelled scorch, scorch in the grass and on her hair, and Skye's mule was sprawled on the grass. Sonofabitch, and him drunk down there.

She clambered painfully to her feet, winded and tired. The mules rolled off the ridge now, scattering into the hollows of the dunes. She rattled after them, against torrents of air that knocked her back and whistled around her skirts. She could scarcely push up the slope because of the icy air that the Thunder Spirits had thrown to earth like sky lances. She heard a new rattle, a thousand rattlesnakes rattling, and the first hail smashed wetly on her black hair, and others slapped her face. She glimpsed a specter up on the ridge, the Lightning Spirit riding a white charger. She'd never seen the Lightning Spirit before, and she clawed away her fear. Across the ridge it galloped, crackling blue bolts following in its wake, a spirit sowing lightning. She'd never seen anything like that.

With her own eyes she saw the Lightning Spirit. She fled downslope, tumbling, air hot and cold in her throat, hail clubbing her, hammering her shoulders and the back of her head. And behind her the Lightning Spirit galloped. She felt it coming, and when it fell upon her she glanced back at the specter and saw it was the Chinese, leading three wet mules. She sat in the grass and held her chest because the pain burst her in two.

"Go down!" the Chinese Lightning Spirit yelled.

She crawled, hail pummeling her back and haunches and splattering up into her face. Sonofabitch, the mules gone everywhere, maybe days away, and Skye sprawled down there. She raged. She'd kick that damn Skye and that damn Boudins awake. And kick Mary too, for good measure, good kick in her soft breasts.

The world whirled. Wind shrieked, and walls of water blurred the way down. She heard Jawbone shriek and wondered how that could be, and then the evil blue roan

minced before her, clacking his teeth and snarling and
nudging her with his powerful snout. She grabbed a leg
and pulled herself up until she could clutch the mane, and
then, from the high side of the slope, she crawled over his
bony back and held on. He flew down the hill, gliding
somehow instead of jolting. She turned cold, and the
numbness penetrated from her clammy skin dress to her
heart and bowels. Ice water sheeted down the knobs of
her spine, dripped from her ears and collarbones, sloshed
between her hard old breasts, pooled on her belly making
her tremble, and then dripped off the fringes of her doeskin skirt. Hail clouted her hair, gouging at her like a
Sioux scalping knife.

He slopped through a roaring bottom, the torrent un-
balancing him until he leapt powerfully to the far side,
and she knew the coulee ran, deluging the camp below.
Near her sat the Chinese Lightning Spirit on its white
charger.

The lodge had been flattened, and lay in a clumsy sprawl
like a dead buffalo, lodgepole poking the sky, rain hammering on parfleches and horse gear and her fowling piece.
Jawbone shrieked, and danced around Skye and Mary and
Boudins, who lay stupefied by whiskey, pawing the air as
if pestered by gnats. The lightning quit and night closed
black like a womb and she waited to be born. Jawbone
stopped, stood for her to slide off, and then began nuz-
zling Skye with his snout, squealing angrily. She splashed
through a raging flow of water, finding Skye first and lifting his head out of it. He coughed. She couldn't pull him.
She found a saddle in the blackness and propped his head
up on it. She found Mary next, and violently tugged her,
got her face up out of the racing water and propped on the
saddle. She felt around in the blackness for Boudins. The
deluge plucked him, rolled him. Sonofabitch, she'd need
a rope. She couldn't pull the heavy man, but she could
keep him from being washed into the Platte. She probed
around the carcass of the lodge, and finally grasped horse-
hair reins, and started toward Boudins, or at least where
Boudins should be. But he wasn't there. Water had rolled

him somewhere. She waited for lightning but the Spirit hid in the blackness. Her heart pattered through the cold winters of time and the Lightning Spirits didn't come.

"Jawbone! Go find the man," she cried. The horse shrieked and she heard him slopping around closer to the river. Even the wide Platte boiled now, not a high flood but a sprawling one. The horse whinnied like a night trumpet and she started toward the sound, but the current snagged at her legs, and some drifting thing upended her. Then Jawbone was butting her, and she grabbed mane and let him drag her to higher ground. Maybe Boudins fell in the river, maybe Boudins had tumbled over to the Spirit Land.

She grew dimly aware of women's screams, but they seemed distant. Her own lodge and everything inside lay in a heap. She heard the melody of a lark and then a crow, and knew the Spirit Helpers walked the earth this night. She listened to the sweet warble of the meadowlark and remembered being a girl and walking through a sunny meadow near Arrow Creek, looking for breadroot and wild onions, and plucking yellow daisies and rubbing their soft pollen on her cheeks.

Lightning raked again, a hollow gray light that hung in curtains and let her see the world with the clarity of noon-sky. Her man and Mary sprawled in a foot of tugging water, their heads half under. Mister Skye roared and waved arms the thickness of tree limbs. Jawbone butted him furiously. Victoria found a woven rawhide lariat on the saddle, slipped the lasso end of it over Jawbone's withers, and wrapped the other end under Mister Skye's shoulders. Without command, Jawbone slid Skye toward higher ground until the man was out of the slop. Then Victoria dragged Mary to the higher earth the same way. She carried household goods, her parfleches, her fowling piece, Mister Skye's new Henry, soaked buffalo robes leaden with water, and the rest, until the lightning flickered out like a burnt candle. She rested, her heart banging, and heard cries in the blackness.

A faint flicker bared the rest of the camp to her. Riddle

had double-reefed his wagon sheet, and his wagon stood upright but fifty yards from where it had been, being tugged mercilessly toward the rushing river a foot at a time by the flood tide from the coulee, up to the hubs of its wheels, and gusts of wind that yanked the unreefed middle of the wagon sheet like a sail, sucking and tugging the wagon to its doom. Under the naked bows at either end, desperate women clung to wood and cried piteously. The other wagons had been blown onto their sides and their pink wagon sheets whipped off into the night. Wind churned their high wheels, making them spin and chatter and vibrate. The wagon goods lay in a spill downwind of each wagon, and even as Victoria watched, wind spun a hogshead of whiskey and rolled it into the moil of water plummeting into the Platte. The bawds clung to the wagon bows like pink caterpillars, their thin wrappers plastered wetly to them so they seemed naked in the sheet lightning, and colder than the blue ice caves up in the Pryor Mountains. And their hair lay death-clamped over their skulls and shoulders. One by one, trunks and bundles floated off, propelled like dandelion fuzz by the gale and the water.

Sonofabitch, but nothing could she do for them. She still had to tie her rawhide lariat to her collapsed lodge to keep it from floating off, marshaling whatever last energy she could muster. With numb hands she slid the lariat loop around the lodgepoles that weren't buried in muck, and tugged. The massive weight of the water-soaked lodge anchored it to mud. The torrent of water now boiling over it added to its weight. She found the saddle in the gloom and found Jawbone, and saddled him. He stood patiently, ears back but obedient. She cinched up with all the energy left in her old cold body, dallied the lariat rope around the horn and barked a sharp command at the trembling horse, who dug into the slop and pulled steadily. The lariat sang and sprayed water but held, and slowly the soaked lodge slid up the gentle slope, one step at a time, until it was out of the clutches of the Platte and the demons.

She released Jawbone, unsaddled him, and sat in the downpour, drawing a soaked four-point Hudson's Bay blanket over her, trapping only cold. There was nothing she could do for the others. The pain in her own breast bloomed so large she thought she would soon go to the Beyond Land, but she didn't.

The storm faded, but the water cascading from the highlands mounted higher. In the fading flashes, she glimpsed the Chinese on his white horse dragging the Riddle wagon back from the Platte, and caught the panic of screaming women. Then weariness folded her soul, and she heard meadowlarks singing and the Spirit Helpers making jokes.

Chapter 11

The gibbous moon reminded him of a war lord flush with victory, fat on both sides and cold yellow. It had reappeared as suddenly as it had been eclipsed by cloud, casting wan beams upon the carnage below.

They called him a Celestial here and mocked as they said it. The allusion was to the Celestial Kingdom, the Middle Kingdom of his ancient people. It all sounded heathenish to them, but these pale barbarians did not understand the ancient ways. To build railroads they had virtually enslaved some of his race, the low Cantonese who didn't even speak the Mandarin of the imperial castes, and it amused him that the whites thought all of China was like Canton. Of the nine grades of mandarins, his family's was the highest, and he could wear the button of power and prestige on his dress cap. But they wouldn't know that here.

Everything he wore oozed water and his bones ached, but he ignored it. He knew of no way to kindle a fire. There wasn't a dry stick or dry tinder for leagues, and no place to lay a fire because the earth swam in slop and the shoulders of the land were still shrugging off water. The coulee cutting into the river bluff still roared and foamed like a hydrophobic lion. He sat his wet white stallion surveying the wreckage, and yawned. One had died, but it didn't matter. Boudins, the master of the nearby wagon train, or what was left of it, had vanished, drunk on spirits. Skye, as much a wolfish barbarian as Boudins, would have died too but for the old squaw. Even now he lay stupefied, along with his younger wife, sprawled on a wet slope.

He'd rescued the Riddle wagon. That weasel had reefed his wagon sheet, so the wagon stood while the others toppled, but the wagon had rested in the very throat of the coulee, careening toward perdition when Seven-Story had roped it and dallied the lariat around the horn of the saddle, the way these Western cattle herders caught a cow. While the stallion braced and held the rope taut, Chang had found slabs of rock and lowered them into a foot of raging water around the wagon wheels, stopping its progress. He offered to ferry the terrified women inside it to higher ground, but they wouldn't. Even now, a river moiled through the wheels, rocking the green wagon.

The bawds had fared worse. Blueberry Hill had known nothing about reefing wagon sheets, and both wagons had toppled in the vicious gusts. Orgasmic wind had tugged the canvas loose, billowed it out like a jib, and flipped the wagons over like a woman waiting. Moments later the canvas had whipped loose and sailed on down the Platte, leaving the bows naked in the night. The storm had spent itself upon the bawds' wagon. Most everything within vanished, the ladies' finery, bedrolls, stored food, tins of delicacies for the new parlor house, shoes and boots and parasols and blankets. All gone.

The other red wagon lost its sheet too, and everything inside. A fortune in whiskey gone, the hogsheads floating and banging their way down the Platte, intoxicating suckers and trout. Vanderbilt's faro layout vanished, cards and casebox and oilcloth. Likewise the furnishings for the parlor house, sconces and candelabra and percale and drapes.

The things in his saddlebags survived, but his clothing and books in Vanderbilt's wagon didn't. For that matter, Vanderbilt had vanished, either caught in the other camp, or dead. Everything of the gambler's disappeared too, along with Blueberry's few things.

In the moonlight Chang and Blueberry had righted the wagons with the help of the stallion, but not the help of Alvah Riddle, who peered maliciously at them from his wagon box. Some of the harness vanished, but Blueberry had hung much of it from a broken limb of a tree, where it still draped. In the morning they would know how many spans of mules they could harness—if they found the mules.

Now the red wagons stood upright and their naked bows poked the moon. The bawds were bare. Their thin wet wrappers felt icier than bare flesh, so they'd stripped them and sat forlorn in their empty wagon box, their flesh dry and goosebumped, unmindful of Alvah Riddle's stare and the huffy mail-order brides who glared at them. Seven-Story enjoyed the sight, moonsprites in the box, their breasts light and shadow. He laughed softly. The ladies had nothing to wear, and that seemed a sublime joke of the storm spirits. Naked they would go to Bannack, advertising their sunburnt wares as they entered.

They were smarter than Riddle's virgins, who sat shivering in layers of soaked clothing, feeling morally superior. There'd be some sharing in the morning. Riddle and his ladies would drive a hard bargain and the sporting crowd would be gowned, at least if Goldtooth had any gold left. Maybe that had bottomed in the Platte too, enriching crawfish. Something would have to be done for Blueberry, now attired in soaked red long johns with a hanging trapdoor for the want of buttons. His black broadcloth suit and patent shoes and white spats rolled along the silty bottom of the Platte. Blueberry was not without resources. He stood up in his soaked wagon, peered at the ladies, and clambered over the side, splashing through muck, trapdoor flapping.

He lifted a foot to a hub and then catted into the red wagon.

"All right, ladies," he grated, "let's get warm."

There were amiable giggles and they all disappeared below the sideboards.

Seven-Story admired Blueberry. There lay a man to make the best of any calamity. He touched heels to the stallion and slopped across to Victoria, who huddled silent under a mud-soaked blanket.

"Sonofabitch," she muttered. "I'm going to kill Skye. In the morning I'm gonna kill Skye and kick Mary in the ass."

"A commendable idea," said Seven-Story. "But now we will put your lodge up and start it drying."

Jawbone eyed him narrowly, ears back.

"Bite your master," said Seven-Story.

Jawbone clacked teeth and snarled.

Chang dismounted and attempted to wrestle the lodge upright but it wouldn't budge. The thirteen buffalo cowhides in it slopped with water and one lodgepole had snapped. Victoria shed her blanket and helped him, tugging poles out of the mess until she had the good ones lying free. Then she found a straight seam in the moonlight and unlaced the soppy rawhide until the skins parted and the heavy cover lay flattened on a rise of land. He watched her, admiring the skills of this Indian woman, who looked so much like the peoples of Asia.

She retied the tops of the poles and soon had a conical frame resting on higher ground and poking toward the stars.

"No way to get that cover up," she muttered. "It weighs more than me and you can lift." But they tugged and wrestled anyway and in a few minutes they had yanked the sodden skins up a bit upon the frame, high enough so they could drain and dry. The result was a low hovel with a lot of night air poking around it.

"I got one more thing," she said. She dug into a parfleche and pulled out a bedroll canvas. "I'm gonna wrap them two in this and maybe they won't get sick and die."

Chang did even better. He lifted Mister Skye easily and carried him up to some relatively dry shelf-rock, and then Mary, and rolled the pair of them in the canvas.

Jawbone laid back his ears and followed, protecting Skye.

Mister Skye opened one eye and then the other. "Why, it's Mister Chang," he said. "Bloody imperial mandarin Chinese won't let a man sleep."

With that, Mister Skye passed back into his own world. Victoria spat.

Seven-Story bowed amiably, boarded his stallion, and slopped his way east toward the wagon-train camp. There was yet a mystery, the fate of Cornelius Vanderbilt. Two mysteries: Vanderbilt and the scattered mules. He saw that the other camp had done better. Wagon sheets had been reefed and the wagons had stood. No coulee had disgorged water into their middle. People wore dry clothes, extracted from dry luggage. No fire flared here—no dry fuel anywhere—but several lanterns burned from wagon hooks, casting eerie beams across water-black earth. Work parties had organized, women repairing loose canvas and men checking harness and hunting for drifted stock in the pale light.

The hour was late, perhaps three, and not a soul slept. Chang rode quietly through the hubbub, wondering who to address, where to look for Cornelius, and who to tell about the death of Boudins.

A red-bearded man waylaid him. "You! Chinese!" he said in a sort of singsong. "You tellee where guidee is, chop-chop?"

Seven-Story Chang smiled amiably and reined his horse.

"Hey! Quick-quick, chop-chop, talkee, yes?"

Seven-Story knew the game, and smiled. It always led to such fun, except the time one ruffian got mad and pulled out a toadsticker.

Others gathered now, pushing toward him, glowering in the faint lantern light.

"Talk-talk, Chinaman, or we cuttee offee your pigtail."

Chang debated whether to respond with an Etonian inflection, or Cambridge, and decided on the latter. "Gentlemen," he said, "I bring you sad tidings. I believe your guide, the estimable Boudins, perished in the river."

They gaped. "He was intoxicated from spiritous liquor and was washed into the river," Chang added. "It is a pity. A most distinguished gentleman."

They stared narrowly. Boudins was dead? Dead? Tough old mountain man dead? Impossible.

"How'd it happen again?" snapped one.

"Mister Boudins and Mister Skye and the younger Mrs. Skye were napping after an amiable evening when a wall of water washed over them."

"Don't you use them fancy Chinee words," snapped one. "Most likely you slit his throat and took his coin, for opium. We know your kind, worshipin' idols, sittin' in joss houses. Slit his throat in a storm and pushed old Boudins in the river."

Chang smiled slightly and bowed from horseback. "I'm looking for the sporting man, Vanderbilt."

One of them jerked a thumb toward a wagon whose sagging wet sheet glowed from a wavering orange light inside. "He's one of your kind. Been in there all night playing poker and skinning some of our young men and bachelors. That there bunch, they hardly paid never no mind to the storm, just dealing and smoking, and him in there sitting with a derringer in his lap for all to see. . . . You're all the same kind, fancy-talking Chinee. You and that crook and the fancy women over yonder, all trouble for decent folks, and now you come telling us our guide is dead, washed away in a storm. We should string you all up!"

"Go back to China, Celestial," said another. "We'll go a-hunting Boudins and when we find him with a slit throat, we'll slit yours, and then Skye's for good measure."

"At your service, honorable gentlemen," said Chang, mocking.

He touched heels to his horse and threaded through them to the yellow-lit wagon.

From the front, Seven-Story could peer through the oval puckerstring hole into its smoky interior. A smudged lamp dangled from the middle bow, casting a jaundiced glow on six males, all of them seated on mounds of cargo. The wagon sheet oozed moisture but the inside of this haven remained virtually dry, including Cornelius Vanderbilt, who occupied a seat at the far end, his back to the rear puckerstring hole, where he could make a hasty exit. Not that a hasty exit would do much good on a moonlit night. The light caught Cornelius's sallow features and made him look oily and skeletal, his slicked-down hair glinting blue. They all looked yellow and purple and blue, like bruised flesh.

He dealt blue-backed cards with paisley patterns on them to the others, seven in all, and they plucked these up furtively from the hairy brown blanket beneath them. In the hollows of this metastasizing wool lay piles of gummy greenbacks, a few small gold pieces, mostly eagles, and little piles of dried peas, counters of some sort. But none of these skimpy piles equaled the hoard of green and gold that humped before Mister Vanderbilt, who fingered them idly after he had dealt.

The mood of this makeshift emporium edged toward sour, and seeped out even to Seven-Story, watching intently. In fact the glowers of these sleepless hostages of Fate grew malign, and Chang wondered whether Vanderbilt fathomed the trouble. Probably not, for he droned on, lips pulled back from yellow teeth, restless crabby fingers diddling the deck as he waited for these soldiers of fortune to make up their minds. The storm had come and gone with only the faintest acknowledgment in here. But shipwreck lay near.

"Mister Vanderbilt," said Chang from without, "the Sirens are singing and it is time to stop your ears."

Chang's presence thus penetrated to those within. The gambler peered into the night, startled, and perceived the moonlit Chang. Then he glanced at his hand and smiled thinly.

"Let them sing," he said.

A black-bearded man turned to him. "He's not going anywhere, Celestial, until we've a chance to win it back. We ain't caught him cheating, but that don't mean he don't. And when we catch him, we'll take care of it, and you, and the sluts and lowlifes, and the dirty Injuns and all the rest over there."

"Ah, Mister Vanderbilt, the Sirens sing, the music is in your ears," said Chang.

Now at last Vanderbilt paused. Here was a white horse to carry him off, and no others remained in this drenched camp. The betting had not begun. He sighed and peered at his cards.

"Gents, I will fold for the night. It grows late and to-morrow will be a wearisome day without sleep."

He set his hand down and waited for the others to do the same. Instead, one of them flipped Vanderbilt's cards over, baring four queens lying on their royal backs.

"Bigawd," he said, "your luck runs a little too strong, Vanderbilt. I think you'll just stay here a while. That or give it all back."

Vanderbilt's claws flicked and in no time he had stuffed his loot into the pocket of his black broadcloth. "As the gent said, you've nothing against me," the sporting man muttered. His other hand plucked the two-barrel derringer from his lap. "Let's have the cards, gents; it's my last deck."

None of them donated the pasteboards.

"The cards, gents. It's been a pleasant little game."

From outside, Seven-Story eased out his revolver, hoping it wasn't waterlogged. He would shoot out the light.

"You ain't going anywhere," said one. "Is he, boys?"

"The Sirens sing," said Seven-Story.

"It is my last deck," replied Cornelius. "My means."

Chang hated to shoot the lantern. It would arouse a camp that had finally quieted down.

"You are the Lamp of the Occident," said Chang.

But Vanderbilt paid no heed. His hand flicked up, and the two bores of the derringer pointed at a man whose fist bent seven cards.

"The deck," he said.

Chang thought to shoot the lantern, but things went too fast. Someone plucked the lantern from its bail and threw it at Chang. It exploded at the feet of the white stallion, scattering yellow flame. The horse leapt and plunged. Inside the blackened wagon, tumult and a muffled shot. Chang steadied his horse and raced to the rear, hoping Vanderbilt would exit. Instead, burly men bailed out of both ends, and dragooned the gambler out the front end with them.

They landed all over him, smacking him with blocky fists and square-toed boots, thumping him into a rag doll. He fought back but there were six. A fist knocked the gambler's head back. A knee rammed into his gut, doubling him up. A boot hit his thigh with an awful crack.

Chang glanced swiftly. The shot had awakened the camp, and heads peered from dark and ghostly wagons. A violent hand ripped Vanderbilt's coat off him, and with it the boodle. Another heavy hand, plow-hardened, yanked white shirt and the linen beneath with a fine shrill rip, baring cadaverous hollow hairless chest to the mocking moon.

A brawl, a thing to enjoy, thought Chang. He slid easily off the stallion onto catfeet, returning the revolver to its holster, and plunged into the melee, feeling the concealed lead weight woven into the bottom of his queue swinging behind him. Vanderbilt sank into the muck now as fists clubbed him. He swung back weakly, no match for the six stomping farmers with mean boots. A rough hand grabbed belt and yanked, popping leather and pulling away shrieking broadcloth. Except for his gummy black boots, the skinny gambler was shorn of wool.

Six Occidentals, about right for one mandarin, Chang thought as he waded in, making deft use of foot and the knife-edge of his hardened hands. Art, not muscle, would punish; the artful chop to the vulnerable point—the thing took years of study and practice, something young mandarins learned—the artful chop to the neck, and one fell poleaxed, and another, and now they wheeled toward him, having turned Vanderbilt into a mudball. And a good kick, yes, favor of the gods, a good kick and a little combination kick-feint-chop, and two more doubled up holding privates and coughing up the contents of their bellies.

Ah yes, the science of the warrior! And now one with a knife, quite expected, the point of it blurring past him a foot wide in the white moonlight, and the tripped oaf wallowed in the slop near Vanderbilt. Ah, these giants of the West! Chang laughed happily and caught the remaining one at the base of his skull with his fist, crumpling him over the carcasses of the others, and then quiet settled— for a moment. Yonder, ghostly wagons rocked and men in nightshirts and boots, carrying Dragoon Colts and barrel staves, came mucking through the slop.

"Cornelius, my friend, the Sirens sang and you are shipwrecked on the rocks. Or is it Blueberry down there?"

He heard only a moan.

"I shall have to sully my knickers," said Chang, plucking up the gambler, who slid in hand like a greased pig. He threw the gambler over the withers of the sidestepping unhappy stallion. Fortunately the gambler weighed less than a pronghorn. Seven-Story stepped into the saddle, steadying the slippery gambler all the while, and trotted toward Mister Skye's camp, nether cheeks before him, laughing softly. Behind, the cards lay scattered.

Chapter 12

The sun pained Mister Skye. He cocked an eye open and peered into a dome of transparent azure, washed clean of the last speck of dust. He felt parched and at the same time his bladder howled, as if his kidneys had sucked his carcass dry and transported everything downward. But canvas entombed him and he could scarcely wiggle. Rock mauled his backbone. He lifted his head and it throbbed, but he could see which way the burial sheet wound, and rolled himself free and stood up. And sat down again promptly as dizziness overwhelmed him. Oh, that had been lively whiskey, and now he would pay a fancy price.

It all seemed odd. Shimmering puddles everywhere, the glint lancing his head. The two red wagons lacked sheets. He lay on a rock bench. His lodge had been moved and squatted grotesquely in the sun, steaming. His silk stovepipe hat had vanished. The sporting girls wandered around shamelessly in translucent wrappers that did little to conceal their charms. Blueberry Hill lounged on his wagon seat in red long johns and needed little more than a trident and horns to look like the devil. But that was nothing compared to Cornelius Vanderbilt, who flaunted one of Mister Skye's own fringed buckskin shirts, which fell to his thighs and barely covered his ass. Beneath this attire two legs, white and green as celery stalks, projected downward into Vanderbilt's boots. Red and purple bruises marked them, as well as his arms and face, and he looked uncommonly scrubbed. Seven-Story Chang and Victoria had gone somewhere, and so had Jawbone. Even Jawbone!

From the Riddle wagon, lines splayed out toward tree limbs, and each line sagged under a vast array of women's things, flapping white and mauve and ice-green. Ah, but there came Mary, poking among parfleches and pulling out pemmican. He slipped behind his tilted lodge and released a great satisfying steam of last night's joy, and then found Mary smiling beside him. It all reminded him of the rendezvous of '36, except for the wagons.

"I'm thirsty," he said.

"There are no cups." She handed him some pemmican. He didn't want any and handed it back.

She looked solemn.

"Where's my hat? Where's my Henry?"

"The hat's gone. The Henry is at the lodge, drying."

"We must have had a rain. I see puddles."

The tears in Mary's eyes startled him. "Boudins is dead," she cried.

It did not register at once. Dead? "Who killed him?" he asked at last.

"The whiskey did. The rain did. We did."

Tears seeped down her brown cheeks now. "He got washed away in the water, in what you call a flash flood. He was drunk. We were drunk. We made our camp here at the bottom of that gulch."

Not Boudins. Not an old trapper tougher than grizzly and a match for ten lions. Not Boudins. A man like that couldn't go under. A bullet or arrow maybe, but a flood, water . . .

Mister Skye groaned and ran a gnarled hand through his graying hair. "Not Boudins. He'll show up downstream. He swims better than beaver."

"He was drunk like you and me."

Mister Skye felt like a man with an arrow through the heart, and sat down heavily on wet rock. "We did it to him. We put him under," he muttered. "What else, Mary?"

"The sporting wagons, they got tipped over, and all they got was washed away. They got nothing."

"Where's Victoria? Where's Jawbone?" he asked sharply.

"Gone to find mules. Them and Seven-Story Chang. All the mules and horses busted loose, long time away."

He sat, feeling the throb in his forehead. "What else?"

"Victoria and Chang saved our lives. He pulled me and you up to here. Chang, he went everywhere. Victoria too. The brides, they're okeydokey. Riddle rolled up the canvas when the storm came. But the sporting ladies, they got nothing. Even the barrels of whiskey, all down the river."

Mister Skye observed the faint tremor in his hand.

"They got no food. Riddle got some but he ain't sharing. He and the brides, they say no food and no clothes for a mess of sluts and lowlifes."

Mister Skye pondered that. There had to be weighty meaning in it, but he couldn't grasp it at the moment.

"What else, Mary?"

"I got a damn headache. I shouldn't drink that stuff."

Cornelius Vanderbilt tottered around his wagon, and then Blueberry helped him up, baring his white buttocks.

"What about him?" Skye asked.

At last Mary smiled. "He was over in the other camp playing poker all night until Chang went for him. But they got mad and beat the crap out of him and Chang brought him home. Now he got nuthing to wear. He's got a funny white behind. Every time he bends, his white behind shows. Chang says maybe the whole outfit there come after us and string us up. They don't like it, Boudins dead and Vanderbilt stealing money. I dug the wet powder out of the fowling piece and got dry in, and dry patch and balls, and I been sitting here waiting."

Mister Skye loped for his Henry, found it warm and dry

to the touch, and loaded. But no targets presented themselves. His head throbbed. He felt naked without his hat.

Unsteadily, he trudged to the river and drank endlessly from cupped hands. It made him feel nauseous again. He found a cast-iron skillet half buried in muck, one he'd seen the sports use. He rescued it and wobbled over to their wagon. They sat desolately in the sun, barefoot, bareheaded, no doubt burning. Their wrappers hid little, but Mister Skye lacked the eye for it.

Goldtooth fumed. "You got us into this," she screamed. "Now I've got nothing. Not even clothes! We'll burn to death! Starve to death! My money's gone and I couldn't even buy clothing to save our lives from those bastards over there. And you did it, camping here at the foot of this coulee, getting drunk, you goddamn incompetent idiot."

Mister Skye nodded. His brain wasn't functioning yet.

"We don't have anything to cook with or eat from! We haven't a weapon between us, not even a knife! All my wealth went down the river. Five barrels of good whiskey! Every stitch of clothes we have! Half the harness! Our mules are gone! The wagon sheets tore off so we'll fry! No bedrolls, no blankets! All our jewelry! Mrs. Parkins's heirlooms! We're hungry! No one in the other camp will lift a finger for—women in the Life. We're going to die because you're incompetent, careless, stupid, drunk, addled, and—" She ran out of steam for a moment, and then wept. All four of them wept. Mister Skye almost wept.

"I found a skillet anyway," he mumbled, "and we can find more."

He summoned Blueberry and Cornelius.

"We'll search the riverbank for things," he said. "Maybe the heavy things will be caught in brush. Maybe even canvas and clothing."

"Mister Skye," said Blueberry, "those folks in the other camp, they'd shoot a black man in red long johns comin' along the shore. They'd horsewhip these ladies, wandering along the shore in little nothings."

"A lot of good a few odds and ends will do," said Goldtooth.

"Mizz Jones," said Mister Skye, "in a wilderness, a few small items can perform miracles."

"You goddamn idiot," she snapped.

"I think we've enough truck—Mary's and Victoria's and my things—to outfit two of you. I'll get it, and all of you get under the wagon and stay in shade."

"But it's muddy!" snapped Mrs. Parkins.

"Mud never hurt anyone. Sunburn will kill."

He pawed through the parfleches Victoria had rescued and found leggins, a breechclout, and an old gingham dress of Mary's. Also some jerky. A few minutes later, Goldtooth wore brown gingham and Blueberry had a breechclout and leggins over his red underwear.

"Find what you can. Salvage everything, no matter how useless it seems," Skye said. He handed them all some jerky.

His head ached but he had a lot of thinking to do. First and foremost he would deal with the threat from the wagon-train camp. He surmised that the men were hunting stock that had strayed before the storm, so he would have some time. The next question was whether he could get the women and lowlifes to Bannack. They'd need everything: food, clothing, bedding, cooking utensils, weapons. Once in Bannack they'd make up their losses easily enough . . . He smiled faintly.

He had, he thought, exactly one eagle, ten dollars in gold, with which to buy something from the other camp— if they'd sell. Riddle and his women had things, and Riddle might welcome a bit of gold. He'd see. Mules and horses and harness would be a question mark. He'd wait for Chang and Victoria, and meanwhile see what was left of Goldtooth's stuff. But food would be something. There wasn't much of anything to hunt along the Oregon Trail because the traffic drove animals far away, dozens of miles away. Maybe this trail wasn't the way to go . . . He and Jim Bridger had always thought wagons could be taken up through the Bighorn Valley and west on the Yellowstone.

The pass into the Gallatin Valley might be trouble, though. There'd be game on the Yellowstone but less in the Bighorn Valley. Might have to eat mules or horses. That would not thrill Goldtooth or Mrs. Parkins.

He felt a bit better now, but the death of Boudins lay heavy in him, along with shame. One thing Mister Skye had learned in the wilderness was to set aside guilt. His task now would be to find the means to survive in the present and future, and take his clients safely to the Bannack diggings.

At Alvah Riddle's wagon he found things in order. Soaked clothing hung on lines, food had survived, and Alvah had rolled the wagon sheet back over the bows, where it baked in the sun. But the brides slumped about in damp and drooping clothing, refusing even to doff a layer or two of petticoats to dry in the sun. They all eyed him narrowly as he approached.

"You did pretty well, Riddle."

"No thanks to you, Skye. You were drunk over there with your slut and that oaf—"

Mister Skye's thick arm caught Riddle across the chest and sent him sprawling into muck. The paunchy man leapt up sputtering.

"Are you crazy? What's your angle, Skye?"

"Mister Skye," he replied softly. "You never call Mary a slut again. If you do I will kill you. And you will never call Boudins an oaf. He stood as tall as the mountains."

Riddle caught something in Mister Skye's tone, and eye, and held himself in check. He reddened, muttering for a moment, and then subsided into his usual craftiness, glancing quick-eyed at Skye, the sporting women, the sprawled lodge, and Mary. "What are you going to do now, eh? They've got nothing over there. I know the angles and I saved everything here."

"With the help of Seven-Story Chang, who kept your wagon from sliding into the Platte. And who's even now hunting down the mules you failed to hobble before the storm. Along with my wife Victoria. You owe your lives to the Chinese. The mules probably scattered over a ten-mile circle, and if they are returned, you'll owe your future to Mister Chang and Mrs. Skye."

"I know your angle, Skye. You're trying to draw attention away from your drunk and irresponsible conduct last night. If you'd stayed sober, none of this would have happened."

The guide glared. "It's Mister Skye. And I don't walk on water or send down cloudbursts. As for the rest, you're right. I've come to borrow some food and clothing and I thought you'd be neighborly enough to supply it. With that, I'll get you all to Bannack City safely."

Riddle eyed him and calculated. "Well . . ." he said cautiously. "I figure that maybe we'll just join up with that other train. I don't cotton to your guiding much, and we'll be safer over there, with good respectable folk."

"Go ahead," Skye said.

Riddle seemed faintly startled. "Well, of course, those oxen, they're slower than snails, and we've got mules to make time with."

"Maybe you have mules. Maybe you won't."

"Well, I think I'll just mosey over there anyway, and let those respectable folks know that we've got respectable women here . . ."

"By all means," said Skye. "And now, I'd like to borrow some clothing for women who could die of exposure."

Riddle laughed nastily. "They got what they deserve. Good Lord's repaying them. I might sell them something—"

Drusilla said, "I have an old dress and a petticoat they may have, Mister Skye."

"Now see here," protested Riddle. "That's your dowry. I got a proper business interest in keeping you all dowered. If Skye or those females wish to pay me for it, I'll consider it. Might be worth a double eagle."

Drusilla glared at him icily. "It is not yours to dispose of." She began to remove a blue checked calico from one of the lines. Riddle leapt toward her. "We have a contract.

Section Four, Clause Twelve, prohibits you from disposing—''

She ignored him, and lifted the damp dress and a petticoat from the line. Riddle snatched them from her. ''We have a contract. We have a contract—'' he snapped.

''I think the lady wishes to give some of her clothing to a charitable cause,'' said Mister Skye gently. ''Is that not correct, Miss Dinwiddie?''

''The contract says that the party of the second part—that's the bride—can dispose of her property only with the permission of the party of the first part—that's me,'' said Alvah Riddle.

Mister Skye yawned. His head throbbed.

''They're suffering. I don't care what they are, they're suffering,'' protested Drusilla.

Flora laughed. ''Let 'em suffer,'' she said.

Mary-Rita said, ''I don't think we should be helping such flamin' sinners.''

Riddle's eyes lit up. ''There, you see, Skye? We're against you. Respectable folk are against you. Now I'll just go on over to that other train and see about things.''

Drusilla said, ''I'm sorry, Mister Skye. He does have that right, and I am bound by my contract.''

Riddle cackled nastily, enjoying his triumph.

Mister Skye yawned again. The morning sparkled but he barely noticed. At his own wagon he found the canvas he and Mary had been wrapped in, and took it over to the ladies.

''Two of you roll up in this,'' he said.

He trudged down to the riverbank and found Goldtooth and Blueberry hunting through the brush. They hadn't found much, but they salvaged a pink wagon sheet, much torn but usable, along with some frayed rope still attached to it. He waved at the pair of them and dragged the sodden sheet back to the red wagon and enlisted Vanderbilt to help pull it over the bows and tie it down. Minutes later, the soiled doves had shade and shelter.

It was getting toward noon. Still no sign of Victoria and Seven-Story Chang.

To Mary he said, "I'm going over to the other camp. I'd just as soon you keep that fowling piece handy."

She smiled and nodded. "I can maybe get a fire going now, and boil some jerky for the sporting women."

"You can make fires in the middle of blizzards using fingernails for fuel, Mary."

He had heard the bawling of oxen yonder and knew the other camp would soon pull out. He wanted to palaver before they got away. When he arrived there, he found them almost ready to go. The slow oxen hadn't been driven far by the storm, and most stood in their heavy wooden collars. He spotted other bunches up on the slopes, being choused down by men on foot.

They saw him coming and gathered around, their faces thunderous. "You're Skye, aren't you? The drunken guide of all those lowlifes yonder. Took our guide from us, right into the grave," said one.

"He was my best friend, and it grieves me more than I can say, mate," Skye replied.

"I bet it does," another snapped.

These were angry men, and they spoiled for trouble, such as maybe a good whipping.

"I came over to apologize about the gambler. He had instructions from me not to come here."

"I'll bet," a black-bearded one growled.

Mister Skye fixed him in the eye. "If you haven't the decency to take a man's word, mate, then have the courage to call me a liar."

It gave them pause.

"My wife and Mister Chang are rounding up stock, and will probably bring in horses of yours. I'd expect them anytime now."

"You lowlifes'll probably steal them from us."

Mister Skye's Henry swung casually toward the man. "I didn't hear you thanking us for the help, friend."

"Nothing to thank you for, far as I can figger," said another.

Here lay a stony wall, he thought. "I've a party that wants to join you," he said. "A man named Riddle and his wife, who are escorting some young women to Bannack.''

"We know their kind.''

"You don't rightly do,'' said Mister Skye. "Engaged to be married—Riddle's a matchmaker—and not what you're thinking.''

"He the one we heard about at Laramie that couldn't get hisself harnessed up in the morning, complained constantly, and dragged down the whole outfit?''

Mister Skye ignored him. "They've had enough of travel with lowlifes, mates, and I thought you might welcome respectable folk to your train.''

The last of the oxen trotted into camp now, and men broke from this gathering to yoke them and be off. Far up on a bluff, he saw something new, a herd of dark mules and multicolored horses winding its way downslope, driven by a man on a white stallion, and a tiny Indian woman, his Victoria, on an ancient, battered blue roan. The man on the white horse he esteemed. The woman and the blue horse he loved.

Chapter 13

Thirteen wagon-train horses were returned to their grateful owners, and hostility to Skye's party's evaporated with the rain puddles. A search party ranged three miles down the rough banks of the Platte, did not find Boudins, but salvaged a trunk of Goldtooth's full of gold corsets studded with purple rhinestones, pink-frilled nightgowns, black bloomers, green lisle stockings, and crimson garters with black roses embroidered on them, caught in bankside brush where a log snared the water. The muscular river had swept everything else beyond grasp.

Alvah Riddle sidled around the wagon train, smiling, howdying, whispering to men yoking oxen that he had grown weary of those . . . lowlifes. "Guess I'll join up with you. Make you a stronger party," he ventured to a busy choleric farmer.

The sweated man paused, his brow wet from dealing with fractious oxen, and glared at Alvah. "Heerd Porter's train had trouble with you," the man said and returned to his task.

"I don't get help from the women! But I got it figgered

out now. I got it all figgered,'' Alvah allowed, confidentially.

"We're moving faster than Porter. Passed them some while back. Three, four, more miles a day than him when it's good. Boudins told us we had the best-disciplined outfit he'd ever guided. Mean to keep it that way. We've been out a long time, have it all down.''

"Didn't know,'' Alvah mumbled. "Not quite what I figgered. You'll plumb wear out your stock. It's a good angle to slow down and keep it fat.''

The drenched man paused. "We got land to clear, cabins to build, crops to put down, fences to build, all before snow, and you talk slow.''

Alvah Riddle found no warmer reception elsewhere, and Mister Skye watched him skitter back to his wagon.

The bright-eyed wagon man who had fiddled the turns last night became, by common consent, the train's new captain, and he began at once to organize a small memorial service for Boudins. No one volunteered, but finally Parsimony McGahan, the atheist, pulled a King James from his barrels of books, and read the Twenty-Third Psalm and recited the Lord's Prayer, the Catholic version, which puckered women's faces. Mister Skye, Victoria, and Mary attended.

Just before the new captain, Gonzales Baer, pulled his train out into the soggy ruts of the trail, Mister Skye caught him.

His face reddened. "Say, mate, I could use some help. I've some naked women over there, lost everything. Need britches too.''

"Why, that is their natural condition,'' said Baer.

"I've an eagle left for provisioning.''

Something bright sparked in Baer's brown eyes, crinkling flesh. Then he laughed, like a cataract on a sunny afternoon. He walked back to the center of the line and gathered people around him.

"Mister Skye, here, informs me that certain of his party are without clothing. We're owing them for the horses they brought back, and I would like those women who can spare dresses and certain other things to donate them to a worthy cause. Also two pairs of men's britches, one skinny, one wide.''

People laughed. This wagon train took life amiably.

"Polly," said one, "ain't you got a spare skirt or two?"

"Never thought it'd cover a Cyprian," she said, digging into a trunk.

"One tall and skinny, three mediums," said Mister Skye.

"You're tall and skinny, Della," said another.

"Well, I never," she retorted.

"Shoes, moccasins, food?" said Mister Skye.

At that they shook their heads. There would be no game along the trail, and barely food enough to last to Fort Hall. As for shoes, they were wearing them out at a fearsome rate trudging fifteen or seventeen miles a day.

"Looks like we can't help you there, Skye," said Baer.

"It's Mister Skye. Thanks for your help, mates."

He turned to leave, his arms draped with fabrics, but Parsimony McGahan stayed him.

"Sir," he said hastily. "Please take this to Miss Dinwiddie, with my compliments." He thrust a slim velour-bound book in the guide's hands, *Sonnets from the Portuguese*, by Elizabeth Barrett Browning.

"Whose compliments, mate?"

The young man swallowed. "Parsimony McGahan, sir. With my love, sir."

"I will do that, Mister McGahan. And where may she reach you?"

"She knows, sir. Virginia City, Nevada."

"I will do it," said Skye. He and Mary and Victoria watched as the men roared and whipped and cursed the oxen to life, and the heavy wagons hissed through furrowed gumbo. They would not go far this afternoon before the oxen played out, but only half a day remained anyway.

Mary and Victoria pawed through Goldtooth's trunk, giggling and pressing corsets to themselves.

"Mister Skye," said Mary solemnly, "if you would buy these things, I will wear these things."

"Mary, if you do, I will sell you."

"Mister Skye, that would be fun."

They carried the waterlogged trunk back to their camp, amid the sudden silence. Anger hung there like fog.

"We got these," said Mister Skye, dumping dresses and britches into the red wagon. The women pawed at them silently, dividing them by fit and pulling them on without bothering to hide themselves. Vanderbilt pulled on some butternut gray britches that fit at the waist but were short. Blueberry set his aside, content to wear Skye's leggins and breechclout. Big Alice encased herself in a blousy shapeless gray dress that could not eclipse her golden charms. Mrs. Parkins found an ice-blue that enhanced her blond beauty. Sable-haired Juliet wiggled into a too-small black twill and looked ravishing. Goldtooth pawed testily through the recovered trunk, cussing, and didn't try on charity.

In the grass before the red wagon lay everything Goldtooth and Blueberry had recovered from the river brush— precious little—and Skye studied it because Fate depended on it. A butcher knife, one tin cup, an empty steamer trunk, an axe, loose pieces of harness.

He sighed. Seven-Story herded the mules yonder, and Mister Skye trudged wearily in that direction, his head throbbing again.

"Five killed by lightning, one missing," said the Chinese.

"Whose?"

"You lost one. Goldtooth lost four. Riddle's is the one missing."

Skye nodded. "Has anyone checked harness?"

The mandarin shook his head.

Beneath a cottonwood Blueberry sorted out collars and bellybands. "We can harness three span proper, and I got stuff to make another if I got rope."

Mister Skye nodded. Victoria could cut strips from the bottom of the lodge if necessary.

The sun baked his head and his eyes ached without the shade of his silk hat. Maybe his eyes would ache anyway

this morning, he thought. At his lodge he found a red
bandana and tied it over his forehead, pinning his long
hair.

"That should get you a new squaw," said Victoria. "Put
an eagle feather in back. You're pretty dumb, drinking last
night. Maybe I quit and go back to the Absaroka people.
Maybe you getting too goddamn old for this."

"Hadn't seen that old coon Boudins for years," he muttered.

He needed to think, and toiled his way up a rise to a
small plateau, overlooking the Platte. Below him his people busied, taking tucks in dresses, harnessing mules, dismantling the lodge, loading parfleches on panniers. He
lacked a mule and the loads pressed heavier now on the
others.

He sank down, thinking about Boudins, gone under.
Right here, plenty of people around to help, and the pair
of them stinking drunk, pair of old goddamn fur men piss-
eyed and careless out where carelessness puts a man under. Should have been himself, not Boudins, not Boudins.
Some poor-meat prayer by strangers and old Boudins
plumb forgotten. Big Beaver that took plews out of ice
water, waltzed with grizzlies, sucked the buffler gut that
gave him his name. Come to think of it, he never knew
Boudins by another. The man never seemed to have a
Christian one, never a Peter or Joseph or Jedediah. No
folks to tell about it either, just Boudins, with no strings
going anywhere, no family save for a few temporaries out
on the trail he'd bought for a few plews, or blankets, or a
crowbait pony or two.

Skye mourned in the high sun for an hour, mourned and
watched them break camp below. It would be an unspoken
thing, but they'd turn back to Laramie. Of course, Riddle'd
bide his time there and hook up with some train that didn't
know about him. The sports would go into business temporarily and reoutfit. . . . In a few minutes they'd line up
facing east, not west, and starve all the way back. Victoria
probably had jerky or pemmican enough for a day, but
they were twelve days out of Laramie. Some army garri-

sons in between, but they couldn't part with food and shoes.

He thought some about going back, giving up on this one he had botched. But he didn't like it. He'd never failed to get his clients to their destination. It ragged him, this defeat. They'd starve all the way back, too, and that bothered him.

Well, why go back at all? He and his women knew how to make do with a lot less. He inventoried what they had and what they'd need. It came down to sleeping robes, shoes or moccasins for the lowlifes. As for the food, there might be a way . . .

He sat there another half hour, working it through a brain still puddling from the night's debauch. Below, they'd finished harnessing and loading and were waiting for him irritably. He stood, feeling the warm brass of the Henry in his hand, and trudged down to his party.

They peered at him angrily. Goldtooth steamed. Alvah Riddle's gaze popped at him like the tassel of a whip. Victoria and Mary had turned surly and silent. Mrs. Parkins exuded frost. The only sign of warmth came from Seven-Story Chang, who grinned mockingly on his white stallion.

"We'll get you to Bannack," he said.

"We're returning to Fort Laramie, thanks to your stupidity," snapped Goldtooth Jones.

"Starve the whole way. No need for it."

"With what? How are you going to get us to Bannack when we have one cup, one knife, and an empty trunk? Where are shoes and bedrolls? Where's food?"

"All about us," said Mister Skye. "But not here on the Oregon Trail, where the game's been run off and everything's been picked over."

"You got us into this mess!" she raged.

"Do you want to go to Bannack?"

He could see the abacus beads of her mind skinning on the wires. "Soldiers earn eight dollars a month—when they're paid at all," she said wryly.

He stared. "You'll starve getting to Fort Laramie, and starve at Fort Laramie, and buck a lot of competition."

"This conversation is disgusting," said Gertrude Riddle.

"What's your angle, Skye?" whickered Alvah.

The mandarin sat on his horse, mocking.

"No need to starve, at least no longer than a day or two. No need for you to be barefoot either. No need to sleep cold in this high country either. No need to turn back. What do you think the Indians do to stay alive and warm, mates?"

"You'd better do something plenty damn fast, Skye, because I'm half starved," snapped Vanderbilt.

"I'll stuff you this evening, but you won't like the meat," Skye said. "It'll be more than you deserve."

"What's your angle, Skye? Me and my women, we're fixed good and can go back and hitch to another wagon train."

"And get tossed out again, Riddle. My friend Jim Bridger and I, we always figured there might be a wagon route through the Bighorn Basin, north of here. Then along the Yellowstone, and over a divide Blanket Jim and I know, and after that it's easy to Bannack or the new Alder diggings. Probably two, three hundred miles shorter, maybe more. Game all the way, once we get a few miles off this trail."

"Go where there's no road?"

"Fur company trails," replied Mister Skye. "Know it like the back of my hand."

"Barefoot!" snapped Goldtooth.

"Yonder, packed on that travois, is my lodge. Good cured cowhide skins for moccasins, made to order for your feet by my two ladies, who can outfit the whole lot of you in a day or two. We'll unstitch the hides, and you'll all have robes. If we find buffler along the trail—should be some north of here—we'll have hump roast and bones for kitchen ladles and such, robes we can start tanning, and rawhide for harness."

"What will we eat off of?"

"Wooden trenchers we'll cut from cottonwood and hollow in a day or two."

"Is there water?"

"There is. As it happens, this is a good enough place to leave the Oregon Trail and strike west. Maybe some will be brackish."

"I haven't a shovel for road building," said Blueberry.

"You will when we get some buffalo bones."

"What will we eat tonight?" said Vanderbilt.

"Mule steaks, if the wolves and coyotes haven't got to them. Victoria will cut the tail hair too, and weave new bridles and halters and even reins from it."

"You get drunk and me and Mary work our fingers off," growled Victoria.

Goldtooth laughed raucously.

It looked good, he thought. Blueberry had jury-rigged some harness from loose parts, and had two spans hooked to each wagon. Each red wagon had started with three, but now the wagons carried little. Riddle had five chocolate mules, two spans harnessed and one reserve tied to the rear.

"I'd suggest you and your women walk as much as possible, Riddle," he said. "You've all got shoes, unlike these others. Until it dries, it'll be hard pulling."

"I'll run my outfit as I please, Skye. I don't know what your angle is, but you rightly got nothing to say about it. Not after what you done to us all."

But even as Riddle replied, Drusilla clambered down, followed by Mary-Rita, and a reluctant Flora.

No one said yes. No one said anything, but Skye knew he had carried the day. They wanted to get to Bannack; they wanted food and shelter and comfort.

"One thing, Skye," said Vanderbilt. "I don't have a weapon. Blueberry doesn't have a weapon. These women don't have a weapon. How are we to protect ourselves? What if we have Indian trouble?"

Mister Skye smiled. "Henry repeater here. In my kit is an old Sharps buffalo gun. Colt's at my side. My women each have muzzleloaders. Double-barreled fowling piece, too. And Mister Riddle is not naked.''

"I'll say not," said Alvah, "Spencer carbine, revolver. Might think twice about letting others use them though.''

"That's not the end of it, Mister Vanderbilt. Each of my ladies has a bow of Osage orange, wrapped in fine sinew, and a full quiver of arrows with iron trade points, and a lifelong skill with them. Very handy for making meat when quiet is needed. I would add, Mister Vanderbilt, that only last night you were well armed with short-range weapons, but lost them because you are a sharper.''

He turned to Blueberry. "You should have some protection at your wagons, Mister Hill. This evening we will lend you the fowling piece and some powder and buckshot. Directly, I will begin to make lances, war clubs, and shields, all from wood and bone and hide and stone. . . . You may wish to observe, Mister Riddle. That's an angle you hadn't angled.''

"I'd be obliged, Mister Skye," said Blueberry.

He waited for objections. No one spoke.

He turned Jawbone toward a long dun coulee rising north, and behind him heard the sounds of hawing and whips, and the rattle of trace chains and harness, and the stammer of wagon wheels turning sharply. They would come, then. Ahead of him old Victoria rode her pony, hunched and small and dry as parchment. She would head for the carcasses of the mules and salvage meat before the predators and sun fouled it. And with a swift hack of her old Green River knife, cut an armload of tail hair which she would plait with dextrous old fingers into reins and halters and bridles. She could make those things more easily from the cured leather of their lodge, but that in the end meant more brutal work, tanning fresh lodgeskins. It would be trouble enough for the old woman to make moccasins from one hide, and separate the other hides for bedrolls.

Behind him wagons hissed through damp earth, extruding thin lines of shining clay behind them, and broken bunchgrass.

"Ow, goddamn sonofabitch," howled a female voice behind him, and he turned. Barefooted Big Alice muttered, limping, and just back of her lay a low clump of prickly pear. Mister Skye smiled. They would soon learn that moccasins would not defend them from the stickers either, and they would need to walk with care, as Indians did. But he didn't say anything then. She clambered into the red wagon beside Blueberry, and blued the vaults of heaven.

When they finally topped the bluff north of the Platte Valley, he could see a vast distance, clear to the Bighorns, baking distantly in July heat. He felt suddenly free. This was the empty West he knew, the untouched lands he had learned and loved as a young trapper. Along the Oregon Trail he had felt imprisoned. He always felt hemmed in by people, but suddenly those iron bands around his heart slipped away in the shimmer of the duned prairies. Here was life! Now the days would run and leap and sing! Off to the east he could see Chang scouting and hunting. Far ahead, Victoria dropped over a low ridge, and he knew when he saw her again she'd probably have a load of fly-bitten mule meat wrapped behind her, and enough hair to keep stiff old fingers busy for weeks. But he wanted something else, the shaggy brown beasts that never ventured close now to the Oregon Trail—buffalo, the food, shelter, weapons, and clothing of all the Plains tribes. He sucked sweet, sage-scented air into his lungs, and laughed.

Chapter 14

She had never been poor before. Her own family, the Sylvanuses, ranked among the Memphis elite. Then she had married Hannibal Parkins, who had more gold than Midas. At Goldtooth's parlor house she had used her perfect body, chiseled features, shining ash-blond hair, and twilight-gray hooded eyes to make herself independent, and it was all hers, too, not any man's.

Then that buckskinned idiot leading this brigade lost it all for her in one night. Everything she owned except for one li'l old white wrapper. And out in a wilderness too, where one couldn't simply call the dressmaker or order dinner at a restaurant. She scorned the lout, but even more did she dread the days ahead. She could scarcely imagine life without the things she had carefully packed in fragrant cedar-lined trunks, her silk gowns and pink frocks and black underthings, Wedgwood china, silver, fine damask table linens; a trunk of shining shoes and slippers, belts and yellow velvet ribbons, lavender scents, rouges, and English soaps.

Her inheritance here had been one li'l old sky-blue dimity dress, badly worn and busted out at the elbows, plus an unbleached-muslin petticoat that smelled of cat droppings. The translucent dimity let the slightest breeze through, as well as men's gazes, which amused her. But nothing more amused her. She wished to go back to Fort Laramie. She might easily have married a captain for a while, long enough to put her life together. She knew what she could do to men. Not that she'd have stayed at a crude army post for long.

That first afternoon had been ghastly. She craved food. Not a blanket remained in the wagon to cushion its bouncing over a roadless land, and she jolted and rolled until her whole torso felt bruised. But she found walking even worse because she lacked shoes and the whole mean ol' prairie contrived to stab her feet. Only Big Alice walked. The Creole woman had gone barefoot much of her life, and the rock and prickly pear and sagebrush sticks didn't bother her.

She was a prisoner. On the driver's seat, Blueberry slouched lazily, enjoying himself. He could enjoy himself in hell, she thought bitterly. Britches had been donated to him, but he preferred his faded red long johns, Mister Skye's leggins, and a breechclout. He too lacked shoes. Like Mister Skye and those squaws, Blueberry seemed to bloom the moment they left the Oregon Trail and started overland through an empty, endless, and desolate wilderness.

Mrs. Parkins peered toward the hazy horizons, deeply afraid. She'd been in cities all her life. What would they do for food? Clothing? Shelter? Would she eat grasshoppers or snakes with her filthy fingers? What would she do for soap and shoes and her monthly time? What if Indians came? Would this harsh dry climate bake her flesh and ruin her beauty, her living? On the Oregon Trail there might be help—garrisoned army posts every twenty miles, other wagon trains. But here . . . That evening the gray mule meat salvaged by one of the squaws had been ghastly. It crawled with green-bellied flies when she first saw it, and then the squaws roasted it harshly in open flame, burning it black on the outside. But she ate it ravenously with her fingers after it had cooled, there being nothing else. They all felt so starved they ate the whole of it, envying the Riddles and their mail-order brides who cooked from airtights.

Mrs. Parkins snorted. Where lay the difference between her and the mail-order brides? Nowhere, really. Some li'l old person would mumble over them, but after that a woman's life stayed the same, only she enjoyed it a hundred times more than they ever would. That's why she had entered the Life. She enjoyed it. All she wanted was a big ol' man! Lots and lots of them!

They had made ten good miles that afternoon, striking just north of west from the Oregon Trail, and Mister Skye camped in a shallow valley choked with brush and trees, on either side of a tiny alkaline creek. After that awful meal, Mister Skye's younger squaw, Mary, beckoned her. Moments later, she found herself standing on a buffalo cowhide that had been snipped out of Skye's lodge, while Mary swiftly outlined her bitsy feet with a stick of charcoal. Beside Mary, old Victoria cursed and snipped leather and poked holes in it with an awl. By twilight, the sporting ladies and Blueberry all had moccasins, crudely made but serviceable. And all of them learned instantly that Indian moccasins didn't keep rocks and sticks and thorns from biting their feet. They begged for liners, and that helped. They could walk at last. Mrs. Parkins felt less a prisoner now that she could at least head for bushes without stabbing her feet.

Still muttering and cursing, Victoria snipped the sinews that had bound the lodgeskins together in watertight seams, and somehow separated four soft old hides for the bawds before the night spun too far along. A sleeping robe for each.

That Mister Skye, off in the creek brush, hacked a cottonwood limb with rhythmic whacks. By the time light dimmed in this shallow dip in the plains, he had cut half a dozen things that looked like thick shingles, oblongs of creamy wood, perhaps two inches thick. He lowered himself before the fire, which Victoria kept burning only for light, and with a hatchet for a chisel deftly hollowed out each slab of wood.

"Trenchers," he said, handing one to Mrs. Parkins. She found herself staring at a serviceable plate.

"If you hadn't gotten drunk, we could be eating from our tin camp things," she retorted nastily. She would not let that irresponsible lout off so easily. He came from the servant class, but scarcely knew it, and needed disciplining.

"Right you are, Mrs. Parkins," he replied amiably.

"You'd better make us some silverware. It's disgusting to eat with fingers," she added.

"Will when we take a buffler."

Across the fire, still muttering and cursing, old Victoria separated tail hair she had sliced from the lightning-struck mules into twisted strands, and plaited it. Did these squaws never sleep? she wondered. Victoria's hard brown eyes flicked at her man, and Mrs. Parkins saw embedded forgiveness there, the kind of thing that lasts and grows beyond lifetimes.

"This is all your idea. I trust you have some bitsy thing planned for breakfast, Mister Skye," she said tartly.

"Last of the jerky, Mrs. Parkins."

She could scarcely imagine anything worse. The hard, dried strips of buffalo eventually melted in the mouth, but never satisfied hunger.

Big Alice commandeered the butcher knife and was off slaying grass and carting armloads of it to the red wagon. Mrs. Parkins suddenly realized that might be a good idea, and helped. Eventually Goldtooth and Juliet helped too, and in a while a foot of soft, sweet-smelling dry grasses lined the wagon bed, along with pungent sage leaves. It dawned on Mrs. Parkins for the first time that comfort might be possible out here. The Indians managed it somehow. After that, she sank into a soft new bed beside the others, wrapped the cowhide robe about her, and slept better than she had hoped, except for the pimple that stung on her inner thigh.

The next day she enjoyed. She walked when she felt like it, learning to cope with moccasins, understanding what they could and couldn't do. And when she wearied of that, she rode in the grass-lined wagon bed relishing the fresh smell, somewhat insulated from the rude jolting, staring at the broad back of big ol' Blueberry and the drops of sweat that rolled down his heavy corrugated neck, darkening the faded long john.

She scarcely noticed the vast land they crossed, or the earth she trod upon. The red wagon and its frayed pink sheet had become a sort of island, a tiny dot of shade under an iron sun. This day she thirsted but they found no water anywhere. She peered through the rear puckerhole, watching Vanderbilt stolidly drive the grimy red wagon behind, dressed now in ancient butternut britches that had probably been part of a Confederate uniform, his dull black boots, and a sagging mud-colored calico blouse he'd scrounged somewhere, maybe on the sly from that bride, Drusilla. Without his gambler uniform he looked odd, she thought. Like he ought to be pickin' cotton.

In the morning those squaws of Skye's had made a stew in a black kettle, with jerky and some white roots with brown skins they'd dug up, and even some prairie turnips they'd found, and added a bit of salt from Mister Skye's parfleches, and it'd been grand. And then during the nooning in willow shade, Seven-Story Chang had ridden in on his white horse with a blood-crusted antelope tied behind the cantle, and they feasted. She loved big ol' Chang. He always mocked her, and that made time fly. She looked up to any big ol' man who could tease her. She decided she'd have him tonight. Maybe Blueberry too. She thought about that big ol' Mister Skye, but he had his Mary. Maybe she could steal him from Mary.

For a moment she envied the Shoshone woman, but not much. So what if the squaw had flesh as smooth and colorful as rosy peaches, and shiny blue-black hair, plaited into two braids? So what if her doe eyes gleamed, and she had a row of even white teeth? Mary had a li'l old scar that started back from her forehead, and that marred her.

Mrs. Parkins envied the beautiful soft tan doeskin blouse that Mary wore, fringed at the hips and quilled across the bodice in bold jags of rainbow color. She wore it over a long skirt of red calico, with high beaded moccasins below that, and all cinched at the waist with a black sash she tied as a belt. Mary was lucky to be so beautiful. Mister Skye was lucky too, but she'd show that big ol' man a trick or two that Mary never learned. Mrs. Parkins lay back in the jouncing wagon, stared at blue sky peeping through furry holes in the wagon sheet, and thought about Mister Skye's leggins and red-beaded breechclout.

The moment Mister Skye turned the wagons northwest, away from the Oregon Trail, Mary rejoiced. She knew Victoria rejoiced, too. They rode out upon a vast sun-danced prairie, and she felt at home at once. An eagle soared on summer drafts, and she felt free and clean. Far ahead, Victoria scouted, a dark dot on a golden land, and off to the right side Mary sometimes glimpsed the Chinese on his white medicine horse, dipping in and out of hollows invisible to the eye.

She rode behind Mister Skye, keeping the packmules in line and watching the travois with the lodgepoles and what remained of the lodgecover upon it. She still had enough skins to erect a small shelter for them if it stormed. Mister Skye's back had changed too, straighter and more erect now. He didn't like the trail either. He had become like her people, even though he was a white man. Even Jawbone looked happier, almost dancing along and gamboling like a colt.

She wasn't really afraid of the whites, except sometimes when hard-eyed ones came, but she could not understand them. These had lost their things and talked of going back. What a mystery! They thought they had to go back because there would be nothing to eat or wear. Were they blind, these white women? Here she could find everything to eat and wear. Here in this moon they called July grew roots and berries and herbs, wild onions and breadroot, raspberries and turnips. It had been thus with every party of whites they had taken out upon the breast of the Earth Mother. They walked through food and did not see it, saw clothing but did not know it. Passed weapons and implements and tools and their minds were shut to all of it.

There were dyes in rock and clay and berries and roots and bark; medicine everywhere in leaves and roots and the pulp of insects; and signs everyplace to tell who had come and gone. Even now, they rode over an oblique path of many small unshod hoofs, made since the big rain but dry and a day old. But she knew the whites had not seen this plain thing, even though Mister Skye had. The white people had great medicine and made guns and pots and wheels, but they didn't see or know.

Mister Skye paused to examine the tracks, and the fresher one of a shod horse beside them. Mary paused too. It had been a hunting party, too small for war. No travois furrowed the earth, but a dog ran with them. They had spare ponies that paused to nip bunchgrasses beside the main trail. The prints were light and that meant the ponies carried no meat. The Chinese had found them, and started northeast along their trail, just to check upon them. They scouted for buffalo, just as Mister Skye hunted for a valley black with them.

She did not talk much to Mister Skye. She had little to say, especially when she knew his thoughts before he spoke them. She knew when he would come to her robes and make her happy. She knew when she made him happy, too. He seemed happy now, crossing the wide grassland ahead of the wagons and far from the Oregon Trail. She remembered when they had made Dirk. It was not at night, but at noon in the mountain lands on a day much like this. They made Dirk beside a raucous creek on the other side of the Bitterroot Mountains, and she knew it at once, and knew Dirk would be a good-medicine child. She missed him now, but her task was done. The boy had wept but she didn't when they had put him on a white steamer at Fort Benton in the care of a rich Frenchman named Chouteau who was a friend of Mister Skye's.

Now he learned the medicine of the white men, the little

figures on the paper, their stories and their way of adding things up. It was good, but she hoped Dirk would not lose the wisdom of her people. He had gone on a vision-quest beforehand, and had come back laughing, with a small medicine bundle dangling from his neck. She would not ask, and he would not say, what sacred things he carried. But he knew who his medicine helper was: the red fox. Good! Dirk would have his helper-fox, even back in the place called Independence; even among the blackrobes who would teach him things. Mister Skye had old friends among the blackrobes, especially Father Kiley, who had made all the arrangements.

She did not want ever to see Independence.

These whites were the strangest Mary had ever known. Two wagons of outcast whites, and another wagon of ones who judged the others, and they barely spoke to each other. The outcasts were friendlier to her. She could talk to the ones who sold themselves to men, and she loved to be around Chang or Blueberry, but the women in the other wagon ignored her or addressed her curtly, as if she were a Cheyenne. The ones in the Riddle wagon would not share with the others, and that shocked her. The man, Riddle, talked about angles, and it took her time to understand his meaning, but then she knew he made evil and contrived to take advantage of everyone. He had tried right off to take advantage of Mister Skye, not doing anything in the mornings, thinking that would force Mister Skye to harness his mules for him. But Mister Skye knew how to handle such a person. Just once he asked Mister Riddle to be ready in the morning. But that weasel-man wasn't. He intended to sit back and smirk and leer and feel lordly and make Mister Skye harness. So Mister Skye had gathered Riddle's six mules and tied them all behind the red wagons, and had driven out, leaving Riddle and his women with a bare wagon, openmouthed behind them.

Riddle learned the lesson. Mary giggled, remembering how the weasel-man raved and yelled and cried theft when Skye returned an hour later. Not that it changed Mister Riddle. The white man spent hours trying to get Mary and

Victoria, or someone else, to do things he could easily have done for himself with half the effort. But that was the way of Riddle, very lazy but very energetic about pressuring others. He would be no help at all in a fight, and would hide in his wagon.

Mister Skye knew that too. She saw it in her man's face whenever he looked at Riddle. What a strange party! Nobody helping anybody! It scandalized her. Her Snake people helped one another. In war, there could be no greater honor than to rescue a wounded or endangered comrade. No chief stood tall unless he made sure the least widow woman of the band was fed and sheltered. Mary sat tall in her saddle, proud of her people and aware of the terrible shortcomings of whites.

Mister Skye looked strange to her without his black hat. He wore a red bandana over his forehead now, knotted at the back, holding his long white-shot hair in place and looking like a chief of her people rather than a white man. It pleased her. His black hat came from the other world.

Far off she spotted Victoria galloping toward them, slouched lightly over her sweated brown pony. She never raced unless trouble neared. Mister Skye saw her at once, and loosened the thong of his revolver scabbard. He turned, nodded to Mary, who knew what to do. She wheeled her pony and trotted back to the Riddle wagon.

"Mister Skye say trouble," she announced curtly. Alvah glanced narrowly around, saw nothing, and smiled lazily.

She trotted back. "Mister Skye say trouble," she said to Blueberry. He peered sharply, lifted the fowling piece, and also a small poke full of shot, and a powderhorn. It made a slim defense. In a hard fight, he'd scarcely be able to reload the two barrels before being swept under.

She continued back to Vanderbilt. "Mister Skye say trouble," she announced. But he shrugged. She remembered he lacked weapons, save for some willow staves Mister Skye had cut for him at the last camp.

She rode up to the Riddle wagon. "The sporting man has no gun," she said to Riddle.

"He's plumb in a fix," Riddle said. "Wish I could help."

The brides scurried into the hot shade of the wagon sheet, and spread themselves below the plank box, a thin inch of hardwood between themselves and bullets. Mary-Rita moaned, scared witless.

No good arguing with Riddle, so she trotted forward again. Victoria hung immobile on her racing pony. She weighed scarcely a hundred pounds now, and rode a light grass-stuffed pad which her pony carried effortlessly, but she lost ground to what raced behind her, a dozen bronzed and naked men raising a long plume of dust like running elk on the drying prairie.

Mister Skye stopped now, and the wagons behind him. He peered not at Victoria, but along the horizon to the north, looking for Chang and not seeing him.

"The gambler man has no gun," Mary said to him.

He glanced back. Vanderbilt had abandoned his wagon and was dodging across the prairie, looking for a rabbit hole. The trotting mules dragged the empty wagon farther and farther off, its body and naked bows shrinking into a red dot on the horizon.

Victoria raced in, saying just one word: Arapaho.

Chapter 15

Eleven, and they were not painted. A hunting party then, looking for sport and finding it. They paused, just beyond rifleshot, assessing their chances, seeing Vanderbilt's naked red wagon far from the others, seeing only two males, Mister Skye and Blueberry.

Beneath him Jawbone pawed and shrieked, ears back, clenched for war and blood. Mister Skye pressed his palm against Jawbone's withers, a signal, and the horse quieted.

"Hunters," he said.

"Sonofabitch," muttered Victoria. He heard her pulling her muzzleloader from its sheath. He knew Mary was crouched back of the mule with the travois, the big Sharps resting on the pack.

The warriors began to spread out now, one party heading for the flank and the other nerving itself for the run. So . . . they would take scalps and count coup this fine summer day. They looked to be boys and young men, he thought, but couldn't be sure. Age had done things to his sight.

They would not be far from an Arapaho village that followed the buffalo. Out yonder, the bronze riders paused to make medicine, each in his own way. They hadn't the advantage of surprise, so this would be no sweeping howling assault, but an orchestrated dance of daring, braving the rifles of the whites.

Seven with bows, four with carbines, of what sort he couldn't imagine. He felt the gleaming new Henry in his hands, with more cartridges in its long belly than there were warriors out there. Beneath him Jawbone shivered.

Two of them raced toward Vanderbilt's red wagon now. That would be the first prize, and a shelter to shoot from.

"Mary," he said.

She swung the big Sharps toward them, and squeezed. The throaty boom echoed in the afternoon. The recoil jolted Mary. It had twice the range of his Henry.

A pony collapsed, red flowering its chest, and the rider leapt free as it sank.

Mister Skye glanced behind him, noting Blueberry at the ready. Alvah Riddle had vanished, but now a gleaming blue barrel poked through a small port in the side of his wagon. Another of Riddle's angles, he thought, and not a good one, blindsided as he was.

The main body of the Arapaho spread into a skirmish line now and trotted fast.

"Mister Riddle," he said, "do not shoot to kill unless they are upon you. They are hunters having sport, and we will avoid war. We'll likely go to their village directly."

No answer.

He nodded to Victoria, and she crept toward Riddle's barrel, pressing hard against the side of Riddle's wagon. She would do what Plains Indians were gifted at doing with tumescent barrels.

The unhorsed warrior crabbed toward the abandoned wagon. The others closed in.

He focused on the sweated chest of the lead pony and squeezed. The Henry bucked. He missed. He levered and fired again, dropping a horse and catapulting its rider. He levered and hit another horse, which kept running, stumbling, falling along a declining trajectory. A whinny pierced the afternoon. He smelled gunsmoke. He heard a flat shot from out there, and another. But they stayed too far away for arrows. He levered and shot, grazing a rump, and the horse bucked violently, crowhopped, head down, spilling a rider.

Behind him the Sharps boomed and the most distant of the ponies stumbled. The several dismounted warriors lay flat. From Riddle's wagon a rifle barked and a warrior's arm blossomed red.

Mister Skye cursed.

The horse warriors milled now, then dashed toward their unmounted brothers, who leapt up gracefully as the hunting ponies trotted by, seating themselves behind the riders.

Mister Skye held his fire. Behind him Victoria grasped the barrel of Riddle's rifle, jammed it inward, knocking the butt into Riddle's teeth, and yanked outward violently. Inside, Alvah Riddle howled and women screamed. Victoria darted under his wagon with the rifle.

"You didn't listen to me, Mister Riddle, and now there's a man wounded out there and maybe war."

No reply.

A warrior had gained the empty red wagon and whipped up the mules. Another darted straight toward the bunchgrassed slope where Vanderbilt had flattened himself to earth. Bad business.

He slid brass cartridges into the Henry's magazine and waited. They lurked just beyond Henry range, making medicine again. They wrapped the arm of the wounded one, who sat in shock on the sunstruck earth.

On the flank, one of them spotted Vanderbilt. The gambler sprang up and lumbered in, with the warrior gliding behind him, scalping knife glinting. Mister Skye nodded to Mary, and the Sharps boomed, geysering dirt and rock just ahead of the warrior. He got the message. Vanderbilt puffed in and scrambled under Blueberry's wagon, wheezing and wild-eyed.

They hadn't expected a repeater. They barely understood the seven-shot Spencers and had never experienced a Henry. Mister Skye raised the weapon over his head and touched heels to Jawbone, who snorted and minced toward the warriors, ears flattened and teeth bared. Behind him, Mary and Victoria lay prone, their rifles resting solidly on packs, ready to back their man.

The Arapaho sat their ponies or stood like cemetery statues in a prairie graveyard, naked except for moccasins and breechclouts, bows and rifles canted but ready. Mister Skye rode steadily, hoping he would not have to do what he might have to do. But they had not left their village as a war party, and their sport had vanished with the dead ponies, probably good buffalo runners.

He reined Jawbone some thirty yards from them, and watched. The recognition came to them then. They knew Jawbone, the bad-medicine horse familiar to all the Plains tribes, a source of terror. Those who had never seen the horse nonetheless knew him by description, the scarred evil blue roan with the yellow eyes narrowly set, owned by a barrel of a man with a black stovepipe hat . . .

They studied Skye's head. No hat, but a red bandana. But this horse could only be the terrible one, and this man Mister Skye. He knew none of them, but their eyes knew him. They lowered their weapons cautiously, well aware of the reach of the big buffalo gun back at the wagons.

They stood immobile, waiting. Arapaho, he thought. Dog-eaters, the other Plains people called them, speaking a tongue close to the Atsina, or Gros Ventre, and similar to the Cheyenne. They roamed this land, here close to the North Platte.

He waited too, sniffing out treachery, ticking off time to see whether he could cradle his Henry in his lap and make his big hands flash the signs. He decided he could. I am Mister Skye, the guide, he told them, making the sign for the heavens. Known to all the tribes by the sign of the sky. I am passing through; looking for buffalo. I am peaceful. I had shot only ponies, not men, and had stopped the one in my party who'd shot to kill. His blunt brown hands slashed air as harshly as his voice did.

They nodded.

Did they want war? he asked.

One among them said no; not war against Mister Skye.

They had been out for sport. Buffalo grazed nearby. But now they lacked ponies. Three of the dead ones were good buffalo runners. They would keep the red wagon and mules they had captured.

No, said Mister Skye, they would not. He would take back the wagon and mules. But maybe when he found buffalo he would leave many carcasses for them. He would shoot them with his big Sharps from a distance, the way of the white buffalo hunters, and would drop many before the herd even stirred, and all but one would be theirs. He would take four hides and the meat of one carcass. But if they wanted war, he would give them war, much more war than they ever imagined.

They muttered, and turned at last to the one on the ground holding his arm, and Mister Skye realized the wounded one was their leader. He looked older, perhaps forty, with a bit of white lacing his parted and braided jet hair. The warrior lolled in shock.

Cover him, Skye signaled. But they had little to cover him with. Their ponies had grass-filled pad saddles and no blankets.

My woman will care for him, Mister Skye signaled. He would not turn his back on them, tempting them to shoot him and take his Henry. But he signaled, and Victoria rode forward, hunched lightly over her pony. She said nothing, always understanding his wishes, and slipped off her pony, carrying with her a kit that had been rolled on the pad saddle behind her. Her eyes glinted hard black, and her face grew grave, as it always did among the enemies of the Absaroka people. But she covered the man with her blanket and then pressed herbs under his tongue.

The wash of blood on his arm had gone brown in the hot sun, but his face looked pale and moist. She felt of his arm, and he groaned.

"Broken," she said.

Damn that Riddle, he thought. He'd be the death of them all.

His hands flashed again. No wood here for splints, but under one of the pad saddles lay a piece of tanned hide.

He asked for it, and Victoria wound it tightly around the bullet-mangled arm, tying it deftly with rawhide thong.

Where is your village? Skye's hard hands asked.

They pointed and signed. Half a day west.

We will go there, Skye's hands said.

It would be all right, he thought, if he could disarm Riddle and keep the women of all sorts halfway calm. But even as he thought it, he knew there'd be trouble aplenty. One of the warriors had already started westward with Goldtooth's second red wagon.

He and Victoria rode back to the wagons, his back itching.

"We are going to their village," he said. "Riddle, hand me your revolver."

"You think I'm crazy, Skye?"

"Yes."

That nonplussed Riddle. "What's your angle?" he said at last. "I want my carbine back. I defend my women and your squaw bashes in my lips with my own Spencer."

"Hand me the revolver or I'll come in there after it."

"Try it. I'll shoot you first, Skye."

The women in the wagon cringed.

Mister Skye slid off Jawbone and leapt in the wagon with one cat-spring, knocking Riddle's revolver up even as he pulled the trigger. Inside the wagon the report was deafening. Women screamed.

"You beast!" screamed Flora.

"I am saving your lives," said Mister Skye.

Riddle lay sprawled over trunks and barrels, cursing. Skye plucked up the revolver and backed out, his eye hard upon the milling Arapaho.

"Now I'm defenseless!" cried Alvah. "What's your angle—killing us?"

Mister Skye didn't answer. Drusilla sobbed.

He spotted Vanderbilt under the bawds' wagon. "Gambler! Drive this green wagon."

The command brooked no delay, and Vanderbilt slunk out from under Goldtooth's wagon and sidled into the seat of Riddle's wagon.

"I want my wagon back, you idiot!" snarled Goldtooth.

Mister Skye handed Riddle's weapons to Blueberry. "We are going on a peaceful visit, make meat," he said. "There will be maybe a hundred lodges of Arapaho yonder. They can be friendly or they can take scalps. If we had won this skirmish, we'd have lost the war."

It was all the message Blueberry needed.

Riddle bawled and raged, and his women wept. Mister Skye stopped again at his wagon.

"Mister Riddle," he said. "When I give an instruction in dangerous circumstances, you will bloody well follow it. If you'd killed that warrior, what's left of your hair would be hanging from a medicine tripod tonight. Along with the sausage curls of your wife, these women, and everyone else here."

He didn't wait for an answer.

They veered due west, steering wagons over rolling dunes of sandy prairie. Arapaho warriors flanked the wagons and rode ahead. One of them drove Goldtooth's red wagon far ahead, almost out of sight, lashing the mules recklessly. No doubt that man's first experience with harnessed animals, Mister Skye thought. Might smash the wagon.

He peered sharply at these Arapaho. Their carbines had been sheathed, arrows returned to quiver. But often coupseekers wanted to make medicine against Skye, the medicine legend. For the moment all seemed well. The older one with the wounded arm looked less pale, and more alert. He rode in close to Mister Skye now, his good-arm fingers asking questions, his bad-arm fingers making tiny motions.

Mister Skye replied. The finger-language of the plains required short answers. They were going far to the northwest, he said. Beyond the spine of the mountains to the land of the Bannacks. The women in the green wagon would be brides for the men there. The women in the red wagon sold themselves for money. The men with them were a gambler and bartender . . .

Which reminded him that he had not seen Chang. That worried him. They had veered west, and Chang might miss them . . . if he lived.

Had the Arapaho seen a man on a white horse? he asked.

Surprised, the Arapaho gazed about, studied horizons, and then shrugged.

They didn't know about Chang, Skye thought, still mystified.

"Where are the buffalo?" he asked.

"North," the Arapaho replied.

"How are you called?"

"Crow Killer."

Just behind Skye, Victoria huddled deeper in her saddle and her eyes turned hard.

Crow Killer urged his pony closer and closer to Jawbone, who laid his ears back and began to mince. In one fluid move, Crow Killer raised his good arm, smacked a hand on Mister Skye's hair and wheeled away on his buffalo pony even as Jawbone exploded, shrieking and snapping.

"You don't count coup on guests and friends," Skye said. "So you have told me you are enemies."

Crow Killer shrugged. The flanking warriors reached for arrows and nocked them.

"You have stolen medicine and I will make your medicine bad," Mister Skye said, his Henry leveled in the crook of his arm. "My brothers the buffalo bulls will kill you soon."

Crow Killer laughed.

Three tense hours later they found themselves looking into a shallow, wide trough in the prairie with a silvery creek oxbowed through it. On a verdant meadow along the creek stood scores of Arapaho lodges, their smoke-blackened windflaps a dark forest in the glare of afternoon. The dog soldiers, or village guards, had long since spotted them and now escorted them in. Ahead rolled Goldtooth's empty wagon driven by the warrior and surrounded now by the curious, who had boiled out of the village to see this amazing sight. Town criers announced their presence. Before a larger lodge, painted with bright yellow medicine symbols, stood a chief, one Mister Skye did not recognize.

Behind him was pure fear. He could smell Alvah's sweat and the women's terror. Fear always stank. Blueberry looked drawn. Vanderbilt as taut-strung as a fiddlestring.

Mary-Rita sobbed and bawled imprecations. Jawbone didn't like it, and walked with flat ears and bared teeth.

Yellow and gray dogs, some half wolf, snapped and yapped and howled. Some of them would be tonight's stew, Skye thought. Women with wide cheekbones glared. Naked boys peered, drew mock bows and loosed mock arrows, and fled behind lodges. A sharp breeze flapped orange buffalo-hide lodges, ballooning them and tugging them from the circles of white boulders that pinned them to dun earth. Before many lodges stood tripods with medicine bundles hanging from them, and black-haired scalps, and feather bundles. Squat bronze men with powerful builds trotted beside, carrying deadly lances with black tips. And everywhere rose cacophony, dogs yapping and howling, horses shrieking, children screaming, women chattering.

Mister Skye did not like the feel of it. Neither did Mary and Victoria behind him, who peered flint-eyed and solemnly at all this familiar village life. These were ancient enemies of both the Crows and Shoshones. The warriors among them pointed sullenly at Skye, at Jawbone, and at Skye's brass-framed repeater, which kindled something wary in their eyes.

They wound past a circle of tipis and into a central plaza before the looming lodge of the chief, which stood at its west side, its doorflap pointed ritually east, as did every doorflap here. The man stood in ceremonial finery, wearing a medicine shirt of elkskin from which dangled human hair, mostly black but blond and red and brown as well. Around his neck hung a rawhide string of dried human ears, separated by elk's teeth. Skye knew the man but had never met him: Old Bull, squat, wedge-shouldered, glint-eyed, and with the arced nose of a hawk above thin cruel lips. Skye had only a moment to glance at this legendary war-prone chief before his gaze was drawn elsewhere, to a familiar white stallion, a giant Chinese who stood with mocking eye, and beside him a young Arapaho woman. A beautiful tall woman.

"Ah, Mister Skye," said Chang. "You were a long time arriving in Paradise."

Old Bull motioned for Skye to dismount.

The guide preferred to sit. Beneath him Jawbone trembled and snarled. Skye's hands flashed: Will you smoke?

The question. If Old Bull would smoke the peacepipe, they were guests. If not . . . captives.

Old Bull nodded. He had the calumet in hand, inside of a soft doeskin bag decorated with fine bonework.

Mister Skye's hands flashed. One of your number, Crow Killer there, counted coup with his hand upon my head, after inviting us here as guests. His medicine is bad. Soon the buffalo bulls will kill him.

Crow Killer laughed, but it had been said. Others who read the hand-signs stared at Skye, and at Crow Killer, noting his wounded arm. Mister Skye felt content. Medicine prophesy could be suggestive. He had learned that long ago. Say it, and self-fulfilling doom will begin. Crow Killer sneered, but Skye read the quake in it.

I will smoke the pipe with the great chief Old Bull, said Mister Skye through his hands. And we will talk. If any here can speak English or Crow or Shoshone, we will talk with our tongues.

Mister Skye dismounted slowly, still cradling the Henry. It would be too large a temptation for those outside the lodge, even though stealing from guests in a village ranked among the most shameful of deeds among many of the Plains tribes.

He turned. "Mister Riddle. Mister Vanderbilt. Mister Hill. And ladies. These people will not harm you if you do not harm them. They will expect presents soon. I will explain that later. Be firm but amiable. Is that understood, Mister Riddle? If you knew the angles, Mister Riddle, then you brought twists of tobacco for these moments . . . I am going to smoke with Old Bull, and then we shall see."

Riddle, subdued and frightened, nodded.

Chang laughed. "When the honors are done, Mister Skye, come meet my high-priced bride."

Chapter 16

The barbaric menace of Old Bull's village was too much for a poor colleen only weeks off the boat from Tipperary. Mary-Rita peered bug-eyed at these naked yellow savages and thought her life would come to an abrupt end. She blessed herself, repeated every form of contrition she knew of, and fumed because no priest was on hand for extreme unction. She'd been mad through and through for three months now, but that was nothing new. She'd been born mad at the world.

Mary-Rita Flaherty had orange hair and midnight tongue, and some of her brothers and sisters thought she was a witch. Her hair was her glory. In misty sun it shone gold, and in lamplight it shone carrot colored and leapt from darkness like a blaze. As for the rest, she wasn't so fortunate. She had distrustful green eyes, a wide wavery pink mouth, and a snotty pig-nose sprinkled with lavender freckles. She stood tall and had a fine willowy figure except for thick white ankles. No one in the Arapaho village had seen blazing hair like hers. And so they crowded about her, almost-naked men with wide cheekbones and black

hair hanging loose or in braids, reaching out, touching hair
the color of rising suns.

She bawled at them. "You idjits! Leave me hair alone!
You blasted savages, get away now! You smell like rotten
potatoes."

They smiled and probed and touched the orange fila-
ments and inspected her freckles. Their touch felt rough
and dry.

"You're the dumbest things! Haven't you got a brain in
your idjit heads? Saints preserve me. Saint Patrick get your
blasted sword out! Smite the heathen right and left! Blessed
Saint Bridget, carry me back to Tipperary!"

She wasn't all that sure she wanted to go back to misty
Ireland. Not after what her own ma and pa and Tommy
and Peggy and Sean and Martin had done to her. They
were all idjits. Sean didn't know which end of a red cow
to milk. Peggy grew so lazy she wouldn't even pull up her
blue stockin's. Tommy would spend hours hunkering behind the stone shed and scratching his brown britches
where he wasn't supposed to touch, and smoke and talk
about stranglin' Englishmen and the hoity-toity rich. But
he wasn't half so bad as Martin, the parish quarter-wit,
babbling about taking vows with the brown-robed Bene-
dictines and warning Mary-Rita to get down on her knees
all the time. And that wasn't half so bad as her watery-
eyed pa, who kept them all starving and hardly a potato
to spare, or her ghost-pale ma with black-shadowed eyes,
who kept nagging and never quit.

But all that was nothing compared to the rest. For half
a year they said nary a word to her, no matter how much
she shouted at them. Idjit silence all the time, like they
were all daft or something. The quieter they got, the more
she'd railed, and the more she bawled, the more they
turned away like she was the divil's own she-child. And
then Pa, he told her she would go on a trip. She yelled at
him she didn't want to go on any trip, but they all made
her pack a bag—not that she had anything. But Pa gave
her a battered black valise he had, and they all stood
around solemn, and Pa made the sign of the cross and

they hiked into Tipperary, and Pa and Martin and Tommy, they came along jist to make sure, while Ma and Peggy just stared, and they got a carmine coach to Waterford and next she knew she trotted the deck of a big gray clipper. Pa's eyes leaked and she'd never seen that.

"Mary-Rita," he said all solemn, "this passage was a scrape and it took even your ma's ring. When you get to the other side of the sea, maybe you'll learn to say a kind thing."

"I'm not ever going to see you again," she wailed.

They filed out and closed the door to this rusty place, and it clicked. She felt the ship roll under her, and hammered on the door. When the idjit purser sprung her, nothing remained but the green swelling sea.

She arrived with three shillings and a sixpence, too mad to be frightened. She didn't know what she'd do. They herded her through a cavernous smelly brickpile in Boston and then she was free to walk through a varnished door into a world she didn't know. That's when a man approached her. He could arrange a good Irish and Catholic marriage for her. And next thing, she met another man, Alvah Riddle, and he said a miner out in the west, Tom O'Dougherty, wanted to marry a sweet colleen like herself, and in the church too. She could barely read or write, but she painfully inscribed her name, Mary-Rita Flaherty, on the line, and added a small cross for good measure, like the priests did.

And now she stood here, clutching her wood beads and getting ready to be burned at the stake like Saint Joan, or beheaded or scalped or . . . like saints. . . . or . . . Aw, these idjits!

"Mary-Rita, stop bawling like a loon," said Alvah. "All they want is to see your hair. You'll get us all slaughtered carrying on like that."

"You idjit! You got me into this, you Protestant heathen pig. You crook. You miserable worm. You son of the divil. You heretic skinflint sneaky dim-witted swine! You pink chinless bald fool! You smelly potbellied conniver! You

dirty-fingered lazy—you can't even harness the mules—
you stupid conniving . . . Protestant!''

Mary-Rita didn't run out of breath. ''Get these creatures
away from me. Heathen! Savages! Murderers! They'll slice
my flesh and wring my neck! Saint Brendan, Saint Peter,
Saint Patrick, Saint Bartholomew, Saint Teresa, Saint Patrick, Saint Elizabeth, Saint Patrick, Saint Benedict, Saint
Francis . . . Pa before me, and beside me, Tommy behind
me, Jesus above me, Peggy beneath me . . .''

Old Bull and Mister Skye and others emerged from the
chief's lodge, the pipe ceremony completed. Old Bull saw
her and stared, hard brown eyes peering straight at that
flaming hair. He rolled toward her on legs bandied by a
long life on horse, and gazed, taking her all in, his eyes
studying the hair, her freckles, her little breasts—oh, the
scandal!—and her hips. Oh how he stared and stared.

''Get this heathen away from me!'' she bawled at Mister
Skye.

Mister Skye said, ''He likes the look of you, Miss Flaherty. He understands a little English too. This band winters over on the South Platte, near Denver City and
Auraria.''

''What's that supposed to mean?''

''Bridle your tongue, Miss Flaherty.''

''Why should I? I want to get out of here. These heathen! These smelly savages! These pagan idjits!''

Old Bull said something to Skye's squaw, Victoria, who
repeated something to Mister Skye. It dawned on Mary-
Rita that the chief knew Crow, and talked to their idjit
drunken guide by speaking Crow to Victoria, who translated. They talked a long time, and Old Bull kept staring
at Alvah Riddle, and at her, and back at Riddle.

Finally Mister Skye turned to her, a faint mocking on
his leathery face. ''Old Bull would like to marry you,'' he
said. ''He likes your hair.''

''Marry me? Marry me?'' Mary-Rita cried, thunder-
struck. ''Why, I'd sooner go to bed with the divil! Yes,
the divil! Marry me! I'm to be wed to the miner, Tommy

O'Dougherty, I am. A good Catholic man. Yes I am, you idjit!''

The guide turned to Riddle. "I've explained your part in this to Old Bull. He wishes me to tell you he'll offer a good bride price. Twenty tanned robes, a dozen prime ponies, and a ceremonial elkskin shirt, fringed, with quill and bead trim. And he'll adopt you as a son, and make you a blood brother of the Arapaho."

Alvah Riddle peered at Old Bull, his eyes darting hither and yon, his mind whirling. "I'll have to consider the angles," Riddle muttered. "Got a contract with O'Dougherty."

"Over me dead body! Saints preserve and defend me!" howled Mary-Rita.

Riddle peered craftily. "Kinda hint to me, Mister Skye. Kinda slip it to me, so the old chief don't catch it—but how much would those tanned robes fetch in Bannack among the miners? And the fat ponies?"

Some vast delight suffused Mister Skye's face. "Why, Riddle, that's easy. Mining camps are plumb starved for anything usable, and a good robe should fetch maybe thirty dollars in dust. Ponies, why, they'll vary. Fifty or hundred each. Lots of miners would like them to pack with."

Alvah Riddle's face twisted with excitement. "Skye, get the old chief to throw in some packsaddles, the kind them miners want, for the bride."

Mister Skye and Victoria conveyed Riddle's request, and there began a long powwow with Old Bull in a tongue Mary-Rita thought sounded like jail bars clanging.

"Mister Riddle." This time Drusilla spoke, and her tone was withering. "You have a contract. A most solemn agreement between Miss Flaherty and yourself and Mr. O'Dougherty. If you are going to violate a sacred contract, why, why—"

"I won't mary that heathen goat!" yelled Mary-Rita.

"Got a clause, a forfeit clause," said Alvah Riddle. "Fourteen B. It says that in the event party of the first part—that's me—can't deliver the merchandise—ah, bride—I get to deduct expenses and return the residue.

O'Dougherty paid me five hunnert and is to pay another five hunnert on delivery. But I spent, let's see, over five hunnert getting her here, at twelve cents a mile . . . I wouldn't have to return anything to O'Dougherty; just not take his second payment, is all.''

"I'm not a slave! You can't buy and sell me! I'm Irish!''

"Old Bull'll supply two packsaddles with panniers,'' said Mister Skye.

"What'll they fetch in Bannack?''

"Whatever the market'll bear. Should be pretty scarce, though. He wants the copper-haired young lady for any price.''

"Figure a hunnert. Twenty tanned robes times thirty-five is seven hunnert. Horses might fetch five hunnert. Packsaddles maybe a hunnert. That shirt, maybe twenty. But I got to rent that empty wagon from Goldtooth. Figger a hunnert expenses . . . Tell my old friend and brother Old Bull it's a deal. Yes, I'd be plumb honored to give the hand of Miss Flaherty to a great chief of the Arapaho.''

"You're cheating Mister O'Dougherty. And you've made a slave of Mary-Rita. I'm an abolitionist and I will see you in Hades for it,'' snapped Drusilla.

"Got a clause in the contract,'' bubbled Alvah. "Maybe I could fetch a price for you, too.'' He laughed nastily.

"You made a contract with me but now you're going to sell me into slavery, to a heathen,'' Mary-Rita blubbered. She was beyond anger, and unfamiliar tears oozed from her green eyes.

Goldtooth raged at that slimy gray-fleshed gambler, Vanderbilt. The coward had abandoned the red wagon and it had become the booty of an Arapaho warrior and maybe she'd never get it back. The warrior had unharnessed the mules and driven them off to the village herd, and now the wagon stood forlornly here, its naked bows against the azure sky, harness heaped in its bed.

"I had plans for that wagon,'' she stormed. "I was going to divide it into two cribs for business while we waited for a proper place to be built. But now look! You get that back or I'll kill you, and I mean it!''

"Luck turns," he said blithely. "Life is a turn of the card. Tomorrow you'll have it all back."

"Get out of this wagon," she snapped.

Vanderbilt clambered down and vanished into a crowd of staring Arapaho villagers who eyed his sallow sour face and stepped aside.

A milling crowd gathered around her wagon, fingering harness, touching the skittery mules so that Blueberry had to tug on the lines repeatedly, peering boldly into the wagon bed, their eyes fastening on the only thing of consequence in there, the salvaged black trunk of sporting duds.

"We'd better smile, ladies," she said to her three companions.

Her girls looked all scared, taut as fiddle strings. Mister Skye had disappeared into the chief's skin lodge with several of the elders, plus Victoria and Mary. She wondered why the squaws had gone inside. Blueberry was a comfort, sitting there on the wagon seat like a black boulder, slapping blue flies. And over in the crowd she found even more comfort in Seven-Story, whose arm encircled a stunning young Arapaho woman with black braids, high cheekbones, golden flesh, and a long slim figure. Goldtooth eyed the glowing girl with professional envy. Seven-Story caught her eye, nodded slightly, and mocked Goldtooth with his wicked eyes.

Goldtooth felt so unraveled and despondent she barely noticed the press of the crowd. Everything lost because of that stupid drunken guide. Rags to wear. All the gilded and velvet things to furnish her parlor house. Her ladies desperate and near tears and hungry, dependent on that barbarian. And now the wagon, too, thanks to that craven slinking worm of a Vanderbilt with his oily black hair and gray flesh and sunken shadowed eyes and dirty fingernails. Oh, she'd scratch his eyes out!

"I keep having the feeling they want something from us," said Mrs. Parkins. "Nasty things. Full of lice, I suppose. Probably pluck them from their greasy hair and eat them. Oh, why did we evah leave ol' Memphis?''

Goldtooth had wondered that herself a hundred times in the last days, now that they were reduced to utter poverty. It wasn't all bad, she thought. They could all do business anywhere, anytime, right here before the chief's lodge if it came to that. The thought amused her.

Some of them milled around Blueberry, touching his skin, poking and probing. One woman wanted him to pull off his shirt, wanted to see if all of him had burnt black. He obliged, and they touched and probed and studied his black torso, and peered at his lighter palms.

''Guess they want to see how much of me got toasted,'' he said. A gray old woman urged him to drop his britches, tugged at his rope belt, but he declined. ''You're too old, woman,'' he said, chuckling. Over at the mail-order-bride wagon, they glared at him. ''No ma'am,'' he muttered testily to an Arapaho woman, ''it do not rub off. Try burnt cork.''

Some of them began unbuckling harness. Mule-snatchers, she thought, suddenly alarmed. She had to keep her mules! ''Blueberry, stop them!'' she cried. ''The mules are all we have left!''

He slid off the wagon and into their midst. The almost-naked men and boys were unbuckling harness. The women, mostly in cooler calico tradecloth, voluminous skirts, and long white blouses tied at the waist with a sash, were busy too, unbuckling, loosening, while the big mules pranced and sidled.

''Here now,'' bawled Blueberry, threading through them.

''Stop them!'' cried Goldtooth.

''Not rightly an easy thing without getting us scalped,'' said Blueberry.

Goldtooth leapt up from the wagon seat and crawled back through the rocking wagon to the trunk. The trunk! She dragged it over the grass bedding and robes from Skye's lodge, and sprung the latch. On the very top lay the gold brocade corset, studded with purple rhinestones, whore's armor. She snatched it out.

"Here, y'all," she cried, waving it like a guidon. "Lookit this, sweeties, look here, slut stuff." She laughed, jumped down among them. She found a young woman and wrapped the corset around her and tied it down the front, compressing the figure over her red calico skirts. "Look at that!" Goldtooth cried. "How's that for class. You'd make a great sporting woman, little lady!"

The Arapaho matron beamed, fondling the fat purple lumps of glass, smoothing a hand over the gold brocade, giggling and dancing while her sisters exclaimed and clucked and cackled and honked and clapped hands. The woman whirled, her jet braids flying, sun spraying off the golden girdle. She giggled. The mules were forgotten, and Blueberry hastily buckled the harness back.

"Ayaa," squealed the Arapaho woman, and ran off somewhere, with a crowd of Arapahos following her.

"Belle of the ball," said Blueberry.

A lithe dusky girl hung back, peering up at Goldtooth hungrily. She was a young thing, barely at womanhood, Goldtooth thought. And wanting something. Goldtooth dug into her trunk and found the pea-green lisle stockings and the black garter belt with crimson hearts.

"Come here, honeychile," she said.

The girl sidled up shyly.

"How's this, sweetie?" Goldtooth said, holding the loot. The girl looked puzzled.

"Up here, honey. In here. I'll fix you up."

Hestitantly the girl clambered into the wagon, and in moments Big Alice and Juliet rolled the green stockings up her legs, hoisted her doeskin skirt, and fastened the gaudy garter belt at her waist. Then they showed the girl how to hook the stockings onto the clips. The girl squealed and leapt back to the earth, and danced around, lifting her doeskin skirts, showing green stockings, black garters, golden thighs.

"She keeps that up and I'm going to get myself scalped by her pappy," muttered Blueberry.

The woman who flaunted the gold corset returned, burdened by something that filled her arms. Before Goldtooth she spread out an exquisitely tanned buffalo robe of light color and summer weight, and presented it to her. Goldtooth Jones exclaimed. So did her ladies.

"I nevah saw such a fine robe," said Mrs. Parkins. "I'd sure like that velvet under my bare back. It'd be like makin' love from both di-rections."

It was dawning on Goldtooth. It took a while, like a bubble rising through cold molasses, but when it finally surfaced in her mind with a pop, she chortled. Wealth. She pawed through the trunk restlessly. There was a ton of it, some a bit water-damaged. A dozen naughty corsets, like the one on top, all black lace with red ribbons running through; or the next one of silver, that tied down the front, and had peekaboos all over it, each the size of a silver dollar. And below that, frilly things in purples, pinks, oranges, fleshtones, and yellows. A pile of skimpy black stockings and black garters. Frilly nothings, black chemises, naughties, slut things for Memphis whores. Riches galore, beyond imagining.

In business! She dragged out the trunk and held up each rainbow thing, one by one, before the enchanted throng, now mostly women. Blueberry sweated and studied the mules and slapped flies. The Arapaho women giggled, tried them all on, sometimes dropping whatever clothes they wore to do it, and snorted and pirouetted and howled, and for each selection they made, they scurried off to their lodges and returned with fine robes, or quilled skin dresses, or exquisite moccasins, masterfully crafted in the tribal style and beauteous upon foot and ankle. Others shyly brought white or blue blanket capotes trimmed with ermine or mink or wolf.

One by one, the ladies put on their new finery and paraded through the village, black and silver corsets, black stockings on garters, purple silk robes, red bloomers, pink bloomers, lavender bloomers. Never had the village of Old Bull been so gaily decorated, nor giggles and laughter so thick through a spacious afternoon.

Seven-Story watched it all, wild mockery in his face, holding his Arapaho lady in hand. But Goldtooth ignored him. For one large trunk of bawd's costumes, she had thirty-two perfect robes, a dozen tanned skirts and shirts, twelve pairs of moccasins in every size, a heavy bag of pemmican, a warbonnet with eagle feathers and weasel-skin pendants, a woman-sized Osage bow and a quiver of arrows, five fired clay jars, a waterbag, and two belts with fine bone designwork on them.

When at last Old Bull and his elders emerged from the lodge, along with Mister Skye and his squaws, the chief's eyes beheld a transformation of his women; beheld Goldtooth and her bawds, now attired like Arapaho princesses, and his face crinkled up. That's when he saw the fiery hair of Mary-Rita. And when Mister Skye lost his aplomb.

"Sonofabitch!" said Victoria, and giggled.

Chapter 17

The joke had gone too far. Riddle had leapt at the chance to make an extra few hundred. Mary-Rita sobbed on the wagon seat. If she knew she would be Old Bull's fourth wife, and no doubt maltreated by the senior ones, she'd cry all the more, Mister Skye thought. He could have stopped it earlier, but Mary-Rita's barbed tongue had stung everyone in the caravan, and she could use a little humbling.

Riddle had been predictable. It would be a better angle. His slippery contracts let him do whatever he pleased, and treat his brides as absolute slaves. But it took courts and law to enforce contracts, and those civilized things didn't exist here. The brides would be Riddle's slaves only if Mister Skye let them be.

Mister Skye gazed at the sobbing girl, and his own memories flooded back. Long ago, so long it lay as a blur in the back of his mind, he'd been a slave. He'd been a boy on the banks of the Thames, son of a merchant, when the press gang found him, snatched him, hauled him bodily aboard a teak-decked man-o'-war and made him a powder monkey, living in conditions so brutal he barely survived until he learned to brawl and fight for his gray porridge.

It had made him strong and wily. He had learned courage and ferocity. He'd learned distrust and hate. That crucible had fired every weakness out of him, and had given him the means to live in this wild blue land. So good had come from that terrible thing. His family surely thought him dead, and now his only family was the one he had created here in the vastness of North America. Good had come from slavery, and good might come to Mary-Rita from slavery. Old Bull and his wives would bridle her tongue soon enough. He'd seen pale boys become sun-blistered soldiers and sailors of the Crown, and come out of it men. It was true enough that women were often given away in marriage, and had no say in it. And most of those marriages turned out fine, too. In Mary-Rita's own Ireland, fathers and brothers and priests were all matchmakers for sisters and daughters and parishioners. And yet . . . he could not permit this. The thought of enslaving an adult competent human being rankled him. In Drusilla, abolition formed a principle, an ideal. In Mister Skye, once a slave, it flared as a rage. He pitied the weeping girl so new to this raw land and thought she'd probably die of heartbreak even if Old Bull treated her well. What a sorry thing it'd be to leave her here to sob and die, to shrivel within. No matter how kind to her the Arapaho might be, this would be more than the lass could bear.

"I think not, Mister Riddle," he said.

"Stay out of my business, Skye. My contract—"

"Judge Henry enforces contracts here, Mister Riddle. Sixteen decisions at a time."

The ferret-faced man with red veins in his pointy nose peered craftily about. "The great chief and I have come to an agreement. He'll have something to say, Skye, and so will his warriors."

"Judge Henry's first decision might go against you, Riddle."

"You—you wouldn't!"

"You beast!" yelled Mary-Rita at Skye. "Kill a man, would you? Heathen savage! Your skull is as thick as your body. I know how you talk; like a heretic Englishman. Killin' your own kind indeed!"

Mister Skye cocked a graying eyebrow. "Victoria, tell Old Bull that the lady is promised, and not available, and thank him for the offer. Tell him he has a fine eye for women, with an especially sharp knowledge of their souls and character."

Victoria translated to Crow, while Old Bull listened intently and Alvah Riddle peered about him.

Through Victoria Old Bull replied that the bargain was sealed. He fancied the white woman with the hair the color of fire. He would have his squaws bring the robes and packsaddles. He would take the bride-man out to pick his ponies. There would be a ceremony of adoption. The tears of the fire-haired woman told him she would be a good squaw.

"You heard all that, Miss Flaherty. Will it be Chief Old Bull or Tommy O'Dougherty?" asked Mister Skye.

"Heretics and heathen! That's all there is here. Don't you be tellin' me what to do, you drunk. Chinless fools and drunken guides and savages, and what's a girl to do? It's not every lass gets proposed to by a chief. Fancy a lass bein' a queen, or at least a princess. You idjit, you stay out of this."

Mister Skye caught Seven-Story Chang at one side of a gathering circle of villagers, mocking as usual.

"Mister Riddle," Skye said, "how do you propose to take all these robes to Bannack? I don't know whether we'll have Mrs. Jones's second wagon. I will discuss the matter with Old Bull, but it's going to be tricky. That's a prize of battle, and whichever warrior got it, he's not likely to give it up, or the mules. And even if I get it back, I haven't heard you making an agreement with Goldtooth to rent it."

"You'd better get it back!" snapped Goldtooth from the edge of the crowd. "You big drunk. If you hadn't climbed into your jug, we'd still be safe on the Oregon Trail and I wouldn't have lost a thing.''

"I imagine a storm had something to do with your difficulties," Mister Skye said amiably.

"What do ya take me for, Skye? A rube? I got that angle figured out first off." Riddle preened a bit. "What do you think I got the packsaddles thrown in for? Five ponies, plus two packsaddles, ten robes to a packsaddle. I don't need that slut's wagon."

Old Bull had had enough of the babble. He abruptly motioned to his squaws. One graying thin Arapaho woman, and three stout ones with glossy black hair and massive hips scurried into his lodge, and emerged with piles of robes. One by one they spread these out on the grass. Each looked soft and tanned, with thick dark—almost black—winter hair.

"Not as good as Crow robes," muttered Victoria nastily.

"I'm not marrying that savage. I'm worth more than a bunch of flea-bit robes," yelled Mary-Rita. "I want Tommy O'Dougherty and a priest, you idjit!"

The women brought Riddle a soft creamy elkskin shirt, fringed on the bottom and sleeves, and decorated with orange and black-dyed quills in a crosshatch pattern.

"Pretty fine stuff. I know Indian stuff. This here'll fetch plenty if I play it right," announced Alvah.

Finally they brought two rawhide yellow packsaddles with buffalo-hide panniers and laid them on the pile.

The chief stared, waiting, daring Riddle to reject any of it. Riddle smirked. The chief nodded abruptly, and Riddle clambered from his muddy green wagon and followed Old Bull out beyond the village, across a tawny bunchgrass meadow where youths watched the horse herd continuously.

Mister Skye followed, along with Victoria and several headmen. They continued onward to a separate band of a hundred or so spotted and solid-colored ponies, buckskins, sorrels, paints, guarded by a sour-looking hard-eyed warrior, his torso laced with white scars. He hefted a new

Spencer carbine. The chief waved a gnarled brown hand at the animals.

"Warned you, Riddle," said Mister Skye quietly.

Riddle ignored him, and plunged in, squint-eyed, poking and probing, lifting tan hoofs, peering at grass-stained black teeth, hunting for saddle galls. In an hour he had his five, all solid-colored, and with a sharp command Old Bull had them separated out by the hard-eyed warrior. Riddle looked ecstatic.

In the larger herd stood Goldtooth's four mules, shining harness marks on their hair, and watching them a thin, concave-chested warrior, their captor. Mister Skye studied the man, memorizing him, noting the hard flesh and the hawknose and the shoulder-length loose blue-black hair and the red bandana, like his own, holding it to the warrior's skull. Their eyes caught. The warrior's glittered, daring Mister Skye to try it, try taking these brown prizes, these coups of battle.

Mister Skye stared back unblinking, and not smiling.

They trooped back to the village, Riddle tugging his ponies behind him on picket lines, the chinless pink man almost prancing with glee. He sidled up to Mister Skye.

"To get ahead, you got to play the angles. I come out like a rose. Likely make five, six hundred more dollars. That's a year's income! Saved me the cost of renting that bawd's wagon, too. Now these ponies—solid colors, Skye, all solids—I'll break them to harness along the way, too, put one at a time in the traces with the mules until they know what's what. So I got two and a half new span, added to my two and a half mulespan, and I'll get the women to riding, and save wear on the harness mules. How's that for angles, Skye? I turned your drunk into a bonanza here."

"If they let you leave the village, mate. I don't rightly trust Old Bull. And you'd better not trust me."

"What do you mean by that?"

"You'll know soon enough," said Mister Skye, as they trudged past skin lodges and barking yellow mutts. "Better tell your women. They're going to have a feast tonight, boil a few dogs. Then tomorrow they hunt the buff. They've been following a big herd for days.''

"Dogs!"

"Better eat it. They don't take kindly to someone scorning their stewpots. They'd just as soon throw a little white man in, too.''

At his lodge, Old Bull barked a command, and the hefty squaws approached Riddle's wagon like oxen on the prod. One of them beckoned to Mary-Rita.

"Go away, you filthy things!" she bawled. "I'm not going to marry some heathen. Go away!"

Drusilla arose, a gray-clad wraith, addressing the chief's women. "This woman has not consented," she said quietly. "Take back the robes and things."

They didn't understand the words, but they understood her message.

Flora tittered nervously, and the chief studied her as well, discovering beauty he'd missed earlier. He approached the wagon and motioned her to stand.

"I don't stand up for red niggers," she said coolly.

He reached abruptly into the wagon seat and dragged her out of it with a powerful grip. She screamed.

"Let go of me! Do you know who I am? My father bought and sold better ones than you!"

He tugged at the yellow ribbon that gathered her hair, and it fell loose around her neck. He stared at one bride, then the other, and finally his eyes settled on Flora. "Maybe I like you better," he said in sudden English. He nodded toward Mary-Rita. "She got bad mouth. You're mean, but I fix that."

He turned to Alvah, who was tugging his prizes toward his wagon.

"Maybe I'll switch," he said, in words Alvah understood instantly.

It had taken a while for Blueberry Hill to understand about Flora Slade of Biloxi. The recognition came slow. He had seen her only from the inside of a cage, and she was much younger. But she hadn't changed any in the

eight years, except for a fine woman's figure and a lush-
ness of body that inspired lust.

That's when her father had sold him, naked, on the
raised auction block fronting the red-brick slave mart that
had housed him in a stinking cage for several days prior.
The bids reached two thousand thirty-seven dollars, and
four bits. Plus one dollar for feed and title. Her father had
called him a fine, strapping young nigger, no diseases,
tractable and hardworking, a perfect field hand. They'd all
stared at him, mostly white men but a few women too,
including Miss Slade, who simply delighted in hopping
around the auctions, whatever her father's wishes may have
been, and lording it over other flesh and blood.

So he fetched that much. That much and no more for
his flesh and bone, his vision, his hearing, his blood. For
his fingers that plucked banjo strings and pounded ivory
and black keys, and his brain that remembered songs and
spoke words. That much and no more. More indeed than
this chief of the Arapaho was offering for Miss Slade,
whose value equaled twenty thirty-dollar robes, five ponies worth perhaps four hundred, and odds and ends. Her
price came to maybe half his own. It didn't please him to
think it: she was quite beautiful.

He watched amiably as the old chief yanked her off the
wagon seat, walked with measured gait around her like a
buyer of fine horseflesh, poked and probed·at her while
she raged. It was familiar, and yet different. If he'd raged
while they prodded his flesh, he'd have been whipped brutally. The memory made him sweat. Any one of these
whites could take him at gunpoint, bind him up and deliver him back to Biloxi, and claim a reward. He might
survive the whipping, and might not. The old white mis-
tress who let him wander and had been kind might be dead
now; her sons would be a different matter.

"Sorry, my friend, Chief Old Bull. She's not for sale.
I got a contract to deliver her. You take this here one with
the flame hair," said Alvah, his lips spouting words from
his chinless pink face. "Yessir, she's worth a lot more.
And we had us a little shake-hand deal, friend."

Old Bull eyed him flatly. "How much more?"

Riddle's Adam's apple bobbled and his eyes darted around. "Why, Flora looks to be ten robes more," he said, hopping about. "She cost me more to fetch up from the South, middle of the war."

"I'll kill you, you slimy thing," yelled Flora. "I've bought and sold better than you."

That, thought Blueberry, was quite true.

"Mister Riddle," snapped Drusilla. "You have made contracts in good faith. If you do not honor them, I'll see to it that your business is ruined. My pen is mightier than swords."

Riddle squinted up at her, a sudden caution on him. Then he leered. "Not likely," he said. "I know your angle and it isn't worth spit."

Flora started to run toward Mister Skye, the only hope she knew, but Old Bull caught her easily. "I'll take this one," he said and wheeled her into the hands of his burly squaws, who dragged her shouting and cursing wild oaths into his lodge. A moment later all sound ceased.

"But you can't— You owe . . . ten robes!" said Alvah, dancing like a boy needing an outhouse.

Old Bull grunted.

Drusilla began weeping. Mary-Rita sobbed. From over at their wagon, the bawds stared, horrified.

"He can't just take her like that!" cried Juliet.

Blueberry found himself feeling sorry for the girl. He'd been bought and sold several times, made to work for nothing—no pay, no hope, no chance of home or family, no future except to toil all his days and then die broken and used. He'd been ripped from a girl he loved, hauled where he would not go, manacled with chains, told his body wasn't his own. He'd been called dumb because he was careful not to be too bright around masters, laughed at for the rags he wore, cast out because of his color. And so he felt sorry for this daughter of a man who'd sold him, knowing she would be taken where she would not go, into a life she did not will.

But not entirely sorry. Some part of him gloated.

"Let it go, Riddle," said Mister Skye sharply. "Unless you want to get us all in more trouble than you ever dreamed of. They know how to peel your skin slow, and burn you with little pine-stick embers so you die a little bit at a time."

"Old Bull and I had us a contract and he cheated," bawled Riddle. "He plum cheated. Crookedest stinking Injun I ever did see."

Mister Skye's slap sent the pink man sprawling into dun earth. He rolled over and sputtered.

"Get into your wagon and stay there, Riddle."

The crowd clamored at this, squaws clucking and staring. Old Bull watched with flat black eyes, his face empty. The women wept, the remaining brides and the bawds alike.

"Old Bull," said Mister Skye, "I mean to powwow with you."

The chief nodded, seeing something akin to murder in Skye's small hooded eyes.

With a short slashing gesture he summoned his elders and shamans and a squat powerful warrior into his lodge. The guide and his squaw Victoria followed. At the flap, Skye's eyes found Blueberry. "Go make camp wherever they want you to. Take Riddle. Take Chang. Stay out of trouble."

Then he vanished inside, and a quietness settled over the villagers, the way breath stops before a trap is sprung or a guillotine blade falls. No one moved. All were awaiting the result of the conference within the quiet lodge. Blueberry hadn't the faintest idea what Mister Skye might be saying or doing. The whores drifted back to their red wagon, thoroughly subdued. Blueberry spotted Vanderbilt, gray-fleshed and sour.

"Cornelius, reckon you'd better drive Riddle's wagon. We'll make us a camp."

No one moved. Riddle hid within his wagon. Vanderbilt stood rooted to earth. Blueberry clambered to his seat and cracked the whip over his mules, sawing on the offside line to turn them, but the Arapahos did not make way, and

Blueberry had a sense of being in an island, surrounded by murderous seas. Near the chief's lodge Jawbone stood, ears flat back, murder-eyed, and yellow teeth bared, grunting softly and snapping when anyone edged within ten or so feet.

"Ah, Blueberry, a wild free land filled only with emptiness and here you are trapped like a rat," said Seven-Story Chang. "It is a puzzle, yes? Something to contemplate. Slave and free, free and slave."

The mock suffused Chang's bony face, but Blueberry found no humor in it. Everything here had struck too close to home.

"Come meet my bride," said Chang.

Fearfully, Blueberry slid off the red wagon, feeling earth shiver beneath him in this terrible silence.

"This is Madame Chang," said Seven-Story, "the fairest maiden on the steppes of North America. I wandered in here only this morning, and was taken for divinity. Something about the way I look, I suppose. I seem to be a great Arapaho creation story come true. They promptly brought me to the most beautiful maiden in the village and offered her to the deity in their midst. Do I look like a god? I suppose I do. I bowed, said, yes the lady would make an acceptable wife for any god stalking North America, and she promptly became mine.

"She's delighted with the proposition, and so am I, my friend. She's the daughter of a subchief and medicine giver, a man who eyed my mandarin face, queue, white horse, and pronounced me divine, as far as I could gather. I didn't dally, Blueberry. I proffered her father a twist of tobacco since I don't exactly know how Arapaho gods behave, and he solemnly accepted. So the deed was done. Her name is Buffalo Whiskers. We have yet to communicate, except by those gentle squeezes of hand that tell her I am smitten blind. Tonight I shall give a nuptial feast—or rather my in-laws will, with my contributions—and then, Blueberry, we shall see. We shall see."

She stood unusually tall for this tribe, smiled serenely at Blueberry, and touched his hand with hers. Her jet hair parted at the center and hung in glossy braids to her breast, encased in soft white doeskin decorated with angling sheaths of tiny hollow bones. Her almond eyes were chocolate and soft, lying above prominent cheekbones that widened her face, and all of her colored a rich light umber that set Blueberry's heart to beating. And plainly she brimmed with joy to be a bride of so great a warrior and lord as this. What she offered Chang could not be bought for gold or any price.

Blueberry bowed. "Madame Chang, I am honored," he muttered.

She smiled, revealing perfect white teeth, and plucked his hand and held it in hers for a moment, eyeing Chang eagerly.

"She bestows her favors generously," said Chang, eyes mocking again. "Ah, how the campfires will change as we forge ahead. If we forge ahead," Chang added.

"Buffalo Whiskers," said Blueberry earnestly, "you are the most exquisite female my sight has seen. You are Venus herself, Minerva and Diana as well. Your sun makes every other lady a moon . . ."

She smiled and pulled Seven-Story close to her side.

For the next hour, all was still. Then at last the flap of Old Bull's lodge parted, and Arapaho men emerged, subchiefs, shamans, and a camp crier. Next, Mister Skye and Victoria. Then Old Bull, carrying a staff of office with eagle feathers flapping from it in the late afternoon breeze. And finally Old Bull's squaws. But not Flora.

They stood solemnly in the racing breeze, long sun shadowing them in orange light. They all looked calm, Blueberry thought. He didn't see mayhem and massacre in these faces. From within the green wagon, Alvah Riddle peered furtively, hiding in the shadow of his wagon sheet.

Mister Skye found Goldtooth and addressed her. "I will hunt buffalo tomorrow with my Sharps. If I am able to drop thirty and help haul them here, I will buy back your wagon and mules. We will be using the wagon to haul the carcasses, two at a time—about a ton and a half a load for cows. I will shoot. Every man of us will help hoist the carcasses into the wagon, deliver them here, unload, and drive back out to the buffalo grounds. This village wants fifty buffalo, thirty of them the price for the wagon and mules. They will save their own scarce bullets for the future.

"Riddle," he barked. "I could not get Miss Slade back. She's his now and that is that. Old Bull wishes you—and the rest—to know that if another word is spoken about it, or there is any trouble at all, the men of our party won't leave here alive, and the women will become slaves."

Drusilla and Mary-Rita began weeping. Gertrude Riddle managed a tear.

"I don't know how that little ol' southern gal can live here," muttered Goldtooth. "It's downright sinful, I think. A wife of red Indians. Poor thing, poor thing . . . "

"Old Bull says that Miss Slade will be comfortable. Perhaps that is more courtesy than she ever knew how to give."

Blueberry said, "You are correct, Mister Skye."

Chapter 18

A sadness fell upon him as he rode Jawbone northeast, accompanied by the hard-eyed warrior who captured the red wagon, and others of the tribe. They were taking him to the herds scattered a few miles from the village. His new Henry stayed sheathed, and in hand was his old Sharps buffalo gun. Among his possibles was a box of paper cartridges, and the caps for them.

As he grew old, he lost his taste for this thing, this taking of life, this reduction of a live, sensate creature breathing the clean air, drinking the sweet water, watching the sunlit prairies with bright eyes, to dead and bloody meat. All the while he had led the fur brigades and trapped beaver, he did what he had to, making meat and drowning beaver, but advancing years had somehow changed all that, and now he largely left the hunting to his women.

He would do what he had to. It consoled him that every scrap of meat and hide and bone would be put to good use by these people. There was no joy in him of slaughter, and men who slaughtered for sport or excitement or trophies puzzled and disgusted him. They were butchers and in their souls lurked something dark and evil. He had shot many an animal over a long life in this empty wilderness, but not a one for the killing. In hard times, starving times, he'd eaten strange food, muskrat and eagle and porcupine and even prairie dog. He was a carnivore and would eat what he would eat, and would kill what he had to kill.

It didn't matter that nature was red in tooth and claw; that wolves prowled the buffalo herds, snaring the old and the very young; that lions and coyotes and wolves and eagles ate fawns and dropped does. Death from his bullets came faster and easier than death from the jaws of wolves tearing out an animal's entrails while it yet lived, but that didn't ease the sorrow Mister Skye had come to feel these recent years about the taking of life.

This day, if he could, he would kill fifty-one animals, one for his own people and the rest for the village that held them all but captive. The young men of the village, primed for a hunt on fleet buffalo ponies, resented him, resented Old Bull's decision to send out Skye. But with summer came war and raids. White men's bullets were always scarce, and Old Bull saw a way to save precious cartridges and arrows and preserve horses, even while gaining more meat than his warriors and hunters could slaughter alone. And so he had commanded it to be. And the one who captured the red wagon, Bad Elk, would have the great honor of distributing meat to the whole band. It would be a high honor, well worth the surrender of the wagon and mules, which were all but useless to his people anyway.

There blew the softest of breezes this morning, lazy air out of the west. He had thrown a handful of grass to the air to test it, and had watched it scatter a few feet east. Now he and Bad Elk and two other warriors rode a large circle compassing the herds, so they might approach from the southeast. The sun lay heavy on the dun dry prairie and no cloud troubled the sky. To the north the Bridger Mountains huddled blue.

They topped a soft rise and the first band of them hove into view half a mile away, thirty or forty. Beyond, similar grazing herds dotted the dun land like dark ponds. This time of year they rarely coalesced into vast migratory herds, but roamed through the lush dry bunchgrasses, fattening in small companies. Their summer hair grew lighter, almost cinnamon at times, and contrasting with the dark hairy collar over their shoulders and hump.

The riders quickly pulled back below the brow of prairie and left their horses hidden from the grazing herd. The buffalo had a keen sense of smell but poorer vision and hearing, and did not observe Mister Skye and the Arapahos with him. He spotted a sentinel bull, but that one didn't worry him. He wanted to find the lead cow, the one who would decide to whip the band away if she sensed trouble. If he could kill her first, or nearly first, he could drop the other beasts one by one and scarcely upset the herd. If these stampeded, they might trigger the distant bands too, and the hunt would be ruined.

They studied the herd for minutes while the sun ticked up the sky. He studied one cow who ate, peered around with weak eyes, ate, and peered again. He would try her first. With a flash of hand and finger, he signed to one of the warriors to have the red wagon that would carry these carcasses back to camp brought near here by the white men. An Arapaho nodded and slipped away on his pony. With a heaviness of spirit that was rare in him, Mister Skye picked up his shooting sticks and possibles and began the crawl that would take him closer, in this case to a slight hummock a hundred fifty yards ahead and downslope. He'd be exposed all the way but the gain of yardage would be valuable. He crawled and stopped, crawled and stopped. Sweaty work in the sun's early forge. Three gray wolves noticed him and slid toward his left flank. Always the cruel wolves circled the herds.

The restless cow stared in his direction and he froze. She resumed cropping, and he slid the rest of the distance fast. The hummock would be a good place, he thought. He spread the sticks, which had been tied at their centers with thong, making an X of them, and rested the barrel of the big Sharps in the vee. The range was ideal for the heavy Sharps, but very long for his Henry or the carbines of the Arapaho. He sweated, and now the bad moment fell upon him as always, the moment when he didn't want to shoot.

He gazed at the cows, twenty or twenty-five of them here. Their summer hides would be scraped clean of hair and would make lodge covers and summer robes. The hides of the bulls would make war shields that could turn arrows and often bullets; horse tack, winter moccasins, and lots more.

The bad moment passed as it always did. He lined the blade sight upon the heart-lung area just behind the shoulder of the cow he thought was the leader, and squeezed. The Sharps roared and its butt slammed into his thick shoulder. Before the day ended his shoulder would be battered and so sore it would take a week to heal.

The shot went true; the cow staggered four steps forward and fell, its legs pawing for a minute and then slowly freezing in place. The others peered dully at the sound and then resumed their cropping. He slid a paper cartridge into the slant breech and positioned a paper cap and was ready again. He selected a smaller cow, also close, but she turned suddenly, denying him the heart shot he wanted. Two others were facing him, heads low, grazing. He spotted a more distant cow who stood broadside, and lined his sight on her carefully. He squeezed again and the throaty boom of the Sharps disturbed the plains again, and his shoulder hurt again. The cow stood, peered around, shook her head violently. He watched. A dark glout blossomed on her side, a little behind the ideal target area. She sawed her head up and down, walked forward, and gently sank to earth.

He shot a bull next. Bull meat was poorer but could be jerked. His Arapaho hosts would want a few bulls and many cows, he knew. The bull bellowed in its death throes, and now the rest of the herd peered restlessly. But it lacked a leader. Mister Skye had found the lead cow right off, so this band did nothing more than mill a bit, and sniff the downed animals curiously. He shot three more cows. One took two cartridges. The big Sharps grew too hot to touch, too hot to load in a paper cartridge, and he let it cool. But it did not cool fast enough so he urinated into its barrel, smelling his water and his sweat and the grimy stink of his own buckskins. The nipple had fouled. He picked at it, and ran a patch through the crusted barrel.

Last evening they had cooked a dog feast, and he had eaten the mushy meat solemnly, and so had the others, although Mary-Rita gagged on it, and Mrs. Parkins managed only a bite or two and looked pale. Flora never appeared and Old Bull's lodge had been guarded by one or another of the dog soldiers. He pitied her, and pondered what he might do.

Tonight there would be a buffalo feast, hump roast of tender red meat more delicious than the standing rib roasts of cattle. And that would be only the beginning. There'd be delicious tenderloin, which most people swore far excelled anything taken from cattle; buffalo tongue, a great delicacy; and sausages of buffalo gut stuffed with minced tenderloin meat and the tasty fat of the animal. Buffalo fat itself was tastier and more palatable than beef fat, especially that long cord of it that ran down the spine of the animal; a part that was carefully recovered and stored as a delicacy by all the Plains tribes. Nor would that be the end of delights. They'd sample hot marrow, too, sweet and juicy, cooked deliciously right in the thigh bone of the animal. The hot bone would be brought from the cookfires, hit adroitly with the back of an axe, and broken open to reveal the succulent treasure within. Before this day was done, everyone in the village, along with his own party, would gorge themselves on several pounds of meat, and find a kind of ecstasy in it. People who considered a pound of meat filling in the East would eat five or six pounds here, and think nothing of it.

In the days following there'd be endless stews seasoned with herbs, boiled or roasted tongue, which kept well on the trail, and all the rest, including succulent dark liver, delicious raw. Some men of the mountains claimed that if a coon could eat buffler liver, he didn't need greens, and Mister Skye had found it so.

Beginning today, every squaw in the village would be busy scraping hides staked out on the earth with small pegs, tanning them with a mixture of brains and liver, cutting meat into thin slices and hanging them on racks to dry in the hot sun, layering thin meat and fat and berries into pemmican, throwing offal to the howling dogs, and saving those bones that would be scraped and hewn into implements.

Green-bellied flies had found him and swarmed around his sweating face, crawling over the gummy stock of his Sharps and even along the hot barrel. The sun rolled high and his own body smelled rank. With the cooled Sharps he sighted on another cow, a distant one this time, and his rifle thundered. He was lucky, he knew: this band had not fled. He felled seven more before the survivors, sniffing restlessly at the black sunbaked carcasses smeared with brown blood, finally trotted over a gentle rise. Mister Skye creaked to his feet and signaled to the observers on the rise behind him. Wearily he trudged up the rise and found on the other side an army of squaws with ponies and travois, ready to butcher and haul meat and hide. Among them, the red wagon with Blueberry reining the mules. Vanderbilt sat beside him, looking gray and dour, and nearby Chang on his white horse, his face forever mocking. His bride had not come. Mister Skye studied the entourage, looking for something and not finding it: Alvah Riddle had weaseled out of the hard work.

He summoned them. The small butcher army scattered out among the dark carcasses and began its swift bloody work under a brass sun. In minutes the women were covered with gore and filth. They slit open the bellies of the beasts and eviscerated them, setting gray gut aside along with the bright red livers. Bold black and white magpies flocked among them robbing carrion almost from the women's hands.

The air was thick with blood-smell and dust and urine, drawing swarms of flies. Arapaho women had been doing this thing for as long as anyone could remember, and very efficiently now that they had white men's knives rather than bone and stone cutting tools. Mister Skye watched, vaguely repelled by the red nakedness of the carcasses as hide after hide was ripped and tugged off. That such noble animals could be reduced to such red and white nakedness, to such indignity, troubled him.

Blueberry pulled up his mules near the first carcass, where three squaws hacked ruthlessly, and soon he and Vanderbilt were dragging and hoisting heavy quarters of cow buffalo into the wagon. On each fresh hide the women piled boudins, liver, heart, tongue, and other parts, and then made a sort of carrying bag of the carcass. Seventeen downed buffalo sprawled here.

Two blood-soaked squaws approached a cow on the farthest side and began slicing its brisket. The animal flayed violently, hoofs catching one woman and spinning her off. She fell on her knife, and began wailing. The other, also thrown by the thrashing animal, lay inert for a moment, shook herself, and crawled toward the wounded one. Mister Skye lumbered down the red slope past carnage and flies and gore, and found a mean gash on the thigh of the wounded woman, bleeding bright and copiously. With his filthy bandana he fashioned a tourniquet and summoned Blueberry. The wagon groaned with raw red meat anyway, and they'd take the sobbing woman back to her village. At some point in all of this, the cow had stopped breathing. The squaws who had gathered around their wounded sister slowly returned to their bloody work, sawing and slicing and wrestling slippery gray gut, and loading it in bundles on travois hanging from ponies driven mad by flies.

Seventeen. Mister Skye clambered wearily onto Jawbone and steered the blue roan northward to the next bunch. The herds had drifted north, away from the butchery, and a half hour lapsed before he found the next group, ranged along the slope of a gentle rise peppered with gray rock and sun-scorched dun bunchgrass. The sun arced high, sucking water out of him, suffocating him. Furnace wind from the west kept the stink of him away from the buffalo. Many of these lay in the grass, waiting out the heat before they returned to cropping. One or two stood, a bull and a cow, staring weak-eyed straight at him. There wasn't a single good lung-shot.

He steered Jawbone directly toward them. There'd be no worthwhile shooting until they stood. But when they stood they'd all stare at him face-on. He might drop them that way if he were lucky, but it would be less certain and he'd waste precious cartridges. He was two hundred miles from a place where he could resupply. The bull saw him and turned belligerent, lowering its massive head, pointing its small curved horns, pawing earth and bellowing. He stopped Jawbone and let the bull bellow. The others in the bunch swung their heads toward him. None rose. He waited, feeling sweat trickle down his neck and chest. The big sun-hot Sharps blistered his hands.

Nothing. The animals lay inertly in the midday heat. He slid off Jawbone, feeling the heat of the horse, and felt his legs give under him as he touched ground. He knew why he felt weary. He walked a hundred yards straight toward the watching bull, and then settled on an ant-bitten slab of clay. He spread his sticks and lowered the barrel of the Sharps into the vee, and fired at the bull. It bawled, sprayed crimson blood from its mouth, shook its head, and then rumbled toward him. He reloaded swiftly, singeing his fingers on hot metal. His lungs sucked powdersmoke and prairie dust and his own stink. The bull tumbled fifty yards from him. Behind the bull, a dozen of the dozing animals jacked themselves to their feet, two legs at a time. He studied them, without an inkling of what animal might be the boss cow.

The standing animals turned more or less to face him. He preferred to shoot from another quarter, so he clambered back on Jawbone and wheeled the reluctant horse to the east. The heatstruck buffalo watched but did nothing, which is what he had hoped. Ten minutes later he was shooting again, waiting long periods between shots for the Sharps to cool, dropping black and tan cows. Seven humped on the ground, three inert and four spasming and

flaying legs, when the entire herd rose and fled, as if
warned by the hand of God. It was one of the mysteries
of nature. He walked out among the dark dead animals,
smelling brass blood and the urine and green fecal matter
that leaked from the doomed. One saw him and in a final
rage tried to clamber to her feet, struggling, and then gave
up with a long sigh. Death, he thought. Death. Flesh to
feed my flesh, Arapaho flesh.

Seven here, seventeen yonder. Less than half. He felt
weary, more weary than if he had been ripping and slashing and sweating the carcasses yonder. He struggled back
to Jawbone, and it took him two bounces to board the
animal. Jawbone turned, curious. He rode south and west,
and met the squaws and their ponies and travois, heading
toward the echoing booms of his Sharps. He pointed the
way, and the women passed him, staring hard at this man
whose medicine and legend they all knew. He spat, scraping his gums to find the juice to do it.

He rode slowly toward the village, following the furrows of innumerable travois poles that had gouged the
dusty earth with their passage. He passed several squaws
and ponies heading back to the carnage for new loads.
Ahead rolled the red wagon, also returning after a long
trip. It was not efficient. The travois and the ponies and
the squaws moved meat and gut and hide and bone faster,
he thought. He tugged gently on Jawbone's rope rein, and
waited.

Blueberry tugged the mules to a halt beside him, and
wordlessly handed Mister Skye a waterskin. He drank,
feeling warm water trickle down his esophagus and spread
loosely through his gut. Blueberry was alone. Vanderbilt
had vanished this trip.

"How many?" asked Blueberry.

"Twenty-four. Enough for one day. All the squaws can
handle, too."

"Not half," said Blueberry.

"No, not half. You want to try it? I'll lend the Sharps."

The man shook his head. "I'm in no rush. Getting to

like the village, now that they didn't slit my throat last night.''

"We'll see," said Mister Skye.

"We saw Flora Slade," said Blueberry. "Out cutting buff, near the chief's lodge. Right between those two beefy squaws of Old Bull's. Big mamas. Every time she slowed down, they whopped her. I mean whopped. Sprawled her in the gore. There's a dog soldier hovering around there too, just in case Riddle gets notions.''

"How'd she look?"

"She ain't dead yet."

"How'd she look, Blueberry?"

"Too mean for tears. Her face is a mess, though. Soft, all that conceit and snob pounded out of it. Whenever one or another of us got near, she started yelling. Says she's going to kill you; that you got her into it. Says she'll escape someday and then come hunting. Better watch your backside, Mister Skye."

"I better had," he agreed.

"I'm not minding it a whole lot," said Blueberry. "Slade sold me once. Ripped me away from my sweetheart and I never saw her again. He said this nigger would make a great field hand. My price, Mister Skye, added up to about twice hers. Good strong slaves have all the luck."

"You sure are lucky," agreed Mister Skye.

He rode slowly toward the village, past dog soldiers patrolling, past gore-soaked squaws slicing red meat, past mutts vomiting up gore and guts, past girls pegging out a hide with tiny stakes, toward his own camp, his Victoria and Mary. He stank. He was filthy inside and out. He would wash with sand in the warm creek, wash until he abraded his flesh, scour his body and soul.

Chapter 19

The wagon stank. In its bed lay offal and guts, now crawling with larvae and coppered with a black mass of flies
that swirled in green whirlpools.

Mister Skye found Cornelius Vanderbilt. "Clean that
thing. Drive it into the creek and scrub it down. I won't
have that flybait around my camps."

Vanderbilt peered back at him indolently. The man puzzled Mister Skye. Without his cards and faro layout, without his gambler's attire, he had ceased to be a person. He
had caved into a sallow hulk, sullen and denuded.

"I have nothing to clean it with," he replied. "I'll find
Blueberry Hill to help you."

Blueberry tackled the job happily because the noisome
rank odor of the wagon pervaded their whole camp. He
harnessed a pair of mules to it and clattered down to the
creek trailing a cloud of winged things while Arapaho children watched. Mister Skye followed, hunting for a smooth
piece of sandstone, remembering how often he had holy-
stoned the teak decks of royal men-o'-war. Blueberry Hill
was a good man, he thought.

In three days he'd fulfilled the contract, recovered Gold-tooth's spare wagon, supplied the whole village with meat and hide with his overheated Sharps, and downed one last cow for his own party. The evidence of it lay at every hand: willow-pole racks sagged under jerked meat. Hides were staked to the ground everywhere, being fleshed or brain-tanned by patient squaws. Camp dogs lazed dolorously, gorged on offal. Buffalo heads and horns were being worked for ceremonial purposes; bone had become awls and knives and forks and ladles. The air swam with the odor of putrefying meat, turning the place foul. The Arapaho had been here too long, and fecal odor eddied among the lodges. The grass wasted down to nothing and the pony herd grazed farther and farther out. Mister Skye itched to be off.

But there was still business to attend. It had come hard to him to do it, but he knew he had to. He padded past cheerful people rejoicing in this buffalo-wealth, toward Old Bull's lodge and waited patiently at the doorflap. He thought briefly about fetching Victoria to translate, but the old chief knew enough English, and he could sign the rest with fingers and hands. A hard thing, what he would do, but the need and duty of it would not go away.

He waited several minutes. It amused chiefs to let business wait and guests stand. But eventually one of the beefy squaws let him into the translucent shade of the lodge. With a curt wave of hand, the chief dismissed the women, including Flora Slade. They rose to leave, but Mister Skye stayed Flora.

"This is about her. I'd like her here," he said.

The chief acquiesced, and Flora settled uncertainly in a far place near the doorflap. She had dark circles beneath her eyes, but her hauteur radiated from her. His eyes caught hers and locked, and he saw no warmth in them.

Old Bull amiably prepared a pipe and lit it with a sulphur match, since the cookfire burned outside in warm weather. The village was tallowed with meat; his lodge-poles groaned with it.

"You will be leaving today," said Old Bull at last. "We will leave in a day or two."

"We'll be off soon. I've come to trade one last thing," said Mister Skye.

The chief peered at him, curious.

"This for her."

He thrust the gleaming new Henry, its brass frame glowing dully in the orange light of the lodge, into the chief's hands. He hefted it, opened the magazine and slid out the cartridges, one after another, counting, and then stuffed them back again and jacked the lever.

"First one in this country," said Mister Skye. "Sixteen shots and one in the chamber, gives you something no chief of any tribe possesses. This plus the two and a half cartons of cartridges I have left . . . over a hundred."

The chief ran his gnarled brown hands down the blued barrel, sighted, felt the balance, and smiled.

"Where will I get cartridges?" he asked.

"Denver City. Maybe Fort Laramie. Maybe Fort Bridger or Fort Hall."

"For her."

"That's what I'm offering."

She spoke from behind him. "It is no use, Mister Skye. You are too late. Two days too late."

A severity he'd never seen hardened her face, and a determination.

Old Bull said, "I will do it. You will take her. This is a good thing. Give me the cartridges now, and take her."

Mister Skye handed over the boxes, feeling something precious slip from his fingers. Now he would be low on ammunition as well as firepower. He'd used scores of the Sharps cartridges and had barely fifty left, tucked in a parfleche.

"Good. Take her," said Old Bull. "I don't need a new wife. But she's a good one, made me happy."

"Come along, then, Flora," he said.

Across her face emotions eclipsed. She peered misty-eyed at him, then hard. Her lips smiled and then drew taut.

"No. I will not go. I am a chief's bride. I am married. I have—been with him. I have entered a new life and don't wish to go back to the other. I am no longer a—maiden. I no longer wish to have a white husband—who'd be my second."

"Come along, Flora. Let's get out in the sun and on the trail."

Old Bull watched closely, fondling his new Henry. "I have given her to you," he repeated.

Mister Skye understood.

Flora's face softened. "I know what the trade meant to you," she said gently. "And I thank you. I am worth one Henry. Also, twenty robes and five ponies plus a few things. I would have been glad of it two days ago. But this man, my chief, has—taken me into . . . a new world. What happened, I enjoyed. I wish to be his woman."

"His fourth woman," said Mister Skye.

"His fourth woman."

"Your mind is set?"

"Yes."

"You are free to come with us. You won't regret it later?"

Her face softened again. "Of course I will. I'll miss everything I am used to, including speaking in my own tongue. And everything is strange and alien. But I am the wife of Chief Old Bull, and I'll be loyal to him."

She smiled at Old Bull, who returned the gaze amiably.

"I have given her. I will keep the Henry. You take her," said Old Bull. "And a good pony. I will add that."

"You will be alone. We will be off in an hour. Who will you talk with?"

"Mister Skye. How often you've spoken against slavery. I'm here of my own free will now. Not at first, but now I am. Will you violate my decision, my choice?"

Mister Skye saw the lay of it and sighed. No, he thought, he would not violate an intelligent, competent, adult woman's will. His hands felt empty, deprived of the comfort and nurture of the rapid-firing rifle. He opened and closed them around nothing. It had all been for nothing.

"Very well then," he said abruptly. "You are made of steel, Flora Slade. I admire that."

He addressed the chief. "We part as friends. I thank you for your hospitality."

Old Bull nodded and stood. Mister Skye squeezed his heavy bulk through the lodge door and into a glaring day. He didn't know what to do with empty hands. What impelled a man to do such things? Why had he given away advantage and perhaps the protection of himself and all under his care, for a woman who deserved nothing? He had put her in her dilemma, that's why.

They were waiting for him at the edge of the village. Mary and Victoria had recovered their lodgeskins from the bawds and sewn the lodge back together, adding a new skin to replace the one cut into moccasins. Now it lay on one travois, with bundles of lodgepoles on another. His mules were loaded. Goldtooth's spare wagon was clean and harnessed, with Vanderbilt driving. Blueberry Hill sat on the seat of Goldtooth's wagon, now loaded with robes and riches, including buffalo dorsal-bone knives and spoons and forks that Seven-Story's wife, Buffalo Whiskers, had ground and carved for the women.

Alvah Riddle sat upon his wagon, now harnessed to three span again, the middle span consisting of a trained mule and one of his new ponies. The remaining ponies were loaded with Riddle's wealth, and tied behind. Mister Skye stared dourly at Riddle, and knew that the paunchy pink man was far more responsible than himself for losing Flora.

And far ahead, Chang on his white mount and his bride on a fat pony waited. Mister Skye sighed, found Jawbone saddled and ready, and mounted, turning the surly half-starved animal north and west. Behind him he heard the sullen rattle of wagons over roadless wastes. There were few to see them off: the women of the village were processing meat as fast as possible before it spoiled, and scraping hides. But the town crier waved, and the dog soldiers saluted Chang and his bride. The mandarin smiled.

Victoria rode beside Mister Skye, watching him sharply. She handed him his old Sharps. "You traded, but no good," she said. She always had it right, a supreme realist, he thought.

"No good," he muttered.

"Plenty good," she said. "Sonofabitch, you are a big man, Mister Skye. You made the medicine but now you kick yourself. I'm gonna cook up buffalo hump tonight and then kick Mary out of the lodge and hug you good."

For days they rode northwest through a duned land, seeing no one, feeling the wind. The rare brackish creeks were easy to cross, and they often discovered buffalo trails down one bank and up the other that the wagons could follow.

Buffalo were plentiful, and Seven-Story Chang shot one daily. He and Buffalo Whiskers usually skinned and butchered on the spot, returning to the caravan with the hump and tongue and liver, wrapped in the hide. Seven-Story found himself immersed in an idyllic life here on these endless steppes of North America, wandering daily forward with his Arapaho bride beside him on a stout bay pony. She was exquisite—far more so than the Peking beauties she resembled in a dusky way—and guileless. She spoke exactly what lay on her mind, contrary to any humans he had known in China, who approached things with mannered indirection. She was equally unlike these Europeans invading this empty land, more natural and without artifice.

They had swiftly learned to communicate, mastering a certain patois composed of English, Arapaho, and such finger-language as Seven-Story had acquired in his months on the prairies. He occasionally added a Mandarin word as well, or a Mandarin inflection of an English word. She laughed and shook her head. They were helped in camp by Victoria and Mary, who knew enough Arapaho to supply details and nuances. Buffalo Whiskers belonged to an enemy tribe, but both of Mister Skye's women accepted her at once, even as she accepted her new friends. Evenings, the three of them industriously haired and fleshed the new hides, and crudely tanned them with brain for a few days at least, keeping them rolled in wet heaps while they traveled. They had a gift in mind for Chang.

They found their private moments far from the caravan, beneath a rare cottonwood, or in a hidden hollow. And there he held her and she clung to him, with a mutual joy that made his spirit sing. He was too much the warrior to dally for long, and always he leapt up and peered intently at empty horizons, and then slipped down to her side once again. Neither in China nor Europe, nor in the settled portion of this continent, had he experienced such indolent isolation. He didn't care if he ever saw the bright-hued palaces of Peking again, or any city. This place transformed a man's spirit into its most primitive and true nature. Someday he would write poetry about this poetic land.

Behind them the wagons toiled. Mister Skye looked serene, except that a lack of ammunition lay on his mind. The newly rich bawds had become content. They wore exquisite Arapaho doe- and elkskin dresses now, moccasins that Skye's squaws and Buffalo Whiskers made as other pairs wore out, and were more handsomely attired— and beautiful—than when they wore sweat-stained, soiled calico and dimity and twill. The French girl, Juliet Picard, was transformed into an Indian by her clothing. Big Alice had always looked like one, and the ash-blond Mrs. Parkins presented an electric contrast in her skin clothes. Except for iron pots they had everything they needed now, plus a wealth in robes to trade when they arrived at Bannack. They were swiftly learning from their Indian mentors how to find edible roots and herbs along creek banks, the meaty biscuit-root, the high-summer berries that added nourishment to pemmican as well as their daily meals. And withal, they felt a lot less helpless than they had in the wake of the storm.

The day before they pierced into the Bridgers along a trail pioneered by old Jim Bridger and Mister Skye himself, the women readied their surprise for Chang. They had made a wagon sheet of half-tanned cowhide sewn together with sinew. At camp one evening they hoisted the heavy skin rectangle over the hickory bows of Goldtooth's wagon and then anchored it with thong thrust through holes awled in its edges. The stiff hide would be difficult to reef in a gale, but usable even so, especially if the thongs that anchored it could be undone swiftly.

Chang stood admiring. "We'll chase Vanderbilt and Hill off and move in," he said. "We have a house."

No sooner did they anchor down the cover than Alvah Riddle sidled up to Goldtooth Jones. "Say," he said, "mind if I store my robes in there? It'll save packsaddling my ponies and unsaddling them each day. Speed us all up."

"Fifty dollars, Riddle," said Goldtooth amiably, watching the shapeless lips on the chinless face pucker over her pickle.

"So that's your angle," he said. "People in your profession, they never do anything free. Never neighborly."

Goldtooth laughed.

For the first time, these sunny days, the brides made timid contact with the bawds. Drusilla paused to admire Juliet Picard's quilled doeskin dress, and shared her Elizabeth Barrett Browning book with Goldtooth. Mary-Rita ventured to ask Big Alice what it felt like to sin every day. Gertrude Riddle didn't approve. She sat like a mound of gum arabic beside the green wagon, and scolded her charges about it.

"What's your angle?" Riddle asked Drusilla. "How come you're lending that book? That's part of your dowry and I shouldn't let you do that, taint yourself like that. In the contract."

"Is kindness in your contract?" Drusilla retorted shortly.

"So that's your angle," he said. "Not bad, not bad. Now she'll owe us. Yes, good, something to use. Call in the marker when we need it."

"You are disgusting, Mister Riddle," she said.

Chang, who had witnessed the contretemps, laughed

softly. Riddle reminded him of a certain kind of peasant found commonly in the hinterlands of his country.

Mister Skye pulled Chang aside that evening. "I get bad feelings," he said. "So does Victoria. There's not much space separating us from trouble. Maybe Cheyenne, maybe Sioux. But I got the skincrawls I usually get. Jawbone's showing it too, mate. Now, I'm so short of cartridges for my Sharps I don't have an hour of fight, much less something to get to Bannack with. The women have plenty of powder and shot for their longrifles, but that's plumb slow. Riddle's well armed, rifle and revolver and cartridges, but he's about as useless as wet powder in a fight. Now I'm thinkin', Chang, if trouble comes, we've got to highjack his carbine, leave him the revolver. That's all I'm thinkin', mate. Just give it your attention."

"Ah, Mister Skye, you can hold off a painted war party with medicine alone," Chang said. "Jawbone is worth ten rifles."

"I'm going to cut your queue, Chang," muttered Mister Skye.

It amused him. At the first sign of trouble, he would assault Riddle's wagon.

Later he caught Drusilla in a place beyond hearing. "Ah, Miss Dinwiddie," he said. "Would you be so kind as to tell me just where in your wagon the esteemed Mister Riddle stores his arms and ammunition?"

She peered through darkness at him. "I will do better," she said quietly. "If the need arises, I will hand them to you. I would feel far more protected if they were in anyone's hands but Mister Riddle's. They are across the front, just behind the seat."

"Leave his revolver for him," said Chang, lightly.

"That's my angle," she replied, and laughed.

They crawled up an alluvial fan the next day, and into a throat of red granite, salted with juniper and silvery sage. The path seemed easy enough for mountain country, but they were occasionally slowed by the need to pull brush and boulders aside. They traversed a hot, dry, sunny wash, but there were springs, and at noon they watered the sweated stock and themselves as one. An hour later they rounded a bend, and came out on a ridge where they could survey the vast plains behind them. They were a thousand feet higher, but could see a vast distance into the haze of nothingness. The plains looked less empty to them then, for below, three snakes of dust marked human passage. Mister Skye pointed and grinned.

They pushed ahead into a narrowing red-rock chasm, where sage grew thicker and movement slowed. Above, along either cliffside, juniper sentinels made a living from rock. It was up-and-down country. Chang and Buffalo Whiskers rode ahead, studying defiles. There could be no scouting on the flanks here, only ahead of the toiling caravan.

Behind them, mid-afternoon, they heard the tattoo of carbines, and then the staccato of shots driving at themselves, gouging earth and shattering rock. Chang turned his horse back, but painted warriors blocked the way.

Chapter 20

"Atsina!" snapped Victoria.

It always mystified him, how Indians could instantly identify each other. He had asked her once, and she had shrugged.

"Maybe Piegan," she added, puzzled. She squinted at darting figures above. "Sarsi? Sonofabitch!" She spat.

A bullet whanged off his pommel. He heeled Jawbone, cursing. He should have had Mary and Victoria flanking the red ridges, he thought. Maybe not. They'd be dead . . .

"Keep moving," he bellowed. "Don't stop for anything. Whip those mules!"

Trapped in a bad place, no defense at all, a bloody defile with Gros Ventre or Piegan or whatever the hell they were peeping and crawling from every pink granite boulder and squat juniper bush up there, and a dozen more vermilioned warriors darting toward them on the trail dead ahead, blurred brown shapes. Broncos, he thought. Mixed bunch of young ones, hating the reservations, hell on whites.

"Hill! Vanderbilt! Whip those mules!"

The bawds were whickering and braying in the red wagon. Behind, Mary-Rita invoked saints in a keening voice, including some he'd never heard of.

Mary and Victoria kicked their ponies, drawing clumsy longrifles from their sheaths, poor weapons for this. A shot creased Jawbone's stifle and he shrieked insanely, kicking at invisible hornets and twisting crazily. Mister Skye hung on, for a moment an impossible target, but also unable to shoot.

He didn't know what lay ahead, but stopping would slaughter them all in seconds. Behind, the green wagon careened to a halt. No one in the driver's seat.

"Riddle!" he roared. "Keep moving, whip those mules!"

Gertrude Riddle wailed like a leaky bellows. Bullets ripped through wagon sheets, feral noises. Above, short bronze naked warriors darted up, fired fusils, loosed arrows, and vanished behind rocks. A bullet smacked a travois pack, bonging a frying pan.

"Sonofabitch!" yelled Victoria, huddling low. One of Goldtooth's lead mules slumped and died in the traces, sighing down. Another shot brained the off-lead mule, and the wagon stopped, forcing Vanderbilt behind to stop. Hill jumped down, shotgun in hand, and began unhooking traces. Three warriors above popped up, aiming for him. Mister Skye methodically unloaded his Colt at them. Only the one-shot Sharps loaded now, and he wished to hell he had his Henry.

Riddle had vanished, and now the blue pecker of his revolver poked through that gunport of his in the side of his wagon.

"Riddle!" roared Mister Skye.

Blueberry jerked spastically, and blood blossomed on his upper arm. He tugged frantically. Mister Skye leveled his Sharps at a warrior upslope aiming at Hill. The warrior flipped and fell on his back, began crawling behind rock. Red rock cascaded.

Ahead, a dozen silent shapes daubed with white chevrons were darting and weaving closer, all scorpion-footed and as elusive as fawns.

Hill got traces loose from the offside mule. Skye rammed home another paper cartridge and cap, and fired again. Hill was the key to everything. The broncos knew it, and five of them rushed him now, dodging and darting to within twenty yards. Hill quit tugging at harness, and blew both barrels of his scattergun at them, bloodying two. One took a ball in the neck but came on, seeing Hill unarmed and pouring fresh powder down a smoking hot barrel. Two others kept coming.

Drusilla suddenly emerged in the seat of Riddle's wagon, Riddle's carbine in hand. She aimed unsteadily at the warrior closing on Hill, and shot. The recoil threw her back. The bullet hit the closest warrior's throat. He fell at Blueberry Hill's feet, leaking blood from neck and mouth. The bawds whickered. Goldtooth leapt out and grabbed the warrior's old carbine, and sprang back into the wagon. Hill got one barrel of the shotgun recharged when the others sprang for him. He fired and caught two, but only one fell. One came on, sheeting red across his chest.

Vanderbilt jumped down from his seat, stone-headed war club in his belt, jabbing the staff Mister Skye had cut for him. The staff knocked the attacker sideways. An arrow gashed Vanderbilt's calf, and he limped convulsively. Mister Skye swore. Victoria snarled.

Mister Skye and Mary fired simultaneously at the darting greased warriors swarming downslope from dead ahead, winging two. Mary threw powder, wad, and ball down her flintlock. Victoria fired at one aiming at Skye, who was fumbling a fresh paper cartridge home. Jawbone shrieked. A magpie exploded from a cedar.

Send him, he thought. He grabbed his possibles from the cantle and sprang off Jawbone. The murderous old blue roan laid ears back, shrieked, exploded like a plugged howitzer, and avalanched into the advancing warriors. He bit one's shoulder, kicked another at the breechclout, folding him in two, stomped on the leg of a downed warrior and broke it with a loud snap, spun into one peering down his rifle, sending him sprawling. He knocked down three with flailing legs. One yellow-daubed giant jabbed a knife into Jawbone's rump before Jawbone caught him with a shod hoof. Jawbone wheeled and charged straight up a slope impossible to horses and chased three warriors from the cover of a juniper thicket. Mister Skye shot the one still standing through a shoulder.

Behind, Skye glimpsed Hill back on his wagon seat, steering his remaining two mules around the dead. Vanderbilt jabbed his willow staff at one springing warrior, but another whirled in with a glinting knife. Drusilla shot him just as his arm thrust out. The blow in his back sprawled him under the wagon wheel, blocking its progress. Hill whipped the two mules mercilessly. They strained, and the wheel rose and dropped over the warrior's buttocks, leaving an indented gray path. A knee rose and the body twitched and defecated. His mouth hollowed and leaked blood.

Three broncos with high scalplocks rushed the blind side of Riddle's wagon. One trotted along just behind Drusilla and sprang up, knocking her sideways. Vanderbilt's stone war club caught him just as he reached for the reins, leaving a caved-in skull with white bone and white pulp poking through jet hair. The gambler wheeled, too late. An arrow hit at the left kidney and pierced clear through, its trade-goods iron point projecting from his abdomen. He slumped silently to earth, staring at his reddening shirt. Drusilla shot again, and a warrior dotted with white clay and grease careened into another, blood gouting from his armpit. They fell and the wagon pulled ahead.

Something heavy clobbered Mister Skye above the ear. He went blind, and the earth rushed up. His Sharps clattered off. Then he saw again, and a wide-cheeked green-greased warrior who shone like an archangel was drawing a sinew-wrapped bow above him, his eyes alight with the knowledge. Mister Skye rolled but the bow followed him. The arrow struck his revolver belt like a sledge and winded him. He found his knife and sprang up, feeling his knees tremble. His knife sliced meat off the arm and the warrior shrieked. Skye twisted, and kicked the bow aside. He found his Sharps and possibles and reloaded. Jawbone's chest gouted red. Skye's breath scraped in sharp hot gasps, and his heart rattled beneath his barrel staves.

From the ridge above he caught a glimpse of a dancing white horse, and the mandarin, laughing wildly, coolly firing his pair of Navy revolvers and reloading with spare cylinders. Around Skye, warriors turned, spotted this flanking menace, and scattered. Chang held protected high ground in a natural purple-rock and silvery cedar fortress. His wild laugh sent chills through Skye, who sat exhausted on the hard earth, the battle whirling around him. But he was not a part of it for a moment. He watched Mary's breasts slide beneath her doeskin blouse, and wanted her. She was alive but where was Victoria?

The wagons were rolling again, now coming past him.

Victoria materialized. "Get up, dammit," she yelled. "You stopping the wagons."

Riddle's wagon rattled by, Drusilla whipping mules and Mary-Rita whining like a sawmill blade in a knot. Mary shot a warrior about to scalp Vanderbilt. He grabbed his crotch and howled.

Goldtooth's wagon careened next, with Hill, sweating rivers and blood-soaked, whipping two weary mules with his good arm. His pants were wet.

The mules of the driverless third wagon followed unbidden. Vanderbilt sat stupidly, watching blood ooze down his britches. Skye trotted that way, and lifted him bodily into the empty wagon, beneath the new skin wagon sheet, which let in pink sunlight like a colander now.

"Five aces," said Vanderbilt.

From above, Chang poured lead and Chinese imprecations at broncos, dancing on a skillet. Warriors broke into flanking parties then and darted upward, tightening the noose. Below, Jawbone butted an aiming warrior and somersaulted him into a ravine. A bullet splintered wagon wood just above Skye's head. A red sliver hung from Skye's vast nose. Three warriors speckled with white dots and ochre heads rushed. He grabbed the burning barrel of the Sharps and scythed, knocking one back and glancing off the burly shoulder of the second. Then the third one was on him, piling him backward. The wagons rolled ahead of him now, upslope, leaving him behind. He kneed the one on him and felt stale air erupt from a wide mouth. The warrior's knife tunneled down. Skye twisted. The blade spanged earth exactly below his armpit, nicking his underarm.

"Smell right, mate?" Skye muttered, rolling hard and throwing off the warrior. A foot caught Skye's groin, and he felt nausea boil up and his remaining strength leak. His bladder emptied into his loincloth. He butted the warrior, feeling warpaint and grease smear on him. He found the man's throat and clamped with his big square blunt hands. The warrior thrashed and stopped thrashing. His tongue went purple, and a green fly landed on it.

Skye lay on his back, willing the nausea away. Above, they closed on Chang. Buffalo Whiskers was visible now, darting toward him with a bow and quiver. The wagons had spun two hundred yards up the grade. Making it, he thought. Getting out. A wounded warrior daubed with yellow clay around each eye spotted him, lifted his dirty fusil. Skye stood up and kicked the black-eyed Susan and picked up the smoothbore. The warrior vomited.

Mary staggered toward him. "Mister Skye," she cried, her eyes leaking.

"I'm here," he muttered.

She dragged him forward toward the train. They were isolated here. A calf bawled ahead, and it puzzled him.

Above, a death-angel swung a blue barrel toward them. The shot hit Mary's moccasin and destroyed her big toe. She danced on blood. She sobbed and staggered forward. Skye set down his unarmed Sharps, and lifted the fusil he'd retrieved. He let his lungs and heart quiet. Another shot from above seared by. Skye shot. The ball hit purple rock an inch below the blue barrel, spraying chips. Someone howled and the barrel vanished. Skye dropped the empty fusil and loaded his Sharps. His possibles bag had vanished and he found one of three spares in the pocket of his fringed shirt. The paper turned pink in his fingers. His breechclout stank.

He searched wildly for his possibles, which contained the other Sharps cartridges. The wagons ahead pulled away. Mary turned stoic and strode deliberately, putting pain squarely on her torturing foot. Skye found his possibles bag, and began trotting. Above, Chang was in deep trouble.

Riddle's peckerpiece popped, and a horse died, but the warrior on top rolled off and bounded toward the rolling wagon. He yanked Riddle's revolver as it ejaculated. Riddle's hand came with it and then darted back in. Skye threw his knife. It caught the warrior's cheek and popped out the opposite cheek. The skinny warrior yanked it out and jabbed at Riddle's porthole, and Riddle shrieked. Skye's boot caught the warrior in the buttocks and drove the warrior's arm into the wagon, up to the shoulder. Skye sledged, the warrior careened sideways, his trapped arm broken and white bone saluting the sun. Skye picked up Riddle's revolver. Jogging ahead, he handed it to Drusilla. Her face shone.

" 'How do I love thee? Let me count the ways,' " she said, and sobbed. "I've murdered," she cried brokenly.

Skye slid to his knees, rested his Sharps on a wind-twisted cedar limb, waited for the barrel to steady and his hands to calm. He sighted on a black-daubed giant who was drawing his bow at Chang. The Sharps vomited and the bow flew up. Chang wore some kind of war vest, thick leather rosetted with shining steel. Three arrows struck it simultaneously. One hung; two fell. Chang danced. A white cloud above unfolded a vision of Buddha. Buffalo Whiskers drove an arrow into the belly of an Atsina cousin. The warrior sat heavily. He wore a crucifix, and he began making the sign of the cross.

Mister Skye rummaged in his possibles for a cartridge.

A fly crawled into the breech just before he rammed home the cartridge and slid up the next cap. He jammed the slant-block shut, shearing off the paper to expose the powder to the cap. Chang wrestled three warriors, one of

them black and yellow stripes from head to foot. No good
shot. Mary's foot would hurt for weeks. The fly emerged
from the muzzle and climbed up on the blade sight, resting
bluely. A greased warrior careened backward from a chop
administered by Chang, Chang-chop. The broncos fled
now, scattering through red boulders.

The wagons had rounded a bend and vanished. He felt
sticky blood dripping over his ear. He heard the soft thump
of Victoria's muzzleloader, and behind him a stark naked
warrior with greased blue genitals and arm chevrons sat
suddenly and clutched his reddening calf. A black horsefly
sucked blood.

Where was Victoria? She was too old for this. Chang
ducked a scything captured cavalry saber and ripped upward with a filagreed gold dagger, releasing gray and red
guts. The last bronco fled, holding his belly. Chang stood,
red at one ear, bleeding from both forearms. The arrow
dangled.

He saw Victoria now, a wizened elf pouring fresh black
powder down the barrel, ramming home a lead ball in a
red patch made from old long johns. She hunched halfway up the pink granite slope, looking like ancient cedar.
Safe. For years he had wondered when the end would
come. Mary, or Victoria, or himself. But their medicine
had been strong once again. One more time.

He reloaded his Sharps and his revolver. The possibles
bag seemed awfully light. Jawbone stood in the sun, his
ears perked upward, his flanks red gore. This bunch
needed following and punishing, he thought. Broncos,
looking for trouble, moochers of the plains, fighting and
stealing, visiting relatives until they were booted out, then
off to find new trouble and more loot.

It took him three tries to board Jawbone. The blue roan
shivered beneath him. "Got to finish it up," he muttered.
He turned the horse upslope in the direction of the vanish-
ing band.

"I am going to kill them."

"Sonofabitch," snapped Victoria. She padded off toward the wagons ahead. Her old cheeks glistened wet.

"Fix Mary," he said. "Find a place up there."

Chang and Buffalo Whiskers joined him, Chang laughing. He let the arrow dangle from his war vest. The horses sagged, weary, especially old Jawbone, who limped a bit from his stifle wound. They followed a red-speckled trail down a defile and up the other side, and at the cedar-crusted ridge they spotted the retreating broncos a thousand yards ahead, doubled on ponies, carrying several limp forms. Sharps range, he thought.

He slid off and found a benchrest of gnarled gray cedar, and sighted down the blued barrel. The Sharps felt peculiarly heavy. He fired, and nothing happened. The retreating party urged tired horses into an uphill trot. Skye fired again, and nothing happened. He shot one more time, missing.

"I'll kill them all," he said.

Chang's eyes mocked but he said nothing.

"Cut your queue," Skye muttered.

"That's original," said Chang.

"Serve 'em notice anyway," said Mister Skye.

He had seven Sharps cartridges left. And they were several hundred miles from Bannack. He slid the gummy weapon into his saddle scabbard.

"Who's alive?" asked Chang.

"Don't know about the women. Vanderbilt's dead. A lot of wounds. Hill for sure, maybe that damned Riddle. Mary's hurt. Drusilla showed blood. You. Me. Jawbone here." He peered at Buffalo Whiskers. "Don't know how you escaped," he muttered.

"They're cousins with Gros Ventre," Chang said, and Skye shrugged, knowing.

Victoria had halted the caravan on a sloping plateau a mile ahead, near the summit. It could be defended, with long fields of fire. Moist July grass too, and the remaining stock was gorging on it. Water dripped from a crack in red granite a hundred yards distant. Mister Skye let Jawbone drink from a natural pool. He splashed his face, his fingers gingerly exploring the clotted furrow above his left ear. Jawbone's wounds leaked red and crusted brown.

Victoria doctored in camp. The ball had amputated Mary's toe and Victoria was preparing to cauterize the leaking stump. Mary looked drawn. Dirt crusted the paths of her tears.

"I'll live, Mister Skye," she said, but she looked like she might not.

Vanderbilt lay on his side in the wagon, still alive. Flies clustered around the two wounds. "Busted hand," said the gambler. "Deuces all my life. Born Homer Donk, two of clubs." Bitter tears welled from his shocked eyes. He couldn't lift an arm to wipe his sallow cheeks.

"We'll make you comfortable," said Mister Skye. He found Chang. They'd get the arrow out and let Vanderbilt die on his back, facing God. Chang sawed at the shaft.

"Godalmighty," said Vanderbilt. "If there is a God." A sob convulsed him.

The iron point fell off.

"Hold him," said Skye. Chang crawled behind and pinioned the gambler. Mister Skye pulled hard. The arrow wouldn't come. Vanderbilt groaned and fainted. "Stretch him flatter," said Skye. He tugged again, wiggling the shaft, and it greased out. "We'll plug the holes, not that it'll do any good." Not much blood leaked from either one. They patched him with his filthy calico shirt and stretched him out in the perforated shade of the wagon.

"He might last a day," Mister Skye muttered.

Mary screamed. The smell of burnt flesh hung in the air. She wept softly, clutching her calf, the pain too large.

Alvah Riddle peered into Vanderbilt's wagon. "Is he dead yet? I'd kinda like the boots. My size, I figure. Mine getting worn through, all this walking."

"Riddle," snapped Mister Skye, "get out of my sight."

Chapter 21

Only moments ago, Alvah Riddle had been congratulating himself. He had come out of it almost unscathed because he had figured all the angles. Gertrude had been wounded. An arrow had ricocheted into her sagging right breast, and fallen out. The women had bound it tight and she was lying quietly in the green wagon. He counted seventeen perforations in the wagon sheet, and seven white-splintered gouges in the green-enameled sides of the wagon box. A wheel spoke had been shattered, but he could fashion a splint. A mule's ear had been shot off. A bullet had furrowed the neck of another. A rein had been severed, and a trace weakened by a shot through its center. A small water cask hanging from the rear of his wagon had absorbed a shot, and bled a third of its water. Three iron-tipped arrows lay inside the wagon, one of them with blood on it.

His shirt was ripped where the warrior who thrust a hand into his gunport had cut it. But no harm had befallen him. Those little gunports on each side made a perfect defense, he thought, congratulating himself. He'd employed a carpenter to cut the six-inch ports before they started, and fashion pivoting metal covers for the holes. When trouble came, he hunkered on the wagon bed, surrounded by high barrels and trunks, and fired in perfect safety. It wasn't perfect: he couldn't see along the flanks. The warrior who had grabbed his revolver surprised him, even as Skye's squaw had surprised him earlier. He'd do something about that: drill tiny peepholes here and there in the box.

"Miss Dinwiddie," he said. "You had no business whipping those mules. Your duty was to find safety among the barrels and goods and not expose yourself. Why, what if you'd been killed or wounded? The ah, contract, ah, expressly provides that a bride place herself under my direction for the duration of the journey. If you'd been ah, killed, we could not deliver you to your husband. Not only that, you commandeered my carbine and used it without permission, and just at a time when I might need it."

The woman's hair sprayed out, half free of her bun. She glared at him through her small rimless spectacles, and turned away. Her gray dress dripped filth and it looked like she had soiled herself. Great wet stains in the skirts. What a loathsome-looking thing, he thought. He suddenly rejoiced that his contract was airtight. She did not reply, but stared at him from a drawn face.

"Clean yourself and start cooking. Poor Gertrude can't cook," he said. "Nobody to help me unhitch the mules and unload the packhorses. No one to help Gertrude, either. Say, isn't it grand that we came out of it in one piece? Let us all give thanks for this blessing. No one badly hurt."

She closed her eyes and that seemed strange to him. He was feeling cocky, having proved to himself that he knew the angles in Indian fighting. He licked a chapped lip and grinned. "You'll feel better in clean duds," he said. "War is hell."

She plucked his Spencer from the wagon seat and started for the spring.

"Leave that here!" he commanded. He'd worked angles

to get that Spencer because the army was eating them all. And she was treating it as her own.

She ignored him.

He let her go. Maybe there'd be a savage lurking over there. He had recharged his revolver and wore it now. The woman lacked obedience, but he was too elated now to fuss about it. How good to be alive! How fine to smell the sweet sage, and feel the brassy sun on him! How marvelous his Gertie could shrug off an arrow wound! Every breath that filled his lungs gave him joy.

Skye and that heathen were off somewhere, still chasing the redskins, whatever tribe it was. When Skye got back, Alvah intended to cuss him out for coming this way and endangering their lives. But just now, feeling himself lord of this camp, he wanted to celebrate victory, and relive his clever defense.

The lowlifes were wandering about now. Hill had a blood-soaked white bandage tied tightly over his upper left arm. The sluts headed for the spring. Alvah sidled over to the second red wagon and found Vanderbilt within, slumped against the plank wall and staring at him, at his arrow, at nothing. Riddle found a twig and held it against Vanderbilt's boots, taking a measure. They were slightly larger than his own. Vanderbilt stared grayly, saying nothing.

The red box was splintered in a dozen places, he noted. That hide cover the squaws had made let sun through to speckle the inside. One beam struck Vanderbilt's nose. Nothing in the wagon but Vanderbilt and blood and a thousand flies. Alvah took a last look at the boots, gauging them keenly for width. He thought to take them now, but that didn't seem a good angle with Vanderbilt still alert. Alvah smiled at the man.

Skye, Chang, and that Arapaho slut rode down a long red slope, and Alvah scuttled away.

"You. Riddle," came an iron voice behind him. Skye's old squaw. "Sonofabitch, unhitch those mules of yours. They need water. And get them ponies on grass, too. One needs sewing up. Got a crease."

He glared back. "I didn't hire you and I don't take orders from squaws," he said loftily. He didn't know about the wound, and sidled around behind his bedraggled wagon. A bay pony had a long red gash across its chest. It slumped beneath its pack load. He cursed Skye for the wound. He'd find some angle to get even. He always did. He began unharnessing, and led his mules and ponies to some thick bunchgrass where Hill had picketed his. The women were at the spring, so he'd water the animals later. His brides and those sluts, they were there together, he noted.

He peered into his own wagon. It stank of urine.

"How are you, Gertrude?" he asked methodically. He liked to humor her.

"Poorly," she said. "I saw it all coming. The spirit writing. Last night on my slate the hand wrote, 'The living dead, the dead living.' You will have to cook, Alvah. Or get these worthless girls to do it."

"You're a brave woman, Gertie, and I'm proud of you."

No flaw marred the sky and the blue scraped these humped red ridges. He peered around him, enjoying the coolness of the mountains after the July heat of the prairies. They'd have a lot of patching to do here, three or four days probably. He'd have the ladies sew up his wagon sheet and mend harness and cook. The whole wagon stank, and he would have them scrub it out, too. He would be busy, but maybe he'd find time to bore some peepholes in his wagon box with his auger. Ahead, that old squaw Victoria—most annoying old hag—had kindled a tiny fire, not two hands wide, and had a knife blade in it. Fool savage, he thought, ruining the temper of the steel like that. The young squaw lay on her back in the bunchgrass, one foot bared and the red pulpy stump of a big toe projecting, along with tan bone.

The old hag stared at the wound and touched the bone. Mary gasped.

"Got to get the bone," she muttered. She peered up at Alvah. "You. Sit on the leg."

She found two jagged pieces of granite and handed them to Mary. "Hold on tight," she said. Mary nodded.

"I have important work to do," said Alvah, backing off.

Victoria opened a barlow knife and stood. "Hold down the leg or I'll cut you to ribbons," she said.

She made him nervous. The old squaw just might. He peered around wildly. Skye and Chang were at Vanderbilt's wagon. Alvah sat gingerly on top of the leg, facing away from the wound. He didn't know which would be worse—staring at Mary's face, or staring at the surgery. Sweat drenched her honey-colored cheeks.

Victoria grunted. The leg spasmed violently, bucking Riddle high. Mary sobbed and clutched the rocks in her hand. Victoria muttered again, and Mary's golden leg shuddered beneath him.

"Good," said the old crone. Alvah peeped around, and she was holding a shattered piece of bone, yellow and red. The wound gouted blood again. "Now hold leg down again," she said.

He heard sizzling. Mary screamed. The acrid smell of burnt flesh scoured his nostrils. Quite unwillingly, he twisted around and saw the heated blade pressed hard against the wound, making purple smoke and blackening flesh. Victoria grunted.

"Sonofabitch," she said. Riddle sprang up and fled, leaving burnt flesh and Mary's sobs behind him.

If they'd fought his way, with total protection, no one would have been hurt, he thought.

Mister Skye approached him that evening, and Riddle began to cringe. "There's a big hot springs two or three days from here. We're going there and rest up. Shoshone place; maybe Mary's people will be there. She needs that right now . . . We're going to need those ponies of yours, Riddle. Goldtooth lost two more mules, and I lost one. You got one of the ponies harness-broke, and we'll break the others, yoking them with the harness mules. Harness one pony as a wheeler on each wagon. That'll be safe enough, and break them fast. And I need a packhorse. You can throw your loads into Vanderbilt's wagon."

Riddle puffed out. "I didn't hire you and I don't take orders. Them lowlifes can suffer, far as I'm concerned. We can stay right here and rest up. When Vanderbilt's dead, that wagon can be ditched anyway. Besides, Skye, one span's enough to pull an empty wagon."

The guide's blue eyes burned brightly. "Vanderbilt might last a week."

Alvah shrugged. "One span's enough. One of those sluts can drive it."

Mister Skye, still bloody and haggard, glared back. "I'm going to harness your ponies in the morning."

"I'll swear out warrants in Bannack," shouted Alvah. "I'm not under your orders. By the time we get there you'll wish you didn't have me along. You like to got us killed, running instead of forting. Now you're wearing down my ponies for those sluts and lowlifes."

Mister Skye's patience was gone; the blow caught Riddle's chinless pink jaw and spiraled him into grass. He sat dizzily for a moment, then sat up. He never got mad, but he felt a little cross. His revolver nestled in its holster. Not a good angle to pull it now, but later he'd catch Skye and pull the trigger. He'd have to get the squaws too, or they'd kill him.

Mary lay in the rocking wagon for two days, watching the sunlight from the bullet and arrow holes knife bright ribbons within. She had wanted to ride her pony after her foot was cauterized, and no one stopped her from trying. But as soon as she had climbed on, that next morning, she felt faint with pain. Her wounded foot throbbed, and shot an ache up her leg and back, until it exploded in her head. Her Shoshone people had always endured such things, and she intended to, but Victoria frowned and Mister Skye had carried her back to the wagon. In his arms, she was glad.

Now she lay next to the wounded gambler, who was taking his time about dying, and who smelled so vile she could barely stand to be next to him. The women who sold themselves had piled the robes they traded from the Arapahos into the wagon, and Mary and the gambler rode comfortably on these. The one they called Big Alice drove, and had no difficulty with the three mules and unbroke pony that Mister Skye and Blueberry Hill had harnessed each morning.

As long as Mary lay quietly with her foot up, the throbbing could be borne. But the moments when she left the wagon to attend to her needs, or just to escape the rank odor of the rattle-throated gambler, which poisoned all the air inside, she gasped at her hurt. The caravan had topped the Bridgers, lurched on down along a small creek into the Bighorn basin, and rolled toward the great hot spring, Bah-que-wana. That pleased her. It would be a place to wash and heal. It was a favorite medicine place for her people, the Snakes. Maybe, just maybe, some would be there, and the thought excited her. She hadn't seen any of them for three winters.

The gambler said nothing the first day. He lay awake and aware, but lolled quietly, his sallow face dark with fatigue and fever. No one had cleaned him because he would be dead soon, when the rest of his blood poured into his belly. But he lingered and stank, and finally Victoria washed him, cursing all the while. No one cared about the man. Mary thought a foul and sick spirit resided in his mind, and it made his body foul too. Victoria had poured a warm stew into him. He could swallow, but lay inertly, his shallow breath wheezing. Then she and Blueberry Hill had tugged his soiled clothing off, changed the bandages on his suppurating wounds, and clothed him in some britches of Blueberry's. The stink retreated then, and Mary no longer felt like vomiting. Occasionally Big Alice peered in, smiled, and spat.

"I hope you make it, Cornelius," she said amiably. "You old sweetie."

After that bawds came regularly, Goldtooth especially, smiling at Vanderbilt and patting him gently. "You ol' dear," she exclaimed. "You get well now."

On the third day they abandoned the mountains and circled west and south over rugged sage-covered foothills through brutal heat. She knew they were close to the healing place. Game never tarried here, but Chang managed to shoot an antelope two of the three days. Victoria brought them both a broth made from the marrow, saying it would heal. She peered narrowly at Vanderbilt, who seemed neither better nor worse.

"I'm slow to die," he said to Mary that morning. "It's inconvenient. No need to bury me. Let the coyotes clean my bones."

"When a person goes to the Spirit Land, he should be buried properly, as he wants. Some people want the earth. Many of the Indian people want the scaffold, high above, where they give themselves to the great sun," she replied.

"It doesn't matter," he muttered, coughing desperately.

She felt indignant. "Of course it matters! Who are you to scorn the Great One above? Do you think the Great One doesn't care? You must find what honor you can, and present yourself to Him with honor. If you can't think how you want to go, I will tell you. We will make a place in a tree, a cottonwood, and lash many poles there with rawhide, and place you on your back so you face Sun and the One Above, and He can see you. And you will be wrapped up, so nothing eats at your flesh and no animal below, wolf or fox or coyote or skunk, eats of you. Then it will be right and you will be given honor."

"Makes no difference," he muttered. "Not for Homer Donk."

"You have given yourself a new name," she said. "That is good. Our people give themselves many names, and sometimes our medicine men give names to people. The new name is good, and gives a new self. What does Cornelius Vanderbilt mean? It is hard to pronounce."

The gambler lay quietly, panting hard and convulsing, until she thought he'd drifted off, maybe to die. But then he said, "I named myself for a very powerful and wealthy man, who earned a lot of—money, gold—and put it to use, making great boats to sail the seas and take things from place to place. They call him Commodore, which is a name for ones who are the chiefs on the boats . . . I didn't take his name to be like him, but to confuse people into thinking I might be him.''

"You took a great name," she said. "A man with much medicine. And so his medicine worked in you. It is good, as I say. You saved the life of Blueberry Hill. You had only a lance, a staff Mister Skye calls it, and a war club, but you got down from your wagon and saved the life of your friend.''

"I don't have any friends.''

"Now you do," she replied. "Blueberry comes here all the time to help feed and wash you. We must bury you with honor for the One Above. You counted coup twice, and saving a life counts for more, and you are a fine warrior.''

"Waste of energy," he said. "It got me killed.''

"No. Mister Skye says that if you hadn't helped Blueberry when he was unhitching the mules, Blueberry would have been killed, the dead mules would not have been unhitched, and the wagons would all have been stopped in that narrow place, and everyone would be dead now. So, Vanderbilt, you must die good now; you tell us how. Mister Skye, he's got the black book and will read those things of your people.''

"I'm Homer Donk," he said, and closed his eyes.

She lay on her robes, wondering about him, about the unclean yellow-tinged man beside her, and the sickness that ate at him. The close breathless heat of midday passed. The mule teams were sweated and white-caked with alkali dust. No shade sheltered, no water flowed where they nooned; only fragrant sage that had snagged the wagon wheels as they rolled over it, and a furnace-hot earth that scorched and dehydrated them all.

Late in the afternoon she knew they were growing close. They struck the Bighorn River and rolled southward over lush green grasses in its bottoms, back into the jaws of the red mountains. Ahead would be a strange dark canyon with layers of red and purple and pink rock, and dun rock at higher levels, an evil place where this river had pierced through. On the other side, whites called it Wind River. Here, the Bighorn. But before they arrived, they would strike the hot springs, Bah-que-wana, the medicine place of her people, except sometimes the Crows were there, and they would fight.

The gambler studied her. "You're excited about something. We getting to this place?"

"Yes!" she said. "Springs so large the whole side of a hill boils with them, and so hot you can't touch the water. The hot water runs south, over white terraces for a little way, and then into the Bighorn River. And there are many places to bathe and wash, where the water is cool enough. It is a great medicine place. Do you see? It has powers from the Unseen Ones. I can feel the powers, and so can Victoria and her Absaroka people, and so can Mister Skye. We will take you to the place and let the medicine powers heal you. You have lived this far; maybe the One Above wants you to make good medicine here."

"Healed for what?" he asked.

"To be what you will be. You need a new name. Vanderbilt was a good name, but now we need a name that says you saved us. You came out of your wagon cave like a bear, a sleeping bear. I will name you Sleeping Bear. No man disturbs a sleeping bear, but walks softly around."

Cornelius smiled at her. She had never seen him smile.

"Maybe I did better than Riddle," he said. "We're both hidey-hole types, but I got out of my hole. Makes me feel not so bad about kicking off."

Mary heard excitement ahead, exclamations and a quickening of the pace, and then they were there, at this familiar sacred place. From the base of a steep sage-covered hill waters gushed from sandstone lips, steaming even on this hot day, and spraying an acrid odor upon the breeze. She clambered up now beside Big Alice, enjoying the scenes, noting the small medicine cairns left here by her people and other people: feathers, small skins, a hawk's head, shining white stones. The sacredness infused her with a rush. She felt the holiness in a ball just under her lungs. This was where Earth Mother and the One

Above brought Snake people to heal body and soul. Mary's eyes glowed.

Game didn't visit here, though sometimes a doe might be taken in the bottoms, or an antelope, so people did not stay long. But she hoped to collect greens and herbs from the Bighorn River bottoms, especially the wild asparagus. She frowned. She could not walk. But it made little difference. Victoria would. The white people were dropping from their wagons now, staring at this place of the hot waters, testing with their fingers.

She felt the power of this place infuse her, and turned to the gambler. "Maybe these waters will heal you," she said.

"Royal flush," the gambler whispered.

Chapter 22

This was a hard-used place, without grass or game. The dun earth lay naked. Mister Skye doubted there'd be an antelope or mule deer or duck or a rabbit within miles, a worrisome thing with most of his party depending entirely on game. Nor would there be vegetables and herbs because it all had been picked over. He thought some of tarrying here an hour or two, and then rolling on down the Bighorn to good grass. But he gave up the thought as fast as it formed in his mind. This party needed these springs and a chance to heal.

A few shallow pools, inches deep, hoarded water cool enough for bathing, but these were as naked as everything else here. The women looked longingly at the delicious water, and turned instead to laundering. They would bathe tonight. Drusilla emerged from her wagon with a small washboard, a ball of orange lye soap, and a pile of filthy clothes. The bawds, wearing fine doeskin dresses and skirts, were less in need, but thought to wash what they could. Mrs. Parkins appeared in her thin wrapper, and proceeded to splash into the middle of a pool. The white wrapper clung translucently to her, and stirred Mister Skye's loins. Mary-Rita clucked and scolded at the sight, finally silenced by Mrs. Parkins's raucous laugh.

Mister Skye sighed. He felt tired and filthy himself, and brown blood crusted the gouge above his ear. He found Blueberry Hill unhitching the mules and ponies from red wagons.

"No grass. We'll have to drive them down the bottoms until we find some, graze them until dusk under guard, and then picket them here," he said. His beaten and wounded animals wouldn't get much of a meal tonight.

Blueberry nodded. "Lots of hours to dark," he said. "They'll get a bellyful. You want me to guard?"

"We'll divide that. There's you, me, Riddle, and Victoria to do it, and I don't trust Riddle. Chang's out hunting and scouting. We'll be lucky if he makes meat. I'd just as soon let Victoria tend to Mary and Vanderbilt and keep things in order here. So it's you and me, Mister Hill."

Riddle's mules and ponies remained hitched, and the man had disappeared toward the springs. Mister Skye found him sitting slightly above the woman, gawking at Mrs. Parkins.

"Unhitch your stock, Riddle. It's a mile or so to grass."

"Mine to do with as I want. You got no right—"

Mister Skye grabbed a handful of sweaty shirt and yanked Riddle upright. "We will walk in one of two directions. Up above there, where the springs boil up, or down to your stock. If we walk up there, I will sit you in a pool and boil your meat."

Riddle grabbed at his holstered Remington, but Skye batted his pink arm away.

"You got no right!" Riddle said. "I'm going to let them graze tonight where there's grass."

"You'd likely never see them again."

"Who says? You think you know everything, but you haven't got half the angles. I'll picket them down there. You can guard if you're so worried about it. They'll be in river brush. Who'll see them?"

Mister Skye dragged Riddle toward the hottest pools.

"You're making extry work. Walking them clear to grass, then back down here. I got enough to do without all that extry—"

They'd reached a hot steaming pool just below the cliff-slope. The steam smelled slightly of minerals. Mister Skye poised the paunchy pink man on the lip, and he shrank from the heat.

"You're trying to kill me!"

"That's about right. Put a finger in, Riddle. The rest of you will follow."

Riddle sank down, and jabbed a finger in, and yanked it out.

"I'll move my stock," he said sourly. "Not that it makes a bit of sense. You make work for everyone here, don't know how to deal with savages—"

Mister Skye shoved him, and Riddle staggered.

"I'll kill you, Skye."

"It's Mister Skye."

They trudged a long way to grass, but eventually the mules and horses spread out on lush yellow-dried bottom grass in an area thick with brush. Riddle complained the whole distance.

"I'll take the first watch," said Blueberry. "I'm feeling poorly, and I'll get this over with."

He carried the double-barreled scattergun. "You need more," Mister Skye said. "Riddle here will lend you his revolver."

"My property! Don't you touch—"

But Mister Skye's massive hands had already pinioned the man and were undoing the belt. He tossed it to Blueberry.

"Here's a few more, for a jam," he said. "I'll be here in a couple of hours." He peered around sharply, studying the low bluffs on both sides. Jawbone looked bad to him, limping slightly and crusted with blood in three places. "Eat," he said to the animal. Jawbone did not lift his head from the grass. In about two hours, the horse would appear in camp. "Jawbone will come in when he wants," Skye said to Blueberry.

Riddle stomped sullenly all the way back.

The women had bathed, and sundry items of clothing lay whitely over sage bushes, leached by dry air and a plummeting sun. Seven-Story Chang and Buffalo Whiskers had returned to camp empty-handed. Mary had scrubbed herself clean and rested before Mister Skye's lodge.

"Riddle," he said. "Maybe you'd be willing to share some airtights and your staples tonight."

"Why should I share—those lowlifes—" he sputtered.

"Didn't hear you refusing when we brought in buffler days on end."

"That's different. You're being paid to—"

"We'll do without, then."

"Now I didn't say that. Didn't say that. Just seems like a little trade here, a little exchange, that's the fair thing. A robe. A robe for—"

"We'll do without. I'd like to borrow your auger and a five-eighths bit."

"What in tarnation do you want that for? What are you offering for the use?"

"Protection, Riddle. Protection."

He didn't wait for an answer, but clambered into Riddle's wagon, pawed among barrels and crates until he found Riddle's toolbox, and the auger and bit he wanted. When he emerged, Riddle hopped from one foot to the other.

"You got no right!" he raged.

"I'll return it directly." Mister Skye turned away.

He found Victoria. "I'm going to need a heap of firewood from someplace," he said. She eyed the auger curiously but said nothing. Then she padded toward the river. She would find fuel, Mister Skye knew. She found it where others found only rock. He would need plenty of it.

He found Vanderbilt sprawled in the red wagon, smelling bad.

"You up to a bath, mate?"

"Makes no difference whether I die dirty or clean. The

wounds aren't closed. Might as well let water in as blood out.''

"I'm thinking you won't die. That arrow missed your lights and you've got most of your blood.''

"Let's go then.''

Mister Skye carried the gambler to a pool and set him in gently. Vanderbilt was too weak to sit up, and lolled back, his head resting on whited rock.

"The flow will do the work, mate.''

"Stings the wounds, but who cares . . . Say, Skye? When I kick off, put me up on a scaffold. Mary gave me a name I like, Sleeping Bear. Say a kind word about Sleeping Bear.''

"She told me,'' said Mister Skye. "It's a name you earned. You did a fine brave thing, Sleeping Bear. Think about living.''

"Water feels good, except for the stings. I must stink. Maybe it's in my flesh and won't wash out. Souls stink too.''

"I'll be back or send someone in a few minutes. If you get too hot in there, speak up.''

The gambler peered up, face gray, and nodded.

Mister Skye sagged on his feet, and his head wound throbbed. He'd dip into the pool himself later, after his guard shift with the stock, and after he had taken care of other matters. He found the camp axe and set off toward the river, passing Victoria, who had miraculously accumulated a pile of small sticks. Everything here had been stripped by passing bands. He found a small cottonwood at last, its lower limbs hacked off to the height of a man on horseback. He ratcheted his way up between two trunks, to a fork in one, and then hacked at a four-inch limb until it dropped. He chopped off two feet of it and abandoned the rest. In camp he skinned two opposite sides flat with the axe and then drilled a dozen short holes in one flattened side, each hole bored five-eighths inch deep.

Seven-Story watched. "You Occidentals are inscrutable,'' he said. "You must be saving face.''

"Something like that," said Mister Skye. He drilled a dozen more holes on the other flat side.

The time arrived for his shift. Victoria was back and soon would have some jerky and herbs boiling into some kind of thin soup, but he would wait. "I'll need some dry wood later," he reminded her. "Relieving Blueberry now. Maybe I can collect some while I guard."

She peered up at him, at his strange stick, and grinned.

It seemed a long walk down the river bottoms in long light, and he felt wearier than he could remember. The fight with the Gros Ventre still lay heavily on him, sapping something vital from him. He'd gotten them through. Vanderbilt might well live. All the other wounds would heal. But he grew tired, tired of guiding greenhorns and porkeaters and pilgrims, tired of dealing with people like Riddle who showed up in some parties. He'd had a full life, had taken his fill of it, and not much mattered now . . .

He found the mules and horses cropping quietly, some of them hidden by brush. No sign of Blueberry. "Hill," he said softly in a voice that would jab through dusk, "it's Skye. Watch your trigger finger."

Silence.

He heard a rustle of hoof, and Jawbone emerged from a thicket, his jaw working methodically.

He didn't like it much. He unfastened his holster, and checked his Sharps. He had one paper cartridge chambered, and his last six cartridges in a pocket.

He prowled the twilight, through grassy parks dotted with thickets of brush. The horses and mules cropped peacefully. Most were free-herded, but Riddle had hobbled his Indian ponies.

"Over here, Mister Skye."

"I didn't see you in the twilight."

"White people don't see blacks."

"There's something wrong with you." Hill lay heavily against an ancient cottonwood trunk decaying in the grass.

"I reckon that's so," said Hill. "It's hitting me bad now."

Mister Skye squatted down, suddenly filled with foreboding.

"I got the distemper of the blood," said Hill. "From the wound. The streaks coming out from it, both sides of the gouge. I've seen those streaks before. It's the distemper. Streaks shooting out."

"Let me see," said Mister Skye. The arm had swollen and Blueberry had slit his sleeve to accommodate it. The guide unwrapped the bandage and stared at the pulpy furrow. Even in twilight it looked angry. "I don't think it's mortifying. It doesn't smell mortifying," he said.

"Nope. Not the gangrene. It's the bad blood, making me hot and sucking everything out of me."

"My friend Jim Bridger always says, 'Meat don't spile in the mountains,' Blueberry. I'll take you back in. Maybe Victoria's got something. She's got herbs . . ."

"I don't rightly think I can make it. I won't get to the mountains, Mister Skye. Not the real ones. Not the ones off west, with snow on the roof, that we've been seeing all day. Maybe up there meat don't spoil, but here it does."

"The Absarokas," said the guide. "The roof of the world, the mountain men call them."

"I'm not going to see them. Not with the distemper of the blood."

"You didn't say anything. How long . . . ?"

"Started to get bad yesterday. No, I didn't say anything. I wanted to do my share and more."

"More? You're the most valuable man I've got."

"Worth more than two thousand dollars?"

Mister Skye nodded. The light was fading fast.

"I don't rightly figure I was a free man until we got west of Fort Laramie. I never knew who'd tie me up and haul me back. Lots of Southerners out here. But after Laramie, and after you took us up, I got to thinking this is how it is, this owning myself at last. But I've been studying and observing, Mister Skye. Long as I didn't own myself, I did as little as possible—just enough to escape the whip and beating. But there wasn't a reason in the wide world to do more, you see? But men who own themselves, they've got to work hard. No one's going to take care of them but themselves. So a free man has got to treat his own property good. I figured I would have to get rid of a whole lifetime of doing as little as possible, and start doing as much as I could so's to make myself valuable. I started that, some, working for Goldtooth, but I wasn't really free there. I figured maybe if I could be valuable, she'd maybe hide me out if they came after me . . . but I wasn't owning myself yet.''

"It's not over, mate. You're my best man. We'll get you to the wagon now. You should have said something—''

Blueberry Hill didn't respond for a while. "No, I can tell I got to be a freeman for a few weeks, and got to taste the burden of it. Freemen got a burden on them, fierce weight. No one takes care of them. They can starve and die too easy. Not sure I want all this freedom and weight on my shoulders, Mister Skye.''

The guide made his decision. He found Jawbone and led him to Blueberry. He hoisted the burly black onto his horse's back, staggering under the man's inert weight. But Blueberry, too weak to hang on, started to slide off. It wasn't going to work. He lifted Blueberry off and settled him next to the fallen cottonwood again.

"I'm going to move camp to here," he said. "I'll bring back Victoria directly.''

He clambered wearily onto Jawbone, and tried to herd the mules back to the hot springs, but they wanted to graze, and dodged around the tired man and tired horse. He finally caught one of Riddle's hobbled ponies, unhobbled it and led it back to camp.

He found Victoria before their lodge. Mary lay there too, on a robe.

"Blueberry's in a bad way," he said.

Wordlessly the tired old woman rose, and ducked into the lodge. He heard her rummaging. He collected halters and picket lines, and saddled Jawbone, who slouched wearily, the feist out of him. Darkness crept close, save for the tiny fire Victoria had built of twigs. Then the weary guide and his tired woman rode down the bottoms of the

Bighorn River, to the herd, and Blueberry. She slid off the pony and pressed her palm to Hill's forehead.

"He is very hot. Get him some water," she said. "I will need a fire to see . . ."

He trudged toward the river with a skin waterbag, while she examined his wound in the darkness. By the time he returned she had gathered kindling from the profuse thickets here, and was striking flint to steel, directing sparks into a tiny ball of cottony tinder. In a few minutes she had a small blaze, and examined the swollen arm. Blueberry watched inertly, aware but not wasting energy on words.

"Sonofabitch!" she exclaimed crossly.

The tired guide bridled six mules and dragged them back to the hot spring.

"We're moving camp about a mile," he said shortly. "Seven-Story, I'd be grateful if you'd harness Goldtooth's wagons."

The mandarin sprang silently to work.

"Not me. We're settled for the night," protested Riddle.

Mister Skye didn't have the strength to argue. "All right then. The rest of us are moving, Riddle, and you can stay here alone."

"Now wait a minute! What's your angle, Skye?"

Mister Skye didn't answer. He hunkered down beside Mary, slipping his hard hand into her tiny one. "I'm going to put you back in the wagon for a bit, and all our truck, too. The lodge and the poles and the parfleches. Hate to do it."

She smiled, and hugged him as he lifted her wearily. "I am glad you are here to hold me," she whispered. "You will tell me soon why we do this."

"Blueberry's dying."

While Chang harnessed, he loaded his whole lodge into the wagon, finding room around Mary and Vanderbilt.

Riddle danced around doing nothing. "Seems to me, you can be harnessing me up, seeing as how you're making the extry work," he said.

Mister Skye addressed Riddle's women. "You will be safer coming with us," he said.

Drusilla and Mary-Rita came at once, and clambered into the bawds' wagon, sitting beside Big Alice.

"Now see here—" yelled Riddle, but the rest rode out into solemn darkness, with only starlight to guide them. Mister Skye rode quietly beside Chang and Buffalo Whiskers, who were driving a red wagon.

"Our friend Blueberry has the fevers and bad blood. Sinking fast. I couldn't get him back here, so we're going there."

Chang said nothing. There was only the soft clop of mule hoofs on the hardpan. "Yin and yang," he muttered at last.

They made a dark camp by the sliver of a moon, on a flat near the river, but far enough back so they could hear the sounds of the night. Mister Skye carried Blueberry Hill from the thicket where he lay, and lowered him onto a robe before his lodge. Victoria muttered and despaired. The swollen arm had a poultice of herbs over it, but Blueberry was sinking.

At last they were settled, and Mister Skye hunkered down beside Blueberry.

"Anyone you want to know? Any message you've got?" he asked harshly.

Blueberry sighed, words coming hard. "Hardly know my parents. I got taken away and sold at ten. They wouldn't know me. No more than a cow knows a calf after a few years. The girl . . ." He paused. "Lou. Bought by Spiller. I don't know the rest. Two counties west, is all . . . No. A slave gets born alone, lives alone, dies alone . . ."

"Not alone," said Mister Skye tightly.

"Alone," said Blueberry. He closed his eyes and wouldn't talk.

An hour later, Riddle drove in and made camp. At dawn, Blueberry lay unconscious. He lingered on for three days, feverish and delirious at first, and finally quiet, hot, and barely breathing. While Blueberry Hill slipped into his death agony, the party rested and healed. Hours on end, Goldtooth held his hand in her own while tears rimmed her eyes. Big Alice, too, hovered over him, caressing him with rough warm fingers. The third night, Blueberry's breathing became shallow and irregular. Then, near dawn, it stopped. Across that morning, Mister Skye built a scaffold. He and Chang wrapped Blueberry tightly in a good robe and laid him on his back, eight feet above the earth, his face toward the sun. Mister Skye found his ancient Bible and read from the last chapter of Deuteronomy. It struck him that Blueberry had left slavery behind and headed for his Promised Land, only to die with his goal in sight. Drusilla led a prayer of her own creation, one she had penned that morning. Her voiced trembled.

Sleeping Bear, propped up in the wagon so he could see, wept bitter tears.

Chapter 23

For two more days they tarried in the bottoms of the Bighorn while stock fattened and healed. Victoria liked the place, except for the swarms of insects, especially the big stinging horseflies. Seven-Story Chang and Buffalo Whiskers rode out each day to scout and hunt, but returned empty-handed. Mister Skye had done a little better. Downriver he found a slough with mud hens, and shot seven with his scattergun. Here the herbs and roots had escaped squaw baskets, and Victoria was able to make a stew to sustain them.

Each day she had escorted the women back to the hot springs to bathe and wash clothing, hovering nearby on her pony and well armed. The barriers between these strange white women had broken down, and the ones who sold themselves mingled with the ones who didn't. Even Gertrude Riddle came along the second day, bathing silently. Victoria watched keenly for visitors, but the hot springs remained deserted in the ruthless July sun.

She thought about the morning that Mister Skye had lifted Blueberry Hill to his scaffold, and the gambler Van-

derbilt had started to weep. That was a strange thing. She
thought she'd never understand white people. But he wept,
lying in his hot wagon with tears leaking from his eyes
and flies crawling over him. What sort of dark spirits possessed a soul like that? No one could know, she thought.

At her lodge, things became happier. She had rolled up
the cover to let the breezes through, and had built a brush
arbor beside it, where she worked. Mary lay on a robe,
making moccasins for the women. Mister Skye rested too.
Like all of them, he had bathed and freshened his clothing. The red bandana that held his hair also covered his
scalp wound, and Victoria had scrubbed it until there was
no blood or grime staining it.

That morning he gathered bone-dry sticks and built a
hot fire between some rocks he had gathered. He borrowed her frying pan, dropped a bar of galena into it, and
waited until the lead slowly dissolved into silvery hot liq-
uid. Then he carefully poured it into each of the holes he
had drilled in the cottonwood stick. It spat and smoked,
and the lead slowly hardened while he watched.

Now she understood.

"I got seven paper cartridges left, and it's getting worrisome," he muttered as he waited for the lead to cool.
"No mould for this .60 Sharps, but here you have to make
do, make do."

When the lead seemed solid, he rapped his stick sharply,
and the bullets fell into the grass. He still could not touch
them, but he filled his bored holes a second time.

When he could pick them up at last, he studied each
one, rejecting two that seemed slightly oval. With his knife
he pared the front ends into smooth cones. "Five-eighths
bit should yield a sixty-two caliber bullet," he muttered.
He slid open the slant breech of his Sharps and nestled a
heavy bullet into the bore. It resisted. He jammed harder
but the bullet wouldn't seat. "Too large," he said. "The
lead burned out the wood. It didn't work."

She understood little of the arithmetic. No bullets. He'd
tried to protect her, as he always did. He had medicine to
make everything work, made do with anything and every-

thing on the trail, but this time he'd failed. She studied him darkly.

Irritably he tried a half-inch auger, but it proved too small. Nothing worked, and he gave up. "Seven shots for the Sharps," he growled. "I'd better buy a sixty-caliber mould when we get there and not rely on paper cartridges."

Over at the Riddle wagon, Alvah seemed uncharacteristically busy. He had stripped off the wagon sheet and had set his three women to sewing up the holes in it. He had heated up the remaining tar in his bucket, and the women daubed each mend with it to waterproof the canvas. He spent a morning fashioning a sort of splint for the bullet-shattered wheel spoke by wrapping it in soaked rawhide he got from Victoria. It dried into a bandage of steel.

At Goldtooth's red wagon, the women likewise worked on the wagon sheet and their clothing and moccasins. They had no needles and thread, having lost them in the storm, but Victoria proffered an awl and thong and the bawds put them to good use. They didn't bother with Vanderbilt's wagon, or the bullet holes in its cowhide cover. Once in a while Victoria heard him weeping there, or muttering to himself, and she knew dark spirits possessed him. She didn't want to go near him or meet this evil of his.

Still, at noon she took him a bowl of broth, and he drank it gratefully. "You are good. Skye's lucky," he said.

"Sonofabitch, but you got the bad medicine in you," she said, tarrying beside this strange white man.

"A good man died and I live," he muttered. "He was a good man. I am a coward."

"Sleeping Bear came out of his cave and fought."

"Names. I'm Homer Donk. Born and raised near the United States Naval Yard in Brooklyn, third largest city in the United States, and they didn't miss me a bit."

"This name you don't like. Homer. What is this name?"

"Bad name to saddle a boy with. All the boys called me Homer the Donkey. They teased and teased, and beat me up. But I got even. I learned to skin them good, get their marbles and jackstraws out of them.''

"What is this name, Homer?'' Victoria persisted.

Sleeping Bear lay back, his eyes soft. "Homer was a great man long ago, long long ago. He made poems, the *Iliad*, the *Odyssey* . . .'' He paused, seeing incomprehension. "He sang songs about the stories of his people, the greatness and courage of his people, and their foolishness too. He was the one to keep their history for them.''

"Ah, we have those too. We have the ones to keep the past and tell it. They are sacred ones among us. But we don't call them Homers. They are the holy ones, among the Absaroka. If you are named for a holy one, how come you don't like it?''

"I was a boy. Boys are cruel . . . They teased until I hated being Homer.''

"Sonofabitch,'' she muttered. "How could that be? You got a good name and you got ashamed of it. What is Donk?''

"Dutch. That's Dutch.''

"What is Dutch? I never heard Dutch. Are they bad people?''

He shook his head. "No, it's just a funny name. Strange name. Vanderbilt is Dutch too.''

"Why do you weep?''

"Because I can't stop it. I took an arrow and should be up on that platform. All I did. All I skinned. All I took. I should be up there.''

"You don't like it that you gambled bad?''

He shook his head and the tears came again. "Wasted life,'' he muttered. "Skinned a thousand people, even the poor, took as I could.''

She shook her head. This was a strange thing. "Can you walk as far as my lodge?''

She supported him as he staggered toward the brush arbor she had built, and soon helped settle him on a robe there.

She eyed him sharply. "We got to make big medicine now, drive away the bad spirits.''

She bustled out, gathering sweetgrass and stalks of sage.

Mary stopped lacing up a moccasin and watched, approval in her soft brown eyes. Victoria kindled a tiny fire in the shade of the arbor, and let it burn hotly for a while.

"Now, Homer Donk," she said. "I burn the sweetgrass and sage and you lean over the smoke, make the sweet smoke flow around your body. You do that, and make the sour go away."

She threw grass and sage into the hot coals and white smoke billowed up, pungent and scented sweet. She beckoned. He stared, uncertainly, and then crawled over and bathed his yellowish torso in the smoke for a moment. Then he pulled back.

"No. Stay in the smoke," she said sharply.

"Now," she droned, "the smoke of the clean sage and the sweetgrass is bathing you, making you clean. Spirits making you clean. Now the One Above likes the scent. Now the One Above looks kindly on you . . ."

For an hour she made her medicine. She painted him with umber clay mixed with grease. She daubed white clay on his chest in the shape of a cross, the white men's medicine symbol. She found her gourd rattles and rattled away the demon spirits. And when she finished, Sleeping Bear was asleep, and his face looked peaceful.

"We make him a child, and he starts over," she muttered. "He's damn sorry about the old self. We give him a new one."

Wearily, she packed up her paints and rattles, and trudged through the hot of the afternoon until she found Blueberry's scaffold.

There she sat. "You," she said. "You had a good spirit and now you gone to the other side. Before you go, you gave it to Sleeping Bear, hey? I watch. I watch all the people Mister Skye guides. You worked the hardest. Never complained. Always helping those women, or the rest. I'm gonna remember you, Blueberry Hill."

She felt an ineffable sadness as she sat there in the shadow of the scaffold. It was good to feel a sadness. That meant that he had made his way into her soul. She sat in

the quietness, and at some time Mister Skye joined her.
They sat quietly in the shadow of Blueberry, and he held
Victoria's hand, loving her.

They rolled north, along the west bank of the Bighorn,
encountering few difficulties except for an occasional draw
that forced them to detour around its head. Often Mister
Skye took them a mile or so west of the river, which lay
greenly off to the right. The sun blazed hot, and dun alkali
dust lifted into the air by metal tires covered them all.
They found no shade in these rolling sage-dotted plains,
and the noonings under the hammering July sun were quiet
and miserable. The air became so suffocating that Mister
Skye let them dally for two or three hours midday, but
pushed them onward in the long summer evenings.

Drusilla had taken to driving Vanderbilt's wagon, and
within a day Mary-Rita had joined her. They both had
come to loathe Alvah Riddle so intensely that it was a
relief to slip away from his green wagon and the increasingly peculiar Gertrude.

"That's a good angle," he said at last. "Lightens the
load on my stock. Yes, good angle. But when we get to
Bannack, I don't want you driving any red wagon or being
anywhere near those lowlifes."

"Respectability is where you find it," Drusilla replied.

She had taught herself to harness, and each day unhobbled or unpicketed three of Goldtooth's mules and one of
Riddle's ponies and readied them.

It enraged Alvah. "If you kin do that for the lowlifes,
you kin do it for me. I got enough work, without any
help from you. The contract says you're under my direction—"

Drusilla wearied of contracts. They made less sense here
in these vast alkali flats. Life imposed larger contracts,
she thought, obligations to one another here where the
well-being of each affected the others. She had simply
turned her back and continued to settle collars over necks,
tighten surcingles, slip on bridles, and hook animals into
the traces.

"I forbid it!" cried Alvah, but he addressed the wind.

With Blueberry gone, Big Alice had taken to driving the bawds' wagon, handling the chores just as easily as Blueberry had. Mary was riding again and ignoring the throb in her foot, herding Mister Skye's pack and travois animals. Victoria scouted ahead and left, while Seven-Story and Buffalo Whiskers probed along the river bottoms to the right, scouting and hunting game. They'd found very little. It seemed as if every deer and antelope in the basin had fled to the mountains until the heat broke. Riddle grumbled about using up his stores. They turned in the evenings back to the river, and there Victoria managed to find roots and herbs, wild onions and turnips, to fill out rabbit or duck or sage-hen stews.

While Drusilla drove, Vanderbilt recovered strength daily, and felt able to attend to his needs and join the others for meals. He said nothing, and Drusilla was in no mood to encourage talk. Her thoughts settled constantly on Parsimony McGahan, wending his way toward far Nevada and the Comstock. She thought also of her husband-to-be in Bannack, and subdued her yearnings with the knowledge that she would be well wed at last, and fortunate for it.

She enjoyed Mary-Rita's company, pleased that the Irish girl kept quiet and held her mean tongue. This vast hot dry land, wild Indians and peculiar Americans, had been so strange to her that she had finally quieted, having run out of words.

"You drive the mules well," Mary-Rita ventured one day, and the kind word surprised Drusilla.

"Would you like to try it? I'll walk a little," she replied.

Fearfully Mary-Rita took the eight lines, and Drusilla stepped down into the dust and began stretching her legs. Her skirts caught on sagebrush, but she had no trouble keeping up with the lagging animals on this furnace of a day.

The next day Vanderbilt asked if he might join them on

the seat, and soon he tried the lines for a while, until he tired.

"Perhaps you can advise me," he said abruptly to Drusilla. "I wish to begin a new profession, or living, and I don't know what I'm fitted for. I have no skills, but I have fast hands."

"You might tend bar in a saloon," said Drusilla.

"I would rather not, Miss Dinwiddie," he replied, and she felt sorry. She had suggested something respectable enough, but he hoped to escape the sporting life altogether.

She tried to think. He hadn't the muscled body of a farmer or teamster, and probably couldn't handle heavy labor. "Perhaps a clerk, Mister Vanderbilt."

He smiled softly. "I'd take it kindly if you'd call me Sleeping Bear. The name reminds me of something in me I didn't know was there."

"I will do that."

"There will be many camps who will know me—a gambler and a . . . tinhorn. I don't suppose anyone will let me try to be something else . . ."

"I will put my mind to it, Mister—Sleeping Bear. I don't know what trades and services are needed in these camps."

"I've never thought about it," he said. "I only know I took an arrow clear through, and I'm alive to tell about it. I suppose if there's a God, he had something to do with it."

Mary-Rita blessed herself. "It was a saint, some saint," she muttered. "Looking out. I don't know the patron saint of gamblers."

Clear across the northern horizon lay a featureless blue mountain, and to the east the Bighorns edged closer and closer as if to herd them west. But off to the west lay formidable peaks still topped with white in late July. Now at last Mister Skye left the Bighorn River, and that night they reached an alkaline slow river he called the Greybull. They crossed it with surprising difficulty, miring in a soft gumbo that sucked at hoofs and wheels. They were heading for Pryor Gap, Mister Skye had explained, and once through that, they'd be in Yellowstone country, and back in the best game area in the Far West, including buffalo.

No Indians disturbed their passage and it dawned on Drusilla that the Indians, like migratory creatures, would be in cooler country this time of year. She learned they were passing through the lands of the Absaroka, or Crow, Victoria's people, but she saw no sign of anticipation on Victoria's face.

One nooning, as she lay indolently in the open shade beneath the wagon, she realized she had changed. In fact they had all changed for better or worse. This hard free land of long peaces and short terrors had annealed her body and soul. She had walked across much of a continent, and now her legs were hard and her ungainly hips much reduced. Her bust and shoulders were fuller and her arms strong. In fact her proportions had found a balance, which pleased her. But beyond that, the rigors of the trail had made her different, more tolerant. She had long since stopped sniffing at Mister Skye and his women. She admired them as models for all who pierced into the wilderness. She had befriended bawds and found them not at all what she had thought. She had always thought that women were forced into that degraded life by desperation, but now she discovered that some women sought it and enjoyed it. Indeed, both Goldtooth and Mrs. Parkins had come from comfortable circumstances. And she suspected that Juliet Picard had a similar background. It surprised her. There was so much that she, in her New England puritan way, had never known and never dreamed.

Sleeping Bear, whose ordeal still crushed him, was being transformed by it, and she felt curious about how he would turn out; whether he'd slip back into his old ways at Bannack. Blueberry Hill had changed, too, becoming industrious and eager and steadfast as the days rolled by. For a while she grieved his loss, coming just as he had blossomed open to the western winds. Mary-Rita, lying beside her, had become subdued and was making some tentative gestures toward accepting others. Would she, too, revert after she married into a vicious-tongued harridan? And Chang. Ah, there was a mystery. She didn't fathom him, and therefore was not sure how this vast exodus across an empty dangerous land had changed him. He was a hard and competent warrior when he began, perhaps as much at home here as upon the deserts and steppes of central Asia. But happy he was, and his bride had become a partner, a unity, with him. Drusilla thought of them riding off each day, beyond the vision of this little caravan, and she knew they found some small Eden and made love there, day after day. The thought quickened her pulse and filled her with some unfathomable yearning for that mystery to unfold in her. For a moment she felt loss.

Curious about herself, she found her looking glass among her things, and stared, barely recognizing the image. Her flesh golden and her cheeks suffused with color. She had gone from soft and white and pinch-faced, to lean and brown. Her lips no longer compressed into lines of disapproval and superiority. Even her hair, sunbleached, seemed softer and looser than when it was severely brushed, parted, and bunned. Oh, if only Parsimony could see her now!

The very thought saddened her, but she dealt well with fragile if-onlys, and thought resolutely instead of the abstract man awaiting her at the end of this journey. It had never occurred to her she had become beautiful, but she knew she was as hard as granite.

A few days later they toiled through Pryor Gap into the Yellowstone country, and the world around her transformed. Here raced icy clear creeks among verdant stretching meadows, and jackpined slopes and yellow rimrock. And the dome of heaven rose bluer than sapphires. They were all wondrously changed, and especially Victoria, who had been reincarnated as a bold young woman.

Chapter 24

Was there ever such a land? Did ever the Absaroka people want for anything in a land like this? This homecoming infused Victoria with an elementary joy that she could not hold within her small withered frame. Each day, as they probed deeper into the Yellowstone country, Victoria grew younger and brighter, until she seemed a shining-eyed girl to those around her.

She had not expected to see her land ever again, or her people, the Kicked-in-the-Bellies band of the mountain Crows. She was old and life perilous, and Mister Skye not as strong and wary as he once had been. So she had made her peace with the future, knowing that someplace unexpected, she would cross over to the Other Side without knowing what children had been born in her village, or who had gone to the Other Side, or who had counted coup against the Siksika, or who had become a war chief or headman.

But here they were, toiling over vast hills that spurred out of the blue mountains to the south, in the land of her fathers and mothers. Almost imperceptibly, she assumed the task of guiding these white people through the tumbled country she knew in her bones and flesh. Each sunny day she rode out ahead of the wagons, finding a path through a tumultuous land full of rushing creeks of clear snow-melt, lush green bottoms, long ridges black with ponderosa pine, and long plateaus of gnarled cedar and purple sagebrush. She spotted game everywhere, does and bucks parading along cottonwood groves or up in aspen, antelope in white-rumped bunches darting down ridges, and grizzly too, although she saw only the awesome scratches on trees, taller than a man could reach. Absaroka! Abundant land! Plain and mountain, buffalo and berries, cool and warm!

This was tricky country for wagons, and often she sat on a ridge, crystalline air playing with the mane of her pony, while far below they double-teamed a wagon to haul it up a steep grade. On top of these vast slopes, they could survey the whole universe, the shoulders of the Absaroka Mountains rearing to the south and west, and the tumbled dun plains north and east, and sometimes the distant tawny cut of the river the whites called Yellowstone, but her people called the Elk. Not the slightest haze dulled this clean air, and sometimes they could look to the edge of the world. Mister Skye called it a hundred miles.

She grew impatient with them and their cumbersome wagons, and at every rise she scanned her world eagerly, with keen old eyes, hunting sign of her people. She would find them eventually. She would cut a trail of ponies, or the furrows of travois, or run into young warriors out stealing horses, or find medicine symbols of feather or hair or birdbone on cairns, or dangling from trees, telling her in their mysterious ways who had come here or what had happened or where someone had gone.

In the camps each evening they noticed the change in her and teased her, and Mister Skye grinned, knowing everything there was to know about her. Meat became abundant, and they grew strong on the best cuts of elk and deer. Even the gambler, Sleeping Bear, flourished on red meat, up and about several hours each day, doing what chores he could. He was harnessing his wagon without help now, and unharnessing evenings, which spread the burdens.

Still her Kicked-in-the-Bellies eluded her, and she decided they were farther west this summer, maybe in the dreaming intimate valley of the Boulder or one of its branches, where game grew thick and the summer breezes flowed cool. She herself left signs of their passage now, the sign for Skye they all knew, the sign for the trapper and guide white man who had become a friend and occasional war ally of the Absaroka people. She felt secure here, even though the terrible Siksika sometimes raided deep in Absaroka, and others as well—the Teton Dakota, the Assiniboin, and even the Cheyenne. They reached the Stillwater on a hot day early in the moon her husband called August. She crossed several trails but they were old and sunwashed and told her only that her people had stayed upstream earlier. But she had come close, and the nearness of her tribe and clan-family infused her. Her medicine toyed with her, delaying the moment she could hug her sisters and babble half a night in the lodges of her brothers, and pay her respects to Many Coups.

Sonofabitch! she thought. How would she explain these strange people to her own? There weren't good Absaroka words to describe the brides, or their chaperones. This man is not their father? they would say. How can that be? The others, the women who sold themselves, she could explain. That practice the Absaroka people knew all about. Her people professed virtue and enjoyed lust. From the days of the fur trappers, husbands had sold wives to white men, often for the price of a cup of mountain whiskey— grain alcohol, diluted with water, with a plug of tobacco and some pepper for taste—or beads or foofaraw. Victoria laughed. Absaroka women had sat at the campfires of these white men and told them the bawdiest imaginable jokes, stories that left the white men gaping at them. She had done it herself. Even now, she could make Mister Skye turn red. Well, what was winter for, if not to steal wives and seduce husbands? She giggled. Her people would understand the bawds, and maybe try them out. But white women were less valuable than whiskey. They'd trade anything for that, and she suddenly felt glad none remained in this caravan. The whiskey hurt her people, but the women would not.

Late that night, when the smell of dew on the grass hung heavy in the air, every mule and pony disappeared. Their night sentinel, Jawbone, shrieked and whinnied beside their lodge, and Mister Skye, Mary, and she sprang up instantly, rushing into a moonless dark, hearing the soft scuff of retreating hoofs. The evil blue roan stood quivering in the night, snorting, awaiting his master's direction.

"Maybe Absaroka," she growled, and the thought mortified her. A terrible thing to think of.

Mister Skye saddled Jawbone swiftly as Victoria threw kindling in the coals to give him light. Then, without waiting to pull on his buckskin shirt, he grabbed his Sharps and his possibles and rode off, letting Jawbone pick the way. Victoria's heart lay leaden in her, heavy with the shame, for the thieves were surely her people, and most likely Kicked-in-the-Bellies. But they would recognize Mister Skye, and they all knew about Jawbone, the great medicine horse.

Dawn broke, and a gray haze rimmed the northeast. Victoria could wait no longer.

"Mary, goddamn, you make the white people stay calm while I'm gone. They gonna go crazy, especially that Riddle. The thieves got Chang's stallion and the Arapaho pony too, and we ain't got anything. But I'll fix it. Fix it good."

Grimly she gathered a sausage of pemmican, a knife, and spare moccasins, and began walking west, along a trail she sensed and smelled more than saw in the ghostly gray of first light. She trotted easily, as she had done as a thin girl and in an hour she had covered a vast distance through tangled hills. Twice she forded rushing creeks, soaking her feet in ice water. The trail grew clearer now, and anyone but a tenderfoot white man could follow it. She found Jawbone's prints and knew Mister Skye rode ahead of her, closing in. Once she found where one of the raiders had dismounted. Yes, Absaroka moccasins! The discovery shamed her. What would Mister Skye think? His mules and ponies, and every mule and pony of the others, driven hard toward her own village?

She trotted west and south, scarcely noticing that the long slopes became harder to climb. She pushed each leg ahead methodically, as she had done as a girl, not thinking of her gray hair or the crevasses lining her weathered brown face. Then at last the sun rose, giving color to a gray world, turning a white sky azure. Muffled on the morning air thumped a single shot, and it filled her with dread. They were cutting across valleys, each a drainage leading from the vast gray and black mountains on down to the Yellowstone River. Still she trotted, perhaps fifteen miles now, by Mister Skye's reckoning. Ahead the thieves were gaining on her; their prints drier now to her keen eye. She topped a long ridge, threaded through loose-knit stubby ponderosa, and down a dun sandstone grade. Ahead lay a mound on the brown grass, and beside it, Mister Skye. Horror rose in her. Now she ran until her lungs ached and her old heart clattered, and still she loped.

The two of them sprawled in a sandy boulder-strewn bottom, surrounded by copses of dark pine, and groves of bright aspen. Jawbone lay inert on his side, his lungs heaving shallowly and his teeth curled back in a death grin. Mister Skye sat mutely, tears leaking down his dark face, one arm cast possessively over Jawbone's trembling belly. She had never seen him cry, except once, when that mad Siksika, Moon-Hides-the-Sun, had struck Mary what seemed a mortal blow in the head.

Stunned, she stopped and stared at the terrible sight, at Mister Skye's torment, at the scarred blue roan gasping. She made her legs sidle closer. She made her feet walk around to Jawbone's chest, where she could see the hole and the froth of blood around it as heaving lungs expelled and sucked red air. She saw no exit wound. The horse's tongue hung in the sand, and its eyes focused on nothing. Jawbone wept from dimming eyes.

"It had to come sometime," Mister Skye muttered. "I just wasn't ready for it."

She groaned with a sorrow beyond words, beyond what her soul could contain. She made her small feet walk the remaining distance to her man, and made her hands take his. He barely noticed.

"I guess I have to do it. Don't have the will for it," he muttered.

He slowly pulled his old Navy out of its holster and stood. He wore only his breechclout and leggins, and she noticed something, that the hair of his chest grew gray. She had not known that his chest was gray. He cocked the Colt and pressed it behind the ear of Jawbone and closed his eyes. Time ticked by, and Victoria wished he would shoot, but he didn't. The horse trembled beneath the muzzle. Jawbone turned his head back, and caught Mister Skye's eye. Jawbone still wept.

"I can't," said Mister Skye hoarsely. "I don't have it in me to do that."

He holstered the revolver and sat heavily beside the trembling horse, beginning his terrible vigil. He seemed lost and forlorn, the smallest speck in a vast wilderness. Her heart ached for him, ached for Jawbone in his pain and dying. She peered narrowly about this place. They perched on a steep slope leading to a sharp cedar-choked bluff. An ambush place. One of them had waited above, shot down the steep incline, hitting Jawbone in the chest. Mister Skye should have been more alert, she thought. The way to her village led through lower hills to the right, not this way to ambush.

Jawbone lay panting irregularly, a horrible wheezing in his chest, leaking blood from his wound. Victoria loved the old gallant horse that had rescued them so often, from so many desperate moments. Softly her old hand found Jawbone's neck, and slid along under the mane. She wished she had medicine in her fingers to heal the animal, medicine to plug the hole and heal the terrible damage within, medicine to pluck out that leaden ball buried in him. Then she knew that her hand did have medicine: her touch along the great stallion's neck transmitted something to the old blue roan, and his breathing steadied and he closed his eyes.

"He knows we love him," she said.

She found Jawbone's half-shot-off ear, and toyed with it, stroked it. Jawbone grew very quiet, eyes closed, awaiting the end.

"Come, Mister Skye," she said. "We must go to my village and see who has done this thing."

He said nothing, sitting heavily, turning old before her eyes. She had never seen Old Man in him, but now Old Man peered from within his haggard face. He could not stop touching Jawbone.

"See?" she said softly. "His eyes are closed and he does not know we are here now. We must go."

He saw it now. He saw that Jawbone had gone to the Other Land. She tugged at his hand. He stood, not wanting to, not wanting to tear himself away from the animal he had trained from weaning day by day to become the greatest war-horse, medicine horse, the people of the plains had ever known. With humans, with herself, he could be taciturn and at loss for words, but between Mister Skye and Jawbone communication had been perfect, and so had love. Through all the years the terrible blue roan whickered his joy at Mister Skye's presence, and Mister Skye's voice and hand and eyes had returned love. Victoria had delighted in this thing, and she had watched it over the long years, this love of man and horse.

"Come along," she said sharply. "We go now."

He followed, unresisting. She did not take him up the trail and over the bluff, but to the north on softer land, and around, picking up the trail again a mile ahead as they descended into an intimate valley curling between sage-crowned hills, not far from the dark flanks of the mountains. And there, ahead, lay a band of blue haze from the cookfires of her people, the Kicked-in-the-Bellies. She would have been so glad. Her heart would have burst. She would have run around the bend ahead, until the poles of the lodges were a forest before her and the people she loved spilled out of the village with open arms to hug her. But she could not run.

They stumbled ahead along the bottoms. The camp police, at this time the Kit Fox Society, aware of them now. The crier racing to spread the word through her village. Now at last her people did boil out to them, and she saw nieces and nephews, a sister and two brothers, a score of friends, all graying now, and far ahead, at the great lodge whose door faced east toward the rising sun, old Many Coups, her cousin. But all of these, her friends and family, the little children she'd never seen, the old ones, the sharp-eyed medicine men, the elders, they saw, and turned suddenly quiet. Once Mister Skye had told her about a man in his black book named Moses, who had been in the presence of God, and whose face was so filled with the presence of God that he had to wear a veil because his face had become too terrible to behold. Mister Skye's face was too terrible for her people to behold. He had not seen God, but he had seen death, and his face became as terrible as the face of Moses, she thought. They knew without being told, and the women wailed. Never in memory had such shame come upon the Kicked-in-the-Bellies.

She tugged Mister Skye along, through a tunnel of silent people, until at last they stood before old Many Coups, who stood on bowed legs with his ceremonial staff in hand, in somber silence.

"My dear cousin and Mister Skye, we welcome you," he said at last. "Only a while ago, our young ones returned in victory, with many prizes, telling us they had ambushed one who followed on a blue horse and killed the horse. Now our victory has turned to ashes. Come, if you will, for the pipe."

They entered his lodge then, and sat in their appointed places, and the elders and medicine men filed in also and seated themselves quietly. It was light within because the cover had been rolled up off the grasses to let the breezes run. Victoria's heart had never been so heavy. She ached for Mister Skye, for old Jawbone, for Many Coups, and for all of her people, who would never forget the shame of this day. Many Coups sighed heavily and extracted his long red pipe from its soft bag of unborn buffalo calf. Silence lay heavy, as he tamped tobacco and lit it with a coal brought to him. The pipe made its passage, and the smoke hung low upon the grass and would not rise.

"Tell us your story," said Many Coups at last.

Mister Skye could not, though he spoke enough Absaroka to do it. So Victoria did.

"Jawbone is dead?"

"He passed to the Other Land before we left," she replied.

The ancient medicine man, Red Turkey Wattle, peered sharply at her, lifted a pinch of dust and let it sift back to earth.

For many minutes no one spoke.

Then, "The young men grieve. They will return what they have taken, and give to you all that they own. The one who shot Jawbone is making a sweat lodge, and when he is sweated he will go into the mountains and fast for four days and four nights, as is the way with us."

Mister Skye nodded.

"I wish to give you my best war-horse, Fastrunner, and your pick of my horses. As many as you will. All of them, if you will."

Mister Skye replied softly. "I am honored by the great gift of Fastrunner, and he will make a good horse for me. We need a few others, humble ones for packs, and for these we would thank you, Many Coups."

The chief nodded. "As many as you need," he said. "I too will enter this lodge and fast, and my face will not see the sun for four days."

"You do us great honor, Many Coups, and return more than was taken away. We—Victoria and I—are friends and kin here."

Red Turkey Wattle said, "I will take my medicine bundle and I will go to Jawbone and help him in his passage to the Other World and bring to his spirit the sorrows of the Kicked-in-the-Bellies."

The old shaman arose then, and walked out into the

sun. Victoria watched him slip into his own tiny lodge—everything he possessed, including each meal, was given to him by the village people—and emerge with his medicine bundle and shuffle slowly off. The village watched solemnly as he left. No medicine had more power than the red throat of the wild turkey.

"The Kit Fox Society will escort you back to your wagon people, and drive the mules and ponies. Take my gifts, and those of the young men, and bring your white people here if you would."

The chief turned to Victoria. "I have not seen you, and thought I never again would," he said. "But now I have seen you, and I say welcome, and say goodbye, because now I will fast."

Her heart grew heavy.

They filed out solemnly into the August sun, and Many Coups had his war-horse brought, and gave it to Mister Skye, who took the unfamiliar rein in hand awkwardly. The powerful buckskin with bulging stifles nudged him hard with its nose. Then they took Mister Skye out to the pony herd, upstream, and there he selected three serviceable ponies that had been broken to pack or carry travois.

"You have taken very little, and do me little honor," said Many Coups darkly.

"I have taken your greatest gift, the best war-horse in the village," replied Mister Skye.

The chief nodded, and began to prepare for his long and mortifying fast. Victoria stayed, but Mister Skye and the Kit Fox Society warriors began the long funereal procession of horses and mules back to the wagons.

Chapter 25

The buckskin war-horse stood small for a man of his weight, but carried him eagerly and responded instantly to the slightest command. Mister Skye scarcely noticed. He rode silently through the afternoon, along with six Kit Fox Society warriors who herded the horses and mules. It dawned on Mister Skye that they were not following any route that wagons could travel. The Kicked-in-the-Bellies had camped high in the roots of the mountains, on a creek that burrowed through canyons, amidst cliffs and bluffs black with ponderosa. The village stood maybe fifteen miles southwest of the wagon train near the Yellowstone River. No, he thought, he would not bring the wagons to the village.

Off to the south a mile stretched the canyon where he'd been ambushed and where Jawbone had died. None of that was visible from where they rode, nor did Mister Skye wish to glimpse the stiffening corpse of the great blue horse. The shaman would be there bringing the medicine of the wild turkey to Jawbone, and that would be enough. Someday, when he could bear it, he'd go back there and bury Jawbone's clean-picked bones, and maybe set a rock up at the place to mark it. He wished he could put sentences together well. He would write the story of that horse. But no one would believe it, he thought heavily. Horses never ran toward trouble; they always ran away from it. Who would believe a horse would fight like that?

Another thought formed in his mind across that solemn afternoon, too. He would urge Victoria to stay with her people for a while. He would come for her after he had delivered his party to Bannack. She had thought she'd never see her village again, and when she finally did, it came in the middle of shame and sorrow. No. She should not come to Bannack. She should stay until her village brightened again, and she could chatter with her family and friends, and meet the little ones. Anyway, he wanted to be solitary now. She would want to comfort him and be with him, and yet it would be the wrong thing for a while. He wanted to crawl inside of his own mortality and meet death alone. We die alone, he thought. Even if we are surrounded by others, we die alone, even as Jawbone died alone while he and Victoria stared helplessly. Now he wanted to prepare for his own dying.

On a hilltop half a mile from the wagons they saw a flash of metal and then the rising figure of Seven-Story Chang. It stirred the Crow warriors briefly, but Mister Skye quieted them. Chang and his tall sweetheart trotted downslope toward them, and Mister Skye could see their eyes were riveted on the buckskin under him.

"Jawbone is dead," he said roughly.

"I have lost an esteemed friend," said Chang. He did not ask for details. Something of the events conveyed itself to him.

"It is Victoria's village and she's there," Mister Skye said, forestalling the question.

At the forlorn wagons the others waited, gladness upon them as they spotted their herd of mules and ponies. Goldtooth beamed. Drusilla and Mary-Rita grinned. Even the inert Gertrude managed a smile at the sight of so many horses.

"I never thought you'd do it, honey. I expected to camp here till— You sure got the magic, Mister Skye," said Goldtooth.

"You dear ol' man. You come fetch your reward anytime," Mrs. Parkins added.

"Royal flush!" proclaimed Sleeping Bear. "How'd you do it?"

Alvah Riddle fairly danced at the sight of his stock, but cast worried eyes at the six powerful Crow warriors who rode solemnly forward, carbines at the ready, and a hard light in their eyes.

"Riddle," said Mister Skye, "these are Victoria's kin and friends."

"You got extry horses. They forked over extrys by way of apologizing. I know Injuns, Skye. That's exactly what they did. Which ones are mine? They paid us all for takin' the stock."

Mister Skye did not feel like answering.

"Say, where's Jawbone? You leave him back with the savages?"

"Dead," said Mister Skye.

He saw Mary's hand fly to her mouth, and tears form; their eyes locked, and they silently exchanged their grief.

"Too bad," replied Riddle. "Pretty decent horse. Might have traded him for something younger but for all those scars."

Mister Skye turned his back. Vanderbilt—Sleeping Bear, he remembered—took charge of the animals now, along with Mary and Chang, who looked over his white stallion and Buffalo Whiskers's Arapaho pony. Big Alice, too, caught Goldtooth's mules and picketed them.

"You didn't say which of these new ones are mine, Skye," persisted Riddle.

"They were a gift to me," Mister Skye replied curtly.

"So that's your angle. Just like I figured. They give us a gift, and you hog it all to yourself. Well, I'm going to take those two there," he said, pointing at a bay pony and black mare. "Ought to pack good. Fetch something in Bannack."

Mister Skye slid off the buckskin and caught the pink man by the scruff of the neck.

"You didn't hear me, Riddle."

The man squirmed in his fist, and tried to swing his Spencer around. Mister Skye let go, and Riddle staggered to earth.

Drusilla exploded. "Can't you see the Crows tried to pay back Mister Skye for Jawbone? Can't you see that, Alvah?"

"That's his story," Riddle muttered.

"Riddle. You point a gun at me again, and you will be dead," whispered Mister Skye.

"If he succeeds, I'll kill him," said Sleeping Bear.

Mary said nothing. When Riddle looked up, it was into the black bore of Mary's cocked fusil. He crabbed sideways, but the bore followed him.

"Tell your squaw to be careful!"

"I understand your English," she retorted.

Riddle peered around, this time into the bores of six Crow carbines, the bore of Chang's carbine, and the twin caverns of Sleeping Bear's scattergun.

"I didn't do anything," he mumbled, terror in his eyes.

Mister Skye lifted his face to the hills. The sun lay low, knifing the land before him into slices, blazoning westerly slopes gold and easterly ones blue. A breeze toyed with his hair and his buckskin's mane. This Yellowstone country . . . if Jawbone had to die, he rejoiced that it happened here, amid clear cold creeks and forested slopes and long grassy plateaus, and huge outcrops of dun rock.

They all stood expectantly.

"I am going back to the village tonight," he said. "It is a long way, over four hours. I will be back in the morning, mid-morning, and we'll start rolling then. You'll be safe here. My dear Mary will keep you comfortable. My friend Mister Chang is a mighty warrior, and wise in the wilderness."

"You abandoning us?" asked Riddle from the earth.

Mister Skye turned wearily, and with a nod he and the Kit Fox warriors rode southward. He knew some of them slightly. They were the cream of all the warriors in the village, and counted many coups between them.

In the blue last light he found Victoria in her brother's lodge. The August nights were chill here, and the covers were rolled to the ground now. Many of the lodges glowed orangely, like dim streetlights through the village, as firelight pierced softly through the cowhide covers. He found a terrible quietness here, and all the familiar joy and cacophony of an Indian village absent. He waited to be invited in, and in a moment he was offered the place of honor, and elk rump stew. He wasn't hungry at all, and declined, with thanks.

Six sat within. Victoria's brother, Arrow Giver, her two sisters, Makes-the-Lodge and Quill-Dye-Woman, a young woman, and two somber youths.

In halting Crow, accompanied by his big hands, Mister Skye asked Arrow Giver to shelter Victoria for a moon or so, while he took people to the mining camp and came back. Victoria could visit her people. Happier days soon. It would be a good visit for them all. He wished to be alone for a little while.

Victoria stared, and then her old face went soft, and its umber creases gentled.

"Sonofabitch!" she exclaimed in English, and hugged him. "How are you going to get along? Cooking, Mary's no damn good. Me, I keep you fat."

"I need it," he said.

"I know."

His business done, he settled into the woven backrest chair given him, and thought of sleep. But he felt an expectancy here, and after a bit he sat up again and waited for whatever would be.

"These young men are my nephews," said Victoria. "They were with—the raiding party. They are like dead men inside of themselves. They wish to—undo what was done. Neither of them pulled the trigger. The one who pulled the trigger waits outside."

She nodded, and one of the young men, a very thin one, rose and slowly lifted the medicine bundle that hung on his chest up and over his head, and handed it to Mister Skye. And the other youth did likewise.

Frightful, terrible gifts. In his hands lay the small leather pouches that contained the most sacred things, sometimes a small stone, or something from the spirit animal that was the youth's guide and protector. These were sacrifices of self, of protection, of help, of courage, of faith, of identity, of tribal connection, of vision-quest and purpose. Mister Skye felt the cold heaviness of these things, gathered now in his hands. These young men had made themselves nameless and had stripped themselves of all that might protect and guide them. He felt the heaviness, and the terribleness, and then knew what he must do.

"The medicine of these young men goes into my heart," he said. "And now, I wish to give the sacred bundles back, each to the one whose medicine it is. They have made Mister Skye happy, and have healed his wound."

He walked over to each, and slipped the thong back over the neck of each, while they gazed at him with wide dark eyes.

He returned to his seat. "There is no greater gift an Absaroka can give," he added.

Victoria nodded. "The other waits outside."

Outside the doorflap stood six ponies and a pile of things hard to discern in the dark. Moccasins, a shirt, a bow and full quiver, a battered muzzleloader—the weapon that had killed Jawbone, he knew—a shield with someone's private medicine daubed in white clay upon it, and more. And off to one side, sitting cross-legged, a youth naked save for a breechclout. The killer of Jawbone.

The boy's entire worldly possessions rested here. Again Mister Skye felt the weight. He could not refuse these gifts and sacrifices for a wrong done. The flap of the lodge closed behind him, and he met the dark. In all politeness Victoria's family would avoid listening, and would talk of other things within their lodge. Mister Skye examined the ponies one by one, and carefully studied the pile of goods, the fine sinew-wrapped bone bow, the skin clothing. Then at last he sat down heavily, directly opposite the youth.

"What is your name?" he asked in his faltering Crow.

"I was named Tobacco Dancer."

"It is a good name. I know of the sacred ceremony of the tobacco."

"I have dishonored the name and now I have none."

"I will give you a new one soon. You have brought me many gifts. All that you have."

"I took away all that you have."

"Much, but not all. I have Victoria, of your people. Mary, of the Shoshone. And my son, Dirk. And more."

"I have had a sweat. Now I must go high upon the mountain and seek the vision. I would like to go now."

The youth twisted uneasily, but Mister Skye did not want him to leave. Not just yet. He stared upward into the mystery of the heavens, wanting guidance. His own spirit lay so heavy he could scarcely decide what to do.

"Red Turkey Wattle has left the village, but is there another medicine man here?"

"There is Little People's Voice."

"We will go see Little People's Voice. Bring along the best pony."

The youth stared sharply at him, and then selected a dun with white stockings, and they walked through the softly lit silent village. Lodge flaps hid those within, and yet Mister Skye felt that the whole village knew exactly where he and the killer of Jawbone were walking.

They stopped at a small dark lodge at the rim of the village, and waited.

"I have expected you," said a reedy voice. "Come in."

They settled down inside a pitch-black lodge.

"You have brought me a pony. We will have a smoke," said the ancient voice.

Mister Skye heard a rustling, and finally a scratch of a sulphur match, and in the matchlight he glimpsed a cragged and seamed face, dark as a saddle. Little People's Voice looked very old. If he was the voice of the miniature people the Absarokas called Nimimbi, protectors of the Crow people, then the old man's medicine was sacred indeed.

He sucked on the long pipe, and passed it to Mister Skye, who drew a breath, and passed it to the youth. The pipe slowly circled among them until the entire charge of tobacco had burned, and the shaman knocked the ashes out. Time for business.

"I wish to adopt this young man as my son, and to give him a new name. I have come to you for the name-giving, and for the blessing."

Silence thickened in the blackness of the lodge. He wished he could see the youth's face. He waited for what seemed an eternity before the old shaman spoke.

"It is good. I am pleased to have the gift of the pony."

The silence folded in again, but Mister Skye sat easily. Careful deliberation was the way of all the Indian people he had known.

He lost track of time in the closed darkness, and heard nothing save for the occasional rasp of breath from the old man. Then at last the shaman spoke. "I see that this young man will be away from the village much of the time. He will often be among the whites learning their ways. I will name him Half Absaroka, or in your tongue, Half Crow."

"That is a good name. Now, Half Crow, in the presence of our esteemed friend Little People's Voice, I adopt you as my own son, with all the honor that I bestow upon my own son, Dirk."

The youth said, "I did not know this would happen. I am very honored. I will always strive to be a good son to Mister Skye."

"Now, a father likes to give good gifts to his son," continued Mister Skye in his faltering Crow. He could not use his hands in this blackness, and the words came slowly. "So I will give you what you gave me, and something more which I will bring back from the mining camp of Bannack in about a moon. Give me your hand, Half Crow."

The boy's hand found his in the blackness, and he held it in his own.

"It is good," said the old man. "Now, Half Crow, give me your medicine bundle. It is dead."

The youth obliged.

"Now, Half Crow, go meet your family. Your new mother is in the lodge of Arrow Maker. Then after you have met your new kin, go up this very night upon the mountain, and begin a vision-quest, and pray that the One Above will send you a vision. If you receive the vision, we will make a new medicine bundle for you."

He dismissed them and they walked back through the quiet village to the lodge of Arrow Maker, and were invited in. Victoria's nephews had left.

"Victoria," he said softly, "meet your new son Half Crow."

"Sonofabitch!" exclaimed the old woman. She stood and peered into the youth's tense face. "Sonofabitch!" she muttered, completely circling him.

"I hope I am acceptable to my new mother," the youth said in Crow.

"Ah!" she cried, her seamed face softening. She hugged Half Crow. And then the others did too, congratulating him, and themselves, and Mister Skye.

"Half Crow will now go up to the mountain for four days, seeking the vision that will give him new medicine," said Mister Skye. "Little People's Voice has declared it."

"I am proud to be the son of Mister Skye, and my mother Victoria," he said, and left.

"Sonofabitch," said Victoria, and hugged Mister Skye.

In the morning Victoria grew cross with him, snapping at everything he said, and serving breakfast rudely. It was her way of saying goodbye, he knew. She couldn't bear any other mood when she and Mister Skye were to be parted for a while. He pressed her to him anyway, and said he'd be back swiftly, and to take care of her new son, giving him gifts.

"Ha!" she bellowed. "You think I don't know what to do!"

He cinched his Crow-made pad saddle over the buckskin while she watched, and when she handed him a small sack of pemmican and berries for the trail, her old brown cheeks were wet. Mysteriously, word of the adoption of Half Crow had spirited through the village, and many people, less solemn now, saw him off. The shame upon the village had lifted. The Kit Fox warriors accompanied him a mile or so, and then resumed their patrolling and policing.

He rode alone. The horse beneath him was not Jawbone. There blew a hint of autumn on the air, but the sun banished it by mid-morning. It was a familiar thing, this aloneness. This vast continent did that to him. Ever since he had jumped ship near Fort Vancouver as a young man, he had encountered this aloneness. He was a Yank now, but not a part of them, and had scarcely seen their civilization, except for one trip to St. Louis. The separateness rose keen in him with Jawbone dead. For many years the horse had been a companion, and they had talked without words. There remained some of the Cambridge-bound merchant's son in him, the youth who buried himself in books, and it was a rare occasion out here that he found anyone who had read the same books and wished to talk of them. This land and its people spoke another language, which he knew and loved, but he rarely found anyone from the East who understood it, or cared about it. So he walked alone among Easterners, and alone among his friends out in this wild.

He rode through a grand and open land, not noticing it this day, once again passing the side canyon where Jawbone lay. His mind went numb and he refused to think about it.

Mary would be waiting, and would share his grief. She gave herself to smiles and tears, and these things of the heart flowed freely from her, while they always caught up in his own throat. He rode into the wagon camp and found it peaceful. The wagons were harnessed and the animals stood patiently in their traces, lashing flies and nipping at each other in their leather prisons. He stared at them irritably, these whites. Over the years in the wilderness he had become more Indian than white. In the village he had understood the feelings, knew what to do, and approved of all that had been done. But here among these people thoughts turned private and sometimes opposite what appeared on their faces. He spotted Drusilla, looking remarkably tanned and handsome, and read pleasure in her eye. He must not judge, he thought. There were people here he would willingly protect with his life.

"You are a fine and brave man, Mister Skye," she said softly.

"Let's be on our way," he said, and heard the wagons begin to roll behind him.

Chapter 26

Sleeping Bear marveled that he was alive. The holes in his belly and back had sealed over and healed into tender dimples. The blood that had reddened his urine had long since disappeared. Day by day the terrible weakness had vanished, and now somehow he felt stronger and healthier than he had been. The sallow yellow-gray of his flesh had turned to tan, and the night-cast of his face had become a ruddy wind-chapped brightness.

He had never seen country like this. Before, he had been indifferent to nature, but now he could scarcely drink in enough. They had struck the Yellowstone River after a hard two days toiling down rugged pine-dotted hills south of the river. Now before him lay a broad tawny valley curling between the great wall of the Rockies to the south, and a jagged separate range to the northwest. The wide clear river rolled between thick green bands of cottonwood that were rife with game, but Mister Skye led them across open grassy bottoms, often a half mile from the stream. The going was easier, he said, and there was less possibility of an ambush.

They were shorthanded now, and Mister Skye and Mary occasionally had a time of it with the loose herd of ponies given to him by the Crows. Sleeping Bear would have liked to help them, but wasn't up to horseback riding yet. So he drove the red wagon, with one of Mister Skye's new ponies as a wheeler, surrounded by well-broke mules and ponies. Another of Mister Skye's green ponies was locked in the traces of Goldtooth's wagon. Sometimes he glimpsed Chang and Buffalo Whiskers far ahead, Chang usually on the hills south of the broad valley, and the Arapaho woman skirting along the river and its thickets.

This land seemed wondrous to him, and he felt like a child in it, seeing it for the first time, noticing gray bluffs, admiring the way low sun sharpened distant black and white peaks, feeling the arch of a limitless and mysterious blue heaven over him. He had never looked into the sky before, or limned its aching distances against his smallness. When white-rumped antelope herds burst away, they enchanted him. When Mister Skye had spotted a prowling grizzly along the river and had given it wide berth, it fascinated him. Why had he never seen or even imagined these things before? How had he crossed a continent without knowing what lay about him?

But most of all he had come to love driving this red wagon, steering it around small barriers, little gullies and boulders, the soft earth of a prairie-dog town, unexpected potholes. He had learned to anticipate, see the earth ahead in terms of his team and his wagon, and choose paths that were easiest on both. Often Drusilla and Mary-Rita joined him on the seat. They couldn't stand Alvah, they said at first, but then it became another reason: the three of them were having fun. Never before had any white women enjoyed his company, and when it dawned on him, it amazed him for hours. Always before, he had bought female companionship for brief impersonal businesslike moments.

They bounced across a rock-strewn tributary river Mister Skye called the Boulder, in a place where wooded islands dotted the Yellowstone and creeks poured in from the opposite bank. Signs of traffic on this great highway lay everywhere, but they saw no one these long August days. Mister Skye had warned of raiding Blackfeet, and even raiding Sioux, far from their home country. From high points now they could see a blue barrier clear across the west, dead ahead. They would cross these formidable mountains by a pass he knew, Mister Skye said. Just before that, the river would swing south, pierce through a mountain gate, and head for the land of the geysers.

A day after they'd crossed the Boulder, Mister Skye led them closer to the Yellowstone until he came to a stretch where the river ran wide and slow, and the gravelly banks were almost horizontal.

"We'll cross here, mates," he said. "Ahead is a narrows I don't want to tackle with these wagons. Might make it, might not. But I want to get on over to the north side anyway. There's a hot springs on that side for those who want to wash. Tomorrow we'll cross. I've seen buffler cross here, and I think we'll have no trouble."

"How deep is the channel, Skye?" asked Riddle.

"Mister Skye."

Riddle was annoyed. "I can't even get an answer to a civil question."

"Uncivil," said Skye. "You'll have to swim the teams and float the wagons. Double-teamed, you'll be all right."

"My wagon doesn't float. I got my shooting ports cut in the sides. All my supplies and robes will get soaked."

Mister Skye seemed to stop a retort in his throat. "I suppose we can put your truck in one of Goldtooth's wagon boxes, if they're tight."

"They should be," said Goldtooth Jones. "I bought the best I could, cash and merchandise." She laughed. "Maybe I ought to charge you for hauling your truck over dry, Alvah."

"So that's your angle," Riddle muttered. "All conspired up against me."

Goldtooth laughed, and soon the others did too. "I might even lend you a team for the double-teaming, Alvah," she added.

They camped in an open grove of majestic cottonwoods

beside the cold river, below a small shelf that would conceal firelight. Mister Skye always selected campsites that would hide fires from night-eyes as much as possible. The women slipped down to the gravel bank of the cold-running Yellowstone for their ablutions, with Mary and the scattergun for protection. Sleeping Bear unhitched both teams, watered and picketed the stock. Riddle did the same, in huffy silence. He had set up his camp at a small defiant distance from Mister Skye's lodge and the red wagons. Chang had brought in a doe, and now it hung from a limb while he methodically yanked back hide and butchered. It was amazing, Sleeping Bear thought, how much work Victoria had done. Not until she had left this party had he or anyone else, except Mister Skye, understood what the old woman's industry meant to them all.

"You gonna share some of that doe, Chang?" asked Riddle.

Chang laughed.

Sleeping Bear found Mister Skye off in deep bunchgrass, combing the buckskin and muttering all the while.

"Need some help?" he asked.

Mister Skye peered up sharply. "No, I guess not. I'm just getting introduced to this bloody horse."

"Is he a good one?"

"He's a horse," said Mister Skye shortly. Then something softened in him. "He's a good horse. Good pony."

"I like this country," said Sleeping Bear.

"Best there is. Heart of Absaroka."

"Why don't you live here? I'm sure Victoria would like that."

The guide stared off into the dusky western hills. "I don't rightly have an answer for that," he said. He finished rubbing the buckskin stallion, and began examining its feet. The animal resisted. Sleeping Bear grabbed the halter rope and held tight while the guide lifted one hoof after another, and checked pasterns and cannons and hocks for heat.

"Thanks, friend," he said. "You know what you're go-

ing to do when we get to Bannack? Get a new faro layout?"

"No . . . no. I thought I'd try to buy the wagons and
teams from Goldtooth after we hit Bannack, start freighting. Fort Hall, Salt Lake. Maybe Fort Benton."

"Hell of a lot to learn about freighting, mate. Competition, dirty tricks, harassment, Indian trouble, drunken
teamsters, ruined goods, breakdowns, bad river crossings,
hail, snow, feed that sickens the stock, alkali water . . .
and road agents. I've heard talk of road agents around
Bannack."

"What else would you have me do then, Mister Skye?"

The guide was visibly startled. "Why, damn, Sleeping
Bear. Why, mate, that's a good plan. It'll take sand. Red
wagons—they'll be . . . a target. Sleeping Bear, freighting
is harder than gambling . . . but . . ."

"I don't know if I can do it either."

"But you're going to try."

The women straggled back to camp, wet-haired and
fresh-scented, in twos and threes that revealed no sign of
earlier divisions. Soon their laundry draped from limbs
and brush, and they were tackling a supper. Sleeping Bear
corraled Goldtooth and led her over to the dark river.

"I've got a business proposition," he began.

"Honey, I'm always open for business, and never turned
down a proposition." She laughed heartily.

"I'd like to buy your wagons when we get there. And
the stock too."

"Now how are you going to do that, Cornelius?"

"I'd like you to call me Sleeping Bear now. It means
something to me. I was hoping—I thought maybe I'd work
off the debt with profits."

"Profits?"

"I thought I'd freight for a living."

"Why, Sleeping Bare—now there's a name for a cat-
house, Sleeping Bare—I thought you'd be my houseman,
now that Blueberry is gone. You silly old thing. You'll
have plenty of time to deal faro on the side. I'll stake you
to a layout. I mean, after we turn a few tricks and get

going. Might put one in my house if I've got room for a saloon."

"Goldtooth, no. I'd like to freight."

She frowned. "You going bluenose on me, sonnyboy?"

"Look, Goldtooth, I've got a new lease on life, and when I lay in that wagon sick of myself, sick of what I was, half dead, I just started to see—"

"Bluenose," she said. "Some people get that way. No, I won't sell the wagons or the stock. I like my wagons. We're almost to Bannack, and they got us here. Tell you what, honey. If you want to start freighting, I'll go fifty-fifty on the earnings. Your business, my wagons and stock. Or are you too bluenosey now to be partners with a madam?"

"Hell no!" he said, and kissed her. It was dark here, and she kissed back, and didn't stop.

"I like being partners," she said.

"We're doing fine, Gertie," said Alvah the next morning. "Why, with Flora sold off, and Skye's people bringing in so much meat, we're going to be ahead. You bet. We'll have airtights and such to sell in Bannack or that new Alder Gulch camp, and they'll fetch fortunes. Sell the wagon and stock and robes too, and we can head back in style, on Holladay's Overland stages."

"The girls are coming along," said Gertrude amiably. "Drusilla is looking nicer each day, and Mary-Rita's holding her tongue. But oh, I'm weary of this."

"It'll be over pretty soon, Mother. We won't be rich, but we'll have comforts. We'll turn heads in Skaneateles. I'm aiming to buy a black surrey and some trotters."

She frowned. "My spirit writers have vanished. I hold the chalk on the slate and nothing happens. Do you suppose that's a bad sign?"

Alvah shrugged. He didn't hold with that nonsense.

He spotted Goldtooth and headed toward her, a little business in mind.

"Say, madam, I'd like to stow my truck in your spare

wagon for the crossing. It'll float dry. And of course I'll
lend you a team, so we can double-team them across."

"Why Alvah, honey, I've already got two teams."

So that was her angle, he thought. "Well, madam, I
thought maybe I could trade two or three airtights for the
use. Got some tomatoes and corn."

"Why, honey, the hunters and Mister Skye's ladies have
brought so much meat and greens, why, we just don't
need—"

"Thought it might be a good angle to trade," he said
shortly.

Goldtooth laughed. "Alvah Riddle, you goose. Of
course you can use the spare wagon. We all help each
other here."

"Well, that's a good thing," he said. "Now I'd like you
people to unload my wagon while I harness up. You ladies, and Vanderbilt, Chang, and Skye, why we can do it
in no time."

Goldtooth laughed again, and didn't reply. He decided
to try Vanderbilt.

"Say, Vanderbilt. I'm borrowing Goldtooth's wagon to
float my stuff over, and I sure could use some help unloading and loading. I reckon I could pay you a couple of
airtights."

The former gambler looked up from the log where he
sat attacking his breakfast. He started to shake his head,
and then stopped. "I've changed my name, Alvah," he
said mildly. "I'll be there in a minute. If you'd get your
team harnessed and pull your wagon next to mine, it'd
help."

"That sounds fine, but let's agree on a price first," said
Alvah.

Sleeping Bear shook his head. "For help in wilderness,
Alvah, there is no price."

Riddle couldn't figure the man's angle, but he didn't
argue. He was tempted to ask help harnessing, but decided
not to push his luck. In half an hour, the gambler had
lifted everything out of Riddle's wagon and set it into the
red one, while Alvah directed.

Big Alice harnessed both of Goldtooth's teams, and now they slouched in the traces of Goldtooth's wagon. Alvah thought it was a good angle to let her go first. He'd see how it went before risking his stuff. On the bank Mister Skye waited, and it startled Alvah to see Mary over on the north bank, wringing water from her doeskin skirt. All of the guide's animals were dripping water and shaking their packs loose over there. Somehow the guide had driven the loose stock across too, including Alvah's ponies.

"Need help, Alice?" asked Sleeping Bear.

"It's my first really big crossing," she said. "Maybe if you'd sit beside me—"

The pair of them drove the loaded red wagon with its ragged sheet down the flat gravel bank and into the swift water, which curled and churned around legs and wheels. As the powerful river pushed and tugged, the going got heavier even for the eight horses and mules. Water crept higher on the wheels, plucking and tilting the wagon, crept up on the red box, splashing and pushing on the upstream side, sucking on the other. The lead team stepped into nothing, splashed almost under, and swam, necks and heads showing. The channel shrank, they found bottom, and bounded in powerful surges toward the far shore, while the teams behind still swam, and the wagon veered crazily downstream, threatening to tip.

The red wagon hit bottom sideways, but the gambler swung the double teams upstream and gradually angled out until the wagon and teams stood dripping in the sun. It worried Alvah. On the far shore, Vanderbilt—what an absurd name he had now—unhitched the teams, clambered up on the lead mule, and swam them back again with Goldtooth and Big Alice whipping the reluctant animals into the water. On the far shore, Drusilla and Mary-Rita emerged from the tarts' wagon. They'd crossed without his permission!

Cussing, he waited for the gambler. In a few minutes the man had the teams hooked to the red wagon, and Al-vah drove into the water. His angle was to steer the teams slightly upstream to keep the current from twisting the floating wagon around behind them. It worked. The wagon lurched and bucked beneath him, and at moments the heads of his team dipped clear under water. Horses coughed and sputtered, but eventually he eased the wagon up and let the dripping animals rest. He squirmed back into the wagon to see if his truck was dry. There'd been a small leak, some robes were wet, but he'd dry them out soon enough.

"I'm plumb tuckered out, Vanderbilt. Do you think you could fetch the green wagon for me?" he said, testing his luck.

The soaked gambler stared. "I haven't all my strength back," he said. He shrugged. "What the hell. This is going to be my business, and I'd better learn it."

Triumphantly, Alvah watched from the wagon seat as Vanderbilt unhooked one team and walked it to the gravel bank.

But Mister Skye intervened. "You've had enough, mate," he said to Sleeping Bear. "Riddle, what's back there? An empty wagon?"

"Empty except for Gertrude."

"One team should do," the guide said. He trotted his buckskin into the water, the pony moving calmly under Skye's firm command. Alvah watched the guide swim the pony back to the south bank and then clamber into the wagon seat. He thought he glimpsed Gertrude poke her head out. Mister Skye eased the team into the water, while the buckskin swam along on the downstream side. When water boiled into the box through the gunports Gertrude lumbered out onto the seat next to Skye, and a few minutes later they were across. They'd tackled the wide Yellowstone and won. Alvah exulted. He'd find some angle to make them reload his green wagon—delay usually would do it—and he would get away scot-free.

Water sluiced out of the wagon, down to his gunholes. But the last eight inches lay trapped in his tight wagon box. That was an angle he hadn't thought of. He peered around irritably. Some of the women hustled into dry clothing behind bushes. On the far north bluffs, Chang and his Indian slut sat their horses, watching. Mister Skye pulled off his leggins and twisted the river out of them.

"Say, Vanderbilt. You mind helping me?"

The gambler trotted over, spotted Lake Riddle, and hoorawed.

"I don't see any trout," he yelled.

That drew the rest, and they all flocked to view Alvah's lake.

"Looks like you'll be our water wagon, Riddle," said the guide solemnly.

"Those gunholes are the best angle I ever had," Alvah retorted. He spotted a sandy hump ahead and whipped his team up it until the wagon hung crazily and water gushed from a hole. That drained half of it. Muttering, Alvah dug through his truck in the red wagon, extracted his auger and bit, and drilled two holes in opposite corners through the bed of the green wagon.

The next day, Mister Skye led them wide of the river, around some ravined hills, and then down into the dun valley again. Ahead squatted a vast impenetrable barrier of mountains the guide called the Belts, and Alvah Riddle knew he'd need double teams again, and that meant borrowing, and he bridled at the thought.

Chapter 27

"Hey, Celestial! Git! Out! Chop-chop! And take that squaw, too. We don't want your kind in here," said the saloonkeeper.

"I can understand the sentiment," replied Seven-Story. "In Peking, we don't look kindly on white barbarians."

The man gaped through his beard, which rolled in salty waves to his chest.

"How'd you git to talk whiteman like that?"

"When among barbarians, do as the barbarians do," mocked Chang. "You have a crude language, but expressive."

"Well, that don't cut no ice here. We don't fancy the yellow race, horning in on our placers and practicing heathen ways."

"A familiar melody. Has no one another tune? You are most unimaginative."

Seven-Story glanced amiably about this saloon and general store, hastily built of massive logs and without windows for want of glass. The open door plus a single lantern supplied quirky light that cast odd shadows.

The sharp-eyed keep studied him distrustfully, his lips forming words under the straggle of his beard. "I don't cotton to what you're saying," he said. "But maybe you're being high and mighty for a Celestial. Git now, chop-chop. We got a boneyard out back to bury your kind."

"Most cordial of you," said Chang. "Western hospitality is legend."

The barkeep reached beneath his crude bar of rough-sawn slab wood and lifted a sawed-off scattergun.

"Most cordial," said Chang.

"You're a big 'un, but that just means you take more buckshot. Now git, chop-chop."

"You certainly speak a peculiar English," said Chang. "Words that have eluded the Oxford lexicographers. Do you suppose you might offer wayfarers some advice? Or sell an item or two?"

"You got dust?"

"Better than that, I have an eagle and double eagles."

The black bore of the weapon, which had never quite reached Seven-Story's chest, wavered downward.

"Well, be quick about it. Don't want you seen in here, understand. You buy quickie, chop-chop, vamoose, yes?"

"Vamoose is more or less Spanish," said Chang. "This is Gallatin City, is it not? We're with a caravan of wagons bound for Bannack City. We'd thought to go down the Jefferson River, and the Beaverhead, but back ten miles we struck a wagon road heading down the Madison valley. Perhaps you could enlighten us?"

"All of you Celestials? I ain't about to sic dogs on a town."

"Ah, I wish they were all Chinese. But I must report that the caravan has less superior stock. A parlor-house madam and her ladies, from Memphis; some brides and their chaperones from all over; and a stray dog or two."

"Whites then. Come down from Benton," the barkeep said.

"No, up the Yellowstone from Fort Laramie."

"Horseapples, Chinaman. There's no wagon road that-away." He swung his scattergun around.

"It is just as you say," said Seven-Story. "Now then, since you are a perspicacious gentleman, perhaps you will divulge—"

"Cut them Chinee words, or I'll cut your queue."

"Say, now that is original!"

The barkeep peered at Chang, and lowered the weapon. "Sure, take that trail south down the Madison. It heads for the new digs at Alder Gulch. Big strike. They called it Varina, after Jeff Davis's wife. But I heered tell Doc Bissell—he's the miners' judge there—said it ain't gonna be named for a Secesh first lady, and he's labeled it Virginia City, nice and Northern. Go there, and if they don't string up Chinee and squaws, there's a good new wagon road west on the Stinking Water and Beaverhead to Bannack City. Hell of a lot better'n hacking down the Jefferson."

"Much obliged, sir."

"Heered tell there's road agents plundering along there. Likely get your gold and string you up. Unless I do it first."

"You barbarians have a fine sense of humor. I am looking for a few provisions. Some cartridges for a Sharps sixty-caliber; some Spencer cartridges. Potatoes or cabbage for the scurvy. A quart of red-eye, popskull, rattlesnake juice—"

"Show me your gold first."

"Ah, you've heard of quartz gold. Well, I have colt's gold and it'll fill your purse chop-chop. That is an interesting term, chop-chop. I try to master your tongue."

"You makin' fun of me, Celestial."

"Well, if you don't want my trade . . ."

The man sighed, tucked his shotgun in his arm, and began collecting goods. "Got no Sharps sixty, but here's the Spencer. One box. Got no potatoes, but here's cabbage. Two dollars a head. Three dollars for Celestials. How many?"

"Six, at white prices."

"I charge what I charge."

"No tickee, no shirtee," said Chang. He nodded at

Buffalo Whiskers, who had been peering wide-eyed into the hostile gloom.

"Hold on, Chinee!" The barkeep was lifting his scattergun. "You kin pay me for my advice."

Chang's shot splintered the stock and bloodied the man's hand. He howled.

"At your service," said Chang. "Most cordial visit."

They rode easily out of the somnolent hamlet. His shot had racketed inside the great log walls, and no one slowed their passage. In moments they escaped the settlement, trotting southeasterly, back to the wagon-road fork where Mister Skye and his party waited.

Gallatin City lay at the three forks of the Missouri, in a breathtaking intermountain valley filled with thick grasses turning dun in the dryness of August. Even now, the tips of the blue ranges that circumscribed the vast basis shone white with last winter's snow. The day shone finer than polished jade, and he heeled his horse into a rack. His smiling bride rode easily beside him through zephyrs—a tall, exquisite woman with features chiseled by the gods, but the whites were too blind to see that. In his arms, she became demanding, mad and delirious, and sometimes comic. Ah, what wouldn't they give for her in the courts of the emperor?

Mister Skye had taken them up a long gentle pass that began just where the Yellowstone curved south into the belly of the mountains, and the teams stood it well as long as they were rested frequently. Near the summit they had double-teamed the wagons the last half mile. On the west slope the descent was so easy they had scarcely paused to lock wheels, but a final sharp grade choked with trees had slowed them. They'd driven along a steep slope that threatened to topple the wagons, and then emerged one sunny afternoon into this valley of the gods. Even Alvah Riddle had exclaimed about the grand vistas, after whining his way up, and whining his way down the mountains.

They were waiting on a sun-swept meadow beside the ruts.

"This goes down the Madison River to the new Alder

Gulch camp they're calling Virginia City," Seven-Story explained to Mister Skye. "From there, there's a good wagon road on over to Bannack, down the Stinking Water and up the Beaverhead. No problem except for road agents."

"You get any truck there?"

"We had a slight problem."

Mister Skye grinned. "You solved it satisfactorily?"

"Call me Bloody Hand. Call me Empty Hand. You barbarians are quite expressive in your naming. An improvement over our Lotus Flowers and Crystal Jades. Here's your eagle back. No popskull, no Sharps loads."

"I'm dry as August prairie," Mister Skye muttered. "Well, mates, we'll head for this Alder Gulch digging—Virginia City—and maybe meet up with a husband or two. If not, we'll keep on going to Bannack City. Wagon roads now all the way."

Even Alvah Riddle nodded cheerfully. The man had taken to bouncing and beaming, and inspecting his robes, and peering happily at his tanned and golden brides these last few days.

They drove easily across a shimmering wide valley, and not even the rushing clear creeks dicing the land slowed them in this last rush toward their destinations, and destinies. Chang and Buffalo Whiskers meandered ahead, less alert for hostile Indians here, although the Blackfeet prowled. In the dappled shade of quaking aspens beside a purling white creek, they made tumultuous love, the thunder music of howitzers, then lay stupefied, staring at humped puff clouds. When Chang looked up, it was into the alert shining eyes of three buffalo cows. They camped beside the Madison that night. At dinner, they feasted on tender hump roast, boiled tongue, boudins stuffed with spiced tallow and meat, and wild carrots and onions and camas root Mary scrounged from the verdant land.

This adventure was coming to an end. Chang had no idea what he'd do next, but his golden-bellied beauty would be with him. The earth was vast and wild, and he was unready to become a dutiful courtier in the shadow of the

Manchu emperor. Someday he'd spin his tales of this endless wilderness and its wild peoples, and they'd lift fans to lips and whisper him a liar. He laughed easily. Mongol blood coursed his veins, blood that would boil even in the cool shadows of the palace of T'ung Chi.

But first he'd see Goldtooth to Bannack. He'd promised her that, and she'd sealed the contract her own delicious way. There were yet perils, from what the oaf in Gallatin City had told him, and his blood raced at the thought of another fine brawl or three. In the settling dusk, he pulled Buffalo Whiskers to him. He'd change her name when at last they crossed the wide Pacific, and hope the emperor wouldn't steal her.

Mary-Rita was subdued. The moment of truth was racing down upon her. What would Tommy O'Dougherty think? Was he rich? Did this endless land bleed his Irish soul, so he'd become something else? He was probably ugly as sin and mean as a lord, or he wouldn't have got himself a bride by mail. Well, if so, she'd give him a piece of her mind, and if he guzzled ale, she'd have a thing or two to say about it.

Still . . . an Irishman here! She stared nervously at her tanned arms with a summer's gold trapped in them. She'd borrowed Drusilla's ivory-handled looking glass and barely recognized herself. Sunbleached red hair tumbled about her now, and hardship and hunger had chiseled her rectangular face into sharp planes, narrowed her nose and turned her freckles into a single tan mass. Her eyes glistened with light caught from the sunny prairies and long blue mountains. She'd become too good-looking for him! She wouldn't let the likes of a Tommy O'Dougherty, up to his knees in muck, touch a beautiful lass like herself! She'd not say a word to some common potato of a man, no matter what that Alvah Riddle might try to do. She'd find a lord and save herself for him. She'd be a lady, and no blarney from some grubby red-faced mucker would turn her cheek!

Her ma told her once to keep her legs crossed and nothing bad would happen. She practiced crossing her legs, and squeezing her thighs together, back and forth, banging her knees. It'd take more than that mean Tommy O'Dougherty to pry them apart, she thought savagely. And probably not a priest in the whole place. She would just keep her legs tight, that's what she'd do. It'd take a rich man or a sheriff or official, Catholic, of course . . .

"There's some bushes up there. I'll stop if you want," said Sleeping Bear.

"None of your business!" she howled.

The trail took them over a tumult of low grassy hills, and down into the vast valley of the Madison River, arching south and flanked by long chains of mountain to either side. Puffy clouds dawdled on the peaks to the west, a range Mister Skye called the Tobacco Roots. The trail veered to the western edge of this vast trough, and turned up the valley of a creek barely two feet wide that raced between long grassy slopes dotted with cedar and sagebrush. The land lay naked, and game stayed distant. She'd never seen such a vast tumbled country, and she felt about the size of an ant in it.

They encountered a hard-looking man named Slade building a toll gate at a rocky choke point. A stone cabin stood upslope.

"Four bits a wagon. I cut this road through," he said.

"You're a long way from the Platte," said Skye.

"You're Skye," said Slade.

"Mister Skye."

Slade nodded and let them pass without paying.

The man scared Mary-Rita witless. They probed through hills so barren and foreboding that she thought the world had ceased to be, or maybe this corner was forgotten by God. She blessed herself. At the low divide they paused to rest. Ahead some vast distance lay black mountains, a devil's kingdom for sure. Mister Skye led them toward hell. Massed gray clouds lowered over those mountains, and the high ridges to the south, sawing them off, bellying down upon the gray land like squatting heathen goddesses. Gold! That's what heathen hunted. Father O'Reilly had warned her about greed, and now she smelled greed everywhere. And Tommy O'Dougherty swirled gold there.

They curled down a sharp slope, rough-locking the wagon wheels to slow their descent. From upland grasses they plunged into gulches of alder, lined with pine, and sweeping around one last curve they beheld an astonishing sight, sprawled cabins and huts, dugouts, a main street with a stone building up and scores of board-and-batt ones being erected, steep-roofed with false fronts. Virginia City. A whole metropolis in September, where none had existed in May.

Everywhere below them men and horses, teams and wagons, swarmed like insects. The sound of hammering lifted to them, and Mary-Rita spotted workmen crawling along walls and beams. She wondered where the sawn wood had come from. Alder Gulch itself curved past the lower end of town, an avenue of bright green alders that shaded the fevered sluicing and panning and rocking of thousands of rough men. Not even the lowering black clouds stayed the feverish swarming of the tiny men below her, gouging gold, guiding giant three-hitch trains drawn by twenty-mule teams from Salt Lake City, throwing together shelter against oncoming winter, buying and selling with a golden dust for money, worth much more than Mister Lincoln's greenbacks.

Somewhere below, Tommy O'Dougherty would probably be washing the gravels. Or maybe he lingered still at Bannack City if he had a good claim there. She had no intention of staying for an hour in this horrible raw place. She'd give him that for starters, she would! Where could she find a priest? She was getting tired of crossing her legs.

Over in the next wagon, Goldtooth laughed. "Oh, we are about to get rich and have fun," she cried. "But maybe Bannack City is bigger and richer. We'll see."

Mrs. Parkins turned wild, peering hot-eyed into the gulch as she stood up the slope in her beautiful doeskin blouse and skirt. Big Alice and Juliet Picard gaped happily.

The shame of it! thought Mary-Rita. And likely Tommy O'Dougherty would prefer such ones to her! Oh, she'd read him her mind, she would! He'd been patronizing them, those evil creatures, instead of saving himself for her. She just knew it! Squandering his gold, wasting his fortune, and not saving a bit of it for her! Oh, she would scold him. He'd have to show her a whole mountain of gold before she'd consent to the sacrament of holy matrimony!

Alvah Riddle's nasal bark snapped her out of her reverie. "You get out of that red wagon, Mary-Rita. We're going in separate. Skye and the sluts, Chang and all, can wait behind. From now on, you keep clear of the bawds and squaws and Chinese and all like that."

Sleeping Bear, beside her, laughed. But it made sense. Lord God in heaven and all the holy saints, she didn't want to ride into this Virginia City in a red wagon!

Alvah skipped around his green wagon, unlocking the braked wheel, and they clattered recklessly into town. Amazingly, Mister Skye halted the rest above town. Mary-Rita felt ashamed—it was almost like betraying friends—but relieved too. Now she was in respectable company, the respectable Drusilla beside her, and the Riddles. Protestants, but she'd escape that soon enough. She pressed her knees together so tight her bladder hurt.

Wallace Street, a crude sign said. There was another rutted thoroughfare running parallel down in a shallow gulch to her right; still others lining the hill to her left. Riddle's mules and horses jangled down the rutted street, past raw plank buildings, log saloons and cabins, an astonishing mercantile called Pfouts and Russell, made of hewn rock. Gusts of icy rain dashed her face but she refused to crawl under the wagon sheet. Alvah Riddle was fairly dancing on the seat, smiling and whistling. Miner and workmen spotted the women and crowded close, galvanized by the sight of white women here, only months after this had been utter wilderness. Bale of Hay Saloon. Dance and Stuart. Idaho Hotel, a squat log structure. Full of bedbugs, she thought. Another one, the Virginia Hotel,

still roofless, its walls wet with rain but the sign in front
new and silvery with water. Mud stuck to wheels now,
making them hiss. Rough bearded men in shapeless black
pants, slouched hats, flannel shirts with faded red underwear peeking from the throat, and square-toed brogans.
All staring. Ox teams drooped in their yokes, chained to
battered wagons with rain-sagged gray sheets. Whirls of
cold water splashed her face, but still Alvah drove, his
itchy fingers making his mules mince, showing off, flaunt-
ing the rarest merchandise in the wilderness, in this camp.

"Whatcha got there, friend?" yelled an amiable young
man whose blond hair glowed even in the gray light. He
walked lithely beside the wagon now, peering first at Mary-
Rita, then Drusilla, then the Riddles, his eyes never stopping.

"Brides!" crowed Alvah like an inflated rooster.
"Spoken-for brides from the states. All spoken-for, fella,
but I'll take your name and put it on the list. And robes—
I've got buffler robes, two ounces of dust for a whole robe,
ounce and a half for a split."

"Name's Ives, George Ives. Put me on your list. And
yours?"

"Riddle," Alvah replied. "Here or in Bannack City."

Mary-Rita and Drusilla glanced at each other. The lithe
blond man wasn't named O'Dougherty or Rasmussen.
Drusilla looked tense, with worry lines radiating from her
mouth. Like Mary-Rita, she refused to take cover, and
gaped at this wild raw place half horrified, half fascinated,
water dripping from her chin and turning her sun-streaked
hair black.

On they went, down the gentle slope. New York Cloth-
ing Store. Variety Store. Gohn and Kohrs butcher shop.
A turnoff with a dripping sign pointing toward Highland,
Pine Grove, and Summit, up the gulch. Nevada, Central,
Adobetown, Junction City down the gulch. Mechanical
Bakery. Morier's Saloon. California Blacksmith and
Wagon Shop. Gem Saloon. Fairweather District. Oliver
Stagecoach Line. Peabody and Caldwell. At the base of
Wallace, Riddle swung his team around while three blue-

jacketed Celestials watched, and onto the lower street, Cover, gawking, hunting miners' shacks and dugouts. But this was not a respectable place. Dusky women lolled here under porches, veiled only by water. He wheeled the wagon up a cross-street, Van Buren, to the safety of Wallace, and pulled up before the Idaho Hotel, which lay squat and cold under the sheeting deluge. He glimpsed Mister Skye and his squaw, the bawds, the Chinese, swinging over to Cover Street, and Daylight Gulch.

Clouds rolled through them now, and Mary-Rita wondered what Alvah would do. He needed to find both of two men, both miners. Men who owed him five hundred dollars in gold, upon delivery. Mary-Rita found herself clenching Drusilla's icy wet hand for comfort.

Chapter 28

Fresh snow bleached the surrounding black peaks and even the lower barren hills, reminding Goldtooth that winter would soon grip this high country of far northwest Idaho Territory. So much to do, and she scarcely knew where to start. She'd trade the robes first, she thought. The ladies needed dresses and underthings, flour and sugar, coffee and tea.

What a mad, vibrant, fascinating raw place! Some called it Fourteen Mile City, because miners toiled from the head of Alder Gulch clear down to the Stinking Water River, with Virginia City somewhere near the middle. A place where a sporting lady could mint a fortune in weeks, but also a place that might not last. These placer camps vanished as fast as they sprang to life, after miners had panned and sluiced and gouged nugget gold and dust from the gravels and bars.

Last night, in the midst of that violent storm, Mister Skye took them into town, his face pinched and suspicious. She could see he didn't like places like this. Mary looked fearful and ill at ease. Sheeting cold rain had

chased men off the streets, but those who braved the wet
stared at Goldtooth's wagons and the women in the seats,
uncertainty written on their faces. Were these women in
water-blackened skin dresses and beaded skin blouses respectable? The gawking men couldn't tell, and it amused
Goldtooth. Let them wonder for a bit. She read the yearning in their eyes though, and their wants pierced to her.
Mister Skye had squinted narrowly through the drip, his
gaze clashing with mercantiles and miners, ox teams and
log cabins. Upslope from the main street rose the begin-
nings of permanent homes. Down on the next muddy street
to the right, though, squatted lines of shanties and tents.
He swung that way.

This gummy street was different. A hurdy-gurdy, the
Virginia Dance, stretched back from the thoroughfare, wet
logs and a peaked canvas roof, and an ornate sign pro-
moting four-bit dances. Goldtooth laughed. What a way
to make a living! Those poor dears clung to respectability
they didn't have, and wore themselves out for pennies. She
found the line across Daylight Creek: shacks, tents, and a
few larger houses half built. Icy rain had chased the girls
inside like the whine of a street preacher, and the travelers
splashed through the raw and sullen district appalled.

She wondered whether she could even find men to build
her a parlor house. The thought of her gorgeous red-brick
building in Memphis brought pangs of regret. How could
she afford such a thing here? How could she and her ladies
even find comfort in a place like this with winter lowering
over them? Maybe Bannack City, almost two years old
now, might be better. Still, countless males tore at gravel
here, thousands of men and almost no women, and most
of these burly rough men had leather pokes full of dust.
She laughed. There was no call to be gloomy, not when a
fortune lay at hand!

Mister Skye found a small bench of level land just west
of town, near the road to Nevada City, that night. His face
became a hard mask as he studied the town, its toughs, the
shanties of flinty miners around the edges, and the hard-
ness didn't soften until they were a few hundred yards out.

The bench had been grazed hard, and little was left for the mules and horses, but it'd have to do. No one except Chang had money for a livery barn or feed.

"I'd suggest you stay here in the lodge tonight," the guide said. "Too cold and wet to cook out there, and your wagons will be plenty chill even if you sleep under robes. In the morning, when it's warmer and drier, do your dickering or whatever you need to do."

That seemed agreeable to them all. Mary and Buffalo Whiskers managed to find firewood in a gulch, peeling back wet bark to make kindling from dry wood underneath. Only Chang prowled, and had returned quickly after a look at the main street. He seemed uncommonly silent to Goldtooth.

"Have a bad time, honey?"

"I tried to buy feed at Boyd and Smith Livery," he said after a moment's silence.

No one spoke for a while.

"It'll take Riddle a day or two to find out whether those husbands are in this camp or Bannack," the guide said. "That'll leave you time to get at your own business. In the morning we'll make camp back away from town, find grass. The farther back, the better we'll be."

He glanced solemnly at Mary and Buffalo Whiskers, who were drying their hair close to the lodgefire.

Goldtooth marveled at the warmth and comfort of the tipi, and understood at last how a man like Mister Skye could choose to live in a skin tent like this. She drifted to sleep easily, and the last thing she remembered was Mister Skye sitting up in the glow of the embers, his Sharps across his lap. No Jawbone lived to warn him, and he wasn't taking chances.

In the bright morning, with ice glinting like diamonds from every shrub, tree, and building, she and Sleeping Bear drove the red wagon up Wallace to Dance and Stuart's big log mercantile for some trading. Men stared but obviously didn't know what to make of the buckskin-clad twosome. Let them wonder! she thought.

They entered a long narrow log cavern, gloomy after

the glare of the sun. Few shelf goods lined the walls, and even the rough tables down the center were bare: the camp devoured everything as fast as freight teams hauled it almost four hundred miles from Salt Lake City. All the better, she thought. If this, the town's biggest emporium had nothing, the smaller places would have less. At one side a bootblack stand projected into the narrow building, presided over by a cadaverous clubfooted dirty man with stained fingers. He studied Goldtooth with calculating eyes.

"I'm Dance," said a brown-bearded young man in a gray flannel shirt. "Need help?" He stared at Goldtooth, unable to make up his mind about her. Sleeping Bear puzzled him just as much.

"Do you trade, honey?"

Dance's eyes went flat and cautious. "Likely," he replied.

"I have a dozen tanned robes. A few pair of moccasins and some fringed elkskin shirts, all Arapaho."

"I can sell pretty near anything here. Good robes fetch three or four dollars at Benton. The shirts—I'll have to look."

"No," she said. "Not three or four for the robes. I'll sell them off my wagon in the streets for much more, honey."

He stared at her. "Let's go look. That your red outfit there?"

"All mine, honey."

She held back robes for herself and her girls and sold everything else. He offered her ten a robe, and twenty-five dollars for the rest, if she'd take it all out in trade rather than cash.

"Suits me, honey," she said. The storekeep became more and more edgy.

"I'll fetch George Lane to help," he said. Dance, the lame bootblack, and Sleeping Bear carted robes to his plank counters while Goldtooth prowled the two aisles, finding little she wanted. In the end she settled for bolts of navy and gray woolen broadcloth, muslin for petticoats, canvas, needles and thread, small sacks of beans, sugar, flour, coffee, a few sprouting potatoes, and ready-made highbutton shoes for herself, in black, and a pair for Mrs. Parkins, who wore her size.

"Is there a dressmaker here?" she asked.

Dance shook his head. "No . . . might be one or two women who could fashion a dress, but Bannack City's the place. Several fine ladies there—" He cut himself off suddenly.

"I run a parlor house, honey. Which place, Bannack or here, is the place to be?"

Dance stiffened, flustered, and peered about the empty store, seeking the funneling ears of customers and finding none.

"This is a rich strike," he said. "Never seen the like. No telling how long it'll last, though. These placer diggings don't settle into keeper towns like quartz mines. Bannack's got quartz, and lots of gold still, though half the town stampeded over here last June. Depends on what you want, ah, ma'am. Fast money here, comfort over there. Maybe they'll find quartz here soon."

"Thanks a bunch, honeypie," she said. She felt Dance relaxing behind her as she and Sleeping Bear clambered into the red wagon and set off for the line.

They halted the mules before the only substantial building, a narrow log affair with lime mortar, a sawn-wood-roofed porch, and a peaked plank roof covered with tar-coated canvas. The morning had scarcely begun and she knew she'd awaken someone. But the Life never stopped for sleep. A place was always open; a lady always available. Leaving Sleeping Bear with the wagon and team, she dodged a puddle and entered. A single tiny window doled grudging light upon a cramped front parlor sided by wooden benches, like a jail cell. The door triggered a small bell, but then silence struck her. She smelled sour whiskey and lilac.

She sat on a bench. Back there, the madam or one of the girls would struggle awake, throw on a wrapper, and scuff in slippers out here to see what sort of male wanted sport at eight in the morning.

A buxom blond materialized, sleepy-eyed, in an open gray wrapper. She seemed surprised to find a woman.

"I'm Nell. Nellie. Strumpet Nellie," she said. "My house here. You here on business or pleasure or both?"

"Goldtooth Jones, from Memphis, honey," she said, rising. "I'm in the Life. I have three ladies out in a wagon."

"I can use you. Always need more girls," said Nell. "Are they pretty?"

Goldtooth grinned. "Knockouts. And they all love the life and won't go running off. But honey, I'm just here to find out stuff, if you don't mind. Like what's the best place to be, Bannack or here? And how can I get a place of my own built?"

Nell laughed sleepily. "Look, sister, you can't get a place built. No workmen will build it. Every goddamn one is building stores or miner cabins or outhouses or driving freight wagons or putting up saloons . . . You think I make money? I do, sister. More dust than I ever seen, but I'm in the hole. I got a note on this place I can't pay off in two years, just because I had to bribe workers—fifty dollars a day, fifty dollars!—to throw this dump up. Makes me want to go back to Bannack. This damned dump. I still got my place there, but it'd be slow now—"

"You've a place in Bannack?"

"Yeah, nice log building, parlor in front all fixed up, cozy little bar to serve spirits, six cribs, plus my private quarters, barn in back for horse and carriage, plus a room there for my houseman. I sure don't know why I left, especially with winter coming on."

"Would you rent, honey?"

"I'd prefer to sell. Long as I'm here, I don't see hanging on to property there. Bannack's down to a thousand people now."

"I'm interested, honey. We lost everything on the trail and I can't pay at once. But in six months—"

"I've heard that song before, Mrs. Jones. I want dust, and now. But if you stick around here, that's just more competition . . . Tell you what: I can tell from the girls. Bring the girls over and let me see the merchandise, and I'll tell you what I'll do. Maybe I'll rent. I've got a man there keeping the place. Some miner who couldn't pan gold out of his navel. Amos Rasmussen. He came to me almost busted after scraping dust off a poor digging, and spent his poke on my girls. So I'm paying him a dollar a day to keep the place. Maybe I'll rent. You'll need a man anyway, I suppose.''

Rasmussen's name seemed vaguely familiar to Goldtooth. He would solve another problem, now that Sleeping Bear wasn't available and poor Blueberry lay on his scaffold.

"I'll rent,'' she said. "And buy in six months, Nell. And we'll be in Bannack, not competing with you here.''

Nell retreated into herself. "So damned early I don't have my head on,'' she muttered. "I'll sell. You pay me five hundred a month for five months and it's yours.''

"That's a lot. And I haven't even seen it—''

"Take it or leave it.'' She yawned.

Goldtooth took it. Five rough months. But she knew exactly what she'd do. Parade Mrs. Parkins through this camp and Bannack until they knew of her from one end of Idaho to the other. And then charge three or four ounces of dust.

Alvah put them up in the Idaho Hotel. He hated to squander the cash, but he wanted the girls bathed and fresh and healthy, and besides, Gertie begged him for the comfort.

It'd be a good angle, though, to make them grateful. "I don't normally waste money like this,'' he said to Drusilla. "But we got some celebrating to do, and I guess Alvah Riddle can afford to put his brides up comfortable. You just remember that I never stint on comforts. Now I'll pay the extry four bits for a hot bath—you and Mary-Rita can share—and you can git yourselves all fixed up, dresses flatironed and all, whilst I go hunt for Rasmussen and O'Dougherty, if they're in this camp.''

Drusilla nodded curtly, and Alvah skittered out to find a livery for his mules and horses. At Morier's Saloon he invested in popskull, privately cussing the two-dollar price, and the price of everything in this camp, and beckoned the barkeep.

"Say, my friend," he whispered confidentially, "I'm new to the diggings, and I've some special merchandise for two men—one named Rasmussen, and the other O'Dougherty. Now how does a gent find these boys in a place like this? I'll make it worth your while," he added craftily.

"Buster, there's three, four thousand men in this gulch and more pouring in daily. It runs from the summit, way the hell south of here, down to the Stinking Water. You'll just have to start at the top and start asking. Might take a few days."

"No message place?" asked Alvah. "No one leaves his name anywheres?"

The barkeep shrugged. "Never heard of either one. You might try the other saloons. Gem, Bale of Hay . . ."

"I'll get cracking," said Alvah. "Say, if I can't find these boys, I've some hot merchandise here. Brides. Both guaranteed respectable, unsullied, know what I mean. Now, for a price I'll—you be thinking of the right customers, eh? I got the rarest thing in the whole camp, and I don't make matches cheap. Understand? I'll pay you a finder's fee."

The barkeep stared. Alvah downed his popskull and sidled out. At the Bale of Hay he got lucky.

"O'Dougherty? Sure, there's one here, man. Thomas. Tommy. He spreads a little dust in here most evenings. He's staked one of the best bars in the gulch, half a mile up from here. In fact, just above Bill Fairweather's discovery claim. Big brown-haired fellow, happy as a king. He's got so much dust he stores it in Dance and Stuart's safe."

"That's the one!" exclaimed Alvah. "I've got something special for him, yes, special merchandise. Say, you've never heard of this Rasmussen?"

"Can't say as I have. You got special merchandise for him, too?"

"Brides!"

He trotted back to the hotel, and pounded on the women's cubicle. "Be ready, Mary-Rita," he cried. "I'll take you to O'Dougherty in the morning."

"I'll tell her," said Drusilla wearily, through the door. "She's in the bath parlor out back."

After a night of no-quarter bloodletting, in which the bedbugs emerged victorious, Alvah shepherded Mary-Rita up a raw road gouged out of red earth, to the gravel bar worked by her intended. He permitted no one else to come, not wanting troubles or diversions. Mary-Rita never opened her mouth, and followed along dutifully in a fresh-pressed pink dimity dress, scrubbed and tanned.

"Now you be nice, Mary-Rita. Remember, I'm Cupid."

He found O'Dougherty easily enough. He had the look of a boxer, and worked shirtless even in the cool air.

"Yas, I'm Tommy O'Dougherty," he boomed in a laughing basso voice. His bright eyes swept Mary-Rita, who stood shivering and speechless.

"I'm Riddle. The broker. The little old matchmaker and happiness man. Well now, I've brought the little lady. Here she be, clear across the continent. Straight from Ireland. Unspoiled—you can have her examined at your expense, and then tie the knot. Of course, I'll need my contract fee first, five hundred in dust, plus a few minor expenses—"

But O'Dougherty's eyes were on Mary-Rita, his gaze sweeping from her sun-gilded carrot hair to the square tanned and freckled planes of her upthrust face, to the fine silky curves that filled out her dress. A grin crinkled his tanned face. White even teeth showed. His brown eyes danced.

"Would you be marrying a rich mick, Mary-Rita Flaherty?" he asked, some comic light in his voice.

"Tommy O'Dougherty, I wouldn't marry you for all the silk in China. Imagine my marrying a man with no shirt! Shame upon you, you ugly beast. I'll not marry the likes of you, you blasted miserable pig."

O'Dougherty laughed.

"And furthermore there's no priest, and you'll have me living in sin, you would. I won't do it, me pure and all, keeping me legs crossed three thousand miles, and now you want to be hauling me off and making babies without even—"

"Why, Mary-Rita, that's a good thing. There's a priest rode into camp a few days ago, held a Mass first thing and married up six miners and their women in holy matrimony. He's a Jesuit, Joseph Giorda, and he's in town. Why, lass, we'll go visit him directly."

"Not on your life!" she cried. "You build me a house first, with glass and lace curtains and doilies on the stuffed chairs."

"Why, Mary-Rita Flaherty, I've done it. I've hired it built while I've mucked gold. Would you come see it, lass?"

"Don't you touch me," she said. "I'd rather die. You take a bath first. Imagine kissing the likes of you, Tommy O'Dougherty!"

Alvah Riddle danced on one foot and then the other, and needed a bush to relieve himself. "Now just a minute, just a minute. I can't release this little lady until I'm paid. Cupid's fee," he said, chortling.

"Where are you from, Mary-Rita Flaherty?"

"Tipperary, and what's it to you? What's wrong with Tipperary, may I ask? Aren't I good enough? You, putting on airs, spending your dust on scarlet women, throwing away money on fancy houses, and drinking yourself into a wreck of a man. I know all about you, Tommy O'Dougherty!"

The miner laughed, a fine roar up from the belly, and he slipped his hard brown hand around her slim one.

"I'm a lost soul, sure I am," he replied. "I think I'm going to love you, Mary-Rita Flaherty."

"I won't love you until after we're married," she replied. "And then you'll stop drinking, stop smoking, and stop going to the Bale of Hay Saloon."

"Let's find the priest," he said, reaching for his shirt. "I've got to pay Cupid here, so we'll be walking to Dance and Stuart's."

"I'll give the bride away!" cried Alvah.

"That won't be necessary, Cupid," replied Tommy O'Dougherty. "I'll pay you now, and that'll be it."

Chapter 29

Drusilla wept through the wedding, more for herself than for Mary-Rita, who beamed pugnaciously through it all. The bride looked ferociously happy, and the groom kept grinning and winking at his mining pals, who had gathered in Tommy O'Dougherty's fine cabin to help him solemnize a union.

Father Giorda looked faintly skeptical about all this, but rattled his way through the ceremony and the Mass with aplomb, after a private hour counseling the betrothed. Alvah Riddle, polished up to a fine gloss and sporting his Sunday suit, smelling of camphor, fairly floated, enjoying his roll as matchmaker and Cupid and successful entrepreneur. Gertrude had spiffed up too, and sat at the rear, a dowager lump, faintly put off by the Romish mumbo jumbo. Mister Skye, Mary, and Sleeping Bear had come to the celebration, but the sporting women stayed discreetly away, and Chang, who had encountered rank hostility in the camp, found other things requiring his attention.

Alvah had plenty to crow about, Drusilla thought bitterly. That morning, just before he was about to ride up and down the gulch seeking Rasmussen, Goldtooth had pulled him aside with her news. A gent named Amos Rasmussen was in Bannack, a caretaker for an empty house of ill fame. The news hit Drusilla like a dropping guillotine blade. In the crumbling moments that followed, all her dreams and hopes disintegrated into dust. The dream of love, of respect, of a good marriage with pleasures of the heart, of companionship, of joy of soul and body, of a part in a new community, a happy home, a place for her books, a hand to hold in the night, a kiss at dawn, a sharing of all that she was, a husband in whom she might find pride . . . all gone in one sagging, caving minute.

She had not known whether she could bear to watch Mary-Rita's wedding, but the girl pressed her, and Drusilla had come with soul and limbs heavier than lead. She'd started this long journey an ugly duckling expecting nothing much, and resigned to a bluestocking life. But along the trail her hopes had risen, not only because her face and figure had changed, but because the long trek had to lead to something good. Surely a woman who had set her small world aside for this, a woman who dared and dreamed, would find goodness and mercy and love at the end of this long rainbow. But no. She grieved. She was widowed before she was wedded. Shorn, doomed. She barely managed to compose herself through the ceremony, and sometimes she failed, and dabbed wet cheeks with a lilac-scented handkerchief from her dowry trunk.

It never occurred to her to break the contract. That wasn't in her. The best she might manage would be a shameful divorce and escape to nowhere, her life a ruin. Even as Mary-Rita and Tom exchanged vows, Drusilla's mind turned to Parsimony McGahan, and suddenly she craved him. Ruthlessly she'd driven every vagrant thought of him from her mind. She managed days on the trail when she didn't think of Parsimony at all. But now the image of him flooded her soul, and she remembered his every word, and the light in his eyes, and the dimming flame when she told him she had committed herself. Now she had only the book of Browning poems to console herself. It was something anyway. After this, she would flee to the wagon and read them, and remember him. He was so far away, far far away, in a place with the same name as this . . .

Then they were all congratulating the bride and groom, handshakes and hugs. Drusilla watched, as if from a distant planet, in a fog of despair. She drifted to the door of Tom O'Dougherty's solid cottage and stepped into bright sun, but Mary-Rita caught her there, hugged her and wept.

"I'll miss you," cried the bride. "We came a long way together, we did, and it all worked out. It'll all work out for you, Drusilla."

"No, it won't work out."

"Come visit. The O'Doughertys will be servin' tea any afternoon."

Drusilla summoned the courage then to congratulate the groom, smile, and slip into the silence of the day. Mister Skye, Mary, and Sleeping Bear all stared at her, she knew, for they had heard Goldtooth's news.

They all drifted toward the wagons. Nothing kept them in Virginia City now. Alvah Riddle danced and skittered behind them, beaming at passersby, doffing his brushed black bowler, smiling his toothy smile from distended pink cheeks.

The lithe blond man who had waylaid them in the rain caught up with Alvah now.

"Looks like you found one of the grooms and had a little wedding," he said amiably.

"Indeed I did," boasted Alvah. "Thomas O'Dougherty, on up the gulch. I believe he's a solid citizen."

"Indeed he is," said the golden-haired man. "He's staked one of the richest bars in the gulch, and coining money."

"He sure is! Paid me my whole fee without a quibble. I charge plenty, you know. He handed over all that dust because I brought him a great bride. Only the best. What did you say your name was?"

"Ives. George Ives," said the man. "Come from Wisconsin, little place you never heard of called Racine."

"Well, Ives," said Alvah. "I have the other groom located in Bannack City. Rasmussen. I tell you, this is a great business if you have the knack and know the angles. Why, my Gertie and me, we'll clear a young fortune, more than most men earn in three years. Brides, and a fine sideline, picked up prime buffalo robes. I sold those for a premium price, too, lots of dust."

"You'd better be careful," said Ives. "This camp has its toughs and thugs. When you get to Bannack, you look up the sheriff, Henry Plummer. He'll look after you."

"Good idea," said Alvah. "That's what the law is for, protecting folks."

George Ives grinned, raked Drusilla with veiled eyes, and ambled off.

Drusilla peered up the long slope at O'Dougherty's cottage, saw the bride and groom standing in the door seeing the last of their guests off. Then the door closed, and Mr. and Mrs. O'Dougherty were alone inside. Drusilla wept, tears sweeping her cheeks as they reached Wallace Street.

"Come along, little lady," said Alvah. "I'll fetch my wagon from the livery barn, while you get your things together at the Idaho. Cheer up now; bliss will be yours in no time."

She sighed, wanting somehow to stay close to Mister Skye.

"Want to talk with you later," said the guide.

She nodded, and made her feet go toward the hotel, walking beside Gertrude. Across Wallace, Goldtooth and Mrs. Parkins promenaded in their beautiful Arapaho doeskin clothing, richly beaded and quilled, turning male heads with every step. Goldtooth was grinning; Mrs. Parkins leveled smoldering gray eyes upon stupefied burly men who didn't know what to make of the pair.

An hour later Mister Skye's entourage swung west down Alder Gulch, with Alvah Riddle's wagon a discreet hundred yards behind because he didn't want to associate too closely with the red wagons and packmules and travois-

laden horses ahead. Drusilla did not sit out on the seat.
She curled into her blankets in the shadow of the wagon,
and hid her tears from Alvah and Gertrude.

He led them along a good stagecoach road that ran down
the alder-strewn gulch between barren broad hills. The
bottoms swarmed with rough bearded men, panning,
gouging, shoveling gravel into wooden rockers and long
toms. They rolled through Nevada City and Central; past
Adobetown and the Granite Creek district. On a wide flat,
they pulled aside to let a Peabody and Caldwell Concord
stage rattle through, swaying on its leather braces. From
above, the shotgun messenger stared at them from flinted
eyes.

Mister Skye sank into melancholy. The men who gouged
these gravels gouged his heart. Settlement would arrive on
the heels of these industrious diggers, and something dear
to Mister Skye would be forever lost. He'd never been a
part of the United States, and hadn't even seen it except
for one journey to the frontier city of St. Louis. He'd left
Victoria's England behind, but was no more a Yankee than
Chang. But the bloody Yanks were swarming, both Northern and Southern varieties.

There'd be no game for miles in either direction. He
knew some of these people did nothing but supply the
camp with meat they shot in distant hills. The bawds had
grub now, and he and Mary would sup at their table, along
with Chang. Mister Skye had hung on to his thin eagle.
It'd buy Sharps cartridges in Bannack, but little more. He
hoped there'd be enough to lubricate his parched throat,
just a bit. He'd lost everything this trip. Bullock would
extend him a little credit back in Laramie, but that was all
he could count on. Maybe, just maybe, he'd winter with
Victoria and the Kicked-in-the-Bellies. His wives would
love that.

The thought turned his mind to Jawbone, and the bitterness seeped through him again, the bitterness of losing
that great horse and treasured friend to the Crows, to Victoria's own people. The buckskin pony he rode was a good

horse, carrying him smoothly along this final stretch, but it wasn't Jawbone, and wouldn't go to war like Jawbone. He knew, hollowly, that Jawbone would not be replaced. He felt too old to start training a colt the way he'd trained Jawbone long ago.

Chang and his tall bride rode close now, subdued by the rank hostility he'd discovered in Virginia City. The mandarin's face had become secretive and Mister Skye privately raged. Civilization brought hatreds and divisions. His memory whirled back to the sprawling rendezvous of the mountain men, wild times among happy barbarians as varied and colored as Joseph's Coat, and as bonded as brawling brothers. Ending, all of it faded away now, amidst these swarms of pick-and-shovel men crawling the gulch, bunched along this road.

They reached Pete Daley's ranch and stagecoach stop at twilight, and he decided to camp there for the night. Daley's place was a two-story log affair with a roofed verandah on one side. Tough-looking gents lounged about the porch. The upstairs room seemed to be a dance hall of some sort. The scratch of fiddle music drifted to him, and in the ambered windows he caught glimpses of bearded men and scrawny women. He wondered where the women had come from and what sort of place this might be.

Two of the loungers unfolded from the verandah and floated across the twilight.

"You putting up here?" asked one. Mister Skye peered into the flat eyes of a rough dark giant. The other was younger and lighter.

"We thought we might."

"Pasture's grazed down, but we have prairie hay. The stagecoach stock takes all we can get. Four bits an animal. You'll have to makeshift the rest. Place there's a saloon and dance hall. Ladies welcome."

Some sharp intuition stole through Mister Skye. "I guess we'll go on ahead a way," he said. "Most of us don't have scratch for a feed bill."

"Now hold up, Skye," yelled Alvah. "This here's a

lively looking place, and a bit of civilization isn't going to hurt anyone after months on the trail. Right, Gertie?''

Mister Skye ignored him, and addressed the heavy rough one: "What did you say your name was?''

The man stared at him. "Boone Helm. This other is Jack Gallagher.''

He'd never heard of either, but he knew the type.

"I reckon we'll go ahead to grass.''

"Mister Skye," said Goldtooth, "we don't have a plugged nickel for hay, but maybe we could make a little ol' bargain with these gents. Listen to the fiddle!''

The guide didn't like it a bit. Beside him Mary frowned, and Chang and Buffalo Whiskers sat their horses silently. "We'll go on ahead a mile or so for grass," he said abruptly.

But here, away from wilderness and back among people, his command had evaporated.

"Boone Helm," Goldtooth said cheerily, "if you're feelin' your oats, honey, we'll make us a little trade, oats for oats.''

"Let's go with Mister Skye," said Drusilla sharply from the green wagon.

"Now hush, little lady," said Alvah. "I'll buy some feed, and we'll just have us a whirl up there. I'll show you off, just in case this Rasmussen fellow can't come up with—''

"I do not wish to be shown off.''

"Now see here. It's in the contract that—''

"I'm coming with you, Mister Skye," she said, stepping down from the wagon. Riddle caught her but she wrenched free.

"Well, honeys, me and the ladies are stayin' for a little light entertainment, and the Riddles too. I guess we'll see you down the trail a bit in the morning.''

"As you wish," said Mister Skye curtly.

Trouble here. His nerves tingled with it. He touched heels to his buckskin and rode into the thickening night, with the amber lights fading behind him. Drusilla walked because the three wagons stayed at Daley's.

A mile ahead he pulled off the two-rut road into a star-washed meadow beside the Stinking Water. It seemed a good enough place, with grass and firewood, and enough open space to prevent surprises. Under a sliver moon, Mary silently erected the lodge, while Chang and Buffalo Whiskers made camp.

Too late, Skye remembered the bawds had whatever grub there was. There might be some jerky in one of Victoria's parfleches, but that'd be it.

Chang approached softly. "I'm going back. But not on the white stallion. Mind if I borrow one of your dark ponies?"

"One Chinese against many."

"One mandarin warrior."

"Helm's a murderer."

"How do you know that?"

"I know it."

Chang stared into the murk. "My little adventure must end happily. What point is there in protecting these ladies of the night across fifteen hundred miles of wilderness only to fail them among the barbarians?" The mock was back in this voice.

"It's Riddle who's in trouble."

Chang laughed. "How do you keep such a one out of trouble?"

He saddled a bay that stood like a shadow in the dark, and rode quietly back, on unshod hooves.

Skye picketed the horses and dug through the parfleches, finding nothing, and hunkered into the cool grass.

"We're going hungry," he said to Drusilla.

"I can bear it."

"Then you're stronger that I am. Miss Dinwiddie, I want to talk."

"About Rasmussen."

"No, not really. About slavery, and contracts that most courts would throw out the window."

"I'm obligated—" she began.

"I'm not going to let it happen, if it comes to that. I

don't think it will. The man apparently squandered his last dime, and hasn't the will or the means to make a living."

"In that case, Mister Riddle has the right to find another—maybe someone better—"

Mister Skye laughed heartily. "You're no abolitionist, but I sure am," he said. "I run my own underground railroad."

A wry smile spread across her moon-touched face. "A few weeks ago I would have stormed at you. I would have insisted on meeting my obligations . . . and ending my life." She paused, flinging herself back on the grass. "Railroad me, Mister Skye."

They laughed quietly, until Mary sat down, frowning, mystified. And then all three laughed. Buffalo Whiskers emerged from the lodge, joined them, and laughed because the others did.

Nothing happened.

The night-peace was broken by two hastening riders going west. With Jawbone dead, Mister Skye's mountain senses had gradually returned, and he slept cat-light, wakening at the slightest change of rhythm in the gloom.

A Bannack-bound Oliver coach awakened him just at sunrise. He pulled aside his doorflap to watch it rumble off into the morning silence. His belly protested its hollowness and made him sour.

An hour or so later, not long after Mary had broken his camp and loaded the lodge on the travois, the wagons rolled in, Big Alice and Sleeping Bear driving the red ones, Alvah the other. Alvah looked gray. Big Alice and Sleeping Bear looked weary and bag-eyed. Chang rode with them, looking taut.

"You missed the fun, Skye," said Alvah. "Not the most respectable place in the world, but we all had a whirl."

"Is that what you call it?" said Goldtooth, yawning. "Mister Skye, honey, you missed the party. I'd sure like to sleep in this mornin', but that damned Sleeping Bear made us all git—"

"It's a long way to Bannack City," growled Mister Skye. He pulled out ahead of them, leading the weary caravan one more leg. His stomach hurt, but that was nothing new. A thousand times, in the high country, cold and hot, his stomach had demanded food.

His sleep-robbed party strung out behind him, Drusilla back in the green wagon and looking brighter, Chang, Buffalo Whiskers, and Mary dozing in their saddles, Big Alice and Sleeping Bear rocking half-awake in their seats. They forded the Stinking Water, cut west, passed another stage stop, and nooned near Dempsey's ranch, in a broad valley guarded by blue ramparts now dusted white. With some of the bawds' grub in his gut, he felt better. The drawn look of hunger had slipped away from the faces of his women, too. Goldtooth joked about how her ladies had paid for hay and spirits, while Gertrude Riddle listened dourly.

"It sure enough was fun," concluded the madam. "You're just an old worrywart, Mister Skye."

"That's what you employed me to be."

In fact he was worrying more than ever. He alone in this party stayed alert and ready. The others weaved in their seats, reins loose in hand, scarcely caring whether they rolled anywhere. Even Chang catnapped on his white stallion.

The guide didn't like it, this vulnerable procession spread out loosely behind him because no one remained alert enough to keep the wagons close. He fought back sleep himself, wiped his face with cold water from springs and creeks, and finally trotted back to the wagons, growling at the drivers, demanding the customary care and wariness. He stomped out of his mind the bad feeling choking him, the sense of trouble crawling down his gut. Only yawns cleaved the afternoon. Maybe he worried too much, he thought, eyeing the still blue peaks and the quiet dun grasslands cupped in the valley.

Late that day they struck the rippling Beaverhead and followed it south along well-worn ruts. A Virginia-bound Peabody stage creaked by, followed by a party of German miners leading packmules, who saluted them in a strange tongue.

Ahead loomed a squat craggy landmark, Beaverhead Rock, or Point of Rock as it was called sometimes. The giant rockpile reared up in the dry valley as if thrown from some distant mountain by a god. The sun lay flat, and the pile of rock flared into orange and black chevrons. Nothing moved in this dry sage-packed bottom. He would camp up the Beaverhead a way, and they'd be lucky to scrounge enough dead sagebrush to build a decent cookfire.

An innocuous crease of land near the river came alive. Masked men swarmed out, six of them on blanketed ponies, just as the last of Skye's caravan, Riddle's wagon, straggled by. Skye cursed. They had the drop on him, six-guns leveled on him, on each driver, on Chang. Their hair lay hidden by wide-brimmed hats jammed down hard and blue bandanas rode high over their noses. And in between, mean cold eyes surveyed each of them.

"If you reach for your guns, you're dead," grated a voice. "You in the green wagon—you step down, slow and careful."

Chapter 30

Alvah Riddle froze, too anguished to do anything.

A shot blistered air inches from his nose. He startled, and trembling, clambered down on shaky legs.

"You. Big one. Drop it." Another shot slashed into Mister Skye's pommel, bloodying his hand. He let his revolver slip to earth, and slowly, slowly raised his arms.

"You! Chinese. Up with 'em. Up with the paws or you're a yellow-skinned dead man." A bullet crashed past Chang's chest. He bowed slightly and raised his hands.

"What you grinning at, heathen?"

"It's a jolly afternoon, Mister Helm," said Chang, mockery in his voice.

The masked road agent lifted his blue revolver, steadied, and pulled the trigger. A black hole in Chang's forehead. Gray and red splattering from the rear of his skull. He sighed, toppled, hit earth with a rolling thud, sprawled on his back. Buffalo Whiskers screamed, wild keening, piercing the sky. Blue powdersmoke curled. Shakily she slid off her pony, ran, sobbing, to Chang, threw herself upon him, hands clutching his chest, her cheeks sheeting with tears of sorrow.

The shot jarred Mister Skye. He rotated his head slowly to see behind him. Buffalo Whiskers sighed, slumped heavily over Chang's still body, twitched and lay quiet, blood leaking from her soft Arapaho skin shirt.

"Don't like colored trash," the road agent said.

Mary sobbed, slumped in her saddle, convulsing with terror and anguish. Mister Skye feared she would be next, but the agent had other things in mind.

Drusilla wept, trembling on the seat of Sleeping Bear's wagon. "You're scum!" she cried. "You're filthy scum! Murderers!"

From behind the dirty red bandana, black eyes glittered at her, and the bore of a heavy Walker Colt steadied on her.

"Go ahead, Boone Helm! Go ahead! I don't want to be in a world with the likes of you!"

"Don't," snapped another one from behind his mask.

Drusilla trembled violently. "Scum! Scum! Scum!" she cried.

The bigger agent nodded to another. "The heathen had gold. Get it, Red." A wiry man with a bit of carrot hair poking from his hat pawed through Chang's saddle kit, snatched out a sack. Then he flipped Buffalo Whiskers off Chang, leaving her in a crumple, and dug another sack from Chang's britches.

"I'm going to track you down. I'll track you down if it's the last thing I do!" yelled Drusilla, trembling.

Mister Skye winced. Miss Dinwiddie had the courage of the deranged.

A shot seared past her nose, making her start.

Alvah Riddle folded into the ground, trembling too violently to stand.

Goldtooth's dander was up. She peered out of the rear puckerstring hole of her wagon. "I know you, Boone Helm," she snapped.

A shot seared through the sheet, just above her. She

jerked back inside. Within, women sobbed and choked. Big Alice sat like a statue holding the reins.

"Get up, Cupid," said the big agent. Alvah couldn't manage it. His muscles had turned to jelly. A shot sprayed dirt in front of him and he bounded up, his hands trembling so violently he couldn't control them.

"Fetch Cupid's arrows," came the dry voice behind the bandana.

A dark one with brown almond eyes pawed into Riddle's coat and extracted a heavy leather pouch.

"No, don't . . ." moaned Riddle. "That's everything I've got."

Helm just nodded, and the dark one clambered inside. Gertrude squawked like a mad hen. "How dare you!" she cried. Chests and cases and barrels flew out of the wagon, popping open, spraying clothing and airtights. A flour bag burst white over sagebrush. Wind plucked every bit of clothing Drusilla owned, and tugged it across the prairie, where things snagged on sage. A sack of sugar burst, revealing a dark poke.

"There's the sweets," said the road agent. He plucked it up and peered inside. "You lied to me, Cupid. It wasn't everything. Do you know what we do to liars?" He lowered the revolver.

Riddle spasmed.

"Company," said an agent, pointing. A party of walking men, miners leading mules, materialized on the southwestern horizon.

The leader stared, and walked over to Goldtooth's wagon. "Give it to me," he said. "Last night's take."

Goldtooth handed him the dust they'd gotten at Daley's.

"The wages of sin is death," said the agent. The others laughed roughly. They clambered onto powerful fast horses, and trotted off, taking everything with them but sorrow.

Mister Skye's rigid muscles eased, and the bile settled back in his belly. He stared at his wet-cheeked Mary, and a shudder racked him. A squaw, nothing, annoyance to them. He stepped shakily off the buckskin and caught her in his big arms and hugged her. She trembled and wept and clutched him, in the tight circle of his arms.

"I can't cope with this, I can't cope with this . . ." Drusilla droned, on and on.

They all slumped, stupefied, too shattered to move. The party of miners found them that way, and took time, in the twilight, to shovel out a shallow grave for Chang and Buffalo Whiskers.

Mister Skye watched silently as the miners shoveled tan earth over Chang's chest and face, over Buffalo Whiskers's soft breast, and into her open mouth. Then they disappeared under the earth.

"Road agent work," said one of the miners, a graying man, leaning on his shovel. "Lots of it. You look pretty bushed. Guess I'll say some words. Heathen, but I'll say some anyway."

They gathered bareheaded in the dusk, and the miner read sonorously, and then they stood quietly, on into the darkness. Goldtooth and Big Alice sobbed softly. Vagrant thoughts hovered and whispered in Mister Skye's mind, and it came to him that he would attempt to contact Chang's family at the Imperial Court; and to bear the news to the Arapahos. They all camped together for protection beside the Beaverhead.

Alvah recovered his wits enough to bluster. "Everything I had, everything I had, except for what Rasmussen owes. You should have defended us, Skye. That's what you're paid for."

Mister Skye walked away.

"He did!" snapped Drusilla, barely containing rage. "He told you—told Goldtooth—not to stop there. But you stopped and had your fun. And it cost lives! Your money doesn't matter. Two lives matter!"

"He should have told me plainer," Alvah whined.

Mister Skye wasn't so sure of Drusilla's view. That Ives, asking questions back in Virginia . . . they knew all about Riddle. It would have happened somewhere.

As fast as gray dawn broke, they set off over frosty ground for Bannack City, the last lap. No one spoke. Drusilla and the Riddles had salvaged what they could. Mister Skye had inherited Chang's Spencer, three boxes of cartridges, his Colt revolver, a fine white stallion, and a bay pony. The trail cut west from the Beaverhead River, climbed steep dry hills, wove through tumbled grassy mountains as barren as death, and settled into an endless downgrade that wound into a hollow cut slashed by Grasshopper Creek. They toiled past Rattlesnake Ranch, a seedy stage stop, but didn't halt. Hard men watched them pass. A Kiskidden Company freight train, twenty ox teams on a three-hitch load, met them. No one felt like talking, but Mister Skye paused briefly to warn the bullwhackers what might lie ahead. They nodded solemnly.

They passed turnoffs into the hamlets of Spring Gulch and Centerville, on Grasshopper Creek below Bannack. Passed Jim's bar, and White's bar, rich diggings. Under a broken sky, with autumnal clouds scudding under the sun now and then, they rolled slowly down a grade into a white and black town, whitewashed plank and black logs, set deep in a hollow surrounded by barren long slopes. The place thrummed. In spite of the rush to Alder, a thousand argonauts gouged gravel here along four miles of the creek. They passed a cemetery hulking on a hill. Below lay Yankee Flats. Two-rut roads cut over slopes to Horse Prairie, and other hamlets in the district.

Mister Skye paused, leaning over the buckskin, staring at an outpost of civilization, such as it was. A ditch had been cut to the left, sluice water, and beside it ran a row of shanties. Storefronts and signs: Chrisman's Store. City Bakery. Bank Exchange Saloon. Skinner's Saloon. Goodrich Hotel, two stories and log. Oliver's Express Office. Aults Hall. Clothing. Pony Express Mail, four bits to Salt Lake. Off at Yankee Flat across the creek, a segregated row of solid log buildings, squatting silently in the cool sun. The line, he thought. He led them there directly, since both Riddle and Goldtooth were heading for the same place. Bannack bustled with freighters and coaches, horses tied to hitch rails, and bearded men hurrying along boardwalks. No one stared at the bedraggled newcomers, except to eye Mary and her travois ponies, an odd sight there.

A wooden bridge, knocking hollowly beneath them, carried them to the edge of town, over to the line slouching on Yankee Flats.

He pulled up before a bald ruddy man of indeterminate age, taking sun on a roofed verandah of a dark and silent rectangle of log.

"Looking for Nell's Place," he yelled.

The rocking stopped, then started again. The gent spat a long brown gob of chaw out upon the dust.

"Guess you found it," he said. "But it's shut down. She's off to Alder."

His blue rheumy eyes took in the red wagons, Goldtooth and Big Alice and Juliet, settled a long moment on Mrs. Parkins, glanced briefly at Sleeping Bear, gazed blankly at Drusilla and the Riddles, and sharply at Mary and her travois. He yawned, stood, revealing a hairy white belly, gaping out of a dirt-grayed buttonless flannel shirt.

"I'm the caretaker, Rasmussen," he said. "You got some business or other?"

Drusilla's face turned to gray granite.

"Home sweet home, honeys," said Goldtooth. "Mister, we're buyin' this ol' place from Nell. We'll just wander in—"

"How do I know that?" asked Rasmussen.

"Right here, honey," said Goldtooth, thrusting a sale agreement before him.

He stared blankly. "Don't rightly know that. My eyes a little weak. Maybe you could read it, eh?"

Drusilla closed hers, tightly.

Alvah Riddle brushed off his dusty clothing, inflated himself, and stepped lightly to Rasmussen.

"My fine friend, I have brought you a great treasure. Yes, Cupid has arrived with a quiver of love darts. Yes, indeed. My name, Rasmussen, is—Riddle!"

The bald man licked lips, and chewed. "Don't recollect it," he muttered.

"The marriage contract. The bride! I've brought the bride to warm your little nest!"

Rasmussen's belly quaked. Hoarse laughter. A wheeze and another brown gob splattered dust. "Aw, shit, I forgot. That's the little lady?"

"You have your fee waiting, of course," said Alvah.

Rasmussen rocked on the balls of scuffed boots. "Haven't got a dime. No gold in my gravel, lot of work for nothing. Sorry, pal."

Something eased in Drusilla's face.

"You can't pay? Can't pay? But you contracted—"

"Go to hell, Riddle." Rasmussen yawned, followed the bawds inside.

"Well, then, little lady, I have the right to make another match. Get you married off. One thousand. Yes, one thousand is my fee. Lots of gold-grubbers got it. Prepare to meet your man, little lady!"

"No," said Drusilla quietly. "No, no, no."

"The contract—"

"You heard her, Riddle," said Mister Skye softly.

"But we have a signed and sealed—"

"Free territory, not slave. Go on home, Riddle. Back to Skaneateles."

"Drusilla, you are obliged to come—"

"No, Riddle."

"I'll sue you in every court. I'll set the hounds baying. I'll—"

He yanked his revolver from its holster. Skye landed on him, driving him back, toppling him hard into dust. The revolver skittered into grass.

"Warned you," whispered Mister Skye, sitting hard on Riddle.

Drusilla screamed.

He rolled off. Riddle lifted his jarred body from the dirt and brushed himself. The guide collected the revolver, and Riddle's Spencer, unloaded them, and handed them to him.

"I think I want to see the inside of this place," said Drusilla.

"It's not respectable. You'll become a slut like the others," said Riddle.

The rest had wandered in. She and Mister Skye climbed the steps, leaving Gertrude and Alvah staring huffily from their wagon. Lampless gloom. A parlor with a bar at the side stretched across the front. Dark and barren now, with the rough plank floor echoing hollowly under their feet. A black hallway stretched back to the rear of the building. On the left, madam's quarters, a two-room apartment with a door into the bar. Whitewashed log, tiny high windows. Behind, six small cribs, bedless and dark, echoing night. Nell's Place sang its sadness.

"Home sweet home," said Goldtooth, unenthused. "Beats livin' in a tent in the middle of Idaho winter. Beats having Union Army bluenoses shutting me down."

"We'll fix this li'l ol' place up," said Mrs. Parkins. "Oh, I wish I had my stuff. But I guess I can replace it fast enough."

At the rear, a door. And down a path, necessary rooms, and a bathhouse with a stove and four-clawed tub. Mary stared at it, clambered inside, sat down and giggled. The bawds laughed. They all drifted back to the front parlor and found it empty. Rasmussen had returned to his rocker on the verandah.

Goldtooth slipped an arm through Sleeping Bear's. "Honey, I know you're leavin' the sporting life. But could you help us get settled in? I want to get rid of that Rasmussen. Definitely not the type for my parlor house. Before you start up the freightin', would you stay, and maybe help find me a good man?"

The former gambler paused, uncertainly. "I'll help you get going, Goldtooth."

"Oh, honey, that's grand! Now first thing, we'll have us a little ride through town. We're gonna sashay up and down Bannack. Take off the wagon sheet! Ladies, we'll get all polished up! Sleeping Bear, you can unload the sleeping robes and things. Haven't got money for beds and ticks and pillows yet, but who cares? We'll open tonight! Money, money, money!"

She turned at last to Mister Skye, Drusilla, and Mary. "Why, honey, you got us here. You got us here, all that long way. You got us through wilderness and hostile Indians and everything. Mister Skye, honey, you're welcome here anytime, for free."

Barnaby Skye laughed.

"What're you going to do, honey?" she asked Drusilla.

"I don't know. Yes I do know. I will find work. And I will save, and buy passage to—a place."

"Well, honey, you need help, you let me know." She turned to the guide. "Goodbye, dear Mister Skye. We'll remember you."

She hugged him. He felt her arms embrace him, felt not lust, but something larger. The others hugged him too, Big Alice, grinning, Juliet Picard, smiling mysteriously, and Mrs. Parkins, who pressed against him too hard.

"Sweetie, I've got treats in the cookie jar for you," she whispered.

Mister Skye laughed, and let her go.

Sleeping Bear caught his hand and pressed hard. The man wept. "Thank you," he said softly. "I'm proud to have known you."

"You were reborn in this free West," said Mister Skye. "Everything is possible for you, Sleeping Bear. You're a good man."

They stepped into blinding sun, leaving tears behind them. The Riddles had driven off, dropping Drusilla's trunk forlornly on the bare earth. The autumnal sky lowered cobalt upon the barren slopes.

"You're penniless. Not even four bits for a cheap room. Trunk sitting here. I've got an eagle I've been saving since Fort Laramie. Meant to buy some cartridges with it, but I don't need them now that I've got Chang's Spencer. Meant to buy—" He thought of the bottle he wanted so badly, to wet his parched throat. "Want you to have it. It'll keep you a week in a respectable rooming house, give you time to find something. Mary and I'll make do, get back to Victoria, spend a fat winter with the Kicked-in-the-Bellies."

"I'd like that. You'll be at Fort Laramie? I'll return the ten dollars when I can."

"Of course, you can stay with us. I hate like blazes leaving you here alone, prey to any—"

"Mister Skye," she retorted. "Look at me. Do I look like prey? After two thousand miles?" She laughed, throwing her loose sunbleached hair back, her eyes shining brightly from the tan planes of her face.

He hoisted her trunk onto a travois, and they rode to-ward the town, Drusilla walking beside them. The line squatted two hundred yards and two thousand miles from the rest of Bannack, and when they thrummed over the bridge, something in Drusilla's face relaxed.

On the main street they spotted a familiar green wagon, with ponies on a picket line behind it. Alvah, talking to a man with a sheriff's badge shining on his black suit, spot-ted them.

"There!" he cried. "That's the one. That woman's got contract obligations with me. He's stealing her. Already lost everything I got to road agents, and now that man—Skye—he's nipping her away! Don't know how we'll get back to New York, less I get my contract rights!"

Mister Skye found himself staring into the bland face of a compact elegantly dressed man, who studied him thoughtfully, his eyes glancing too casually to Mister Skye's fringed shirt, holstered Colt, and the Spencer he now cradled in his arm. Then at Mary. And then his gray eyes studied Drusilla, admiration kindling in them.

"I'm Plummer. Henry Plummer. You have a very beau-tiful woman there, Mister Skye. This gent says he has a contract, but that's a civil matter and out of my hands."

"Civil matter! That Skye almost killed me!"

Plummer turned to Riddle. "As I was saying. I see a thousand dollars here in the wagon, the mules, the ponies and harness. They command fine prices here, where things are short. Try Oliver's over there. Enough to get you and Mrs. Riddle home. Passage to Salt Lake is seventy-five each. And east on Holladay's Overland . . . you'll have enough. But watch out. Those road agents are a problem, so guard your poke.''

Plummer smiled, dismissing the Riddles. ''Now, Mister Skye, Miss Dinwiddie, if I may be of service . . .''

''Need a rooming house for the young lady. Say, where can I trade ponies? Forgot I had ponies to trade.''

''Indeed, Gibson's very respectable, over in that block there—and any livery barn. Oliver's . . .''

They turned onto a side street, with Mary and her travois ponies drawing stares, and eyes curious upon the burly guide on the buckskin horse, leading a long picket line, and the tall woman striding boldly beside him.

Two workmen on ladders were bolting a gilded sign onto a log building with a rough-sawn board front, whitewashed fresh. McGahan's Books. Drusilla gasped. Something feral caught up in her throat, erupting in a cry that shivered Mister Skye's flesh and spun Mary's head.

Drusilla Dinwiddie raced. But she'd been seen by a young man inside, who erupted from the door. They caught each other in the middle of the sunny street, caught and whirled, speechless.

''Parsimony!'' she wept. ''Parsimony! Parsimony!''

''I turned off at Fort Hall. Couldn't stand the thought of the Comstock. Thought I'd have a chance. Thought I might pay Riddle, outbid—thought I'd better find the woman I love, only woman I'll ever love . . .'' he babbled.

Drusilla clutched him and sobbed.

''I love you, Parsimony McGahan. I want you, now, with or without clergy. Married or not. Right now, forever . . .'' She buried her face in his chest, wetting his suit with flowing tears.

'' 'How do I love thee? Let me count the ways,' '' he whispered and she clutched him.

Burly men stared. Mister Skye coughed. Mary unloaded Drusilla's trunk and hauled it into the store, gawking at shelves of books. They all strolled into his store and found it half put together, books in barrels, books in stacks, books tumbling across white enameled floorboards. Lamps glowing, smell of leather and paper.

"Oh, Parsimony. What a place! What a good life of the mind you have!" cried Drusilla.

"Do you like it? It's yours, my darling."

A battered black top hat perched on a stack of books in a dark corner, looking forlorn and homeless. Barnaby Skye stared at it, recognition coming slowly. His own hat. The mark of an English gentlemen, the very hat that separated him from these Americans, the topper that fit his head so well that gales couldn't dislodge it.

"My hat," he said, picking it up and clamping it down.

Neither Parsimony nor Drusilla heard him.

"My hat!" he exclaimed.

"Found it," muttered Parsimony, never taking his eyes from the woman he loved.

"Where? How?" demanded Barnaby Skye.

He got no answer.

Mister Skye twisted it slightly, until it canted to starboard. "Haw!" he roared.

Mary giggled.

An hour later, Mister Skye and Mary rode east, up the long dry slopes out of Bannack City. His elkskin shirt was wet with Drusilla's tears. Beside him rode Mary, smiling, and behind them a picket string of ponies. Minus one he had traded at a livery for the grub that now burdened his parfleches. And a crockery jug corked tight, for the moment.

"Looking forward to tonight," he said, and she beamed.

Chapter 31

Outside the lodge, a horse stopped.

He and Mary were five hours east of Bannack, camping in a wooded draw among barren slopes. She'd scarcely gotten the parfleches put away. He sat in the dusk. Later he'd pull the cork. At the sound, he lifted the Spencer.

"Sonofabitch," yelled Victoria, outside. "You too close to the road, too easy to find. Get your horses stole."

He peered out, astonished. His Sits-Beside-Him-Wife materialized in the lavender twilight.

He hugged her, his mind full of questions.

In the wavering light of a smoky new fire, she settled herself quietly and grinned smugly, saying nothing.

Wait her out. He knew the game.

He yawned, scratched his belly, and formed in his mind the things he'd tell her, good and bad, bright and tragic, about what had happened since they parted. But why was she here?

"Yes, Victoria?" he asked, driven to surrender.

"Sonofabitch! Look here!" She dropped a flattened lead ball into his hand. He stared at it, finding no meaning.

"From Jawbone. He's feeling pretty good. Gonna be fine when we get back. Red Turkey Wattle, he made big medicine. He found the ball, down under the skin, between Jawbone's front legs, and he told bad medicine to come out. Jawbone, he's coming along. Half Crow, our Half Crow, he takes care of Jawbone like a mother. Jawbone likes Half Crow. You come on back now, and we'll stay with my people, and in the spring Jawbone will be good as new, right, Mister Skye?''

She grinned, but Mister Skye couldn't see her through the blur welling over his eyes.

She spotted his hat, picked it up, turned it around, and screwed it down on his head, scolding the wind.

Printed in the United States
6690

9 780812 510713